Also by Amitava Kumar

FICTION

A Time Outside This Time
Immigrant, Montana
Nobody Does the Right Thing

NONFICTION

Every Day I Write the Book
Lunch with a Bigot
A Matter of Rats: A Short Biography of Patna
A Foreigner Carrying in the Crook of His Arm a Tiny Bomb
Husband of a Fanatic
Bombay—London—New York
Passport Photos

POETRY

No Tears for the NRI

MY BELOVED LIFE

MY BELOVED LIFE

A Novel

Amitava Kumar

ALFRED A. KNOPF

NEW YORK

2024

THIS IS A BORZOI BOOK
PUBLISHED BY ALFRED A. KNOPF

Copyright © 2024 by Amitava Kumar

All rights reserved. Published in the United States by Alfred A. Knopf,
a division of Penguin Random House LLC, New York.

www.aaknopf.com

Knopf, Borzoi Books, and the colophon are registered
trademarks of Penguin Random House LLC.

Grateful acknowledgment is made to the following for permission
to reprint previously published material:
Excerpt from "Aubade" from *The Complete Poems of Philip Larkin* by Philip Larkin,
edited by Archie Burnett. Copyright © 2012 by The Estate of Philip Larkin.
Reprinted by permission of Farrar, Straus and Giroux. All Rights Reserved.

Library of Congress Cataloging-in-Publication Data
Names: Kumar, Amitava, [date] author.
Title: My beloved life : a novel / Amitava Kumar.
Description: First edition. | New York : Alfred A. Knopf, 2024.
Identifiers: LCCN 2023018114 (print) | LCCN 2023018115 (ebook) |
ISBN 9780593536063 (hardcover) | ISBN 9780593536070 (ebook)
Subjects: LCGFT: Novels.
Classification: LCC PR9499.4.K8618 M9 2024 (print) |
LCC PR9499.4.K8618 (ebook) | DDC 823/.914—dc23/eng/20230421
LC record available at https://lccn.loc.gov/2023018114
LC ebook record available at https://lccn.loc.gov/2023018115

Jacket inset image: Royal Geographical Society/Getty Images
Jacket design by Oliver Munday

Manufactured in the United States of America
First Edition

For

MONA

death cannot harm me
more than you have harmed me,
my beloved life.

—LOUISE GLÜCK, "OCTOBER"

Contents

Part I

JADU

The sure extinction that we travel to
And shall be lost in always. Not to be here,
Not to be anywhere,
And soon; nothing more terrible, nothing more true.

—PHILIP LARKIN, "AUBADE"

All his life Jadunath Kunwar remembered this from before he was
born:

There was a crack in the brick wall next to the front door of
the small house in which his mother gave birth to him. The crack
stretched up from the door like a well-formed branch reaching
skyward, or, if you were so inclined, it was like the line of destiny
on a man's palm describing the tremors of his fate. In 1934, the year
before Jadu was born, there had been a terrible earthquake. The
earth split wide and swallowed huts and cattle. A widow and her
new daughter-in-law both disappeared into the hole that opened
up on the road on which they were walking home after collecting
spinach from their field. A hotheaded young man sprang on his
horse, wishing to ride away from this calamity, but the animal
only reared up and refused to move when the ground rocked and
shuddered under its hooves. Thirty miles away from Jadu's village,
the Scottish owner of the sugar mill near Sugauli was driving his
prized Wolseley when the ground opened under the rear wheels
and the motorcar toppled backward into a sudden abyss, the white
man buried under the machine. Everyone in Jadu's family survived
unscathed. The small unfinished brick house did not collapse, and
a part of the reason for this was that instead of a concrete ceiling it
had a thatched roof. Thirty thousand clay bricks were piled a little
distance away because construction on the house was still going

on—the tower of unbaked clay bricks buckled and fell into a giant hole and became mud.

The house didn't fall down but the crack appeared near the frame of the front door. It was about five or six feet long. The jagged space that opened up in the exposed brick began to be turned to good use. At the highest edge, just above human reach, a pair of sparrows built a tiny nest with dried grass and what looked like a piece of red ribbon. But at a lower height, letters and receipts and Congress Party bills were often tucked into the gaps between the bricks. They stayed there sometimes for a day or two, and were retrieved when needed, and there were also a few that had been put there and forgotten. Higher than the receipts but lower than the sparrow's nest there was a narrow fissure where each evening Jadu's mother, Sumitra, inserted a twig that she had broken from the neem tree that grew in front of their house. This was her daily routine. In the morning, when it was still dark, she would step outside the door, a kerosene lantern lighting her way. The village had no electricity, and would not have it for another fifty years. Shivnath, Jadu's father, would already be up, putting feed in the troughs for the cow and buffalo. From the crack in the wall, Sumitra would pull out the twig and chew on its tip before using the crushed end to brush her teeth.

A little before dawn on a wet July day, Sumitra gingerly crossed the threshold with the lantern in one hand. The earthen floor was slippery from the rain. Sumitra was still in the early stages of her pregnancy, Jadu making his presence known only through the bouts of morning sickness that his mother bore without fuss. The air felt damp on Sumitra's skin. When she put the lantern down and reached up to remove the neem twig, she was stunned by a bite on her hand. At first Sumitra thought that she had disturbed a wasp but then she saw the snake slither down. The cobra, probably attracted by the eggs in the sparrow's nest or maybe only seeking shelter from the night's rain, had hidden itself in the crack. Sumitra gasped more in surprise than in pain. Shivnath later said that he was emptying the bucket of fodder for the horse and, on hearing Sumitra's small cry, the animal turned its head toward her.

When her husband reached Sumitra, she was sitting on the ground holding her hand. The bite was on the ring finger of her right hand. As soon as Shivnath touched her, Sumitra sighed and stretched out on the wet floor. She wanted to say something about the child that was inside her but she only told her husband to be careful of the snake.

Shivnath took her finger in his mouth and sucked on it before spitting out whatever he could taste. He wasn't sure he had been able to get at anything that had already entered Sumitra. He removed the gold ring from her finger and then, with a mix of practical wisdom and a desperate energy, he drew out his penknife from the pocket of his kurta and made two sharp cuts in the skin right over the fang marks. Instead of crying out in pain, Sumitra raised her head an inch and threw up a foamy white and yellow liquid. Her finger felt hot and Shivnath could see that the whole arm was beginning to blacken and swell. Shivnath called out to his cousin whose hut was across the narrow lane. About a five-minute walk away lived a pharmacist who had worked at a small hospital in a nearby district town. Shivnath could think of nothing else to do—it was as if he too had been bitten by the snake. Dazed, he first fetched water and cleaned Sumitra's face and then picked her up in his arms. Slowly, as carefully as Sumitra herself had walked on the wet floor, he crossed into the house. Sumitra hadn't spoken a word, her eyes were closed; her whole body convulsed without warning, and she vomited again. The cousin hadn't come back yet with the pharmacist and unable to do anything else, Shivnath rubbed ash from the previous night's cooking fire on Sumitra's cut to stop the bleeding. Then he ran outside to get neem leaves, thinking that the juice would be an antiseptic.

When he was plucking the leaves, he caught sight of Babulal Mishra, the pharmacist. Like a woman holding up her sari as she wades into a pond, Babulal, dhoti clutched in one hand, was cutting across the field where only weeks earlier Sumitra had planted turmeric and tomato.

In one pocket of his shirt, Babulal had a small bottle with purple crystals. Pouring a small amount on a spoon, he brought a match to it. Shivnath watched as pink flames quickly glowed on the dark metal and he stood watching in surprise and pain as Babulal wordlessly transferred the flaming crystals, bubbling now, from the spoon onto Sumitra's finger. She woke up with a scream, and Shivnath saw that Babulal held Sumitra's shoulder down with his fingers spread wide as if it were he who was her husband. After more crystals had been dissolved in water in a small brass lota, Babulal asked Shivnath to unlock Sumitra's jaws and then he poured the pink liquid into her mouth. After that, they began the three-hour journey by bullock cart to the hospital where Babulal had once worked as a pharmacist.

Shivnath drove his bullocks hard, glancing back now and then at his wife's prostrate form while Babulal tenderly wiped the white foam that occasionally escaped from Sumitra's mouth. When the bullock cart jolted over a rut in the dirt road, Babulal's hand steadied Sumitra's shoulder and he cupped her head with the other. And, while this odd intimacy between not just Babulal and Sumitra but also between Babulal and Shivnath never got lodged in Jadu's memory, the journey to the hospital and Sumitra's recovery became a part of the strange and glorious story about how he had entered this world.

When he was very little, Jadu once heard an older cousin's wife joke that the reason Jadu was dark-skinned, and so unlike his fair-skinned mother, was because of the poison injected by the snake. In this telling, it was as if his father, Shivnath, had been replaced by the snake whose bodily fluid had entered Sumitra and produced the child that was born some months later. This remark had disturbed the boy and then it got pushed aside and forgotten in a dark part of his brain. What remained was the story of Sumitra's anxious concern for the unborn baby and her struggle in the hospital over four difficult days and nights. And this story had been told in one form or another so many times as he grew into boyhood that Jadu had come to accept the memory that he himself had survived a cobra's bite and emerged triumphant into this world.

Jadunath was Sumitra's first child. She gave birth to two more children, both girls. On a night in March or April, just weeks after the Holi festival, Sumitra was sleeping with her daughters outside the house on mats that she had spread on the ground. Laali was asleep on a mat by herself; she was two at that time. And the youngest one, Lata, still an infant, barely three months old, lay facedown next to her mother. Sumitra was trying to escape the heat that was still trapped inside the brick house. Shivnath and Jadu were away. They had gone in a baraat, as a part of the bridegroom's party, to another village for a wedding. Sumitra woke up when she heard the baby crying. There was enough light from the moon for her to see that a fox was trying to drag the child away by pulling on the cotton vest she wore. She got up in a blaze, screaming, still believing that this was a nightmare and she would wake up and come out of it if her screams were loud enough. The fox dropped the child and vanished into the darkness. Sumitra gave herself permission to wail loudly after she had picked up the baby and found all her limbs intact. Remarkably, there were no teeth marks on her skin anywhere. Her neighbors, some of whom were relatives, had woken up when they heard Sumitra's loud wails. No one could remember a fox trying to do anything like this in the past. Once a wolf had come to the village and there were tigers in the forests a few hours north. But, a fox? Those more skeptical of this possibility were willing to believe that this was a ghost or an evil spirit that had visited the house.

Sumitra accepted this last reading. The next morning, even before Shivnath had returned with Jadu, the priest came to sprinkle ganga-jal around the house to purify it. The priest was old but he had a strong voice, and he recited the mantras in a sonorous manner. His one eye would close, and he squinted with the other, as if he was peering into the world of demons and ghosts. He burned camphor on the doorstep and threw sandalwood chips into the flames. Then he prayed some more. But his prayers hadn't reached their destination because that very day, while the infant girl, Lata, remained healthy and cheerful, the older girl, Laali, fell sick. A mysterious fever seized her. It seemed her limbs were becoming rigid. After three days she clenched her jaws and refused to take food or water. Ten days later, she was dead. People said that the fox must have licked her and that was what had caused the child's death. Others in the village were all the more certain now that the creature that Sumitra had seen was an evil spirit and it had now carried off one of her children.

This was Jadu's first real memory, his sister's death, except that it rested on a shaky foundation. The cause of the death was never clear. It didn't make the tragedy meaningless as much as make it unmanageable. Better to adopt the indubitable fact of the snake biting Sumitra as his first memory. Also, in that instance, no one died, not even the snake. That story had a better ending. The purple crystals of potassium permanganate had burned Sumitra's skin, and a scar disfigured her finger for the rest of her life, but it was proof that all the terrors that life held could not destroy you.

———

When Jadu left the village and came to Patna for college, life became more real. In fact, he began to think of this time as his birth or even a rebirth. No longer was he surrounded by relatives; he was living in a hostel named after an Englishman; in a row next to him in class sat attractive young women who, just till yesterday, had been strangers. Jadu was convinced he was now going to have *experiences*. And chief among them was the feeling that he had become modern.

A few months after climbing Mt. Everest, Tenzing Norgay visited Patna. This was in May 1954, and Shri R. R. Diwakar was the Governor of Bihar. He had invited Norgay to Patna to lay the foundation stone of a sports stadium. The students in the first-year history class at Patna College were taken to meet the mountaineer at Raj Bhawan, the Governor's residence. The invitation was for high tea.

None of the students had ever met a governor before. There was excitement also about meeting the man who, along with Edmund Hillary, was the first to set foot on the roof of the world. For Jadu, a student from Champaran, there was the magic of the term *high tea*. On the rented bus, he discovered that none of the others around him were familiar with that phrase. Naveen Kashyap asked nervously if they would be required to use forks and knives. Now a bit of nervous uncertainty began to dissolve, like sugar, in a cup filled to the brim with anticipation.

All the students lived in the hostel on campus. The road overlooking Patna College was often crowded with cars, buses, rickshaws, sharing this choked space with pedestrians, some of whom were shoppers but others just sick patients on their way to the hospital next door. A little distance away was the tonga stand where ponies stood with their faces in bags hanging from their necks. The bags were filled with grass and horse gram. (Why did some of the animals stand with one of their hind legs a little off the ground? He was learning new things in the classroom but for answers to questions like this one he knew he would need to go out into the world.) When their bus got close to the Raj Bhawan, Jadu noticed that the wide road with its gleaming black tarmac was free of people and noisy, crowded traffic. It would perhaps be possible for four elephants to comfortably walk abreast there and still keep distance between their swinging trunks. Glorious yellow amaltas and several gulmohar trees with red flowers lined the pavements on both sides. When the students stepped off the bus, next to a fountain outside the gates, they saw that the steps of the Raj Bhawan were covered with colorful dahlias blooming in clay pots.

Professor Dey went ahead and the students in a straight line followed him into the main hall. The waitstaff, in knee-length red tunics and black Gandhi topis on their heads, were lined up against the far wall. Tables covered with white cloth were stacked with food. The spicy scent of just-fried samosas and something sour and stinging, which they later found was pudeena chutney. They had not imagined this by themselves until they had bitten into the small crustless sandwiches—a layer of spicy green mint in the middle between pieces of soft buttered white bread.

Professor Dey had a reputation. He had published a paper on modern Indian nationalism. More interesting, it was said that each evening he got on a boat on the Ganga that ferried passengers to the opposite bank. He drank country liquor sold in one of the many shacks that were visible from this side. Professor Dey's elder brother held a clerical position in the governor's secretariat. This explained the invitation to high tea. Professor Dey had probably wanted to meet Tenzing Norgay himself; the students had discussed whether they had been the excuse that got Professor Dey inside the building and this thought pleased them. But no country liquor this evening then for Professor Dey. He was here with them, an anxious presence, his hands a bit shaky, at the Governor House.

Jadu and his classmates were standing in a neat row like the members of a cricket team before a match. In front of them, the trays of food stood untouched on the tables. And on the other side, the waiters wore impassive expressions, their postures alert but immobile. Another quarter hour passed. Then, an officer in military uniform stepped out smartly from a door on the right and held the heavy curtains aside.

The Governor wore khadi. He, too, had a Gandhi topi on his head, but it was white. The smiling, younger man next to him, his black hair sleek and parted in the middle, was the mountaineer. He wore a Western-style suit. All the students instinctively greeted the men with folded hands. Shri R. R. Diwakar only nodded but Tenzing Norgay smiled at them and, bringing his hands together, bowed in their direction.

The Governor assumed the position of the umpire on the field addressing the assembled team. "Welcome. We are glad you are here. This is Mr. Tenzing Norgay. Why is he a hero?"

"Conqueror of Everest," a voice shouted.

The Governor smiled. Norgay too.

The Governor said, "I'm a Gandhian. I do not believe in conquest. Let us celebrate Mr. Norgay's feat. He is a hero because he has climbed Mt. Everest, the tallest mountain in the world."

He looked toward Norgay, who nodded and smiled.

The Governor said, "Do you have any questions?"

A student called Radha Charan Tripathi half-raised his right hand and asked, "Sir, who stepped on the summit first? You or Edmund Hillary?"

Both Shri R. R. Diwakar and Tenzing Norgay laughed. There had been some controversy because of rumors. Was it really the white man Hillary who had reached the top of Everest first, or had Tenzing pulled his semiconscious partner up the last several feet to the summit? In newly independent countries like India, which had thrown off the foreign yoke, these were critical questions.

A crease appeared on Norgay's forehead. He said, "We are a team, not just the two of us, but many more. You help to me. I help to you. All same. We cannot do anything alone."

Another student was asking a question. Jadu noticed that the quiet youth next to him, Ramdeo Manjhi, was wearing shiny leather sandals that must have been borrowed. His customary rubber chappals, cheap and worn-out, had been discarded for this visit. Ramdeo didn't speak up in class and he was silent now too. Jadu's parents were village people but they owned land; Ramdeo was dirt poor. The matter of his caste was something that Jadu had been aware of but he hadn't broached it in conversation. He looked now at Ramdeo's dark-skinned face, serious and shining, thick hair curling back over a tall forehead.

"Mr. Norgay, sir, what did you do on the top?" This question was asked by Gita Mohan Singh; his father was an advocate in Darbhanga.

Again, that easy laugh.

"For Sherpas, the mountain is a goddess. Chomolungma. I did a prayer and made offering. I placed a chocolate bar and biscuits on the top. My daughter had given a pencil. I buried that under the snow."

The Governor liked this mention of prayer and smiled approvingly. He said, "Prayer is important."

Norgay smiled too. He said, "We had camera. We took pictures of each other on the summit, holding flags. We did not have too much oxygen in our tanks. So, we hurried back after eating a bit of cake."

The mention of food made the students silent. None of them wanted to ask a question now. Professor Dey cleared his throat. His hand went up to his head to straighten his hair. His students were looking at him.

"Sir, you were part of the British expedition. Your success was greeted with great joy in London because the news reached there on the same day Elizabeth was going to be coronated."

"Yes, that is true."

"But in these parts, our happiness was of a different nature." Professor Dey had put a hand on his heart. He said, "An Indian had climbed Everest. What did you feel inside?"

Tenzing Norgay paused. He began to explain that once they had climbed to the top of the mountain, Hillary and he planted the flags of Britain, Nepal, India, and the United Nations. Professor Dey smiled and kept nodding his head. Earlier, Professor Dey had told the students that Sherpas were a nomadic people from Tibet. They had migrated down to Nepal to farm small patches of land. Many of the young came to Darjeeling at the northern tip of West Bengal. Tenzing had taken Indian citizenship. Jadu understood that Tenzing Norgay had given a diplomatic answer.

Shri R. R. Diwakar said, "We are proud of Tenzing Norgay. But we understand that with his great fame, he now belongs to the world."

The students clapped at this remark. Jadu saw that, with a politician's deft touch, the Governor had taken the white dove that was hidden in Norgay's answer and released it gently into the sky above him. The Governor glanced at the tables laden with food and looking at the students opened his palm and pointed toward the stacked plates.

A waiter wearing white cotton gloves brought the Governor and his guest of honor tea on a silver tray. The students were led by the military attaché to the food. The general feeling was that if you ate what was on your plate, you could return to get a cup of tea. Professor Dey did not take any food or tea; he was standing close to Shri R. R. Diwakar, listening with his head tilted toward the mountaineer.

A student approached the trio. Atul Tandon didn't stay in the hostel, his father was a local Navy man. (Why was there a naval officer in the middle of the plains? Who among these students had even seen the sea? Had Tenzing?) Slightly tentative but curious, Tandon asked Tenzing, "Sir, do you have any other goals left in life?"

Tenzing said, "Do you know the name Lhakpa Chedi?"

Tandon took a guess. "Is it the name of a mountain?"

Tenzing laughed. "No, it is the name of the most famous Sherpa mountaineer of the past. An important British climber once said that Lhakpa Chedi's name should be written in gold alongside George Mallory's. Do you know who is Mallory?"

"Yes, sir." Tandon said, "Everest pioneer, sir."

"You see," Tenzing said, still smiling. "You know the name of the Englishman Mallory but you do not know Lhakpa Chedi. Lhakpa is now a doorman at a hotel in Calcutta. I have ambition to set up a trust to take better care of the Sherpa climbers."

Professor Dey looked at the students intently. Most of his students did not come from wealth. But they were also impressed by its trappings. They were excited to be standing in the Governor House. Perhaps Professor Dey realized that this feeling of awe was what his students would carry away with them. He wanted the young men to know that just as Tenzing Norgay had carried the flags of several nations to the summit, he also carried his many worlds with him, the world of George Mallory but also, definitely, that of Lhakpa Chedi. But this was one lesson that Professor Dey's students didn't need. Many of them had come from villages across Bihar; they took a train or a bus, and then maybe also waded across rivers or walked over muddy fields, to reach their homes. Moved partly by nostalgia, and partly also guilt at having left their parents behind, they told themselves repeatedly that during their time in the city they would remember their village. They were never going to abandon their past. This was a mantra that they would cling to piously until with age it had lost its meaning.

The Governor suggested that it was time now for a photograph to be taken of the group.

The students were asked to line up on the steps outside for the photograph. Jadu stood next to his classmate Mani Shanker. Jadu owned two shirts, one white and one blue. He was wearing the white shirt, which was newer; Mani had borrowed his blue shirt because his own dress shirt had an ugly tear on the left sleeve. On that afternoon, with the two friends positioned in that way, Jadu felt there was some poetry in his shirts standing together with their shoulders touching.

The Governor and Tenzing Norgay had joined them on the steps of the Governor House and stood in the middle of the group.

"Smile, please. Thank you," the photographer said three times.

The next morning, in the student mess hall, Ashfaque Alam, a science student from Sitamarhi, brought the newspaper to Jadu. In his right hand, he held his breakfast plate of puri-sabzi, and in his left, a copy of *The Searchlight*. Right on the front page, there was a picture of Tenzing Norgay with Shri R. R. Diwakar. The two men were looking at each other and smiling. There was no photograph of the students.

Jadu was disappointed. He would have liked to take the newspaper home to his village to show his parents. However, there was comfort to be found even in disappointment: the students were all well versed in that art. Seated beside him, Lallan Yadav said that they had at least met a great man. This statement took residence in Jadu's mind. It announced a break from his past. If his mother were asked what her goal in life was, she would try to describe an exalted purpose linked to God. She would mention not the crops or her children, or even her husband's welfare, but her desire to visit all the seven sacred places she had heard about. These were the pilgrimage towns, near and far, Deogarh and Benares, with temples consecrated to Lord Shiva. That morning when Lallan declared that they had met a great man in Tenzing Norgay, Jadu realized that this was his truth now, and it revealed how he had moved away from the village life of his parents. God had his place but man was important too. Professor Dey had been the first person that Jadu had revered after becoming an adult—and Professor Dey had now led him to Norgay, who was famous all over the world.

Three months after the visit to the Governor House to meet Norgay, there was trouble at the college. After the government announced a fare hike for buses and trains, students set fire to a state transport bus. In response, the police shot at the protesters and two students were killed.

The next morning, a senior student in history, a tall fellow with a gaunt, bearded face, knocked on Jadu's door. Jadu was sitting on his cot with his friend Ramdeo. The senior looked at the two young men but addressed only one of them.

"Jadunathji, please join us today in our march. The common man is being made to suffer. We must protest."

Jadu went.

The previous week's rain had dried in the ditches but the humidity was such that the air was heavy with heat. His shirt was soon soaked. Sweat trickled into Jadu's eyes and made them sting. Traffic was piled up because half of Ashok Rajpath was taken over by the protesters. The thick band of students closest to Jadu jostled for space with the others on the road, a jeep carrying a wedding party, a minibus, numerous rickshaws trying impatiently to find a way forward, rickshaw pullers, their limbs oiled with sweat. All this just where he was standing in the stalled procession.

Above him, Jadu saw a crow on an electric line, its beak open as if waiting for rain. After what felt like half an hour, the students moved forward. A handful of policemen struggled to hold back the students, who carried banners and chanted slogans. The protesters would be pushed back a bit with sticks and then they would surge forward again. Then there was more commotion in the front, angry shouts, maybe someone had been hurt. The procession had now reached Elphinstone Cinema Hall. In a minute a buzz went through the crowd and it became clear that there was going to be trouble. Word filtered back about a police vehicle having been set on fire and then Jadu could see black smoke rising in the sky.

Jadu didn't want trouble. He knew what his father would say. There had been a fare hike but had he needed to set fire to public property? "You could have asked us for more money. We would have forgone vegetables and eaten rotis with salt. But you had to go and get arrested!"

He turned back or at least tried to do so unobtrusively. It wouldn't look good if the students who were his seniors saw him escaping. But a large police party had arrived by now at the back. They were holding the students in place. And then came the warning that the police had grown in number in the front and there was a scuffle. Jadu felt his eyes burning. Was it just smoke from the burning van or had tear gas been used?

Moving quickly to the left, Jadu ducked past a bank of parked rickshaws and, sprinting over three cement steps, he entered the dank interior of Sharma Vegetarian Bhojnalaya. Acting as if it were an ordinary day, he spoke formally to the young waiter in Hindi.

"Kindly give me one vegetarian thali."

Next, Jadu wet two napkins with water from the glass that was put on his table and soaked his eyes; there was some relief but the burning sensation didn't disappear entirely. The angry shouting outside grew louder. A little distance away, the sound of whistles being blown and the singing of sirens. His food arrived. Using a spoon, Jadu first swallowed the yogurt to ease the itching in his throat. He had barely taken the first morsel of rice and dal when three students came rushing into the restaurant. There was a scramble on the steps because a hand was pulling them back. A police inspector's brown uniform now appeared on the steps. He was grabbing the students by one hand and hitting them with the baton held in the other hand. He pushed the boys out, and then turned to survey the room, his eyes taking in the seated patrons, lingering on Jadu for just a beat longer. Jadu pushed another bite into his mouth. When the policeman stepped back into the street, an exchange began to take shape inside Jadu's head.

"What are you doing here?"

"I'm having my lunch, sir."

"Were you not out there with them?"

"Ask the waiter, sir. I've been peacefully eating my food."

The waiter was standing impassively next to the tiny sink, a grimy mirror nailed above it. Jadu looked at the waiter and his eyes watered more.

"What happened to your eyes?" the policeman might have asked.

"There is so much masala, chili, in this potato curry, sir. I am sensitive."

If the policeman asked him his name, Jadu thought he would try a trick.

"Vidyarthi."

Vidyarthi, which also meant student. A common name, nevertheless.

If the policeman had asked if that was really his name, Jadu would have clarified that he was simply saying, "I am just a student, sir."

"Are you trying to be clever?"

The day passed without incident for him but it cast a shadow over the weeks that followed. By evening Jadu had learned that six more students had been killed that day and several more injured. Jadu was aware that he hadn't been brave, but he asked himself what good was bravery if you were dead. He decided that he had acted cleverly by slipping into Sharma Vegetarian Bhojnalaya. He felt pride at his bold escape; it was as if he had passed a test. He told himself that here was proof that he could be worldly and overcome his bookishness. Was it wrong to be clever?

At the end of the month, Jawaharlal Nehru arrived in Patna to address a big rally. At the rally, the Prime Minister delivered sharp words about the protesters who had set fire to buses. He said, "Intellectual politics is one thing. To take part in demonstrations and hooliganism in the name of politics is, apart from the right and wrong of it, not proper for students of any country." There were many among Jadu's friends who said that Nehru was wrong. Fewer than ten years ago, students all over India had taken part in demonstrations and driven out the British. Why didn't Nehru chastise the police instead who had shot at students in Patna just as the colonial police had done earlier?

But Jadu wasn't on the side of these radical students; it was clear in his mind that he wanted to participate in nation-building. It might have been selfish to want to simply improve his lot, but not if in trying to better himself he was also contributing to the betterment of the nation. In other words, Jadu didn't want to be clever, he wanted to be mature. He wanted people to say that he was serious.

And then, during his tutorial for the Independence Movement class, Professor Amar Sahay said that Mahatma Gandhi had been clever when he gave the call for the salt satyagraha in January 1930. The British had imposed an excise duty on salt and the government held a monopoly on the manufacture of salt. Gandhi announced a civil disobedience campaign in which the salt laws would be broken. For many people, however, Gandhi's choice of salt as a central issue in the fight against British rule in India appeared eccentric. Just a few weeks prior, Nehru had delivered a stirring address at the Lahore Congress, speaking as a socialist and sketching out a new internationalist and radical perspective for the freedom movement. Gandhi's narrow insistence on salt left Nehru feeling bewildered. Even the British were lulled into inaction. Lord Irwin, the Viceroy of India, wrote to London: "At present the prospect of a salt campaign does not keep me awake at night."

"He should have stayed awake," Professor Sahay said with a smile.

The salt satyagraha linked up in a flash the ideal of self-rule with a concrete and universal grievance of the rural poor, and also offered to the people in urban areas the possibility of a symbolic identification with mass suffering. Gandhi began the march from his ashram. When he bent down on the shore to pick up salt, in the coastal town of Dandi, his act electrified the masses. Every Indian heard his call: from now on, they would make their own salt.

Gandhi's triumphant march to Dandi, a distance of 241 miles, had stretched over twenty-four days. It was covered by journalists worldwide. Gandhi had started with only seventy-eight volunteers but each day thousands more had joined his march. Many of those who joined were Indians who, at Gandhi's behest, had resigned from their government jobs. The salt satyagraha was a victory for nonviolent resistance. A year later, Lord Irwin conceded to Gandhi that the latter had "planned a fine strategy around the issue of salt."

When Professor Sahay said that Gandhi had been clever, Jadu again began thinking that this was a good thing and he too wanted to be like that. If he was clever, he would be able to act. It would be possible to bring about change. Seriousness could be his armor and cleverness the weapon in his hand. Jadu was thinking mainly about his village, and his parents in particular, but also the others who lived there. When a snake bit his mother, she had to be taken to a clinic three hours away. There was a need in his village for a small hospital.

Some years earlier, Aslam Master, the teacher in Khewali's primary school, had told Shivnath that Jadu was special. There was no other student who had his quickness or grasp. And that is how Shivnath decided to put Jadu in the nearest middle school, which happened to be in the next village, and then in the high school in Raxaul.

All that was behind him now. Jadu had made his way to the college in Patna and was sitting cross-legged on the hard wooden bed in his hostel room with a history textbook by Professor K. K. Datta open before him. The walls of his room were stained with age, the light from the naked bulb dangling from the ceiling was dim, but there was so much to learn. Jadu was up for the task. He knew he was determined; the only thing he lacked was sophistication and he was uncertain what could be done about it. A few days earlier, after the morning class, some of the boys had gone near the college gate to drink tea. The tea was hot and Jadu had poured it into the saucer. When he was blowing on the hot liquid and relishing the noisy sips, Atul Tandon mocked him. He had called him a *dehati*, a country yokel. *Cheeks glowing . . . breeze blowing . . . tea flowing . . . Are you enjoying your life in the city?*

When he remembered these small humiliations, Jadu would no longer think of uplifting the life of the people in his village. Instead, he wanted to start speaking English casually. *Good morning . . . thank you.* He also wished to have a new walk and a new way to talk. He wanted to wear that jacket that Atul Tandon wore, one which he had inherited from his father, and maybe wear a tie. Tandon's father, while studying at the Warsash Maritime Academy in Southampton, had acquired the blazer made from a material called Harris tweed. You looked at that wool jacket and you could feel the warmth inside you, as if you were back in your village sitting around a blazing fire. Wearing the blazer, Jadu would declaim in English with confidence, like Nehru, who had been educated at Harrow and then Cambridge: "Fine buildings, fine pictures and books and everything that is beautiful are certainly signs of civilization. But an even better sign is a fine man who is unselfish and works with others for the good of all. To work together is better than to work singly, and to work together for the common good is best of all."

———

Nehru was an aristocrat who had pledged himself to the service of the nation. Gandhi was different. Nehru regarded Gandhi as

a man of the people, an embodiment of the Indian peasant, close
to the ancient traditions of the land and the ideals of asceticism
and renunciation. No silk tunics with rosebuds tucked in the buttonhole for him! No gold-tipped 555 cigarettes in a holder for a
postprandial smoke either!

If you were poor, your friends in college mocked you by calling
you Gandhiji.

When Atul Tandon called Jadu that name, he didn't know Jadu's
story. This bothered Jadu. It was true that he was poor, and this
embarrassed him, but what annoyed him was that Tandon had no
mental picture of Jadu's poverty. When he was called Gandhiji,
Jadu laughed, revealing his well-formed teeth, and he passed his
hand through his hair. His greatest desire during those early
months in Patna was to tell people about his past.

The name of his village, for example.

*The name of my village is Khewali. I was born there and so was my
father and my father's father. Our family has always farmed the land.
We are not rich, that is correct, but we have never gone hungry.*

That is what Jadu felt his elders would have liked him to have
said. He was first in his family to go to college. The outlines of
his life, his status, altered when he began to teach. Nevertheless,
there wasn't much money in education. By then, however, Jadu had
lost his embarrassment and he had adopted a different declaration:
I am, by profession, poor.

There were other things he would have liked to tell the likes of
Atul Tandon if only to shock them.

He was a boy once. When he went into the fields next to his
home to relieve himself, every time that a blade of grass tickled
his behind, his heart jumped into his mouth. His imagination was
run over by spiders, scorpions, snakes. He was very little when he
looked down at his shit and saw tiny forms writhing there. Without even washing himself, he ran back to tell Sumitra what had
come out of his body. She had him take her to the place where he
had been squatting. She said he had tapeworm and would need to
get medicine from Babulal Mishra. In the meantime, she gave him

turmeric to swallow with honey and ajwain seeds to chew with a lump of jaggery. After he got the medicine, round tablets that he took for five days, he didn't see those worms again. But they had been a revelation. He learned that his body held secrets and could surprise him.

Let Tandon call him Gandhiji!

Jadu felt an instinctive affinity with Gandhi. And not just because Jadu had been born in a village and his parents were peasants. Ever since he was a little boy Jadu would be taken to a temple on the edge of the village. The temple was a small brick building with whitewashed walls and a triangular red flag atop a small bamboo pole. Abutting the temple was a straw hut. Jadu's family always visited the temple on auspicious days, ringing the tiny brass bell at its doorway, as if waking the gods from their sleep. At the sound of the bell, the priest would emerge from the darkness of the hut. He was a dark-skinned old man with a white-and-gray beard and shaggy braids that fell about his shoulders. Everyone touched his feet and Sumitra, with great reverence, drew out the aanchal of her sari so that when she touched the holy man's feet a triangle of bright cotton or silk was spread on the ground. The old man opened his palm to bless her and kept his palm raised for a long moment as if he were raining coins on Sumitra's sari. Everyone called the priest Baba and showed him respect. Jadu must have been five or six years old, or even older, before he realized that the priest was his own grandfather. He was Shivnath's father. Fifteen years earlier, after his wife had died, Jadu's grandfather had renounced the world. He lived alone in the hut he had built and prayed at the temple. Like Gandhi, he had very few needs.

Jadu knew that Tandon had attended a Catholic school run by white Jesuit priests, in spotless cassocks, men who spoke to the students in English. At the village school that Jadu himself had attended there was only one teacher, Aslam Master. He had always needed to go away into the fields when the harvest had to be brought in. It wasn't just the teacher; often the students, even

while very young, were needed to lend a hand in the fields during the planting season and again during harvests. Aslam Master
was also a wrestler. He earned five or even ten extra rupees from
his wrestling bouts in other villages and towns. Often after his
fights, Aslam Master would lie down on the cot and ask two of
his strongest students to massage his limbs. When this happened,
the other students were asked to loudly recite the multiplication
tables. *Nine times one is nine, nine times two is eighteen, nine times
three is twenty-seven . . .*

The daily-wage laborers were the poorest in the village. Most
of them were low-caste. When there was a drought, and the yield
was small, their share of the crop was paltry. They were forced
to go into debt. If there was illness or death, their troubles were
only compounded. Some years before Jadu was born, his father
had taken on the role of a moneylender. He offered petty loans to
farmers and landless laborers in Khewali and surrounding villages.
These loans were for short periods and came with high interest, a
little over 50 percent. Shivnath owned a horse, a tall black animal
with a white forehead. His debtors were often forced to beg and
plead when they found it difficult to return what they owed. It
was difficult at times to recover what Shivnath felt was rightfully
his, particularly if he was in a distant village. He would arrive on
horseback; doing so made the journey easier and his arrival a little
more intimidating; he addressed people from an unaccustomed
height. One summer day Shivnath came back home in the afternoon on an even gallop so as to have time to talk to his field hands
before his evening prayers. One of his men gave the horse a bucket
of water and then wiped the animal down. That was the last that
Shivnath saw the horse alive. In the morning, a youth who worked
for him in the fields brought the news that he had seen blood leaking out of the hut where the horse was kept.

Inside the hut, Shivnath found that the horse's head had been
severed from its body. The killer had used a hammer to smash the
skull and then had expended considerable effort and time on saw-

ing off the head. Who would have done such a thing? A policeman came from the nearby town to investigate but the ground outside the hut had been trodden by far too many people and there were no other clues inside. This had happened a few years before Jadu's birth but it was an event that was often discussed among his relatives. The death of the horse, a horse which unlike the horses in storybooks had no name, belonged to that group of events that, while normal and quite acceptable in later life, crowd the short length of a childhood and inevitably give it the character of a tragedy. Also mystery because there was a hint of his own family's crime or complicity. Had Shivnath been cruel with his practice of usury? Had he taken away a debtor's land? It had been an unpleasant experience, and Jadu understood why Shivnath had soon afterward given up the practice of moneylending.

The horse's death, how it might have weighed on his father, was a question that young Jadu had entertained whenever he saw his father praying. The boy, especially in his teens when he started taking prayer seriously because he was scared of his new interest in masturbation and considered it a moral failing, wondered whether his father was seeking atonement. And then the memory faded. He certainly wouldn't have brought it up for discussion among his classmates like Tandon at the college. But the horse's story came back to him one morning in the college library. Jadu was reading an administrative report from the years during which the First World War had been fought. The subject of his research was the role of the Indian cavalry as a part of the British Expeditionary Forces. He was noting the number of horses shipped from the Punjab and Uttar Pradesh to the killing fields of Europe—the Battle of Bazentin, the Battle of Flers-Courcelette, the Battle of Cambrai—when he saw in a flash his mother, Sumitra, saying to him when he was a boy, "I had never seen so much blood." As if he had witnessed the scene himself, he now remembered the slaughtered horse in Khewali, its head massive and long, blood pooling on the ground.

There was also an elephant. Jadu was perhaps four years old. It came when Shivnath's younger brother, Manjunath, was getting married. The elephant was a loan from Jadu's maternal uncle. Sumitra came from a wealthy farming family. Apart from owning fifty fertile acres of land for crops, the family also counted among its possessions several mango orchards and a pond that yielded a rich supply of fish. Sumitra never failed to remind Jadu that she got married to Shivnath because her father had been misled about the actual wealth that the groom possessed. Shivnath and his brothers were organized as a joint family; the eldest cousin, the principal operator in the marriage negotiations, was the British government's junior advocate in the court in Motihari. He wore a monogrammed blue blazer when he spoke to Sumitra's father and brothers. A guard stood at his door. The junior advocate's officious air and his use of random English words had cowed Sumitra's father. He had assumed his daughter would be introduced to a life that was comfortable and close to power. Instead, she had become a peasant's wife. She barely laid eyes on any cash, making and accepting payments almost entirely in loads of grain. It is true that the storerooms were never empty but there was no denying that Sumitra led a circumscribed existence. The story that she told of her marriage, of being cheated of her true destiny, was yet another lesson in tragedy in Jadu's early life.

Jadu would not have known why the elephant was requested on loan for a day. It is quite likely that it was because Manjunath was so entirely without accomplishment that there was some surprise in the family that the bride had even said yes. It was an arranged marriage, of course, and the bride's brother was a police officer, a daroga, with a fearsome reputation for having once chased down a marauding band of dacoits. The bride's family lived in a village near Bettiah. Her siblings had received education and also owned property. Jadu was too young to know such things but his father had asked for the elephant so that they could make a good impression on the girl's family. *We are not beggars. We will give your daughter a home.*

The night before the wedding, a cry went through the village. *The elephant has arrived.* Jadu peered out and he saw in the shadows, close to the clump of banana trees, the flapping of a gigantic fan. It was the elephant's ear. Jadu woke up at dawn to see the animal. It was chewing on a pile of bamboo leaves that had been placed in front of it. The mahout, a young bearded sadhu, took to the road to Bettiah with his placid but ancient-looking beast early in the day. The journey would take him four hours with a little rest along the way. Then, three bullock carts brought the rest of the groom's family to the dharamshala in Bettiah, where they were to spend the next three days immersed in the rituals of marriage.

Just after it grew dark outside the dharamshala, a small band arrived. Thin men clad in shabby white uniforms with piping of red and golden brocade. They were carrying drums, trumpets, horns, even a tuba. Six Petromax lamps perched on the shoulders of the servants. When the marriage procession was assembled, the band led the way while the elephant followed—the groom and young Jadu sitting high atop the animal, the rest of the party trailing behind on foot.

The images that formed in the dark became imprinted on young Jadu's mind. They stayed there, apparently unchanging, and he later returned to those pictures in the dark cave of his mind as if they were still happening in the present.

The elephant seems to rise above not just the people but also the thatched roofs of the huts they pass on the way. Jadu is looking down at the world from a height that makes him appear unreachable. The surrounding darkness is deep, even intense, despite the bright Petromax lamps. The men pump the lamps and the sac-like filaments in the center glow a hot white. When people step into that glare on the road and turn up their faces to say something teasing to Manjunath, their faces appear unreal to Jadu, harsh and cut by dark shadows, like the animals in his picture book, peering out from behind trees in the jungle at night.

Any memory he might have once had of the festivities is gone, lost in the dark of night. Now, in college in Patna, he connects that night with another memory. He is in his teens now. It is as if he fell asleep in his uncle's lap and then woke up in some future where he is a bit more grown up, and everything around him is normal, and he is running beside the shining waters of the river to the high school in the distant village where he lives with his father's relative. He feels the sunlight on his face while sitting beside the river with his classmates—a morning in winter, the boys sitting on the brick embankment, two cigarettes being shared among them—and Jadu asks the boys to share their first memory. One boy named Chandu talks about his grandfather's body being taken out of the house. (*Wait, do you remember your grandfather only as a corpse?*) Chandu has an image of his mother hitting her head against the wall as the grandfather's body was being taken out. No, he says, he has no memory of his grandfather while he was alive. Another boy says that his earliest memory would have to be of his bathing under a water pump. His sister stands close to him, and, holding a towel and smiling, his aunt who later died of cholera. A Muslim boy remembers sitting at night watching a Ramlila performance with his Hindu neighbor: the monkey god Hanuman onstage, setting fire to Ravana's palace. Hanuman was played by a man wearing a monkey mask, but the little boy hadn't known. He was fascinated by the monkey he saw onstage speaking a human language and touching the feet of Lord Rama.

Jadu, what about you? Why are you asking us this question?

Jadu has been waiting for this moment. He wades into the shallow part of the river and then turns around to face his friends. He mentions the huge elephant, its trunk so monumental and yet so mobile. The elephant could use its trunk to pluck a coin from the boy's palm.

Jadu uses one foot to splash the boys with the cold water. He has discovered the idea of sex, and so have the boys, and he has been waiting to take the conversation there. He lays down a theory he has borrowed from a Hindi magazine that his uncle Manjunath was reading and had hidden under a pillow. The article's author was a man who had put doctor in front of his name: Dr. P. P. Mehta. The doctor urges his readers to search among their memories for their first experience of sex. Dr. P. P. Mehta has quoted from the accounts of his patients. *(But is he really a doctor? Or is it some frustrated fellow sitting in Meerut composing letters from his fantasies?)* Jadu tells his friends what he learned from one letter sent by "Geeta from Hoshiarpur." Geeta is thirty-two and a mother of two and has only now come to understand why she loves eating kaju barfi, and, in fact, craves it when she wants any pleasure in her otherwise hard life. When she had just turned sixteen, a young man named Santosh on her street joined the army. He was tall and strong like a young rosewood tree. Geeta often thought of him. They were cordial with each other, and their families were friends, as happens with neighbors. Once Santosh was on a brief visit home, and it so happened that it was Geeta's birthday. How did Santosh find out? He came to her house in the afternoon. Geeta's mother welcomed him and then Geeta came down from her room. Her mother went to the kitchen to make tea. Santosh had brought a box of kaju barfis. He took one out and put half of it in Geeta's mouth. It was sweet and she half-shut her eyes, only to feel the crush of his lips on hers. Santosh was kissing her and he pulled her to his chest so that Geeta's breasts were pressing against him. This embrace must have lasted only a few seconds but to Geeta it seemed to extend forever. Then, the next day or soon thereafter, Santosh was gone. A year later Geeta got married to a man who had a good job in the local bicycle factory. She never saw Santosh again but someone said he had become an officer in the army. And Geeta, living her own private life, had remembered the secret of her hunger for the missing half of a kaju barfi.

Jadu tells his friends that he read in Dr. Mehta's column in the magazine that our earliest memories are of sexual experiences. *(Is that really true?)* And because sex is taboo, certainly at the age we become conscious of it, such experiences are often repressed in our memories. A shocking discovery, for example, is covered over by another memory. Jadu looks up from under his thatch of thick black hair and tells them that, as they are no doubt aware, a young male accompanies the groom to the bride's house. He was that young male at his uncle Manjunath's wedding. Jadu proposes to his classmates as they sit at the river's edge that his fascinated recollection of the elephant, the strange animal with the enormous trunk, is so fixed in his mind because later that night, as a little boy sleeping in his uncle's bed, he had heard Manjunath having sex with his bride. The boy had known nothing of sex. It is likely that when he heard the strange sounds at night, he imagined the elephant rampaging in a farmer's fields in the dark, opening its mouth to suck the juice from the clump of sugarcane it had pulled out of the ground with its trunk. Then, the boy probably turned on his side and fell right back to sleep.

Laughter and shared joy greet this novel tale.

Jadu will not know this but one of the boys in that group, a sallow-cheeked boy named Paras, who has a younger sister, maybe six or seven years his junior, will enact his own little drama of early sexual memory and repression. A few years will have passed since that winter morning when the boys had sat laughing beside the river. Paras will inaugurate a routine of quiet nightly visits to his sister's bed—two cots set a few feet apart in the same musty room where pots of curd and ghee hang from the ceiling—and not encounter any resistance from the quietly surrendering body in the dark. After suffering several nocturnal visitations, while sitting across from her brother eating from his thali on the kitchen floor, the girl will suddenly blurt out to her mother, "Mai, just after I shut my eyes to sleep, a demon takes a human form and frightens me at night."

The mother will laugh but then turn to Paras. "Do you ever hear anything?"

Paras will push another ball of rice in his mouth and shake his head.

The mother will ask the village priest to conduct a puja to cleanse the home. Both siblings will sit cross-legged near the fire. The sister's life will now shift gears. She will be taken to the city to have her photograph taken in a studio. Her mother will make her wear a sari and the photographer will add a beauty mark on her right cheek so that she doesn't attract the evil eye. By the time the wedding season arrives, her marriage will be arranged with a clerk in the transport department in the government of Bihar. After the priests from both families have finalized the dates, Paras will wear new clothes and travel to the city, carrying for his sister's future husband a bolt of cloth, 501 rupees in new notes, and, on a mango leaf, an areca nut, the root of turmeric, and a twist of cotton, to protect with good luck, as the priest has advised, the auspicious marriage.

———

In his second year of college, Jadu attended the wedding of his classmate Radha Charan Tripathi in Dibrugarh, Assam. The family of priests that presided over the Shiva temple there had moved from Gaya fifty or sixty years earlier. It had become a tradition among them to find spouses for all the boys and girls in the family not in Assam but back in Bihar, where the family had its roots. Radha Charan was from what used to be called a learned Brahmin family, which meant that he was poor; the Brahmins from Assam came looking for him with a suitcase filled with cash. The elder Tripathi was immediately interested in the wealth but he tried to protest, saying that his son's education was still incomplete.

"Perhaps it would be better to wait, until he finds work?"

"He has found work now, his work is to be the husband to our daughter." *(Laughter)* "All the tea gardens of Assam are looking for honest men to be managers."

And that is how Radha Charan, seen to be working in concordance with the guardians of divine will, was appointed assistant manager of a large tea garden near Naharkatia in Assam. He left Patna six hours after writing the last answer in his final history exam a year later. "Discuss the causes and consequences of the burning of the library at Nalanda in 1193 A.D." He didn't even wait to collect his degree; he felt he had burned down his own little library and sought salvation in the mist-covered tea gardens.

But before all this happened—the arrival of a black-and-white photograph showing Radha Charan standing next to a jeep on which the painted letters said MANNAGER—there was the wedding. What a lovely occasion that was! A card had come inviting Professor Dey's students. *Radha Charan marries Vimla. May heaven bestow choicest blessings on the new couple.* Jadu and many of the others had never left the state; now they journeyed to a place they had never seen, and maybe had never even imagined. The bare plains gave way to green hills and lush fields. All those hours spent in the company of close friends. The students, young and lighthearted, kept the whole train car amused with their banter and intermittent arguments and fights. More than once, at their insistence, Mani Shanker would sing for them the Dev Anand hit song *Yeh raat, yeh chandni, phir kahan.* Many years later, a British film director made a film on Gandhi: you saw the young Gandhi, after his return from South Africa, traveling across India in trains. That was the journey of his discovery of India. Jadu and his friends were doing something more modest and necessary. They were finding out how little they knew of their land and, a twin discovery this, they were also learning that they belonged in places that they had so far so little knowledge about.

On their second night in Dibrugarh, six bottles of Old Monk rum were brought by a member of the bride's family. He directed a servant to put the rum next to the mattress where some of the young men were sitting playing cards. The transistor radio they had played on their train journey was now playing Hindi film songs on *Binaca Geetmala* on Radio Ceylon.

Mohabbat kar lo, jee bhar lo, ajee kis ne roka hai . . . (Go on, fall in love, until the heart's full, who is there to stop you . . .)

The man from Vimla's family, probably an uncle, said, "You are young. Please enjoy."

Lallan Yadav's father had died from drink. Lallan had vowed to never touch alcohol. Ashfaque Alam also didn't drink. No one drank in his family except for an uncle who wanted to be the next Mohammed Rafi and spent most of his time in the bathroom singing or combing his hair in front of the mirror. For the teetotalers, the kind and elderly gent had also brought several bottles of Coca-Cola. Atul Tandon had a father in the Navy, and he knew more about alcohol than the others did. The bottles of rum had an emotional impact on him. He said, "These people are going out of their way to please us. I had only heard about this rum. It is new in the Indian market. If only they had also brought us some slices of lime . . ."

Jadu had never tasted alcohol before. After the first sip, which didn't suit his tongue, Jadu said to his classmate Gita Mohan, "I like Coca-Cola better." This was greeted with great merriment. One of his friends sprawled around him even kicked Jadu playfully. A blend of affection and abuse. *"Piyo, bhonsdi ke,"* said Gita Mohan and poured him more rum and mixed it with a splash of Coke. This time, the drink went down better. Jadu felt the muscles in his face relax. A warm glow seemed to have taken residence in his body.

After two hours, Jadu was quite drunk even though he had not been given a lot. The aimless mirth of his companions didn't suit him. Frankly, he was disappointed in them. Especially in Krishna Murari Sharma, who had suggested they go out and find someone to fight on the streets. Krishna Murari's uncle was a well-known rangbaaz in Kadam Kuan: he went around on his Royal Enfield Bullet motorcycle, molesting girls and extorting payouts from neighborhood businesses. Going against Krishna Murari's proposal, Jadu appealed for peace. He wanted all of them to embrace each other as one did at Holi or Eid: a genuine expression of love. For a moment, moved by his own words, he felt he might cry.

Outside the dharamshala, the black Ambassador that had ferried them from the train station the previous day was parked in the driveway. Seated in a cane chair on the veranda, poring over what looked like a wad of receipts, was the thin man who had been supervising the delivery of meals to the visiting guests. He looked up and saw Jadu holding a fountain pen in his hand.

Jadu felt he had found a fellow human after a long search. He spoke with great feeling.

"Brother, what is your name?"

"Subhash."

"Do you have some paper? I want to write a letter."

The man was affected by the emotion in Jadu's speech. He half-rose from his seat and extracted from under his buttocks a thick hard-bound register. There were plain sheets of paper between its covers.

The man paused. He asked, "Did you want to mail the letter? Would you prefer a letter form?" The word he had used was *antardeshiye*. As in, inland letter.

Jadu was struck by the magic of this communication between two human souls. He replied in the affirmative, at least thrice. From between another set of leaves of his register, this helpful man named Subhash, who could well have been his own brother, now extracted a crisp, blue inland letter form. Subhash rose up to give his seat to Jadu and offered the use of his register as a surface for writing. Jadu was nearly moved to tears again. He took what was so generously presented to him.

Just ten minutes earlier, Jadu had thought he would write a letter to his parents. But now he entertained a more attractive proposition. He was going to write a love letter. But to whom? There were the two classmates, the Bengali twin sisters, Ananya and Sukanya, daughters of the local eye doctor in Patna. The problem was that even if he could decide which of the two he liked more, which he couldn't, Jadu didn't have their postal address. Where would he send the letter? The only place he would not need to know anyone's address was if he mailed a letter to his own village. He liked a lower-caste girl there, just a few years older than he. He

suspected that the landlord's son, or if not him, then the landlord's
younger brother, had carnal relations with her. No one, he was
sure, wrote letters to that girl. Probably, she was also illiterate. He
would be found out if he sent her a letter. The thought of writing
to her disappeared as soon as it had come even if the tight stretch
of her mustard-colored blouse and her insouciant walk lingered
in his mind as a tantalizing memory. Then another possibility
swam into view. He thought of Mamta Tiwari, the daughter of
a Brahmin farmer in the village, a year younger than he, terribly
thin and quiet but beautiful with her high forehead and a single
curl of hair falling over her cheek. He could write her name, her
father's name, the name of the post office and police station close
by, Sabor; the name of the village, Khewali; district, Champaran;
state, Bihar. The letter would be delivered to her door. He saw in
his mind the white flat rectangle of her house with the tiled roof
and maroon trim around the windows and doors. Instead of his
name and return address on the inland letter form, he would only
put his initials and let her guess.

He was writing in Hindi, of course. प्रिय ममता, he began.

*You will no doubt be very surprised to receive this letter from me. You
will never be able to guess where I am writing from. No, not Patna, but
a town called Dibrugarh, far away in Assam. I'm here for the wedding
of a classmate of mine. It is almost nine at night. I thought of you just
now because we were listening to Binaca Geetmala on the transistor
radio—and when I heard Lata Mangeshkar singing* Mera dil yeh
pukaare aaja, mere ghum ke sahare aaja *it struck me that it is
likely that the song was playing in our village too. Were you listening
to the show on the radio tonight? I want to believe that you were. These
are the ways in which one misses home. My thoughts tonight turn
toward our village, my parents, my friends, in a way very different from
how I usually feel when I'm in Patna. The whole world is the night
around me; home is the lamp burning in the distance. Do you know
what I mean?*

I hope you are well.

In English, he added, incongruously but with a flourish, *Health is wealth.*

And then signed his name.

Subhash was still around. Jadu gave the letter to him. His thin frame erect, Subhash said, "This will go out at nine forty a.m. tomorrow from the Main Market post office. That is when the first collection takes place."

What did Jadu know? He went to sleep feeling self-satisfied. While his friends were getting drunk and whiling away the time, he had set words down on paper. He had given shape to his emotions; this act had given him a sense of achievement. Or purpose. He didn't have the imagination to look further into the future, but when he returned home for the summer holidays, Mamta Tiwari was waiting for him. On the evening of his arrival, she came over with *prasad* from a puja her father had performed. A perfect excuse. She smiled and said, "I got your letter but didn't know where to send a reply."

The truth was that Mamta had felt it was an important event in her life: in a strange and unknown city, a young man was thinking of her and had written her a letter as proof. Standing in front of him now, unable to stop smiling, she waited.

Did Jadu respond? Jadu didn't know how. For one, he wasn't drunk on Old Monk rum when he saw her back in the village. Also, the letter was all that he had meant to give of himself to her. There was nothing more to be said. On this visit home, in front of his mother, he was without longing. *I owe you nothing*, this is what he would have said if he could. If someone pointed out that this wasn't fair, that he had aroused expectations in another heart, he might have responded that life wasn't fair at all. We are full of mistakes; he had made a mistake. Please . . .

One day at his hostel in Patna, an *antar-deshiye* letter arrived for Jadu in an unfamiliar hand. He turned it over. In the space for the return address, Mamta Tiwari had written her name and the name of their village.

प्रिय जादू she had addressed him in the same way that he had.

This is the first letter I'm writing to you. With the blessings of Goddess Durga, my parents have arranged for me to get married on June 25. I know that Babuji will send the proper invitation to your parents, but I wanted to inform you of this personally. I have known you since childhood and I will feel more full of courage if you are here to give us your best wishes. Promise that you will come!

I hope you are well and still listening to Binaca Geetmala on Wednesday nights. My current favorite is Na yeh chand hoga, na taare rahenge, magar hum hamesha tumhare rahenge. *I hope that song touches your heart too.*

Heart! Touch! Jadu felt pierced. He went down to the Ganga and walked beside the river with the letter in his breast pocket. Mamta was a simple village girl but she had composed a brilliant riposte! He was charmed. No girl had ever written a letter to him. This could be love, he thought, except the amazing thing was that Mamta had also freed him. She had mentioned the song after announcing that she was getting married. What a gesture that was! And a fine song too, a promise of eternal love. He couldn't say anything to Mamta but in his head he admired her boldness. Her boldness and her beauty.

Mamta Tiwari was married off to a prosperous businessman in Valmikinagar. Had Jadu returned to the village to be present at that wedding? He had. Mamta Tiwari's husband turned out to be a skilled horticulturist. During the early years of his marriage, he made money as a building contractor. The foundation of his wealth was laid deep in the ground: he had bribed the right people and won lucrative government contracts to sink tube wells in the Gandak region. He was given other government contracts to build roads and, when he had time to spare, he grew roses on the land around his house. Mamta Tiwari's husband was responsible also for bringing the first rosebush to Jadu's village. The bush with small cream-white buds that he planted outside his father-in-law's house. When asked, the man informed the villagers that this particular rose—Jawahar—had been named after India's first prime minister, who always wore a rose in the buttonhole on his tunic's lapel.

———

Professor Dey was delivering a lecture on the Constituent Assembly. Jadu was not really listening. One solitary boat floated on the Ganga outside the window. The previous evening, he had sat on the steps near the river and bought salted peanuts for twenty paise. The peanuts came in a cone fashioned from a scrap of newspaper. On that scrap was printed the news that a goat with two heads had been born in Darbhanga. Now Professor Dey was talking about the framers of the Constitution. Bhimrao Ambedkar. Ambedkar was born in a village in Maharashtra. He belonged to the Mahar caste, considered untouchable, living on the edge of the village, responsible for removing filth and with no expectation of payment. The family survived on scraps thrown from a distance. It was not from his lessons at his village school but from his observations of life that Ambedkar learned the cruel lessons of caste. He became one of India's greatest jurists. Jadu was listening now. Professor Dey wrote on the board behind him: Justice, Liberty, Equality, Fraternity. Under Justice, he drew three lines branching out: Social, Economic, Political.

Professor Dey asked, "Do you understand how his experiences have shaped what he has drafted into the Constitution?"

Next to Jadu, Ramdeo Manjhi snickered. This was unusual. He was often quiet and impassive. Jadu looked at him. Indeed, he was smiling. When Jadu jerked his head, as if to ask what had happened, Professor Dey looked at them.

He said, "Manjhiji, did I say anything wrong?"

"No, sir."

"But something has amused you. What is it?"

"Sir, in my village there was no school peon. Even the teacher only came occasionally."

Professor Dey must have known there was something more. He waited.

When Ramdeo didn't speak further, Professor Dey said, "Was there justice, equality, fraternity at your school?"

Several students started laughing. How many schools in the vast country stretching from the Himalaya in the north to the Indian Ocean in the south could honestly make that claim?

Professor Dey was still looking at Ramdeo, who didn't raise his eyes to look at the professor.

After a moment, Ramdeo spoke again. "There was an earthen pot from which students were allowed to take water. I had even seen a crow regularly drinking from it. But once I made the mistake of pouring myself a glass of water from it. The teacher saw me. He kicked me so that I fell on the ground. For many days, he made me sit on a sack outside the door. It wasn't bad. There would be a breeze but the sun was hot."

Ramdeo looked up now and smiled. He was speaking plainly, and somehow without any bitterness.

"I think my skin turned black that week and has stayed that way since."

This was the first time Ramdeo had mentioned that he was an untouchable. Jadu had known of this in the way that people knew such things. A chance remark, a well-aimed insult, a savviness about last names. It is likely no one felt too guilty about it in Professor Dey's class; after all, they had all gone to the Raj Bhawan and eaten samosas together. But then it turned out that Mritunjay Rai, Ramdeo's roommate, wasn't much of a believer in the Indian Constitution. On more than one occasion, he had asked Ramdeo to wash his clothes or even clean the room. When Ramdeo had said no, Mritunjay had laughed. "Stop complaining," Mritunjay told him. "*Phokat ka kaam nahin hai*. I'll give you two rupees." The matter reached the warden of the hostel. He was the same caste as Mritunjay. The Bhumihar warden tried to resolve the matter by saying that Ramdeo could sleep in the sickroom on the first floor. But this wasn't acceptable to Ramdeo. He said he wasn't suffering from tuberculosis or smallpox, he didn't like being dumped in the sickroom. He had every right to his original room, and that is where the matter remained. No punishment for Mritunjay Rai.

There was silence after Ramdeo had spoken in Professor Dey's class. It became clear that it wasn't Ramdeo who was untouchable; instead, it was the subject of caste itself. It was a given, everyone knew about it, but it wasn't spoken about much. Therefore, no one offered sympathy to Ramdeo after his brief, unexpected speech in class.

One afternoon, after the bus had dropped him off at Gandhi Maidan, Jadu was walking to his hostel room in the college. He thought he would cut to the banks of the Ganga and walk up to the campus. But on returning to the hostel, he knocked on a door.

When he answered the knock, Ramdeo looked sleepy. Jadu apologized for waking him up and Ramdeo said, "It is okay. I seem to have had a fever for the past two days."

Jadu asked if he had eaten anything and Ramdeo said he hadn't. The mess hall wouldn't be open but Jadu liked a tea shop near the nurses' hostel on the other side of the hospital wall. En route, they passed a man squatting outside a shack. Naked except for a blue lungi wrapped around his torso, he was cleaning his teeth with a neem twig. Ramdeo greeted him in the Patnaiya dialect, which always sounded alien to Jadu because he himself spoke the Bhojpuri that he thought of as having the sweetness and charm of the rural districts across the river. The man answered Ramdeo cheerfully.

Jadu said, "Is he a *karmachari* from the college, a peon in the main office?"

Ramdeo said, "I don't know. The other day he was feeding his children slices from a watermelon. I had no money, and I was hungry. I saw that he had grown the vine on the roof of his shack and asked him if that big melon had grown right there. He said yes, it was all Mother Ganga's blessing. They are sweeter than sugar, he said, and then gave me two slices . . . I was saved."

It occurred to Jadu that both Ramdeo and the man by the side of the road might be from the same low caste. A moment later he was embarrassed at the thought. It was conceivable the two had connected simply because they recognized each other's humanity. Or just each other's need. Jadu remained silent for the rest of the walk.

At the tea shop, they asked the old woman for tea and two plates of *litti-chokha*. While they were eating, Jadu sought an opening. He said, "When I was sick in the village, my mother would boil rice with a bit of salt and as soon as the rice was a little bit cooked she would pour the water out in a bowl for me to drink . . . What was considered a cure for fever in your village?"

Ramdeo appeared lethargic. He was making an effort to eat. He understood that Jadu wasn't really asking about medicines. He said, "All our days were the same. When we were kids, we would find our own food because our parents were in the landlord's fields. We ate snails or caught small fish in the ponds which we turned on a twig over a small fire. Sometimes, rats."

Was it poverty, Jadu thought, that gave Ramdeo his directness? He spoke without inhibition or hypocrisy. Jadu had been standing while eating, while Ramdeo sat on the bench. Now Jadu sat down next to him and said, "Ramdeo bhai, tell me. What is your earliest memory?"

The question reflected a preoccupation on Jadu's part; he tried to know people by what they remembered. As an adolescent he had believed that this memory would need to be a sexual one but Jadu was now a social historian. In asking people about family, school, and religion, he sought a key to the self and society.

"I was four years old. My village is in Gaya district. There was a flood and our hut was washed away. We climbed up in a tree to escape the rushing waters. There was always the fear of the branches breaking but what I have never forgotten is that on a branch below us a long, brown snake had wrapped itself. My father said that the snake wasn't going to bite us and it didn't."

Later, when he was older, Ramdeo had collected other memories of that time. He was told that a woman whose hut had been close to theirs was forced to give birth on the dry patch of highway half a mile away. A few of the upper-caste homes were made of brick: the people who lived in those homes, or even if they didn't live there but were from the same caste, climbed onto the roofs of these houses. All the Musahar families like Ramdeo's were without shelter. Their mud huts had been swept away. There was no privacy. A piece of the highway had collapsed and people would climb down the few feet into the debris to shit. It was worse for women, who had to wait until it was dark. Ramdeo had probably observed all this himself, taken it all in, as a boy, but he harbored some uncertainty about these early memories. It was likely that his psyche had tried to erase the memory of humiliation. The past wasn't a blank slate, it was a dark hole.

Jadu was listening to Ramdeo deliver this report from his childhood. It sounded familiar, and yet it was alien to his own experience. He said, "It is good for you to be out of that room, to be taking the sun. Let's have one more glass of tea."

It was understood that Jadu would pay.

The old woman poured them more tea in the glasses from which they had been drinking.

Ramdeo told Jadu about the six huts outside the village that made up the untouchable settlement. His people did the jobs that the upper-caste people didn't do—dragging away the carcasses of dead animals, for instance. There were two other families, a different caste, whose job it was to collect shit from the toilets of the upper-caste homes. Only three houses in the whole village had toilets. For this work the payment from each house was only one roti left over from the previous night's dinner. After collecting and depositing the shit in a ditch and covering it with soil, the men and women would rush to the fields. Ramdeo's parents didn't at least have to carry human waste on their heads.

From the building closest to the tea shop, a group of Malayali nurses emerged and walked past the two seated classmates discussing caste. The women, all of them thin, as if they had chosen a hard life of sacrifice that involved forgoing food, were dressed in white uniforms. White blouse, white skirt, white stockings. Ramdeo pointed with his chin at the nurses and said, "My face is darker than those Malayalis. However, my father has fair skin." His father had aged now. He used to be good-looking and was a wonderful dancer. Ramdeo said that despite being illiterate, his father could recall hundreds of songs and bhajans. He was a *netua*, which meant that during festivals and on other special occasions, he put on women's clothes and danced.

Was Ramdeo feeling better? The food and drink had taken away some of his lassitude.

"Ramdeo bhai," Jadu said, "what are you going to do after graduation?"

Even as he asked the question, Jadu was flung into confusion. He himself wasn't sure what he was going to do and the thought passed through his mind that he had only addressed this question to Ramdeo because he was an untouchable. It was as if he had asked his friend: your father tilled the landlord's field and during Holi he danced as the *netua*, tell me how your life is going to be different?

But Ramdeo did not hesitate. He said, "I will enter politics."

Politics! To be a politician you needed to be either rich or a gangster. Ramdeo was neither.

"Really, politics?"

Ramdeo said that ever since he won a scholarship in middle school and then again in high school, upper-caste politicians would take him around on their campaign vehicles. He would ride in rickshaws in small towns or in jeeps traveling through several villages. They would come to a stop in a slum or a mosquito-ridden mohalla of the low caste, where what you first saw were pigs rooting in the rotting garbage. Ramdeo would be given the microphone. His voice would emerge from the loudspeaker that was turned toward the electorate. He was there to tell the people that he was a Musahar boy who, because of his caste status, had been given a stipend by the government. He was able to study and improve his lot. The politicians were there to express support for such policies. They were making an appeal to those who were called the downtrodden. Ramdeo's exalted fate could be their fate too, or, at least, the fate of their children. This was Ramdeo's rote speech and a part of how democracy worked. Every few years, the powerful set foot in your part of the town or village and asked for your vote.

Ramdeo looked at Jadu and said, "This formula worked every time. The upper-caste politicians used me and got the votes. Ever since then the thought has been in my mind: if I can get votes for others, why should I not get them for myself?"

These words entered deep into Jadu's heart. There was such clarity in Ramdeo. This was an important lesson in language: if your head was clear, your words would be strong and direct. Jadu got up from the slab of stone that served as the bench at the old woman's tea shop. He wanted to go back to his room and study. In high school, he had read a story about Ishwar Chandra Vidyasagar, who had acquired knowledge in Sanskrit and had advocated for widow remarriage in Bengal. The story was about a young Vidya- sagar studying under a streetlight because his home was dark. All knowledge could be gained only through adversity. There was something suspect about that moral tale but Ramdeo's story ap- pealed to Jadu. It was more immediate and real.

When they were walking back to the hostel, Jadu had one more question for Ramdeo.

"How did you know what you must do?"

Ramdeo said, "Two years ago, my grandfather died. We didn't have money even to buy firewood to cremate his body. What could be done? We threw the corpse into the river. My father was cry- ing. We all were. But I thought I was going to make sure that when my father died, there would be enough money for wood."

Jadu absorbed this lesson too. Maybe he looked serious, because Ramdeo laughed. And said, "Tragedy is a demon that has a tail attached to it. The tail is the lesson that you are supposed to draw from the tragedy. This is the truth that civilization has recog- nized through the ages so that you don't feel robbed of everything.

The demon burned down your house. Oh, but at least you got the chance to warm your hands on the fire."

———

The most beautiful woman in the world was Madhubala. Sitting one summer night in Regent Theatre, Jadu watched her in *Mr. & Mrs. '55*. The captivating, tragic face framed by her black sari and her long slim fingers—she is watching the plane leave with the man she realizes she loves. Then, a close-up revealing a pitted right cheek. Such endearing imperfection! Geeta Dutt's melodious voice provides the backdrop: *Preetam aan milo . . .*

Madhubala was her stage name. She was a Muslim and her real name was Mumtaz. She was a distant star shining in the sky at sunset.

When Jadu thought of beauty and fantasized about its pleasures, his imagination conjured the faces of the Bengali twins in his class, Ananya and Sukanya. They were a remarkable pair. If Jadu was lingering in the corridor outside Professor Dey's classroom, he would see them arrive on a rickshaw. They sat with their backs erect, heads held high. Ashfaque Alam once said that Rani Laxmi Bai going into battle against the British Raj had probably sat on her horse like that, but that wasn't an accurate comparison. There was no urgency of battle in their stance or movement. The twins were regal, like queens sitting on a chariot. The eyes of the adoring throng were fixed on them, all those upturned faces on both sides of the street, while the gazes of the two gliding along on the rickshaw were set on a point in the far distance.

The twins were particular about attending lectures. Yet, what was their punctiliousness in the service of? It had been observed by all the young men that neither Ananya nor Sukanya took notes. This was considered a singular feature of their educational life. Radha Charan Tripathi wanted to suggest an economic model to the sisters: as the two of them were enrolled in the same classes, there could be a division of labor and only one of the sisters need take notes in any one class. But he remained silent on this issue.

Of all the males in the class, Radha Charan was the only one who had ever conversed with the twins. The sisters looked upon their admirers with disdain. This was what their classmates always complained about among themselves—that the twins never met their eyes. It was a belief held among the rest of the males that the only reason the twins spoke to Radha Charan was that they knew he got married during their second year at college and he would not spread gossip. Regardless, there was a lot of talk about the twins.

One rumor was that the twins had appeared in some ad for Bombay Dyeing. They had stood on either side of Dev Anand, their hands on his arms. He had flirted with them and offered them roles in one of his future films. Someone also said that the reason the Bengali girls didn't take notes in class was that they were related to Professor Dey. They received private tuition from him. A rumor took root that the girls were related to the royal family of Nepal and owned a five-star hotel in Kathmandu. Lallan Yadav suggested at dinner one night that the girls' father was on the lookout for two young Bengali doctors who could help expand his business. It turned out that Lallan was the closest to the truth, but he was only half right.

Ananya was a little shorter than Sukanya, with sharper cheekbones and thin lips. The full-lipped Sukanya had large round eyes and possessed the kind of beauty associated with fair and curvy Hindu goddesses displayed on calendars given out by businesses at the start of a new year. During their second year in college, when the students returned after the break for Holi, they learned that the twins were going to appear in a play that Professor Dey was directing. The play was a Hindi adaptation of Chekhov's *The Cherry Orchard* and would be performed not in the college but in the town's Rabindra Bhawan. Tickets were priced at five rupees, a bit more expensive than the cheapest cinema ticket, but it was all for a good cause. The proceeds from the play would be used to give free eyeglasses and medicines in an eye camp run by the twins' father, Dr. Birendra Ghosh.

Jadu and his friends went on opening night. Beautiful, slightly plump Sukanya, with a part of her hair painted gray, played a land-owner named Madame Lyubov. Professor Dey had cast himself in the role of another old landlord, Boris Simeonov-Pishchik. Ananya, who seemed to conduct electricity every time she spoke, had been given the role of Madame Lyubov's adopted daughter, Varya. A Sikh girl who was a first-year student, and was talked of as the heiress of a sports equipment business in Patna City, played the role of Madame Lyubov's teenage daughter, Anya. Anya is visiting from Paris. There were various other small roles being per-formed by other students. The most important role was that of the young and wealthy merchant Lopakhin, a loud member of the nouveau riche. Lopakhin was played by Krishna Murari Sharma. He brought a brash swagger to his role. The backdrop to a part of the stage was a painted wall with trees that were dotted with red fruit. This was the cherry orchard that the aristocratic Madame Lyubov could no longer afford to own; it was being taken over by Lopakhin, the son of a former serf, and he was going to cut down the trees.

Jadu felt all this was familiar, and yet, the play kept him at a dis-tance. Although all the dialogue was in Hindi—and the characters wore saris, and sherwani, and kurtas—the names of the charac-ters were in Russian. Why the Russian names? Why had Profes-sor Dey not substituted Indian names? This was the question that Jadu asked himself on the way back to his room. It was drizzling and, by the time he had cycled halfway back to the hostel, he was already drenched. To keep his mind away from the misery, rain-water in his eyes, rainwater running down his back, rainwater in his shoes, he asked himself if Professor Dey wanted them to under-stand that the role of art was not to simply stage stories where you could, as a reader or a viewer, identify yourself with the character. The goal could well be to create a sense of alienation and even discomfort.

The next day, during a discussion in the mess hall, Ramdeo manufactured a different kind of alienation. Atul Tandon was say-ing that he had found the staging of the play very realistic. He was thinking, he said, of the way the audience was able to see how the old feudal order was fading in India too. At which point Ramdeo looked up from his plate and asked if the play had said anything about low-caste laborers tilling the landlord's fields. "No, no, the play was set in Russia, Ramdeo bhai," someone said, and then there was silence of the sort that suggested the curtains had come down prematurely onstage. The stage that was their social life was a dark place.

The fact is that it is not just art but life itself which keeps you at a distance or surprises you with its turns. A year after the staging of *The Cherry Orchard*, Dr. Birendra Ghosh found a doctor for Sukanya—a Bengali boy from Asansol who was a dentist and who moved to Patna after his marriage. The other sister, Ananya, married a cause. She joined the Ananda Marg group, which some people called a cult. The Ananda Margis wore saffron and meditated in front of skulls. The movement had been started a couple of years earlier in Jamalpur in Bihar by a man who was an accountant in the railways. When their leader was arrested under the charge that he had a hand in the murder of seven of his followers, Ananya left the country (some said she had gone to nearby Seychelles but others said she was in Switzerland) and her former classmates, or at least Jadu and others, didn't hear anything more about her.

The sense of wonder that Jadu had experienced ever since he arrived in Patna from the village started to fade, or at least changed, after a year or so. He had become more independent, and his engagement with the world around him deepened. Young men like him worked as tutors of schoolchildren, helping with homework, and this allowed them to earn a bit of money. Jadu was now able to buy tea and jalebis without feeling guilty. Also, he was acquiring knowledge in his classes. After the experience of attending lectures and living in the hostel, he felt himself growing into the role of an assured citizen of the academy. The earlier feeling of surprise had given way to familiarity—routine, planning, and even ambition. He was still serious about his studies but he was pulled by the currents of intellectual energy that swirled around the others, who were much more creative than he was.

When Professor Dey directed *The Cherry Orchard*, Jadu had been an eager spectator. He was not an actor—wasn't this true in every sense? He asked himself if he was only to watch others perform on the stage of life. This question nagged at him.

Jadu felt deeply that those who asserted themselves, whether in a play or in real life, were attractive to him. But what about the innumerable others? A blind man, led by his son, came each month to Jadu's village when he was a child. Unlike all the other blind men, who sang, especially in Hindi films, this blind man was a bad singer, his voice like the engine of an old car. He remained an exception in Jadu's mind. Otherwise, people seemed to possess some talent or another. No one was without a gift that was unique to them. Maybe the blind man who visited Khewali was good with his hands or he had an amazing memory or, who knows, was an incredible cook. This belief in others had settled as a conviction in Jadu's mind. And yet, he was also troubled that he had considered his own compensating virtue to be nothing other than the peasant simplicity of his origins, his directness, his ability to remain grounded and to see things as they are. He felt that this was a meager accomplishment. *To hell with humility!* When he contemplated the performance of *The Cherry Orchard*, especially the way in which Krishna Murari had spoken and put his arms around the Sikh girl Prabhjot and, more than that, the way Ananya moved on the stage as if she owned it, he was conscious of his smallness. Ananya had impressed him. How she had appeared to possess not just the stage but also the cherry orchard and, beyond it, the whole world and the air that Jadu and the rest of the audience was breathing.

That is why, barely a month after the performance of *The Cherry Orchard*, Jadu started attending kavi-sammelans, where both well-known poets and some unknown ones stood up to recite poetry. There was much to learn from them about language but also about how to live life. Each week there were crowded evening gatherings at the Janta Hotel on Govind Mitra Marg, or at the India Coffee House on Exhibition Road. Poets presented their work to an eager audience. There was some charm in being a poet. It appeared to Jadu that if you were a poet, it gave you the right to attach a lyrical title to the end of your name. A fiery local poet, famous all over India, was Ramdhari Singh "Dinkar." Another luminary was the curly-haired Phanishwar Nath "Renu." Then there was Baba Nagarjun. Another student, Jamal Ashraf, had added "Darbhangiya" to his name to indicate that he was from Darbhanga. Shatdal Verma cleverly changed his name to Shatdal Kamal, which was quite something, because now his name was "Lotus Lotus." A tall, long-haired man who wore colorful kurtas called himself Shyam Manohar "Sheetal." *Sheetal*, as in cool and calm. A postgraduate poet was Ram Niwas "Mohit." *Mohit*, or entranced, as when one is in love. Mohit was mostly in love only with himself but it didn't matter.

At times, these names appeared trite, but at other times, they added magic and piquancy to one's existence. Jadu looked on these poets with admiration because, with the simple use of language, the mere adoption of one word, they had altered their identities. They were telling the world who they were or wanted to be.

A young man in Jadu's hostel, a master's student in Hindi literature with a room at the end of Jadu's corridor, had taken to calling himself Saurabh Kumar "Jigyasa." One evening, Jigyasa knocked on Jadu's door. He was holding a few books in his hand and wanted to know if Jadu could return the books to the library. Over the past couple of weeks Jadu had asked Jigyasa if he could accompany him to readings, and they had made several outings to India Coffee House together, and now Jadu saw that he was being asked to do something in return.

"But, Jigyasaji, where are you going?"

Jigyasa said a telegram had come from his father. He needed help bringing a pair of new bullocks back from the cattle fair in Sonepur.

Jadu smiled. He said dreamily, wistfully, "The life of a poet . . ."

Jigyasa waved away Jadu's silliness. "My father probably doesn't want to be ambushed by cattle thieves. That is why he has summoned me. But it is true I like the red color that the peasants rub on the horns of the bullocks they are selling. A pair of handsome white bullocks with red smeared on their horns, their humps. To hear a villager singing *alhar* or reciting from an epic while his fresh bullocks, their bells tinkling, are raising dust on the rural roads . . . It touches my heart."

The telegram had arrived that morning. It wasn't just a poetic interest in the rural landscape that exercised a draw on Jigyasa's heart. There was a stark material reality to consider. Jigyasa's father must have walked or ridden a bicycle from their village to the junction five miles away, from where he would have caught a bus, after a wait under a tree, his faded black umbrella folded in his hand. The bus would have brought him to the small town of Narkatiaganj, where the tiny post office with its telegraph machine was located. The telegram had taken time and effort to send. It demanded action.

If he was his mother's son, Jigyasa would not ignore it.

Jigyasa was considered a prodigy by many. The child of peasants, he had written some memorable pieces about village life even when he was just twelve. His teacher in middle school was a cousin of the famous Hindi writer Satyadev and had sent the latter some of Jigyasa's writing. Satyadev was very likely drunk when he was reading his cousin's letter: he wrote back to say that if the young student Saurabh Kumar had any curiosity about literary life in the city, he should come to Patna and stay with him. The first thing that happened in response to Satyadev's letter was that Saurabh Kumar adopted the Hindi word that Satyadev had used for "curiosity"—*jigyasa*—as his nom de plume. That was how he had become Saurabh Kumar "Jigyasa."

Jigyasa spent a summer with Satyadev, attending poetry readings and doing errands for the poet, and then a year or so later, when still in high school, he moved to Patna to live in Satyadev's home. Satyadev would proudly tell people, "If you are a musician in this country, you live in your guru's house and learn the craft at his feet. Why shouldn't literature be an art like that? It is not right that a young poet today should learn about poetry only from a two-inch report in a newspaper."

And now, in college, Saurabh Kumar "Jigyasa" was a hostel mate of Jadu's. He left his library books with Jadu and then walked over to Mahendru Ghat to board the steamer ferry that would take him to Pahleza Ghat on the other side of the river. Ten days later, when he came back from his village, Jigyasa brought fresh vegetables and a small sack of aged basmati rice. The two young men took over one of the *chulhas* in the mess, where the firewood was still burning. Jadu chopped the okra and fried the sticky green vegetable with mustard seeds and onion. While he was doing this, Jigyasa tossed the eggplants on the burning embers. When they were black, steam hissing out from the cracks in the skin, Jigyasa peeled them and sauteed the smoky pulp in oil and sprinkled minced garlic on it. Radishes they washed and bit into while still attached to the leafy stalks. The basmati rice that they ate that night, Jadu felt, was more fragrant than nearly anything he had eaten before in his life.

Jigyasa took him to a reading by the poet Agyeya, who had arrived that morning by train from Delhi. Although he was nearly fifty, the poet appeared youthful. Agyeya's poetry was experimental and philosophical: he was known as a proponent of *nayi kavita*, or new poetry in Hindi. Jadu bought a chapbook of Agyeya's poems and back in his room, reading late into the night, he found the lines that he knew he would translate from Hindi and use as the epigraph in his thesis. Agyeya's poem referred to the tale told in the *Ramayana* about the bridge built by the army of monkeys so that Lord Rama could cross over into Lanka and rescue Sita from the demon-king Ravana. The lines that Jadu translated into English for his thesis were the following ones: *Those who build bridges / will necessarily / be left behind. / Armies will cross over / The demons will be defeated and die / The deities will triumph / Those who were builders / in history / will only be called monkeys.*

————

Four years had passed since the time Jadu found admission in First Year, History Honors. No one, certainly not someone like Ananya Ghosh, had asked him to tell them his story. In 1935, on a rainy night, Jadunath Kunwar had been born in a hut in Khewali village. When he turned nineteen, he had crossed the Ganga at Hajipur on a steamer. On his first night in Patna, he slept on the riverbank. In the morning, after a breakfast of fresh jalebis and tea, he had walked with his blanket and his higher secondary certificate to the gates of Patna College. After successfully acquiring his bachelor of arts degree, Jadu had enrolled in the master's program even though his mother, Sumitra, had expressed a desire that he join the police force and become a daroga or inspector.

After graduation, several of Jadu's classmates were planning to sit for the entrance exams for the civil services. Ramdeo Manjhi, who had wanted to enter politics, took a job as a postal clerk instead. Ramdeo's father had died suddenly, and his brother needed money for college. Jadu also wanted to earn a little money and send it to his mother, so he decided to take the job of a lecturer in history at Langat Singh College in nearby Muzaffarpur. During this time, already enrolled in the class for master's students, he continued to live in Patna in the university hostel. On some days, he offered private tutoring in the evenings to schoolchildren of doctors and government officers. In these homes, he got used to being served tea and dry snacks that were often stale. For his trips to Muzaffarpur, he took the early-morning steamer across the river to Hajipur and then traveled second-class on the local train, the grit from the train's coal engine lining his scalp and his eyebrows.

That first summer as a postgraduate, Jadu arrived home in Khewali on a visit. His mother said in her own indirect way that so-and-so's wife had remarked that Jadu would look handsome and imposing in a policeman's uniform. He could not see himself with a baton in hand or wearing boots with nails in them. He told Sumitra that the man who was the President of India, Rajendra Prasad, had once taught in the same room he did at Langat Singh College in Muzaffarpur. This was true.

Sumitra did not say anything in response and, still sitting in a semicrouch on the floor in the tiny hut that served as the kitchen, she began lighting the fire to heat the food she had kept aside for her son. In his small suitcase, between the pages of a history textbook, were twenty-five rupees that Jadu had brought for his mother. This fact gave him belief in himself but looking at the crouching figure of his mother he was also seized by shame. He was embarrassed that he had mentioned the President of India. Was the President's mother at that moment getting smoke in her eyes from blowing into a wood fire in a dark hut? Jadu told himself that his own work, teaching students at a small regional college, had dignity. He wanted Sumitra to have some pride in her son's job. But by making it sound more important than it really was he had made matters worse. During his second year at college, the government had opened the State Bank of India and in his account Jadu had saved around 250 rupees. That was enough money. He decided that he would give his mother the 25 rupees now but also send another 25 rupees by money order.

Two weeks later, Jadu got the opportunity to invoke Rajendra Prasad's name again.

He had returned to the hostel from a round of tutoring sessions. Once he had locked his bicycle, he found waiting on the table in the mess hall a letter addressed to him. The letter was from Ramdeo. Jadu was being invited to a dinner celebrating the birth of Ramdeo's daughter. A daughter? When did Ramdeo get married? Jadu rode his bicycle to the dinner party. He held a flashlight in one hand, lighting his way in the dark, while with the other hand he steered his bicycle around puddles. The house that Ramdeo was renting was in Mithapur, next to the Ramakrishna school. Both windows facing the street were thrown open and brightly lit. Inside, there were at least a dozen other guests, men and women, children too. No sign of Ramdeo. Had Jadu come to the wrong house? Then he saw Mani Shanker sitting in the corner and next to him Lallan Yadav with a bandaged hand.

Jadu went straight to Lallan to take a closer look at his hand. Lallan had accepted a part-time job teaching history as well as physical education at Miller School. In the meantime, he was preparing for the civil services exams. Jadu asked if the injury was from the physical education class or from teaching history. Lallan had been trying to separate two boys who were fighting in the corridor and he had crashed against a window.

"Jadunathji," Ramdeo was saying from somewhere behind him.

Jadu folded his hands and bowed to Ramdeo and then in the general direction of his guests. Ramdeo said to the men and women all sitting in two small facing rows, "Jadunath, my friend from college. Those were the days!"

Holding his wrist, Ramdeo led Jadu to the next room, where a tall woman, taller than Ramdeo at least, was arranging bolster pillows around a sleeping infant.

"Jadunath, this is my wife, Reena. And this is my daughter, Rani."

Jadu said, "Wah, all three names begin with *R*. It was all predestined! Ramdeo, Reena, and Rani. Very nice."

Ramdeo and his wife laughed.

Jadu said, "But when did you get married? I didn't get invited to the wedding!"

Ramdeo laughed harder now. Reena covered half of her face with her sari to hide her amusement.

"We got married when I was only fifteen," Ramdeo said. "She was fourteen."

"A month short of fourteen," Reena said.

Jadu's face must have shown surprise. Ramdeo said, "It is common among our caste. You get married early in the village."

Jadu had recovered. He said, "You are in good company. I think

Gandhiji got married when he was fourteen. And our President, Rajendra babu, was only twelve when he was married off."

Ramdeo held up his hand. "No, no, don't give us those examples from the past. This is a big problem in my community, second only to that of alcoholism. If I had gone into politics . . ."

Once again, he took Jadu's wrist in his hand, and led him into the room where the other guests were gathered. Reena followed them out. She had a younger brother in high school; he was bringing out food from the kitchen. Puris, dal, vegetables, raita. Vegetarian fare because it was an auspicious occasion. A clay pot of warm gulab jamun for dessert. They drank tea from tiny china cups that, Ramdeo said with his customary frankness, they had borrowed from a restaurant in the neighborhood. The milk in the tea was smoky—how did that happen? After dinner had been eaten, Jadu asked Mani Shanker to sing a song. Mani began with a pleasant imitation of Talat Mahmood singing *Ae mere dil kahin aur chal*. A song about the eternal drama of escape from misery to prosperity, from the country to the city. On his way back to the college hostel, the flashlight casting weak light into the night's liquid darkness, Jadu wondered when he too would get married. The future took shape in his mind. It had the shape of the letter *J*. Jadunath would marry a girl with a name like Jaya and have a son named Jeet or a daughter named Jugnu.

Another night. Jadu had eaten his dinner early in the mess hall—there was fried fish but the dal too watery. A new film, *Insan Jaag Utha*, had been playing for a week. A light drizzle began to fall as soon as Jadu stepped out and he was glad to step inside the foyer of Regent Cinema. He bought hot tea. Jadu had come because the leads were Sunil Dutt—and Madhubala! The lights dimmed in the cavernous hall and the film started. Just like Jadu, the Madhubala character in the film was a villager. He identified with her and not with the male lead, who was from the city and wore trousers and a shirt. In one scene, Madhubala leaned her head against a haystack. Jadu knew the touch of that hay, he knew the fragrance that the hay released in the sun, and the tiny scratches he knew the stalks of hay were leaving on Madhubala's skin. In the film, a large dam was being built. Giant machinery and the tires that were bigger than humans featured in the songs. Why dams? Because the idea that was central to the film was that of everyone coming together in the act of nation-building. Nehru himself had stood close to the concrete expanse of the Bhakra-Nangal Dam in Punjab and called it "the biggest temple and mosque and gurdwara."

But there was evil in the film. The male lead was a criminal-turned-crane-operator at the dam site. Yet, even he appealed to national ideals. He sang a song about Madhubala—she was the moon, he crooned, the moon that belonged not to Russia, not to Japan, not to America, but to India. (As he sang, how Madhubala's eyes flashed! How she wrapped her arms around her shapely bosom—a divine embrace!) When the heroine sang a song about labor—everyone on the screen joined in the national effort—it aroused our hero's conscience. He turned from villainy to good. The whole song presented a united chorus of national striving and development. India had been free from British rule only a few years. The giant black-and-white figures singing and dancing on the screen were telling Jadu to embrace idealism without irony. When Jadu stepped out of the cinema hall he dreamed of being in a relationship—he was ready for love—so that he could also be a good citizen.

———

During the monsoon, rainwater collected in drains and ditches in Patna; ponds overflowed and water covered the fields where only a month before there was burnt stubble; stagnant water also stood in potholes and in trashed tires or small discarded tins rusting on rooftops. Dark water pooled under air conditioners in the bungalows of the rich, and that same water also formed puddles through which the poor waded to get to their rotting, ramshackle dwellings. Mosquitoes laid their eggs everywhere in the standing water and just two or three days later the eggs hatched, releasing into the water the tiny wriggling bodies that were mosquito larvae. They developed into adult mosquitoes, with the female mosquito needing a blood meal in order to reproduce. There were over three thousand species of mosquitoes in the world and one of them, the anopheles mosquito, was the main transmitter of malaria. One female of that species found Jadu.

Jadu felt alone in his illness, but he also felt foolish for not having taken the right precaution. He had denied himself what he had seen Radha Charan Tripathi doing in his own hostel room—which was the daily use of Flit, the insecticide sprayed from a small pump that always resided under Radha Charan's bed. Jadu didn't want the expense, and he didn't like the smell. He thought the mosquito net he used at night was protection enough. It wasn't. For days on end, sick with fever and chills, Jadu stayed in bed, racked by nausea, often feeling that the white net around him was in reality a shroud and that death was near. His classmates brought him food from the student mess hall. Gita Mohan Singh had chloroquine tablets left over from his own illness, and he gave them to Jadu. In Hindi films, when the hero was dying, his mother appeared somewhere in the sky and a beam of light flowed out from her upraised palm toward her son about to breathe his last. Now, filled with self-pity and dread, Jadu waited for his mother's disembodied shining face to materialize above him. As soon as he saw her, he would know that he was about to die.

During the second week of his illness, when Jadu was feeling better but still weak because the fever would return now and then, he opened his eyes and saw Professor Dey standing near the bed. He was holding a paperback novel for Jadu to read. Jadu didn't know how to pronounce the name in the title but he read the book with interest and cried at the fate of the heroine when the book ended. The novel was Thomas Hardy's *Tess of the d'Urbervilles*. In his thin notebook, Jadu noted down the new English words he had learned from the novel. *Unsullied; betrothal; dissembler; imbibed; purport; lambent.* The list went on.

When he recovered, Jadu decided to go to Khewali. He wanted

to be home. There wasn't much money because he had been unable to do any tutoring during his illness. Still, he went out and bought a new mosquito net for his parents. And bright new notebooks for his sister Lata. Notebooks and a new pen and a bottle of ink.

He knew his parents would first be alarmed when they saw him. He had grown thin and pale. But they would be alarmed also because he had arrived without being summoned. Usually, in the days before every festival, a yellow postcard would come from Khewali. Sumitra couldn't write and the letters were in Shivnath's handwriting. In small, irregular letters, his words looking like scratches from a language entirely different from Hindi, Shivnath would write down what Sumitra was saying to him. Nearly all the postcards said the same thing. They would remind Jadu of the upcoming festival and express the desire that he return home for a few days. Each postcard closed with a prayer for his good health. A line here or there would be different. For example, that Jadu's sister Lata had passed her annual examination at the Janaki Devi Girls School in a nearby village.

Jadu always wanted Lata to write to him, but she was a shy girl, and she never sent him a letter. There was a lot of love between them, of course, and Jadu never went back to Khewali without a special gift for his sister. When he arrived, late in the evening, Lata brought him water. She soon put on his cot a clean dhoti and a towel. With a smile, she asked if he wanted to eat puffed rice before dinner could be served. Inevitably, Jadu only asked for tea. When his tea came, Jadu would laugh and say, "Ah, this reminds me . . ."

Lata then smiled and smiled while Jadu looked in his suitcase for the present he had brought. He would have something for his parents too, but he felt abashed offering it to them himself. Often, after they had eaten dinner and only two lanterns remained lit, Jadu would give to Lata the things he had brought for Sumitra and Shivnath. She knew what to do. Jadu would watch from a distance his mother's face near the lantern's glow, searching her expression, hoping for the look of surprise to change to one of pleasure.

Lata would then go to Shivnath. Jadu would hear his father in the next room, beyond the straw partition, saying something about how expensive the flashlight must have been or how the old slippers were still holding together fine. But the next day, Jadu would see his father early in the morning take his bath and then use the new slippers or move around in his new blue striped shirt. Once Jadu had brought for his father a heavy bronze lock, to be used on the iron trunk where the land deeds and other papers were kept, but all of that first day Shivnath simply carried in one hand the lock, key attached, as he went about his business in the village. He was ready to answer any question about this new gleaming lock. The brand name Harrison was etched in the metal. In reality, the lock company owed its name to an entrepreneur named Hari Monga; the business was started by this Hari's son: that explained the name. Shivnath didn't know this, of course. To anyone who asked, he said, "Jadu has brought it from Patna. English-make. See the name . . ."

The new mosquito net that Jadu had brought had a pale pink hue, the light shade you glimpse on the stomach of the rohu fish pulled fresh from the river. Sumitra liked the net at first sight and took it to the room where Shivnath was already in bed. The old net had acquired holes in a few places. When Lata came to report on this to Jadu, he said that in the morning he would read to her a poem in English and that the two of them could work on a translation.

Translation? The word itself was new to Lata. She knew only a handful of common words in English. Jadu knew this. He translated the word for her.

"Good morning," Lata said in English when Jadu woke up. He laughed.

What other words did she know?

She made a zero with her thin index finger and thumb.

But Jadu wouldn't accept this answer. He tossed words in the air to tell her that she already knew a few.

Yes. No. Good morning. Good night. Bus. Train. Station. Telephone.

Jadu also wanted to know if she knew the word *tea*. Lata smiled and turned away.

When she came back with his tea, she brought one of her new blue notebooks (on the cover, a print of a young maiden, perhaps a princess in an ancient kingdom like Magadha, reaching for a high branch laden with flowers while behind her a flock of deer look up). Lata was ready for her lesson. The morning sunshine poured in through the window. Short shoots of sugarcane that would take a whole season to grow to full height and ripen to sweetness stretched in neat rows to the visible horizon. In the distance, the rapid chugging of the flour mill. The siblings sat on the cot with the notebook and an orange textbook that Jadu had been required to purchase for his mandatory English-language course. The poem was a short one by an Englishman named Edward Thomas and was titled "Adlestrop."

On a summer afternoon an express train has stopped at Adlestrop station. No one boarded the train or got off on the empty platform. Lata said she had seen such stations, small and desolate, where no express train stopped except in an emergency. How would she write Adlestrop in Hindi, he wanted to know. They struggled over it. It was absorbing to discuss the precise details described in the poem and then to pluck Hindi words from their shared vocabulary; sometimes they would scratch out one word and then insert another. The poet had used simple words and Jadu saw how such words arranged in the right order could surprise you with their beauty.

But how to translate the words for English flora? Example: *willows, willow-herb, meadowsweet*, and *haycocks*. Or *blackbird*. When the train stops, the poem's narrator hears the hiss of the steam from the train engine and then the sound of someone clearing his throat. There is a description of the rural landscape outside, the varied vegetation and the cloudlets in the sky. And then the poem comes to an echoing end: the song of the blackbird seemingly spreading farther and farther, joining the song of the birds in the surrounding counties. What to do? Lata had stopped writing.

Jadu asked her to go on composing in Hindi. She ought to imagine a train stopping in the middle of nowhere between Muzaffarpur and Motihari. "Which trees would you see outside? And which bird are you likely to hear singing in the summer?"

They soon had a poem. A train has stopped to take water at a small station called Sugauli. The passengers don't want the train to move yet because a singing mynah sits in the branches of a mahua tree.

Jadu told his sister that the note on the young poet in his college textbook said that Edward Thomas had joined the army in 1915, soon after writing the poem. This was during the First World War. He was killed in action in 1917 shortly before the poem was published. There is no mention of war but it is a poem of war because its history, and the history of its creator, tells the story of war's destruction. Jadu saw that Lata's eyes were shining. Jadu didn't want his sister to cry and so didn't see it fit to ask what had moved her so much. Instead, he congratulated his sister for her poem, and she, finding herself praised by her brother, the college student, spoke to him in English. "Thank you," she said, before rushing out of the room.

————

Jadu had become a part of the campus scene, one of those people who arrive young and then one day notice that their walk has slowed down and a bit of gray is beginning to show in their hair. He now returned to his old room in the hostel in Patna with the air not of a student but of a householder; nevertheless, he was still officially a postgraduate student and he planned to submit his thesis the following year.

The weather hadn't turned hot yet but winter was fast becoming a distant memory. One afternoon, Jadu found himself thinking again of the time he was a new student at Patna College and had shaken hands with Tenzing Norgay. Tibet was in the news. The tiny country had declared its freedom from China and there were rumors that the young Dalai Lama had been arrested or maybe even killed by the Red Army. Then the news came that the Dalai Lama—he was twenty-three, the same age as Jadu—had made a daring escape from Lhasa and crossed the Himalaya into India on foot. He was accompanied by his mother, his siblings, and members of his cabinet. Wasn't that also what Tenzing Norgay's ancestors had done each year in their own way? They would find a path down through the treacherous passes when the weather turned, and then they farmed in the foothills, or sold merchandise like yak wool blankets in places like Darjeeling.

The Dalai Lama's journey had been filled with danger. He was being hunted by the Chinese army. The fugitives had walked for two days and two nights without stopping. On the Himalayan terrain, where they would be visible from the air, they traveled only at night. The newspapers said that the party had crossed the Brahmaputra on a boat made of yak skin. Then, soon after arriving in Dharamsala, the Dalai Lama announced his government-in-exile in India. Chinese planes had been searching in the mountains for the party making their escape, and many Tibetans believed that the group had been screened from the planes by mist and low clouds conjured by the prayers of the Buddhist priests.

During the years that followed, there would often be Tibetan families, in small, sad, always quiet, colorful groups sitting on the platform at Patna railway station. Jadu would look at them during his own journeys but he did not feel they even shared a language with him. Year after year, during the winter months, a Tibetan man came down from the mountains with a litter of pups to sell. He stood under a tall tree outside the courthouse, not saying much in response to questions. Jadu had walked past the dog seller on several occasions. The puppies had thick fur, small ears, small snouts. Their faces were stained with dirty tears. It had occurred to Jadu that he should stop and ask the man how much a puppy would cost. Yet, even at that moment, Jadu would be conscious of the approaching summer and he would think about the tar melting under his feet in May. The heat would become unbearable. How would these mountain dogs be able to tolerate it? The dogs were like their Tibetan owners, displaced, searching for a home, forced to live in a land where their customs, their clothes, their very bodies did not belong and were markers of a tragic destitution.

When the Dalai Lama first entered India, fleeing the Chinese authorities, the Indian magazines gave magical glimpses of his early life. His parents were poor farmers in Taktser village in the northeastern part of Tibet. When he was only two, a search party of monks had arrived at a nearby monastery. They had been led there by signs and wonders. A vision had come to an old lama as he stared into the waters of a sacred lake—a vision that gave a clue about the location of the house where the future Dalai Lama lived. The lama had seen in the lake's waters an image of a three-storied monastery with a gold and turquoise roof and a path running from it to a hill. This turned out to be the Kumbum monastery. The lama's vision had given way to a small house with strangely shaped gutters. That was where the boy who was to be seen as the reincarnation of the previous Dalai Lama lived.

The story was rich with details that excited Jadu's imagination and even raised doubt in his mind. The two-year-old village child had recognized among the visitors the lama of a distant monastery. He had picked up the objects that had been brought to his house—those items had belonged to the previous Dalai Lama, and now drew from the boy's lips quick cries of "It's mine, it's mine"— and he ignored the other objects that the monks had cunningly put in the mix to test him. The visiting party took the child away to the nearby monastery, where he stayed for several months. He had been separated from his parents and the rest of his family. That same summer, Jadu had been two years old. How he would have cried if he had been torn away from his mother and from his simple home in Khewali! While he was reading the details of the young Dalai Lama's life in a magazine in the college library, Jadu's eyes misted over. He had a sudden longing for the dirt road that passed by the village pond in Khewali and turned right near a banyan tree before coming to a stop outside the thatched-roof shed where his father could be seen putting feed into the troughs for the cows.

When the boy from Taktser village was taken to the Potala Palace and installed as the Dalai Lama, he was given a new name. His head was shaved: he would now be free of vanity. He was dressed in the maroon robes that were going to be his attire for the rest of his life. Among the subjects he was taught (apart from metaphysics, logic, epistemology, the philosophy of the Middle Way) was Sanskrit grammar. This was a subject in which Jadu had scored high; all that had been required was that he memorize the rules. The magazine profile also mentioned that the Dalai Lama's education was in the Nalanda tradition. Nalanda was only two hours away by bus from the small whitewashed library building in which Jadu sat reading the magazine while from outside came the cries of a man selling guavas. In Nalanda, the ancient Buddhist monastery that functioned as an important university had flourished for several centuries and then an invading army around 1200 C.E. had set fire to the library and most likely executed the monks who were studying there. All this history had taken place close to where Jadu had lived and studied these past few years. He had not worn saffron robes but had he not left home and given himself up to a life of dedicated study? The life he had led over the years in tiny hostel rooms, rooms that were damp during monsoon, burning hot during the months of summer, and cold in winter, were these rooms not like monastic caves? Had he not known hunger and suffering in his search for knowledge? Jadu asked these questions and saw himself in saffron robes—and then he quickly realized that he was being piteously vain and self-indulgent.

The Buddha had achieved enlightenment in Gaya. A giant banyan tree stood at the site where a starving Gautama resisted temptations and then entered an exalted state where a halo formed over his head. Jadu could walk out of the library in which he was sitting and a train would deliver him at Gaya train station in a few hours. Gautama Buddha's statues were everywhere in Patna and the rest of Bihar. But these were recent constructions. As a result of the devastation caused by the Turkish invaders, Buddhism had retreated from India by the end of the twelfth century, moving into the mountain fastnesses of places like Tibet. There was a history that linked Patna with Potala Palace. And now the Dalai Lama, a world leader of the Buddhist faith, had found refuge in India. How wonderful to know the connection between cultures!

Jadu put the magazine aside. He had a question that the Dalai Lama hadn't been asked by the journalist. Did he dream of beautiful women? Did full-breasted apsaras, dressed in the simple, seductive style common during the Buddha's lifetime, approach him with serene, downcast eyes? Did the Dalai Lama find himself waking up at night, troubled, telling himself sternly that he was a monk and must only have pure thoughts? From a library book in his bag, a book about the Indian Constitution, Jadu extracted a three-by-five, black-and-white studio portrait of a young woman. His mother had sent the photo to Jadu. A smile, the gentlest sort, played on the young woman's lips. Her name was Maya, a good name for an apsara, suggestive of beauty and wealth but also tantalizing and elusive like a dream or illusion. She lived here in Patna with her mother and an elder brother who was an advocate at the High Court. This elder brother had brought Maya's photograph to Jadu's mother and with a great show of humility put forward a proposal of marriage. Would Jadu marry Maya? Sumitra saw this as a chance for her son to move up in life. These people were not peasants, they were professionals in the city. The girl's father had been a government official in the Revenue Department but had died young. Another brother, a year older than she, was a lieutenant in the Bihar infantry regiment but stationed at that time in the western sector near Ladakh.

Three days later, it was Diwali. Maya's elder brother, Manoranjan, came in a car to pick Jadu up from the college hostel. It wasn't dark yet; diyas were being arranged on the parapets and railings of the houses they passed. Soon, the diyas would be lit and the city would glow with the light of tens of thousands of lamps. Maya's house was in one of the outer suburbs and overlooked the railway line. There was a small station there for local trains. Manoranjan said that on the days she had to attend college, Maya caught the local train to town, traveling in the ladies' compartment. The journey took twenty minutes to half an hour. The mother, short, bespectacled, kind-looking, asked him to sit down on the plastic-covered sofa. Then, Maya came with a plate of sweets. She didn't look at him.

Less than a year after the meeting, this girl with the thin arms, a dainty watch on her left wrist, would become his wife.

———

In April 1960 the Chinese premier Chou En Lai arrived in India. He was welcomed by Nehru but there were angry crowds in different cities holding aloft black flags to protest Chinese incursions into Indian territory to the north. On the same day that Chou landed in Delhi, Jadu and Maya got married in Patna. A minibus brought the groom's party from Khewali to Patna. Others had come by train or ferry. Jadu's college friends were there. Saurabh Kumar "Jigyasa" in a white kurta and a necklace of round rudraksha beads, and Ramdeo Manjhi with his wife, Reena, pregnant with their second child. Mani Shanker with his wife, who was a scholar. Lallan Yadav with his ever-present stubble. Krishna Murari Sharma in a white safari suit and white leather shoes, wearing dark glasses even at night. The presence of these friends, sitting on plastic chairs in a line behind the priest, was important to Jadu. They represented a link to the past and they were also witness to his becoming a family man.

The ceremony was held in Lady Stephenson Hall, where Maya's elder brother had received a rental discount. As Maya's father had died so long ago, his garlanded portrait was placed on a chair near the sacred fire. Manoranjan, the elder brother, and Maitreyi, the army captain, performed the rituals while their mother hovered nearby. It was a hot day and there weren't enough soft drinks for all the guests, but other than that no one had any complaints. The general feeling among Jadu's relatives was that the bride's brothers had appeared so humble, so full of apology, that there was no question of blaming them for anything. One of Jadu's distant uncles went so far as to say that Maya and her brothers were orphans— he used the English word—and should therefore be pitied.

Truth be told, Jadu was relieved that Maya's father was already dead. This feeling had to do with a story he had been told by his friend Rishi, who had got married two years earlier in the winter. Three days after being appointed a lecturer at the local engineering college, Rishi had received a marriage proposal from a family that owned a jewelry business in Ranchi. The night when the wedding took place was especially cold, and just as the priest was carrying out the complicated final rituals the bride's father collapsed.

He was seated close to Rishi and simply slumped against him with a loud sigh. The old man had suffered a heart attack, and people quickly covered him with a blanket. "Give him some warmth, give him some warmth," said one of the middle-aged women who was standing nearby. She was a cousin of the bride's and she appeared to be wearing more gold than anyone else at the wedding. The same woman then bent down and said to the priest that he should ask the groom to put the red sindoor in the bride's hair to mark the completion of the marriage. The priest balked but the woman touched his arm and said, "There is no time left."

When Rishi saw this unseemly haste, he knew that the old man was dead. He also understood that this death would be seen as inauspicious and, if anyone from his side objected or if the rituals were not quickly completed, the young woman he was about to marry would remain unmarried, perhaps forever.

The priest was racing through his chants. Quickly, he asked Rishi to put the sindoor in the parting on the bride's head and then the newly married couple was led into the room that had been decorated for them with long lines of jasmine with dark red rose petals and bits of silver tinsel.

Rishi's wife was the dead man's youngest child, and when she was given the news about her father's death it was necessary to sedate her. In the morning, Rishi was politely asked to leave for Patna and to return in a month. He was told that his wife had suffered a nervous breakdown. He had married into a rigidly traditional family—the women observed purdah and didn't appear in public. They were vegetarians and extremely religious. Rishi slowly became aware of the fear that had arisen among his wife's relatives: they suspected that Rishi would abandon his wife because she would be seen as a bad omen. But he had never entertained such superstitions. Over the next few months, when he visited his wife, whose name was Namrata, he would gently introduce himself again. "I am Rishikesh. I am your husband." After a year or so, Namrata began to see Rishi as a friend and he saw that his wife looked forward to his visits with some excitement and even joy. In time, Namrata came to Patna—fifteen months had passed since that night when her father died. Rishi told Jadu, "She has come to accept that her father is gone, and she sees me as someone he had left behind for her."

Rishi's story had injected fear into Jadu's heart. He fully expected things to go wrong, but no tragedy marred his wedding. The morning after, Jadu took Maya to Mahendru Ghat on the river. Maya had been raised in a home overlooking the railway lines: she had never stepped on a ferry. The trip on the boat across the Ganga charmed her. The idea of a crossing seemed laden with symbolic meaning. Two blasts of the horn and the ferry began chugging north. Pressed against the iron railing on the steamer's bow, their bodies close to each other, Jadu and Maya looked at the brown water churning below them. Then, as they began pulling farther away from the city, Jadu pointed out the buildings that they were leaving behind, including the giant dome of the Gol Ghar, the granary that the British had built as a protection against famine. There was some problem with the door, which only opened to the inside and so there had been trouble and the granary was never put to proper use. Jadu wanted to tell Maya this story but he didn't want to bring bad luck. He focused on Maya's hands, which clutched the metal railing. The scent of the flowers woven into her hair felt pleasant to him and he drew closer to Maya. When Jadu put his hand on her hand, it was the first time that they had touched in public.

After the ferry, they took the train to Sugauli, the same train that Jadu had boarded so many times when he used to teach at Muzaffarpur. In the past, he had always been alone, but now there was Maya in her new red sari. Her hands had henna on them and the soles of her feet were painted red. She drew the attention of their fellow passengers, who cast admiring glances at her. When they were eating aloo-puri in the moving train car, Jadu told Maya that they were lucky. The rest of the marriage party, traveling in the rented bus, would be taking a longer route. Jadu was saying this because he was afraid that Maya would grow weary of the trip soon. But he needn't have been nervous. Each part of this journey held the surprise of novelty for her. At Sugauli, the family's bullock cart was waiting to take them to Khewali. Jadu and Maya stepped on a wooden box and then climbed onto the cart, which had a tarp covering on a bamboo frame. A rug lay thrown over a pile of straw and there were two pillows added for comfort. A hand fan, fashioned from dried palm leaf, rested on the rug. Beeda, the old farmhand that Shivnath trusted the most and had asked to wait at the small terminus, clucked his tongue to signal to the bullocks that they could start pulling. Letting out a laugh, addressing no one in particular, Beeda said proudly, "They always know when they are going home. They will now dance all the way back."

Most of Maya's jewelry as well as the cash that the couple had received as gifts had been put in a new metal trunk with a conspicuously new lock. That metal trunk was traveling with Shivnath on the bus which was bringing home the rest of the wedding party. Shivnath felt safety in numbers. Two of Jadu's cousins had brought their guns to the wedding and they were also on the bus. In the bullock cart, Jadu put his head on the small suitcase they had with them and stretched out his legs. He wanted Maya to have the pillows to protect her from the occasional jolt. They had left the small town behind and were in the countryside. A dirt road stretched out ahead of them. On both sides of this narrow road, dark water gleamed in small plots of land. Men and women were hunched over in horizontal lines, planting rice seedlings as they advanced in slow, straight rows. In some of the paddy fields they passed, one or more people were keeping up a chant as they worked. There were small sections of fields where a bund had been built with mounds of mud: the water in those portions of the field, Jadu explained to Maya, would be bailed out and the people working in that field would take home the walking catfish as well as the needlefish that were found wriggling in the gray mud. Men and women in the fields, their clothes pulled up and tucked high on their waists, raised their heads when they heard the bells that Shivnath's bullocks wore on their necks. Children by the wayside, village children, saw that a bride was riding in the bullock cart and they ran alongside singing snatches of songs sung at weddings. A boy held out a gleaming fish for Maya. Jadu said that it was a tengra. Maya had never before seen a fish like this, small, silver, with elegant whiskers.

"The air is so pure here," Maya said after they had gone farther.

Jadu laughed. The remark had made him happy.

"That is because there are no trucks or cars here. No industries. That will change once we get electricity."

"It is nice," Maya said. "We are close to nature."

Nature?

Jadu wanted to say something but didn't. The picture that had first appeared in his mind was of being a child in Khewali and coming across a little rag doll on the dirt road. He remembered his mother warning him not to step over the doll but to walk around it. Under the surface of the world that they inhabited in the village was another, darker world, a hidden world of secret spells and black magic. You would be walking to school and come across evidence of what had taken place in the night: mysterious mud altars visible in the bushes and sometimes even on the road. On the altars would be signs of worship, a smear of color, some scattered grains or offerings, and also signs of animal sacrifice, drops of blood, feathers, and human or animal hair. That was the unknown world that Maya's remark had conjured in Jadu's mind.

When he was around twelve or thirteen, an evil spirit took possession of a girl in the village. Her name was Tanu and she was no more than a year or two older than Jadu. The man who had been called to get rid of the demonic spirit had a dark-skinned face covered with white ash. Tanu's screams were heard from the room in which the man with the white face tried to get rid of the spirit. It seemed he was asking her a question but the girl only screamed. After a while, the man came out of the room and demanded that a Brahmin boy who was a virgin be brought to him. A child of eight named Gagan was brought to the man. The door was closed again and after an hour when the sorcerer opened the door, people saw that Tanu lay tied to her bed with rope. It wasn't clear whether she was resting or asleep. Gagan's eyes were wild and he was reeling as if he was drunk. The man took Gagan by the hand and led him out of the house into the streets of the village. He would stop and loudly ask Gagan to point to the person who had put the evil spirit inside Tanu. Gagan would jabber for a while and then take a few more dizzy steps.

In a nearby cowshed, a thin, young farmhand had fed the cows and had sat down on the ground to eat rice from an aluminum plate. Gagan didn't know his name but he pointed at the farmhand. The man with the white ash pushed Gagan away, slapped the low-caste, and kicked him viciously when he fell down on the ground. The villagers now pounced upon him, this confused young man who had been singled out by Gagan. Tanu had been found to be pregnant despite being unmarried and so young. This was the evil spirit that had possessed her. She did not survive the efforts of the sorcerer to rid her of the demonic possession. The farmhand also didn't survive the beating he received and, therefore, he didn't get a chance to say whether he was guilty or innocent.

Jadu did not recount any of this to Maya. Instead, he said, "Yes, we are close to nature. But that means we don't have plumbing in the house. We use the hand pump. You will find the water sweet here."

———

Before she was allowed to step down from the bullock cart, the new bride was asked to dip her right hand into a copper jar filled with water. A mango leaf, a live fish, and two silver coins had been put in the copper jar for good luck. Then, Jadu's sister Lata helped Maya down. The embroidered aanchal of Maya's sari was pulled over her face and this made it difficult for her to find her footing.

Lata collected the currency notes that the village women gave Maya. It wasn't a lot. The women, young or old or very old, would peer at the bride's face and make approving noises. They touched her hair and also the gold jewelry she was wearing. The money was rolled up in their palms and they handed it to Sumitra, who passed it on to Lata, who made an entry for each amount in a notebook. When she brought the money to Maya, Jadu spoke up. He said that they must start putting aside a bit of money, however small the amount, in savings for their future. With this remark he was giving Maya a glimpse into his authentic self.

When he was hired to teach at the college at Muzaffarpur, Jadu earned 310 rupees per month. He lived simply and like others around him he sent money home to his parents and he also put into another account a small amount that he knew would be needed for Lata's wedding. His salary increased to nearly 400 rupees when he got the job at Patna College. Yet, he was afraid that after his marriage, his financial situation might become dire. Maya was an urban and educated woman. She was likely to have needs that he would struggle to meet. They moved into a small flat in Kankarbagh, not far from the house in which Maya's mother and brother lived. Once or twice, when he was in Khewali after the marriage, Sumitra tried to say gently to Jadu that his bride's needs were more pressing, and that he should stop sending money to them. But he knew this was out of the question—not only would it disappoint his parents, but it would make life more difficult for them.

Jadu would always remember that during the year he got married a dozen hens could be purchased for just ten rupees. For a rupee, he could buy several kilos of tomatoes. Petrol for the scooter that he had bought was sold for eighty paise a liter. Same price for mustard oil. For three rupees, you could get a kilo of ghee. When the two of them started life together in Patna, their daily expenses, including what was paid to the milkman or the money spent on vegetables plus the weekly payment to the maid who came each day, were all recorded in a diary that Jadu kept next to the bed. Maya noticed that when he went out to teach or left the home for any reason, the diary would be slipped under his pillow. She teased him about it, asked him if he hid it so carefully because he wrote his secret thoughts in its pages.

He was amused. Laughing, he opened the diary's pages for her to see. There was a black-and-white photo of Maya inside its front pocket. It was the picture that had been sent to Sumitra before their marriage had been arranged. And on the pages inside were little daily jottings, rows of items and numbers next to them indicating expenses. It was now Maya's turn to be amused. She asked her husband why he hid the diary from her if this was all there was in it. He said he wasn't hiding it from her. He didn't want the diary in plain view in case a thief stepped in when they were not at home. In the back of the diary, he showed her he had kept a hundred-rupee note. Folded inside the hundred-rupee note, there was a ten-rupee note. Jadu pointed to the money and said, "This money here is for emergencies. I have kept the ten-rupee note inside the hundred because sometimes you can't get change easily. If you have a small expense, like paying for the rickshaw, the hundred-rupee note is useless. Use the ten if you can't find your purse. This money is always there if you need it in a hurry."

Maya was still laughing at this demonstration of practical wisdom but she also felt love for her husband. She saw the years unfolding into the future and she had the clear sense that she would never lead a luxurious life; she also saw that her life would not be without an ordinary contentment, and that unless something utterly tragic and unforeseen happened, she would enjoy a secure life.

Feeling a sudden emotion, Maya asked her husband, "Do you want some tea?"

As they sipped tea, Jadu started outlining his financial plan, a combination of schemes that Maya liked hearing about but whose differences she didn't fully comprehend. Life insurance policy, retirement fund, and pension. He was trying to tell Maya that at the end of their lives there would always be out there in the world a large folded bill and, inside it, yet another, smaller one. They would have something to tide them over during difficulties, including death.

Maya wanted to get away from the seriousness, even the morbidity, that had come into the conversation. She said, "Tell me, what is the most amount of money you have held in your hands?"

Jadu thought for a moment. He said decisively, "I've never carried a large amount. I paid for the scooter with a bank draft. Only people engaged in illegal activities deal in cash."

This was news to Maya.

What Jadu and Maya did not know was that after twenty years had passed, they would need to withdraw all the money available from Jadu's retirement fund savings in preparation for their daughter Jugnu's wedding. It was a large amount. Jadu had been saving money; after selling his old Vespa scooter, he hadn't bought a car. He could have bought a used car but it was more prudent to save the money for the wedding. At the bank, he asked the teller to give him seventy thousand rupees in hundred-rupee notes and then requested that the remaining balance be put in his checking account. The teller asked him to fill out a deposit form. The man was rude. He didn't even bother to reply when Jadu asked him if he could give him a manila envelope to keep the money he was taking out. After making the deposit, Jadu wrapped the notes in a large red handkerchief and put the bundle in his cotton shoulder bag.

Jadu was angry with Satish Pathak, the father of the young man his daughter was marrying. He had requested this amount in cash as part of the dowry. It was out of the question, Satishji had said, when Jadu proposed bringing him a bank draft. The practice of dowry was illegal. "You will go to jail," Satish Pathak had said, but what he must have meant was that *he* would end up there. Maya had wanted Jadu to take a briefcase or a leather satchel, but he had said no. The leather satchel was a feminine style and the briefcase, so shiny and new, would have drawn attention. Jadu had passed unnoticed through much of his life and he wished to pass unnoticed when he was carrying such a large amount of cash.

But he hadn't passed unnoticed. Did the teller have a contact on the outside and had he sent him a signal? Or did pickpockets linger at a tea shop on the other side of the street from the bank, waiting to see who came out looking nervous? Did Jadu's face tell a story of fear and he had only tempted a man in need? These and other questions never left him in the years that followed, not even when the worth of seventy thousand rupees became much less during those years of inflation. And he wasn't surprised when even on his dying day what appeared in his mind was the scene from the bus station. He had noticed the lightness of the bag when he got up from his seat. He first looked under the seat. The bus had reached the Khajpura terminal and people were getting off. Maybe the money had slipped under an adjoining seat. But there was no bundle wrapped in a red handkerchief anywhere in sight. A couple bumped into him. The conductor came up to ask him what the matter was. Jadu said, "My money. My daughter's wedding." He couldn't think of anything else to say. He must have been wailing—or was it just his body crouching on the dirty ground after he had staggered off the bus?—because a crowd had gathered around him.

"All my money. My daughter's wedding," he repeated.

A man in the crowd bent down and touched the bag that still hung from his shoulder. The man murmured knowingly, "A razor cut."

The bottom of the bag had a neat slice. When Jadu saw it, he wanted to put the bag on his head, so that people would know he had been a fool. He thought of Maya telling him to take a brief-case. Then he imagined his daughter's face. He could return home but he had come far and he was expected at the groom's family's home in half an hour. He didn't know what he would say to them and, as if this was the only answer he could gather, he again spoke to the air in front of him. "All my money. My daughter's wedding."

Then they brought the youth with the bleeding lip. Jadu could still see clearly in his mind's eye the man wearing a blue cap who led the boy to him, their fingers interlaced like the sticks in the wattle fences that farmers put up outside their animal sheds in Khewali. Who were these strangers whose paths had so strangely—and so briefly, and yet decisively—got entangled with his? When the crowd started beating the youth, Jadu was led away by a man who first offered him water and then the advice that the money was now probably gone but he should make sure to file a report to the police.

Jadu didn't go to the police. Instead, he walked to Satish Pathak's home. The door was opened with a smile. They had invited a rela-tive who had dressed up in a silk kurta. Jadu felt he should deliver his report from the threshold and leave, but they were solicitous and urged him to come inside. Sit, they said, and they too offered him water.

Jadu was distraught but he didn't fail to notice that the young man Jugnu was to marry, Ranjit, was watching his own father closely. Ranjit seemed to sense that they had arrived at a crisis. He didn't know how to respond; his father would be his guide. Satish Pathak was a bureaucrat in the state industries and handi-crafts department. His first question was about the man who had led Jadu away from the crowd.

His eyes were narrowed, and his brow furrowed as he addressed Jadu. "Do you think this man was himself mixed up with the pickpockets?"

"I don't know."

"Where did this man get the water for you?"

"A sweet shop. You must know it. It is right there on the side of the road where the buses stop."

"Did he tell you who he was?"

"No."

Jadu wanted these questions to stop. He wanted Pathak to say that the money was now gone, they shouldn't worry about it any further. It would not be needed anymore.

Ranjit's mother, Kalyani, brought tea on a tray. She sighed sweetly when giving a cup to Jadu. But Satish Pathak retained his severe look.

"No use going to the police. What will you say to them anyway? Let it be. The main question is whether you can recover from this loss."

No one spoke. After a while, Jadu realized he was expected to say something. But he didn't know what he could say. He stayed silent.

Satish Pathak was still in charge. He said, "Please drink your tea."

The tea, hot and sweet, revived Jadu and he took another sip. Before he had taken a third sip, Satish Pathak got up and, touching Jadu on the shoulder, asked him to step outside for a second.

Outside his own living room, speaking conspiratorially, Satish Pathak said, "This is extremely unfortunate what happened to you. What solution is there?"

Jadu said, "I cashed in my retirement fund today. I have eighteen thousand left from it, which I was saving to buy other things, including a fridge. It was on the list you had given me."

Pathak said, "Yes, the fridge is important, of course. What about the money I need to buy the jewelry for your daughter? I cannot welcome her empty-handed."

Jadu glanced toward the door. All conversation had ceased inside. Had he spoken too loudly? Satish Pathak shifted his body a little so that he was blocking the door.

As if the wedding was part of a criminal plan they were hatching together, Pathak brought his head close to Jadu's. "It is good to meet misfortune with resolve. I'm trying to be clear so that there is no misunderstanding."

Lowering his voice even further, Pathak continued, "My son is hoping to move to Delhi to find more professional opportunities. The prospects here are close to nil. He has big plans. I do not have a paisa to spare."

Jadu said, "I'll do all I can."

"Yes," said Pathak, nodding approvingly. "It is a matter of your daughter's honor. Let's go inside."

But Jadu lingered at the threshold a moment longer. He wanted to catch hold of Pathak's arm and plead with him. His appeal had already taken shape in his head. "Pathakji, my daughter is now your daughter too. I have been a humble teacher and I have led an honest life. I have done everything I could to give my daughter a future. She is a very good person, intelligent, alert, and enormously kind. Please do not let cruel fate deny her what is her due."

Satish Pathak had probably seen the look on Jadu's face and guessed that an act of begging was soon to follow. He quickly stepped away from Jadu and went inside. Jadu followed him back into the room but didn't want to touch his tea now. Kalyani scanned her husband's face and she struggled to smile when she looked at Jadu. Kalyani had liked Jugnu. She had said to Jugnu that she was the kind of girl who was educated, and at ease in the city, but with respect for her elders.

By the time he was on a bus taking him back home, Jadu already felt better. All the money he was to give to Jugnu's future in-laws had been stolen, yes, but Jadu had had the foresight to carry his wallet in his pocket. This meant that, at least, he had been spared the humiliation of asking Satish Pathak for bus fare. Jadu was feeling better also because he had come to a decision. He had held on to all the land in Khewali that he had inherited from Shivnath. In Jadu's family, the rice, dal, turmeric, ginger, all came from their own land, which was cultivated by tenant farmers, families that had known each other for generations. His gains from the land were small; the real wealth lay in capital and in attachment to the land of his ancestors. He had kept this property as protection, and now the need had arrived. It would hurt him to part with the land but he would do it. His sister had received from Shivnath a small plot near the village pond. On that plot, there were two beautiful mango trees, a tiny bamboo grove in one corner, and a champa tree in the other corner, where it dropped its flowers on the water in the pond. After Lata's wedding, her husband had asked her to quickly sell this piece of property and use the money to build their house in Purnea. It hadn't hurt Lata even though, at that time, Jadu had entertained doubts. He had wanted his sister to hold on to that land; it would have been her protection.

Jadu himself would not sell all the land he owned. He was going to sell only the plot that each year yielded a fine crop of sugar-cane. That would give him the money needed to pay for the dowry and maybe even help with the wedding. This would leave untouched the parcel of land on which rice was grown. Each year, he would receive grain from home. He was also not going to sell the land in Khewali on which the brick house still stood; it was crumbling, and good only for cattle seeking shelter during heavy rains, but still, it was his home. He had been born there. A snake had bitten his mother on the steps of that house but she had defeated its poison and a few months later given birth to him. They had survived whatever fate had thrown at them. He would let the other piece of land go. His father had tilled the land but that life was not for Jadu. Life is long and the real wealth is time; you have to fight to not let it slip away. He must not abandon faith or squander his days. That ought to be life's goal. This thought took hold of Jadu as he sat on the bus and he raised the glass window so that the rushing wind kissed his face.

———

The stained yellow walls of the apartment building, its window ledges painted red, overlooked an alley filled with bicycle repair shops and ramshackle dhabas serving tea and cheap snacks. On a particular Tuesday morning back in 1965, anyone standing at any one of the building's windows would have seen Jadu walking home with a bag in his hand. He had stepped out in the morning to buy dried coconuts. This was because his wife, Maya, was pregnant with their first child and craving the taste of coconut—she wanted to chew on the grated shavings—and later, nearly every night, she demanded salted cashew. Never had she demonstrated such an intense desire for any food. This sudden interest was of a limited nature; there were some dishes that she could no longer prepare. Among the smells she now found unbearable was that of meat cooking. It made her throw up. Vegetables didn't fare much better. All strong odors were unpleasant to her. A part-time maid, a mother of three children herself, visited twice daily to cook plain meals for the couple. When Jadu wasn't around, this woman also dispensed advice about the complications of pregnancy and childbirth. She knew about all kinds of tragedies that befell women: water breaking early; babies stillborn because of various delays; umbilical cords choking the babies; babies whose shoulders got caught in the vagina; tears in the mother's vagina or excessive bleeding for other reasons; the flourishing trade in kidnapped babies. Maya began to fear any conversation with the maid and she soon asked Jadu if they could move to her mother's house sooner than they had planned.

The pregnancy presented no real complications. The gynecologist, a brisk and confident Sikh woman, conducted routine checkups. She would begin the visit to the clinic by asking the expectant mother if she had chosen a name for the baby and, without meaning to be secretive, Maya or Jadu would say that they were still thinking about it. No choices yet, they would say, even though this wasn't true. They had discussed it between themselves, and told each other that they were both a bit scared, and that they wanted to keep their hopes and also their fears private. Even before her third trimester had started, Maya moved into her mother's house. The family of Maya's brother, Manoranjan, occupied much of the space in the flat—Maya and Jadu were given a room next to the one in which Maya's mother slept. No more morning sickness for

Maya but her back hurt and her feet were swollen. When Jadu sat at the foot of the narrow bed massaging his wife's feet, the two of them took turns guessing whether the baby would be a boy or a girl. In the West, people named their children in honor of their dead relatives. Jadu knew in his heart that in a society like theirs such a practice would be considered in bad taste—or worse, a taboo and an invitation to bad luck. To make Maya laugh, Jadu cheerfully disclosed that, returning from Ramdeo's one night, he had decided that he would like his child to share his initial. If a boy, Jeet, and if a girl, Jugnu.

When Jugnu arrived, Jadu was told that he couldn't see her for twenty-seven days. The alignment of the stars and of the planet Saturn during the child's birth was such that a dark fate would visit the father if he caught sight of the baby before that time was up. This knowledge had come from Sumitra herself. She had made the trip from Khewali with a gold necklace for Maya and tiny silver anklets for Jugnu. Also, a tiny silver spoon and bowl. Also, a silver coin embossed with the head of a bald, bearded sovereign (EDWARD VII KING AND SOVEREIGN). Also, as the chief determinant of Jadu's immediate fate, a yellow document, each page fingerprinted in the lower right corner with turmeric paste—the fingerprints belonging to an astrologer who lived near Khewali. The world was passing through an inauspicious period, he had written in Hindi, and given the position of the planets and the stars, Jadu was to wait till the twenty-seventh day to first glimpse the infant's face as it was reflected in a dark bowl filled with mustard oil. Lacking the courage to argue with this logic, Jadu decamped to his apartment near the college. A cot was put in Jugnu's room for Sumitra, who would collect the baby from the mother's breast whenever needed during the day or night. Maya was too tired to come to the phone, which sat in its wooden cradle in the living room, but Jadu called every day from the college office just to confirm that no celestial body had interfered in any way with the happiness of his family.

When Jugnu was about to turn four, she stood with her palms

facing each other, about six inches apart, and asked her father if that was her size when she came out of her mother's stomach. Jadu said she was probably a bit bigger than that and then he added that he hadn't seen her till she was almost a month old. Why, the child wanted to know, and Jadu was stumped for an answer. We often put our faith in strange superstitions? That wouldn't do. He remained silent for a moment and then said something about having been sent away on duty. The child waited for more and when Jadu said nothing further she only asked if he was going to be around for her birthday.

When she was seven, Jugnu fell down a staircase at her friend Manju's house. Maya learned that the child's body had bounced down several steps and there were bruises to show for this. No broken bones, however. But by later in the evening, Jugnu had a high fever. Next morning, Jadu took her to a doctor. It was puzzling, had the fall damaged an organ? After examining her, the doctor said that the illness had nothing to do with the fall. He wanted a blood test done; he was certain it was malaria. While they were still at the clinic, Jugnu also vomited twice. On the doctor's face, Jadu thought he read concern.

In a soft voice, the doctor asked Jugnu if she had hit her neck on the stairs. The child looked sleepy, exhausted, and didn't answer. The doctor asked her to bend her neck and Jugnu refused, saying that it hurt. Taking Jadu aside, the doctor said, "Take her to the hospital immediately. We don't want it to be meningitis."

Jadu called Manoranjan from the hospital and asked him to bring Maya. The malaria had led to meningitis. After a three-hour wait, a doctor came to Jugnu's hospital bed to tell the parents that the child would have to be kept there the next few nights. Maya gasped. The doctor was calm and dispassionate, and this should have been reassuring, but Jadu too reeled from the news. Jugnu's spinal fluid as well as her brain lining were probably infected, the doctor said, and what was now necessary was just watching to assess how quickly the antibiotics worked. Maya was getting more agitated and she had questions but Jadu didn't want to hear more. He said, "We are going to wait and see, wait and see."

Maya's mouth tightened and she didn't want to talk to Jadu after that. When Jadu suggested that he was going to call Manoranjan so that he could take Maya home, she replied tersely that she would spend the night there in the hospital. Jadu was free to go home and return early in the morning.

In the bedroom that night, Jadu extracted from a low drawer in Maya's dresser a thin yellow notebook. Its pages had turmeric marks in their lower right corners for good luck.

Jadu was searching for something specific. He had only read the astrologer's words once before, soon after Jugnu had been born, and he had then put the book away. Now he found what he was looking for. All these years he had believed that the astrologer had noted that a grave illness ("a threatening affliction"—was that a better translation?) would befall the newborn when she turned three. But now Jadu saw that the astrologer had actually written six. The numeral three in Hindi is the mirror opposite of six, an easy mistake that Jadu had made earlier too. Was this the illness that the astrologer had predicted years ago? Jugnu had just celebrated her seventh birthday. That was pretty close to six, wasn't it? Why was he doing this, he asked himself next. And even as he asked this question of himself, he was curious about what else the astrologer had said. He continued reading.

It was clear that whatever it was that Jugnu was suffering would soon pass. There was proof right there on the page. The astrologer had written in his sloping hand that Jugnu would grow up to be a caring, sensitive woman who genuinely loved her parents. Like her father, she would have an interest in history. She would make an able administrator. She would be troubled by minor problems to do with her ears, nose, and throat. The astrologer advised her to wear the color green and, after reaching puberty, she was to wear emerald to strengthen the role of Mercury in her chart. It would help with her powers of reasoning. The child would be a world traveler. She would marry at nineteen and bear two healthy children. She would need to be careful when she was thirty-three years of age . . . Jadu stopped himself, asking if the astrologer had written sixty-six instead. But the truth was that Jadu didn't care, it was all so distant in the future. Bending down, he hid the yellow notebook in the dank interior of the unused drawer from which he had extracted it.

What the astrologer could not foresee: Jugnu at eight making a card at Christmas for her father as part of a school project and after pasting the envelope shut making a tear in the corner to make it easy for Jadu to open it; Jugnu at ten telling her teacher that her mother had died from cancer and later the teacher bursting into tears upon seeing Maya buying sweets during Dussehra; at thirteen, Jugnu taking care of the little girl downstairs, whose mother had indeed died of cancer, reading aloud stories and thoughtfully altering all references to death ("when Cinderella's father *went away to the city*, she lived with her stepmother and stepsisters"); Jadu entering Jugnu's room to turn off the light and finding her reading his old copy of *Lolita*—how old was she at that time, maybe fourteen?; a year or two later, winter holidays, Jadu coming upon his daughter with a newspaper in her lap, she somehow not conscious of his presence and he finding her examining an ad for Charminar cigarettes—a young man with a dark mustache gazing dreamily into the camera under the words "It takes Charminar to satisfy a man like you"—and Jadu's first thought, clearly wrong, that Jugnu has started smoking; also unforeseen, the disaster of her marriage.

———

Maya had made a promise to Lord Shiva. If a child was born to her, she would make the long pilgrimage to Deoghar. She was determined to join the thousands of pilgrims walking barefoot for a hundred miles carrying the sacred water from the Ganga at Sultanganj. Jadu didn't protest. Sumitra had always talked about such a pilgrimage and now she believed that Maya was fulfilling a desire that had long resided in the family. Jadu and Maya waited after Jugnu was born. When she was three years old they left the child with her grandmother in the village.

The train from Patna brought them to the small station at Sultanganj. The summer light lingered in the sky even though it was nine in the evening. It had rained earlier but the monsoon clouds still hung heavily over the horizon. Pilgrims in saffron garb filled the wet streets and were crammed into every eating place. Jadu and Maya paid for a tiny room at a dharamshala that was charging sixty rupees each night. They bought a simple meal of khichdi and plain yogurt at a small restaurant whose signboard showed the Ganga flowing out of Lord Shiva's knotted hair atop his head. Each painting, each statue of blue-skinned Shiva fascinated Jadu, not least because of the snake, the cobra with the expanded hood, that sat coiled around the divine neck. This neck that gave Shiva the name *neelkantha,* the blue-throated one, because he had drunk the world's poison and turned blue. Jadu felt the snake's gaze focused on him and, all through dinner, he looked back at the painted image on the signboard as one might examine a photograph of a long-dead ancestor, feeling distant and yet mysteriously connected.

Just before dawn, Jadu and Maya walked to the river ghat. The steps were slick with mud. They waded into the river and lowered their small brass pots into the water. Each pot came with a tight seal: the holy water was not to be spilled. It was to be poured on the *shivaling* at Deogarh at the end of their pilgrimage. Thin blue nylon rope secured the pots to each end of a flexible length of bamboo that was balanced on their shoulders.

Bol Bam! Bol Bam! The chants rang up and down the streets as the procession moved in the direction of Deoghar. Every few miles, tents rose up out of the green, fertile earth. Tents had been erected by the government for the pilgrims to rest. Outside each tent, policemen in khaki uniforms sat on metal chairs, looking like bored minor priests before the beginning of a ceremony. Painted signs everywhere warned people of pickpockets and thieves who would give you food that made you lose consciousness.

When they rested the first time after an hour and a half's walk, Maya read the warning signs and asked Jadu, "Can that be true? Who is going to dare steal under God's nose?"

He laughed at her innocence. He understood she was trying to make conversation. She had made a joke. Jadu was weighed down with worries about his wife: a slight woman, unused to walking long distances, how was she going to complete this pilgrimage? As they sat sipping tea, they watched the dense crowd, the faces of the men and women hurrying past. The faces bore a uniform look of attention, each one tense with determination. The test was difficult and drawn-out, and everyone was rushing to their goal. Close to her, Maya heard a woman walking with her chappals held in her right hand asking for tea, and her husband, breathing hard through his mouth, saying loudly, "Only after we have reached Tarapur!"

Jadu and Maya tossed their baked clay cups on a pile behind the tent and joined the flow of humanity. The sun warmed the asphalt on the road and although they were wearing sneakers their feet were hurting by lunchtime. When they stopped at one of the many wayside vegetarian restaurants in Rangaon to eat, Jadu wanted to take off his shoes and soak his feet in water. Was it possible that walking made blood pool in your feet? He asked Maya this question and she said calmly that the pain might go away after their feet got used to walking.

Jadu had noticed the pilgrims walking barefoot. But there were sharp stones everywhere. When he voiced this thought aloud, Maya said that it was a matter of faith. Jadu didn't argue. In the distance, he saw hills and small green trees growing on the red earth. Clouds were approaching from the direction of the hills and then it began to rain. So, in the end, Jadu's feet got the soaking he wanted. His shoes filled with water and made a squelching noise. The other pilgrims continued to chant in the light drizzle; their chanting grew louder with the rain. They were keeping their spirits up by repeating *Bol Bam, Bol Bam*. Then, a skinny dog appeared from nowhere, running alongside the procession, sending the pilgrims lurching away because they didn't want to be defiled. And then soon, the dog was gone, an emissary from another world.

That night, when they stepped into a dharamshala in Mahadev Nagar, it was as if they had arrived at a leper colony. Everywhere Jadu looked, in the dimly lit rooms and in the crowded corridors, men and women sat or slept swathed in bandages. No one walked, everyone only limped. Such a parade of afflictions. Once again, Jadu fetched khichdi for dinner but Maya only accepted a couple spoons of yogurt and after quietly writing in a small green diary she quickly fell asleep.

It was a struggle to walk the next morning. Sore limbs and, more serious, blisters on the feet. But the pain eased again—or maybe one just got used to it. And after a while the only thing to do was to put one foot in front of the other. It was an act as simple as faith. Later in life, Jadu would remember this journey and how the difficulties that had appeared intolerable at times had in the end not mattered so much. It had become possible to overcome everything simply by not giving up. Perhaps this was the lesson that the gods wanted you to absorb.

A tent came into view at midday with a sign outside identifying it as a first-aid station. Jadu and Maya stopped to ask if they could get medicine for their blisters. A man with only one leg was sitting on a metal foldout chair and he squeezed out an antiseptic ointment on a piece of cotton and handed it to Jadu with a tiny roll of gauze. Maya did not have any blisters. When they thanked the man, he nodded his head wordlessly, which made them suspect he was perhaps also deaf and dumb. But how had he understood what they needed? Maybe because Jadu had taken off his sneakers and pointed at the blisters.

They left the tent and sat on the stone parapet of a well nearby. In the shade of a tree next to them there were other pilgrims also sitting, resting. An enormous weariness overcame Jadu. He joked that this was what it must have looked like at the end of the day when the battle of Kurukshetra was being fought in the *Mahabharata*. A koel was calling from some hidden place in one

of the surrounding trees. Maya looked in every direction, wanting to catch sight of the bird. A woman her age sitting under the
umbrella that she was sharing with her husband pointed at a tree
to Maya's right. And yes, partially hidden among the leaves of the
mango tree, Maya caught a glimpse of a dark shape. As long as the
koel kept up its call, Maya didn't even feel like leaving. But then
Jadu said that they must keep walking.

When they stopped at another vegetarian restaurant that evening, Jadu and Maya were tired and impatient with each other.
While having dinner, they argued over whether or not they ought
to stop at a medicine store to buy bandages and a healing ointment
for Jadu. It was Maya's idea but Jadu thought they would be wast-
ing money. After all, he could get those items at a first-aid station.
Maya said that there was no need to spend money on the food they
were eating in the restaurant.

"After all," she added preposterously, "we could try to find a
charitable temple where food is given free to beggars."

Jadu's expression must have revealed his irritation or anger,
because Maya stopped abruptly.

Later, while looking for a room in a dharamshala or even a
hotel room if there was one to be found, they happened to pass a
pharmacy.

"One minute," Jadu said and stepped inside, where a man was
standing under a lightbulb glowing red.

When Jadu came back to the street where Maya was waiting for
him, she saw that he was holding a wad of gauze, a tube of antiseptic medicine, and, to show that he could easily spend money,
a small tin of Pond's talcum powder for her. He had seen fellow
pilgrims sprinkling talcum powder on their feet and then pulling
on socks. Maybe this reduced friction and the chance of blisters.

Maya smiled and said, "What need was there for this?"

Jadu said huskily, with sudden, unnecessary emotion, "Keep it,
keep it."

At the dharamshala in Katoria, they had to separate. Women
were sleeping in one large hall and men in another. Stiff carpets

covered the floor in each room. For five rupees, each person could borrow bedding. A pillow and two thin sheets. Jadu gave the man ten rupees. Lights were turned off at nine and Jadu was too exhausted to be affected by the snoring and shifting in the dark, the small moans of men with hurting feet and knees. He was worried about Maya. She had said that the women's bathroom was attached to the hall in which they were sleeping. But he wondered how she would find her way to it in the dark.

Long before dawn, men were up, brushing their teeth, spitting, chanting *Bol Bam*. Should he go and find Maya, or should he get ready first? Jadu took his bag into the bathroom and waited in line. When he came out, he found Maya outside the hall where he had left her the previous night. She smiled when she saw him.

"Shall we start?"

"How did you sleep?"

They talked while they walked. Maya asked Jadu if he remembered the kind woman who had shown her where the koel was hiding in the tree. That woman had spent the night in the same hall she had. Maya wanted to know if Jadu had met her husband. He hadn't. Maya thought that was unfortunate. She had liked making a friend. The woman's name was Chitra, and she was Bengali, with two small children, whom she had left with her brother in Bhagalpur. The two women had slept next to each other.

Maya wanted tea. Jadu bought two bananas, which they ate, and then waited for tea. The name of the small town was Kalakatia. If they walked for two hours without stopping, Jadu said to Maya, they would reach Deoghar. He had been surprised how calm and constant she had been during this long trek. And she had not complained once while he had said at least a dozen times to her, asking for sympathy, "We are not used to this."

But now Maya wanted to know how long they would be standing in the line outside the temple. How long before they would stand in front of the *shivaling*?

"At least one hour," said the man making the tea.

Not too long, then. With this in mind, Maya suggested to Jadu that they wait a bit and see if the Bengali lady, Chitra, passed by. It would be wonderful to walk with her.

But Jadu would not listen. He said to his wife, "Gajender is expecting us."

Gajender, a Brahmin from Jadu's village, was one of the priests at the main temple in Deogarh. Jadu had written a letter telling him that he would arrive on this date with his wife. Gajender had sent back a postcard to confirm that he would wait at the temple and that he would also make arrangements for their stay in a cheap but comfortable hotel.

Jadu and Maya resumed their walk. The country was more hilly now and mica glinted in the gravel at their feet. They passed an orchard with cashew trees. Maya wanted their journey to end. She imagined herself soon pouring the holy water she was carrying on the *shivaling* in the temple, but she had liked observing the landscape that stretched out on both sides of the road. "Your father did not take me to the Taj Mahal," she would tell her daughter many years later, "but we had a good time walking to the temple in Deoghar."

Sensing that he had disappointed his wife by telling her that they couldn't wait for the Bengali woman whom she had befriended, Jadu thought he should talk to Maya as they walked. Maybe tell her a story to take her mind off the grueling trek. He tried to engage her interest by talking excitedly about Gajender. Jadu called him Gajender Bhaiya, as if the priest were really his elder brother. But that was the way of the village and this was part of what Maya was learning. Jadu said, "Gajender Bhaiya is no longer in his prime but you should have seen him when he was young."

When Jadu was still a boy and on his way to the middle school in the next village, he would often be looking past the sugarcane fields at the rosewood trees in the distance. That was where the tarred road began. And then Gajender would appear through the mist, his bare feet thundering on the ground as he ran past. This daily run of ten miles was a part of Gajender's regular routine. His father had once served on the railways as a ticket collector but then returned to Khewali to follow his own father's profession and serve as the village priest. Gajender had a younger brother named Mahender, whose ambitions, to the extent that he had any, lay elsewhere. Mahender wore shiny clothes and, unlike Gajender, he wore shoes. Mahender died a drunk when he was only thirty.

Gajender went barefoot everywhere. As he was tall and well built, he had declared that he was going to become a police constable. He was from a poor family but he was also a Brahmin and he was literate. He ran every morning, performed exercises under the bel tree in front of his house, and then drank a liter of milk after eating a fistful of raisins.

"So, instead of becoming a policeman he became a priest?"

"No, no," Jadu said with a laugh. "That is why I'm telling you this story. My father used to say that Gajender was so good at running that he galloped straight into history."

Gajender had gone to Patna to take a test for entry as a constable into what was called the Home Guards. But the only young man who was faster than him, one Umesh Yadav, told him that he was headed to nearby Danapur cantonment to undergo a written and physical examination for the army. Gajender ran his race at the cantonment so well that the British colonel doing the recruiting took an instant liking to him. He was asked to return the following week. A sense of gloom descended on the village when Gajender came back with this news. His father, the priest, had wanted to see his son in a policeman's uniform, a man that people in the village would be afraid of and would wish to bribe with money and invitations to feasts. Instead, Gajender had joined the army. The priest's wife was afraid that her son would be sent away to fight and die in foreign lands. She was only half right.

After Gajender left for the army barracks, the village did not see him for five years. His letters came, separated by several weeks and, toward the end, even months. In these letters addressed to his parents, Gajender first sent one half of a five-rupee currency note, and then in a later letter, he would send the second half. He explained that this way there was less chance of the money being stolen. Gajender's father would take both halves of the note to the bank in Motihari and request smaller denominations in exchange. Was it from Gajender's letter that the village learned that a war had started? Jadu wasn't sure. But the letters made the war real. Japanese forces had launched an offensive in Burma. Gajender's regiment was 1 Bihar and it was sent to the northeast. Shivanand Tiwary, the Congress Party volunteer in the village, told everyone that Gandhiji wanted Indians to help the British in the war—it was the right thing to do and it would help India get freedom when the war was over. Jadu said that this made them feel good about Gajender's role in the army.

From Gajender's brief, infrequent letters the people of Khewali village learned the names of places like Rangoon and Imphal and Irrawaddy. When Jadu was twelve or thirteen, a belief took root in people's minds that Gajender had been taken prisoner or, worse, that he was dead. Several months had passed since his last letter. Unexpectedly, a letter turned up from Manipur with details about heavy losses in the war. The bombs were still falling, Japanese planes arriving like news from a distant land, and then came the incessant rains. Gajender was part of a tiny party of soldiers who had been isolated in a village near Jiribam, where some inhabitants had served as porters in the British-led army. The people were friendly and hospitable. The small group of 1 Bihar soldiers labored in the paddy fields alongside the villagers and went on hunts in the forest. Gajender wrote that he and his companions were liked by the Manipuris. The soldiers spent four months there before beginning a brutal trek back home. Not all of them returned. Two of the soldiers had got married in the village, and stayed back there as if they had indeed died in the war.

Gajender's mother was told by a boy who had come running into her hut that her son had returned from the war. Where, where was he? Gajender was outside Nazir Tailor's shop, where people had stopped him to ask for news of the war's end. The mother clutched her throat and asked the boy to find her husband. *Panditji*, she shouted for Gajender's father, and then, her head uncovered and also barefoot, she ran wailing outside. She was shouting her son's name but the pain was too much, and so she sat down in the middle of the road, unable to see or speak, capable only of an animal howl. It was understood by everyone, including Jadu, who was the boy who had given her the news of Gajender's arrival, that the Pandit's wife was only getting rid of all the sorrow she had gathered while contemplating her son's death in the war. She was emptying her heart of the pain so that she could make space for the relief and joy that she was now feeling. As she didn't want the good news that had been given to her to be proved false, she didn't have the courage to walk one more step toward her son. She waited in the middle of the dirt road until, half-smiling, half-weeping, Gajender touched her shoulder and said, "Mai."

Two years later, when a priest from Deoghar offered his daughter's hand in marriage and said that Gajender could take over from him as the priest there—a huge temple, the saawan mela, where hundreds of thousands came, an earning more secure than that of a government which Gandhiji was soon to drive out of the country anyway—Gajender collected his discharge papers from the army and began walking around in a white dhoti, a sacred thread crossing his chest, a round red tilak on his fair forehead.

And that is how Jadu brought Maya to Deoghar, telling her a story about the long journey that had been Gajender's life. And in a way Jadu's too, from middle school to his marriage to Maya. From the road where they stood for a moment, they could see the tall white spires of the temples, and the red ribbons that linked the iron tridents on the tops. They said *Bol Bam* and shut their eyes. With heads bowed, each murmured a soft prayer that the other could not hear and then they started walking again.

———

Upon their return from Deoghar they went to Khewali to fetch Jugnu and found out that she had changed. The child had begun to think that Sumitra, Jadu's mother, was also her own mother. She now called her Mai. This was perhaps because many people in the village, young or old, called Sumitra by that name. The child had also decided that she was going to stay in Khewali instead of coming back to Patna with the two people whom she now wanted to address by their names, Jadu and Maya.

For their part, Jugnu's parents watched helplessly as the child insisted on eating from the same large brass plate from which her grandfather, Shivnath, ate his meals while sitting cross-legged on a plank on the floor. Shivnath would draw a line in the plate with his finger, dividing the food, and then he and his granddaughter would eat their separate portions, rolling the food and picking up each mouthful in unison from their designated areas. As they chewed their food, Shivnath would smile, and Jugnu smiled back, and if he mock-frowned, the child also drew her eyebrows together in an intense frown. At night, Jugnu slept with Sumitra. The two pilgrims who had come back from Deoghar with sweet, round *pedas* for her to eat were nice enough people that she could talk to, but Jugnu would no longer consider them her parents.

All this was cause at first for jokes but when Jadu and Maya were by themselves in their room they breathed an air filled with guilt. This bedroom had been added to the brick house at the time of Jadu's marriage. More than once, Maya wondered aloud if they had been right to leave Jugnu behind. But how could the little child have walked on that road to Deoghar? When Jadu asked his wife this question, he was trying to gently tell her that she was being irrational. Even as he did this, he was secretly troubled by the complete and indeed logical coherence of the three-year-old's response. She had thoroughly reimagined her nuclear family and made that act of imagination real through her actions. It was funny, and also unsettling.

Sumitra owned a nanny goat that had turned mean after Shivnath had her offspring butchered for a feast during Holi. That at least was Sumitra's theory. Visitors from the village were a bit scared of the goat; her horns were small but she was prone to throwing down her head and fearlessly advancing into battle. Sumitra was fond of the animal and gave her vegetable leaves instead of the insults and shouts that the others threw her way. One afternoon, the goat headbutted little Jugnu when she was crossing the yard in front of the house. A vicious push from the goat sent the girl flying. The shock of the attack and then the fall, during which Jugnu scraped her knees, caused her to burst into tears. She cried out and both Maya and Sumitra rushed to the rescue—but the child only wanted Sumitra to touch her. Now there were two people crying, Maya as well as Jugnu.

To placate the child, Sumitra said she would have the goat slaughtered very soon and Jugnu would get to eat the mean creature's delicious meat. Sumitra was a vegetarian but she became eloquent just then talking about the grilled heart of the goat, its ribs cooked in a thick curry, the skill with which the goat's brain could be fried by a talented cook. "Think of that," the otherwise gentle Sumitra said, "that brain which made the goat cruel, hurting my precious child today, that brain will sit sizzling and tasting just wonderful on a plate." A few minutes later, the child was laughing. Sumitra had struggled to say something to make Jugnu feel better but it is difficult to find the right words for adults: she stole a glance at Maya, who sat mute on a cot, and Sumitra did not know what to say to her.

Thirteen years later, Jadu was sitting in a train and trying to recall what they had needed to do to placate Jugnu. He could not remember. How had they won her over? She was stubborn as a child, and more stubborn still when she was older. On the train, Jugnu was sitting next to him, silent, simmering with resentment. They were returning that afternoon to Patna from Gaya, where they had gone to catch a glimpse of the Dalai Lama. It was a day in early April. The train was crowded. At the Jehanabad station, a few college students had clambered on board. There were about eight of them, identifiable as college students not just by their youth but by the fact that some of them carried notebooks. The notebook as an ID card or a badge that says we are not devoted to study, but look, we are carrying this rolled-up notebook and this means we are scholars and tomorrow's rulers. The young students, ruffians really, took in the sight of Jugnu, an attractive teenage girl, and chose to place themselves nearby. There were no seats available for them but they urged the lady with her small children on the berth across from Jugnu to make space for two of them. Two others climbed to the upper berth. Two others stood like guards on a stage, framing a performance unfolding in the middle.

A commentary began to emerge from the upper berth. "The color green is a calming color," declaimed the rogue in a cream kurta, looking like a sailor perched on a tall mast. "It induces a state of relaxation among those who wear it. It also calms the senses of those who perceive it. Green allows you to relax."

Jugnu was wearing a green shalwar-kameez.

His companion on the high berth now filed his own report like an orator addressing his audience of fellow buffoons.

"In nature, green is to be found on the leaves of trees. Leaves give us life by releasing oxygen into the air. If we did not have green, we would die. So, thank you, green!"

The rest of the boys, those sitting across from them but also two others who were sitting farther away across the aisle, kept their gaze fixed on Jugnu's face. She remained impassive, not saying a single word. She had clearly faced such harassment before. None among the other passengers found it necessary to react; Jadu didn't look at anyone but he heard the silence around him. Despite the mirth in the voices, the air had become tense. No one was in any doubt about what was taking place. And yet, not one person had said or done anything to stop it. Jadu told himself that he was waiting for the youth to cross a line. *I didn't know what I could do, or even what I should do.* He asked himself if Jugnu was waiting to see how her father would respond to this abuse. As soon as this last thought formed in his mind, Jadu felt his anger spill.

When he spoke up, he heard Jugnu's sigh. He had disappointed her by opening his mouth.

"Gentlemen." Jadu addressed the men in front of him. "Which

institution of higher learning has the good fortune of having you all as students?"

Jadu's diction was that of a highly educated man. He had used the same tone he adopted sometimes in his classes, except that there he had power and here he had none. The youth were not impressed by this display of irony. They countered it with their own brand of sarcasm. Although he had spoken in Hindi, one of the commentators on the high berth pretended that Jadu had used English. The boy said, "Ask your question in Hindi, please."

His friends enjoyed this show of wit.

Jadu chose not to repeat his question. The atmosphere grew more strained. Jadu's protest had been registered. The students became quiet. Jadu was aware, however, that if things weren't simply fun anymore, they could easily also turn vicious. He was on guard. To distract himself, he went back in his mind to that episode from long ago in Khewali when Jugnu didn't accept them as her parents anymore. She had been stubborn beyond reason. How had they won her over?

Jadu was so tense that he could smell his sweat and his mouth was full of ashes. He turned his mind to the days when the young woman seated next to him was just a child and refusing to be his daughter. He thought that the reason he was remembering that long-ago episode was that Jugnu perhaps did not want to be his daughter right then too. He ought not to have tried to hotly engage the misbehaving youth. But it was just as likely that Jadu was simply trying to escape into the past. He was returning to a moment when his child was little and not likely to attract the attention of lascivious youth. In any case, he felt he was being cowardly.

After the train left Taregna, a boy of maybe thirteen or fourteen with a basket hanging from his neck appeared in the train car. He was selling jhaal-mudhi. The pungent smell of spices and finely cut raw onion and lime now mingled with the other smells in the car. The boy would mix the puffed rice and other ingredients in a tin mug before filling thin newspaper cones for his customers. The students wanted to buy jhaal-mudhi. The boy sensed trouble but he remained calm. Jadu watched him pour a few drops of mustard oil in his tin mug and then pause to ask the youth if they wanted the mixture to be extra spicy.

"Extra spicy! How old are you, fucker? What the hell do you know about extra spicy?"

They had found a new target.

The boy didn't wait for them to answer. He had a tolerant half-smile on his face and he went on with the business of preparing the mixture. When he handed the boys the cones of food, the youth sitting closest to Jadu asked, "Uncle, would you like some?"

Jadu shook his head no and then, in a gesture that he thought must have further annoyed Jugnu, he made a show of folding his hands together and declining with a formal show of gratitude.

The boy was waiting for his payment.

One of the students on the high berth reached into his front pocket for money. He asked the boy, "Where are you from?"

"Punpun."

"Punpun? Every day the papers carry news of illegal guns being made there. Why don't you just buy a pistol and rob a train every day?"

The boy kept his smile but said nothing.

"Four rupees," he said.

A thin middle-aged man on a side berth had been waiting patiently to buy a cone of jhaal-mudhi. Jadu had heard him earlier telling the old man seated beside him that he was a cloth merchant—his shop in Gaya stocked polyester saris and children's clothes. He was holding out a one-rupee note in his hand and addressed the boy's back. "Eh, jhaal-mudhi, let me also see some of it."

The boy turned. "Spicy?"

"Normal," the man said, patting his stomach, as if he was listening carefully to what his body was saying to him.

After giving the man two cones, the boy faced the older youth again and held out his hand.

"Babuji," he said, "four rupees."

The college students began urging each other to pay. Each said it was someone else's turn. They were all laughing. Not the boy with the basket of jhaal-mudhi, a keen and forbearing spectator of this drama. His posture suggested that he was resigned to this behavior and maybe even familiar with it.

Were others in the train car waiting to buy a cone of jhaal-mudhi from the boy? It was quite probable that people all along the length of the train were waiting. This polite and hardworking boy was losing business while these young fools exchanged jokes. That is what Jadu was thinking—and then, without further thought, removing his wallet from his kurta pocket, he extracted a five-rupee note.

When he held it out in front of him, the boy began to fiddle with his cones and Jadu said that he didn't want any jhaal-mudhi. He just wanted to give him the money.

But the boy wouldn't take it.

"Good boy," Jadu said, switching to English, as if this would do the trick.

The college students were not laughing anymore. Jadu had felt noble, he was restoring justice and helping the boy, but now he feared he was going to be embarrassed if the boy refused the money.

Help came from an unlikely direction. One of the two students perched on the upper berth, the connoisseur of the color green, spoke to the boy, urging him to take the money as a blessing. "*Le lo, aashirvaad hai.*"

The boy took the five-rupee note. The tension had eased.

The same student from the upper berth now commanded the boy. "Touch the old babu's feet!"

"No, no," Jadu said and laughed girlishly, pulling his feet away as though he were being tickled.

Everyone was laughing with him and Jadu gave in to the temptation of looking at Jugnu. But her face gave nothing away. She was gazing into the middle distance, apparently seeing nothing.

By this time the train had reached Parsa Bazar; it was only a matter of another half hour before they would be in Patna, and an unbidden memory opened in Jadu's mind. After their return to Khewali from the pilgrimage to Deoghar, Jadu had found his child playing by herself with a doll and bits of hay. Jugnu was allowing her grandmother Sumitra to shut herself off in her room for her daily nap. Jadu decided to read a book while also keeping an eye on his daughter. In the tall jamun tree that spread its branches over the hut, there was a commotion of wings. A small hawk had occupied a place on the top of the tree and it had got a drongo in its claws.

Using its hooked beak, the small but majestic hawk removed the bird's feathers and pulled out delicately a glistening red entrail—while around it two drongos called out incessantly and beat their wings. The hawk hadn't made a sound: it was acting without mercy and with complete calm. Jugnu looked at Jadu, did not call him Papa as she used to do in Patna, and asked, "What are the birds doing?"

Jadu had been watching the scene in silence: the hawk sat dipping its head toward them, the bird under its claws. The drongos were relentless, repeating their futile calls, fluttering close to the hawk in swooping circles but never touching it. Putting one hand on his daughter's shoulder, Jadu said, "The small birds are the parents. They are trying to protect their child from the hawk."

But the little drongo was being dismembered before their eyes. He hadn't acknowledged it, seemingly willing that fact away. Jugnu must have understood what was happening, she had stayed utterly quiet, and he wondered now what she thought of her father's attempt at dissembling, his pathetic effort to divert her attention from a clear recognition of cruelty. And how brutal was the implied lesson about listening to your parents!

Did the child resume talking to them after that conversation? He doesn't remember. He must have felt some guilt about it—why else has this memory been so long banished from his consciousness? He has a notion, sitting in the train with the eight male students arrayed around him, and Jugnu not talking to him at all, why the memory has returned to him now.

————

Jadu's own students weren't hooligans. He wouldn't have tolerated this behavior from them. He had tried to like them all; it was difficult, he had his favorites. At his first job, as a lecturer in Langat Singh College in Muzaffarpur, he had a student named Amol Thakur. Amol had been born in poverty and his life had taken unusual turns. His mother was a widow from an untouchable caste and his father was a priest at a village temple near Mokameh. The priest had begun spending his nights at the widow's hut and then something like love had taken root between them. The relationship had no social sanction, of course, and it caused great suffering to the couple and their child. Once, when Amol's father was away, trying to earn a few rupees by taking his fellow villagers on a pilgrimage, the father's elder brother put Amol on a train and then disappeared.

Amol was only four years old. He was lost for almost a year. The train had taken him to a town in the *terai* forests near Dehra Dun and before his father found him, Amol was mauled by a tiger. You could still see the scars on his chest and the back of his neck. Through all these travails, his mother had never given up and his father, a weak and delusional man, had tried his best to keep supporting his illegitimate son.

Jadu encouraged Amol to write a memoir. When Amol completed his bachelor's degree, he was admitted for graduate studies on a scholarship at the capital's Jawaharlal Nehru University. Two years later his memoir was published under the title *Daldal Mein Kamal* (Lotuses in the Swamp). And Amol, whose parents had been social pariahs and had survived with so little to their name, was now a professor of humanities at the Indian Institute of Technology in Delhi. Jadu had not seen him for years but he would occasionally read Amol's column in *The Indian Express* commenting on everything from fashion to fascism. After all these years, when struggling with a recalcitrant student or even one who seemed overwhelmed by self-doubt, Jadu would mention Amol or press on the student a well-thumbed copy of *Daldal Mein Kamal.*

A small beginning need not be an obstacle, he was telling his students, but Jadu also knew in his heart, of course, that Amol was special. He often wished that it was he and not his student who had written *Daldal Mein Kamal.* In Amol's book there was a description of the village school that he had attended. The classroom had two doors, one that students used to enter the room from the open field outside, and the other, which wasn't really a door but only an opening in the wall with naked bricks and a wooden frame. A door was meant to be there but either it had been stolen or it had simply never been attached to the frame because the money hadn't come or had been siphoned off by the headmaster. This opening in the wall overlooked the village pond and sometimes when the students came to class they found little bits of uneaten fish and bones and bird droppings on the rough floor. Amol had written that egrets slept in the room at night. In fact, Amol dreamed of catching one of those birds and when he was hungry, which was often, he thought of the fish in the pond. A bird in your classroom, leaving bones on the floor. Jadu never forgot what Amol had written and when he was teaching, he would gaze at the faces in front of him and think there were so many stories in the world just waiting to be told.

When Jadu was hired as a lecturer at Patna College, it occurred to him that Professor Dey had perhaps regarded him as special too. It was he who had recommended Jadu to the department for the position. Later, Professor Dey encouraged Jadu to pursue a PhD and Jadu began working on the topic "the oppressed peasantry and taxation in nineteenth-century colonial Bihar." Ten years after Jadu met him, Professor Dey was to die from cirrhosis of the liver, his body laid out on a bier of bamboo. A roll of gauze went around his head and face to stop his jaw from falling open. The dead man's nostrils were stuffed with cotton. A round and shining one-rupee coin had been put on his forehead where his third eye would have been. Jadu could not find the courage to offer any word of consolation to Professor Dey's wife, but he walked in the small group to the cremation ghat three miles away. Earlier that year, Jadu had become Professor Dey's junior colleague at the college. This was something he had wanted. He had long fantasized about one day having Professor Dey's office. Standing next to his old teacher's funeral pyre, Jadu guiltily wondered whether he wasn't like one of those usurping princes in medieval India who greedily took over his father's throne.

When discussing their students, Jadu had once asked Professor Dey whether it was easier for those from affluent homes to do well on examinations. The daughter of a senior police officer as well as the son of the state's chief secretary, one a Bengali and the other a Tamil, were at that time Jadu's top students. Professor Dey asked Jadu about Hira Mirchandani. Wasn't he a very capable student? Jadu said that he was but Hira, too, simply proved his point. Hira Mirchandani was the son of a businessman whose clothing and dry-cleaning shop, Tip Top, was on Patna's Fraser Road. He came from a rich family. Professor Dey admitted that that was true but he also pointed out that Hira's father had migrated across the border from what had recently become Pakistan. He had come all the way from Karachi to Patna and taken shelter in his uncle's home. The uncle was an official in the postal service. They hadn't always been rich. Lalit Mirchandani, Hira's father, had arrived with only four gold bangles sewn by his mother in a hidden pocket in his vest-coat. He was the sole survivor of the trek across the border. In less than twenty years—even less than that, fifteen—he had become a rich man.

Professor Dey wanted Jadu to consider whether Hira's determination to succeed was related as much to his affluence as it was to the grit that had pulled the family through the horror of the Partition. Jadu felt that Professor Dey was making a subtle point about writing history. Money didn't explain everything, you needed to think of culture as a whole. It was important to consider who you were, how you thought of yourself, and what struggles had shaped you. When Professor Dey said this to him, with all the gentleness of a man who knew he was dying, Jadu thought of his mother. This was the first time he had thought in an intellectual way about Sumitra's experience of being bitten by the snake, and then surviving it and completing her term of pregnancy. He thought of it as a cultural experience that had affected not just Sumitra but also him. Sumitra's strength and resolve had given him courage as a birthright.

There were very few women in Jadu's history classes the first few years. More women studied English or Hindi literature and other subjects like psychology. But even in those early years, there was a young woman in his class named Ayesha Shaheen, who Jadu had always known was going to excel because he could not ever anticipate the breadth and depth of her responses to whatever she was learning from him. Her thesis was on progressive Urdu magazines in Patna in the late nineteenth and early twentieth centuries. Her father and brothers were lawyers but she chose to study history. When Jadu asked her whether she hadn't been tempted to go into law, she replied that while the men in her family dealt with criminals in court, as a historian she was only going to study those who had been remembered as criminals by posterity. Within ten years Ayesha was the head of the department of history at Patna Women's College. She had heard her own grandfather talking about a satirical magazine called *al Punch*, and that is where her search started, broadening over the course of several years into a serious commentary on the social, political, and linguistic life of educated Muslims in Bihar, particularly in Patna.

Did Jadu learn from his students? Yes. From Ayesha's thesis he learned that Maulana Azad, Nehru's education minister and widely respected as one of the country's foremost intellectuals, had begun contributing to *al Punch* when he was barely thirteen years old. There was more to learn. After the publication of her book, Ayesha took her interest in popular magazines and the public sphere in a new direction. She translated from Urdu into English the journalism of Saadat Hasan Manto, and this shocked some of the Muslim elites in Patna, including her own aunt, an educated lady who declared her niece now forever unsuitable for marriage. Jadu said to her, laughing, "I will be your father and your mother whenever you decide to get married."

Jadu had to take on that role not only for Ayesha but for another couple too, both of them his students, who were getting married against the will of their families. The girl's name was Alankrita, and the boy she was marrying was Surendra. The families belonged to different castes, but this difference wasn't as significant as the class difference between them. Surendra was very poor and it was going to be difficult for them if Alankrita received nothing from her family. But they wanted to marry and Jadu went with them to the magistrate's office. Maya said Jadu was going to get into trouble, the families would blame him. Perhaps there would have been more to answer for if the two had been from different religions, but it had worked out in the end.

So many students, so many stories. Some of them remained puzzles.

For example, Dina Nath. Had he dropped his surname to hide his caste? Jadu always wondered about that. Serious, he hardly spoke in class; he turned in the most cogent tutorials, written in a neat hand. He was interested in researching the Razakars, the private militia that had supported the rule of the Nizam in Hyderabad. In the year after Independence, the Razakars had been defeated by the Indian army. Jadu hadn't been able to find out why Dina was interested in the question; this would have been taken up once he started working on his thesis. But that process never got under way. Dina had been in Jadu's world for ten months when, in April 1969, he just disappeared. What happened to him? Another student had told Jadu that Dina's father was a police constable or maybe a railway guard on a train; Dina had been married early and his wife, who lived with her parents in a village near Siwan, was schizophrenic. Jadu had not asked Dina anything himself. He had found Dina's quiet intensity forbidding and he wasn't sure that his inquiries would even be entertained. A year later, at a history conference in Aligarh, a professor of history from the D.A.V. College in Siwan surprised Jadu by talking about his student Dina Nath.

"Where is he these days?" Jadu asked, pleased at getting news.

The man from Siwan said, "Who?"

"Dina. He was suddenly gone."

"Oh, I thought you knew. He is dead."

"No. What happened?"

"How much did you know about Dina?"

"Not much. He was a very good student."

"We don't know exactly what happened. Siwan is a dangerous place for communists. One night a man knocked on the door of the house in which he lived with his father. The man said he had bad news from his mother's village. Dina went with—"

Jadu didn't want to hear more. He clasped both his hands in front of his chest and turned away.

———

During the monsoon season in 1971, when the street outside his apartment building turned into a dirty brown stream, his neighbors holding aloft in one hand their shoes and pulling up the hems of their saris or their trousers as they gingerly walked up to the main road, Jadu had to make a more difficult crossing near Khewali in an effort to reach his village home. His mother had died. To make matters worse, there was an epidemic of a new type of conjunctivitis called "Jai Bangla." Next door, in East Pakistan, the struggle for liberation was gathering strength; "Jai Bangla" was the slogan in this fight for the creation of what would become Bangladesh. There were reports that the disease had come with the refugees pouring into India from East Pakistan. When he returned to Patna, his eyes inflamed and itchy, Jadu went to the doctor he had known for a decade. The elderly physician, Dr. Asim Chatterjee, said, "You are a historian. You should know how diseases often get their names. It has nothing to do with science."

Dr. Chatterjee told him that earlier, in Ghana, the same strain of conjunctivitis was called the Apollo 11 disease because its arrival coincided with man's landing on the moon. There were many who believed that the disease was caused by the soil brought back from the moon. Jadu had imagined the conditions in the refugee camps at the border with East Pakistan, and now he felt a bit ashamed about the conclusions he had drawn by himself. But Dr. Chatterjee wasn't interested in embarrassing him. He noticed Jadu's shaved head and asked if there was a reason for it.

Jadu said, "My mother died last week."

Dr. Chatterjee asked if she had been sick and Jadu shook his head. "It was an accident," he said slowly, and the doctor, sensing a reticence in Jadu, didn't press on the pain.

But the whole thing, apart from being painful, was also embarrassing. Jadu had come back from the cremation in Khewali with his eyes red and tears flowing. It was because of the disease he had picked up there. Those who saw his shaved head and the red eyes often assumed that he had been crying and treated him with exaggerated sympathy. He began wearing dark glasses but this didn't cure the problem. The illness lasted about ten days.

Soon, Jadu returned to the classroom. As the reports of Bangla freedom fighters filtered back to them, a few of the progressive faculty decided to hold a symposium on the war. During the Dussehra festival each year, many well-known poets and musicians, as well as dancers, would be invited to Patna. Jadu's colleagues decided to poach, if only for an hour or two, two notables who had well-deserved reputations for being antiestablishment writers. Letters of appeal were mailed to their addresses in the town of Allahabad in nearby Uttar Pradesh and, without too much delay, they also received responses assenting to the requests. This was thrilling to Jadu: literary giants responding to unknown teachers who had written on behalf of their students. And so it came to be that Mahadevi Varma and Firaq Gorakhpuri came to speak at Patna College in a borrowed car.

Mahadevi began with a poem about widows, then she spoke of the ordinary citizen in East Pakistan fighting the well-equipped army under the direction of the generals in West Pakistan, and from there she took a further step away, talking about the war being fought in Vietnam. It was now Firaq's turn. He threw his cigarette on the ground and said that a worldwide war was being fought—everywhere the weak against the strong. That was one thing no one ought to lose sight of: don't let the flags of nations hide from sight the fact of the people in rags. Then he recited a poem about the small, seemingly weak fingers that had joined together to fight the iron fist of U.S. imperialism. He wove together English poetry written during the Second World War in the fight against fascism with his remarks on the devastation in Vietnam. A current ran through the audience. Change was coming. When at the end Firaq recited a couplet to predict that the Americans would lose and Saigon would fall, the students in the front rows cheered and shouted slogans. The odd thought that came to Jadu was that the Americans would return home with itchy, red eyes and this time the conjunctivitis epidemic would be called the Saigon disease.

With the arrival of winter and even before the semester ended it was clear that there would be a war with Pakistan. From the office of the college registrar, Jadu got many of the used carbon sheets discarded by the typists. These sheets he glued to the window-panes of his home. When the siren sounded, everyone was supposed to turn off the lights. Only use torches or candles, they were told. Draw the curtains. Danapur Military Cantonment was just next door. Patna could easily be bombed by mistake. Cars too were not permitted on the road when the sirens wailed at night: drivers were instructed to pull to the side of the road and douse their lights. In Agra the Taj Mahal was camouflaged with the use of bamboo scaffolding and burlap—otherwise, its marble dome and walls gleamed in the moonlight. Everything else remained normal. Grains, vegetables, milk, such essentials were all still easily available. The people were asked to donate what they could to the war effort. Women knitted cardigans and gloves; thousands of blankets were dropped off in the bins outside military cantonments. Jadu became familiar with the sight of Maya knitting woolen caps, soft skeins of yarn the size of week-old kittens in her lap, the labels identifying their color as "military green."

A decade earlier a Hindi film song had become popular—*Jaane waale sipahi se poochho* . . . "Ask the departing soldier, where is it that he is headed . . ." It had been sung with great feeling by the Bengali singer Manna Dey; it was a melancholic anthem, made more poignant by the stirring chorus, with both male and female voices joined in a collective appeal. But it was also a prophetic anthem, seemingly anticipating the massacre that was to take place a year later on the Indian side in the war with China. Now, in 1971, during the conflict with Pakistan, it would play on the radio at least once every day. It raised the question of bloodshed and sacrifice, and perhaps that is why it wasn't aired as often as a few of the other patriotic songs. It would be bad for morale. Jadu liked the song but would switch the radio off if Maya was nearby. Her brother's death in the war with China was the one thing that Jadu knew not to discuss with her ever. Two years after his wedding, on a Thursday morning in November 1962, Jadu had opened the door to find his brother-in-law Manoranjan standing outside, looking drunk. Manoranjan didn't want to come in. He wasn't drunk, it was just that he hadn't slept, and his eyes were puffy. He said he had brought bad news about Mantu.

There had been fear and anticipation for the previous two weeks. This was because fighting had broken out on the frontier between China and India. A small, unprepared Indian army was vastly outnumbered by the enemy. A little after midnight, an army truck had arrived outside Manoranjan's house. First the officer delivered the news and then four soldiers carried in a coffin that was packed with ice and draped with the Indian flag. It contained Mantu's blackened body. Jadu had known Maitreyi, whom everyone called Mantu, as a cheerful young man during the days of his wedding. He was twenty-three years old and recently promoted to the rank of captain in the 4th Infantry Division. They were told he had shielded the body of his injured subedar. None of this could be shared with Maya. She was wild with grief; first, she screamed as if she were falling down a steep cliff, the bottom nowhere in sight; then, her voice rose again, shrill this time. She flung herself in rage at Jadu, who had brought the news to her. Jadu felt utterly helpless and broken when this slight and beautiful woman, who had been too shy to look at him at their first meeting, bunched up her fists and struck him repeatedly on his chest. He held her as her bangles broke against his body and her wails rent the air.

For days after that, Maya's mother didn't want to put on the lights in her house and preferred sitting in the dark. She stopped speaking. Maya also slipped into a depression. She had been very young when her father died; she had probably only felt the enormity of that loss slowly with each passing year. But that old trauma returned with this new blow. In the years that followed, it became clear that Maya never really recovered from the terror of losing the beloved family member who was closest in age to her. After that time, Mantu was to be remembered formally only on the anniversary of his birth and death with visits to the temple. But even during these visits, his name was never uttered. Jadu had begun thinking of his dashing and now dead brother-in-law more as a date that came twice each year.

The war with Pakistan started in December; there was sadness and anxiety, certainly, and some undeniable excitement too. Radio bulletins mentioned battles for places with names like Chittagong and Jessore; and there were reports of successful attacks on the enemy because of the clever use of the tank T-55 and the fighter-jet MiG 21. So, there was tension, but also jubilation. Jadu remained distant from the national obsession because during that fortnight his energies were focused on attending to the needs of his downstairs neighbors. These were the Chackos. The nation was at war, prayer meetings were being held for soldiers fighting at the border, everyone was in love with the mustache of the handsome General Manekshaw, and Jadu was buying two kilos of fresh sweet lime each day because in the flat below a young woman named Jyotsna was dying.

Jadu's downstairs neighbors were a young chemistry professor from Kottayam, Mathew Chacko, and his sick wife, both Catholics from Kerala. Maya went down each morning with sweet-lime juice for Jyotsna and then came back up with the empty glass, her eyes brimming. Jyotsna's bed had been moved to the living room because it received most of the winter sun; the disease but also the chemo treatment left Jyotsna weak and unable to hold down normal food and there was a bucket next to her. The medications had made her face swell up, and after her treatment, her hair fell out. One night, Maya was telling Jadu about how Jyotsna had started crying earlier that day, crying not for herself but for Mathew's sake. Jyotsna had said to her that for the past four years, ever since she got married, she had wanted children. She had been ready. And then she fell sick. Her tears now weren't for her unborn babies. She said she just felt stupid. She repeated that word. Her tears flowed when she thought about how unlucky her children would have been if they had been born and then if she was dying like this. So, were those tears of relief? But Jadu couldn't ask this question because Maya was now sobbing as she told him this story.

The war lasted only thirteen days. In Dacca, the Pakistan Army surrendered on December 16, and soon afterward the provisional government of the new country called Bangladesh returned from exile. Three days later it was going to be Christmas. On Christmas Eve, Jadu knocked on Mathew's door and invited him to come up for tea. The two men stared at a plate of Britannia biscuits in front of them. The tea that Maya had made was excellent, not too sweet and fortified with ginger. In a voice that was compassionate but restrained, Jadu asked Mathew what he was going to do for Christmas. Then, seeing that his words were sinking into Mathew seemingly without being heard, Jadu said, "Maya was hoping that we could all go together for the midnight mass."

And that is how Jadu and Maya both stepped inside a church for the first time in their lives. The service they attended was in the chapel at Patna Women's College. Jyotsna had been a student there. She must have come to the chapel between her classes or during weekends and sat in these pews, Jadu thought. The nuns were kind to Mathew, reminding him about the blessings of Christ, and consoling him on his loss. He was given three slices of fruitcake to take home; one of the slices, Sister Sushma said to him with a smile, was baked with cherries soaked in rum.

When they returned home and Mathew had shut the door behind himself in his apartment, Maya shared her theory with Jadu. Mathew was now a bachelor, and suffering had made him vulnerable. "All those scheming nuns," Maya said, "with all their sweet words and prayers. They are going to convince poor Mathew to join their Catholic order." He was going to turn into Brother Mathew. Maya had studied at the Catholic English Medium School and believed, as many other Hindu girls in her catechism class did, that the nuns were just waiting to pounce on them—they were all to be converted to Christianity. But that didn't happen. All that the sisters took from the students was their money and what they gave in return was access to the English language spoken with a Malayali accent. Jadu foresaw a different future for Mathew: bachelorhood, loneliness, death. He also knew that Mathew would be there as a friend to them in old age: when Jadu died, Mathew would take Maya to the temple just as they had taken him to the church. History would provide balance to the story they had started this Christmas.

Both Maya and Jadu were proved wrong. Mathew married the younger sister of one of the sisters whom he had met that day in the chapel. The young woman, who had just finished training as a nurse in Kochi, was quickly summoned to Patna. Her name was Alphine, a name that Jadu had never heard before. She was a slim, smiling woman who seemed happy to be so far away from home. So, the story had a happy ending after all. Yet, Jadu had never imagined that the little girl who came from this union—the child always reminding Maya of Jyotsna—would excel at sports and would one day, at the 1994 Asian Games, win the gold medal in the 400-meter track event. Years earlier, Mathew had taken charge of a teacher's college in Palakkad and Jadu had lost touch with him. But he immediately recognized the girl, Anju Chacko, on his television screen, smiling on the red running track with white stripes in a city in Japan. He remembered how much she had loved singing songs for Maya. And then, a decade later, there was Anju Chacko on his screen again, being sworn in as social welfare minister in the communist government in Kerala. Alone in his flat, Jadu was suddenly with Maya crying tears for Jyotsna and he was convinced that there was a little bit of Jyotsna still living in the figure of the erect woman smiling as she took the oath of office. The next day, he cut out the newspaper report about the new government in Kerala and, having circled Anju Chacko's name with red ink, he took an envelope to the post office to mail it to Jugnu in Atlanta.

———

Years ago, Jadu had been among the mourners in the procession to the burning ghat when Professor Dey died; after his daughter's birth, and then through the years when students passed through his classroom, Jadu would now and then imagine his own death. He didn't have any afflictions, no diseases, no weakness in his heart or an infection of the liver or kidney, but the thought of mortality began taking a seat close to him during lonely evenings or early mornings. His mother had died and then, more recently, his downstairs neighbor Jyotsna. Jadu would see his corpse being lifted on the bamboo bier and taken out of the apartment. Cries of *Ram Naam Satya Hai*. "God is Truth." A fairly short walk to the ghat, though a lot depended on the traffic. He didn't want it to be raining—wet clothes, wet hair, wet wood. The body's stubborn refusal to burn, testing the grief of the mourners. He imagined his voluble colleague Professor Misra at the funeral observing Jadu's last minutes on earth. Among all the mourners, Professor Misra's kurta would be of the best quality. He would probably not walk in the procession, arriving separately, driven to the ghat by his extremely polite driver, Niranjan. Professor Misra would observe everything and then report to Roopa when he was back home. A shower first and a Scotch, and then a few minutes later, he would say to his wife, "I expected more of Jadu's favorite students. He gave them a lot of his time."

A pause and then Professor Misra would add, "Everyone is busy these days."

Jadu could see this very clearly in his mind. And in a sense, it had all already happened. Jadu's students went out into the world, some struggled, several failed, and a few leapt on the footboard of that fast-moving vehicle called fate and became powerful. One of them was Amitesh and he was responsible for Jadu going to jail.

On a morning in March, in 1974, Maya was making tea. She looked out the window and, in the distance to her right, she saw dense smoke climbing into the air. She called Jadu. The smoke was dark, almost like an inkblot. Jadu stepped out on the street for a minute, but finding no one there, he came back inside and turned on the radio. The local station of All India Radio was reporting that the police had opened fire on students in Patna. There was no mention yet of any deaths.

The students of the Chhatra Sangharsh Samiti had been restless for some weeks now. At his own university, these students wanted better education and better food in the hostels. Jadu had been observing the students. Their demand for food, clothing, and shelter (roti, kapda, aur makaan) was exactly what Indira Gandhi had promised—back in 1967, when many of Jadu's current students were still in middle school. Now, in the face of rising prices and growing unemployment, the youth had come out to protest in the streets.

After lunch, Jadu was reading in bed when there was a knock on the door. It was his colleague Saeed Anwar, who taught medieval history. Anwar had come to tell him that the students had set the Income Tax building on fire and then the home of the Bihar education minister. In response, the police shot at them, and at least three students had been killed. Jadu found his heart was racing; he asked for their names. His student Amitesh was active in the agitation. Amitesh was inspired by the leader Jayaprakash Narayan who, the boy claimed, was his paternal grandfather's brother-in-law.

Had Amitesh been killed?

But Anwar said he didn't know the names of the dead students. Like everyone else, he said, "Keep listening to the radio."

At eight that night, before the family had sat down for dinner, another knock, louder this time. Jadu asked Jugnu to open the door. If it was the police, he wanted them to see that this was a family home. The person who stepped inside was Amitesh, red eyes, face haggard. Jadu thought that perhaps a close friend of his had been killed, and that was why Amitesh's eyes were red. But Amitesh clarified he didn't know the dead boys. His eyes were red because the police had used tear gas.

"These deaths won't be in vain," he said, sounding like a politician, full of bluster. "In five days, a massive general strike."

Amitesh looked at Jadu and added that every teacher should support the call. The students were demanding a complete overhaul of the system, particularly of education. Jadu felt he was being urged to discard his passivity. When Maya came into the room with a glass of water, Amitesh removed his shirt and showed her the welts on his upper arm and on his back where the police had beaten him during the lathi charge.

Faced with this youth who had so calmly removed his shirt in front of her, Maya became maternal. She said, "Wash your face and hands in the bathroom. Dinner will be ready in ten minutes."

On the day of the general strike, Jadu put on a clean kurta and joined the march. He caught sight of his old friend Krishna Murari, who waved at him from a distance. Krishna Murari was walking with a group of politicians, all of them minor leaders in the opposition. His old college friend Ramdeo had also joined the agitation. Jadu saw him standing atop a crowded van which had a megaphone attached to it. Some years earlier, Ramdeo's younger brother had found a job in the police and was posted in Ranchi as an inspector; now that someone in the family held a government job, Ramdeo had been freed at last to try his luck in politics as a Dalit leader. Jadu didn't catch sight of Amitesh in the procession and, at one point, when he stopped to buy a glass of water from a boy selling iced water from a cart, Jadu wished Amitesh would see him. If he did, Jadu would have furnished proof of his commitment to democracy and he could then return home. But Amitesh was nowhere to be seen in that large crowd and when the procession reached the gutted Income Tax building, Jadu decided he had had enough. He began to walk home. It took him forty-five minutes to reach Gandhi Maidan, and from there he took a rickshaw.

The student movement didn't die over the summer. Instead, there was news of police shootings and strikes in different parts of the country. In July, when classes would ordinarily begin, Jayaprakash Narayan, universally known as JP, called for a boycott of colleges. Amitesh told Jadu that the students were committed to an agitation without end. No one was going to attend classes. Students were ready to lose a year of their lives if they succeeded in bringing about change.

With no classes being held, the college took on an abandoned look. Gusts of hot wind blew dust across the campus. Sitting in his office, looking at the faded posters on the walls of the corridor outside, Jadu decided that he would write a memoir-essay. He had written enough history; now, with half his life over, he would try his hand at giving meaning to his own experiences. His daughter was almost ten now. What would she know of him when she was older? He struggled with the story he had always remembered about his mother being bitten by a snake when she was pregnant with him. He wrote a short paragraph but was confused about the details. Sumitra had told him once that after she had been bitten, Shivnath had gone looking for the pharmacist Babulal Mishra, and then things had taken a bad turn. Babulal had mistakenly given her pills that were meant to induce diarrhea when, if he was remembering this right, she was supposed to be given an emetic to induce vomiting. There was too much uncertainty in the story. A postcard could be sent to his father asking him for details, but his father would find this odd and it was possible he didn't remember much anyway, or maybe even remembered incorrectly. Jadu threw away what he was writing. And he didn't think about it again until

a few months later when he found himself, much to his consterna-
tion, sitting in a crowded cell in Patna jail, not knowing when he
would be released.

This is what happened. Jayaprakash Narayan had called for a
three-day strike that was to begin on Gandhi's birth anniversary,
October 2. By this time, it was understood that a major movement
was afoot. If proof were needed it was visible in the barricades that
had been built in town and the number of police deployed everywhere. Huge crowds showed up for JP's speeches despite attempts
by the government to prevent the people from reaching the capital. Although Jadu didn't go to any of the public meetings, he
read the reports of the speeches carefully. He told anyone who
asked that he fully supported his students. Then, in the face of
attacks by the police and the ruling party's indifference, another
march was planned for November 4. This time, Amitesh came to
Jadu's home and took him along. A few of Jadu's other students were
also in the group. JP addressed a huge rally at Gandhi Maidan and
then he led a march to the legislative building.

After they had walked for about an hour, Jadu saw the policemen swinging their bamboo lathis, striking the men and women
who were leading the march. This was happening just about fifty
yards ahead of where Jadu stood with his students. And then, right
in front of him, he saw an old man and his wife, both stick-like figures, possibly peasants, being contemptuously pushed by a policeman who looked as if he were only twenty years old.

Jadu spoke loudly, "They are as old as your grandparents. What
are you doing?"

The remark enraged the uniformed youth. He swung his lathi
back in an arc, aiming to hit Jadu, but Jadu had found a hidden source of strength, or maybe it was fear and the desire for
survival—he lunged at his attacker with a voice screaming inside
his head. Instinctively, the policeman raised the khaki shield held
in his other hand. And while Jadu clung to the shield, attempting
to wrestle it from the cop, he felt his arms being torn away from
him. Two policemen had caught him, one at each arm. One of

the cops brought his elbow down savagely on Jadu's face and then he was hauled to a waiting police bus. He wasn't alone. Scores of student leaders and their supporters were taken to the local jail. The fact that there were so many witnesses watching and people being dragged to prison brought a sense of calm to Jadu's mind. He told himself that Maya would learn about what had happened to him. She would know that he had only been taken to prison and he wasn't dead.

Jadu's section was on the second floor of Patna Jail and over-looked a busy street. Next to a newspaper office and a gas sta-tion, Jadu could see a line of other businesses. A restaurant and a Mafatlal clothing store and then an upscale grocery store called D. Lall & Sons and then another, smaller store selling electronics. Inside Jadu's ward, the students stood facing the street at all wak-ing hours, singing songs and shouting slogans for the pedestrians below. None of the students were family men. They didn't have the worries that paralyzed Jadu. He only left his place on the floor, a thin mattress with its shifting rectangle of sunlight, when it was essential. Otherwise, he remained prone on the ground. There were so many questions troubling him. How was Maya coping? How many times during the day and night did Jugnu call out for her father? Would his salary be paid in time or would it be stopped?

In another few months, although none of them knew this, the country was going to change, all fundamental rights suspended for nearly two years. Indira Gandhi's Emergency Rule. When those two years ended, the student leaders would emerge trium-phant. Many would become ministers. Amitesh was one of them, and so was Krishna Murari. But all that could not yet be foreseen, far from it; during the two weeks he was in jail, the future was unclear and Jadu felt his world shrinking and he slipped into a feeling of dark despondency. The jail resembled an overcrowded railway platform more than it did a prison. Jadu felt he needed a space of quiet. The local newspapers could be read downstairs if you jostled with others at the public stands; there were three such structures in the square below, a sloping desk with a metal ruler holding down the middle of the newspaper. If you turned a page to read the rest of the story, someone or the other always said, "One minute. Let me finish what I am reading."

How did all the great leaders—Nehru, Gandhi—write so much in prison? It wasn't just the crowding. The uncertainty about the future, as far as Jadu was concerned, made all thought impossible. Time had been reduced to a blankness called waiting. He saw others writing letters but he didn't feel the urge. After four or five days, he felt the need to find a different way to mark time's passing. He once again entertained the idea of writing about his mother's death. This time he wrote a paragraph. And then he kept it aside. It was painful to remember everything. He had much preferred the distance of writing national history: mass movements, the confluence of events and characters, the vast, invisible forces bigger than any individual. He thought he would wait a few more days but then, one afternoon, there was a roll call and 179 political prisoners, all recently arrested, were let go. Jadu was among them. He took a rickshaw home. He smelled a little, his hair was unkempt, and in the pocket of his kurta he had a paragraph he had written out on prison paper. When he arrived at his door, Maya shouted Jugnu's name and then, turning back to her husband, asked with a smile if there wasn't even a single barber in such a big jail.

I am a historian by training but this account is from my own past. When my mother was pregnant with me, she was bitten by a snake hiding in the house during a period of heavy rainfall. I grew up with this memory, and, as far as I am aware, everyone else in my native village was also familiar with this fact. My mother carried on her finger the memory of the snakebite: a scar where my father had made cuts with his knife to suck out the poison. No one asked my mother about this mark because everyone knew. This was the story told about my mother, she had been bitten by the cobra and she had survived. But in the year 1971, in the last week of August, when she was in her late fifties and in generally good health, my mother met with an accident. She was a devout, God-fearing individual and all her life she had followed a daily ritual of offering prayers in the morning before sunrise and in the evening after sunset. On this particular evening, as it was Ganesh Chaturthi, my mother was offering special prayers. Following his own pattern of activity, my father was out taking care of the cattle, feeding them before they were tied up for the night. The three or four farmhands my father employed in his fields would have long gone home. Our village does not have electricity and people tried to complete the day's work before darkness fell. This was the routine. My mother had taken a bath and then, clad in a silk sari because it was a special occasion, she had lit an oil lamp and taken it into the puja room to say a prayer in front of a small statue of Lord Ganesh. My mother was largely illiterate but could recite Vedic hymns as well as the Hanuman Chalisa. In what was a repeat of an event from nearly four decades ago, when my father, Shri Shivnath Kunwar, had heard my mother's cry after the snake had bitten her, this time my father heard a similar anguished call. Naturally, his first thought was that my mother had been bitten by a snake again. In fact, his first, irrational thought was that it was the same snake that had returned to our house. In 1971, when this event took place, my father was sixty-five years old. He was unable to run but he moved quickly toward the house because my mother's cry had turned into a terrifying screaming. Even before he reached the brick house in which my parents had lived from just before my birth, my mother appeared in the doorway. She was on fire. To my father, as he told me later, my mother resembled for a moment a dry branch that was burning. My father understood at once that my mother had accidentally set herself on fire in the puja room—her sari set aflame because she was leaning over the oil lamp or maybe she had shut her eyes to pray and knocked the lamp over. The silk sari had turned black and there was the smell of charred flesh in the air. My father swooped down and picked up a burlap sack from the floor of the cattle shed, it still smelled of fertilizer and wheat seeds, and he threw it on my mother's body. It was an indescribable sight. Her hair was scorched and her body was black except for parts like her nose that had seemed to melt. My mother had collapsed near the front steps, in the same place where she had laid herself down following the snake bite. My mother, Shrimati Sumitra Devi, died before a doctor could reach her. Her badly burnt body experienced fire for a second time when we cremated her the next day. I had traveled through the night to reach my village. In my grief I asked my father why this had happened, why my mother, a pious and kindhearted woman, had suffered such a painful death. It was an absurd question, trying to ascribe a cause to a chance happening, an accident. But my father had thought it through. For him, there were too many coincidences. He was convinced that the snake had taken the form of fire and come back to complete its unfinished business. For a fortnight after my mother's cremation I stayed in the village and each day I pondered a simple question. Every day I asked myself whether, in telling a neat story with an ascribable cause, my father was acting more like a professional historian than I was—and whether it was simply beyond me to tell a different story.

Jadu missed the news of the Emergency being imposed because he was in the hospital ward with little Jugnu. She had come down with a high fever and the doctor discovered that her tonsils had become infected. He said removing them was a simple operation. For a day or two after the operation, he said to Jugnu, she could eat as much ice cream as she wanted. So, it was not till the next day, when he could see how bloody Jugnu's throat was, and he stepped out to buy vanilla ice cream, oddly self-conscious because who buys ice cream at eight in the morning, that Jadu learned that all the main leaders in the opposition had been hustled into jail. Censorship had been imposed. It was difficult to know what this meant but all constitutional rights had been canceled. In the days that followed, newspapers like *The Indian Express* published blank editorial pages because the censor had cut out whatever the editors had written. In another paper, a brave editor replaced what had been excised with the words from a famous poem of Tagore's: *where the mind is without fear, into that heaven of freedom, dear God, let my country awake . . .* The Bombay edition of the *Times of India* carried an obituary notice: "D'Ocracy—D.E.M. beloved husband of T.Ruth, loving father of L.I. Bertie, brother of Faith, Hope, and Justicia, expired on 26th June."

A disturbing kind of peace descended on the town. People said to each other, "You have to be careful," but it wasn't clear what exactly was meant by this. Jadu didn't hoard grain that he then sold on the black market. He wasn't blowing up railway lines or participating in secret meetings. It had been a long time since he had even attended a poetry reading. Months passed. A few people, including newspaper editors and reasonable others, talked of the trains running on time. But Jadu's students had told him that if they were caught traveling on trains without a ticket the only way to get off free was to show a sterilization certificate. The Prime Minister's son had started a campaign to limit the growing population. It wasn't clear if the government was creating new jobs but it was certainly opening new clinics for tubectomies and vasectomies. On all the main roads in Patna there were huge signs about the Prime Minister's twenty-point program and the need for discipline and hard work: at each roundabout a billboard assured everyone that the nation was marching toward a golden tomorrow. Jadu saw that one of Indira Gandhi's slogans had been borrowed for the urinal in the college. On the wall that he faced while peeing, someone had scribbled the government's slogan: *Aapka bhavishya aapke haath mein hai* (You hold your future in your hand).

Jadu felt that one could get used to anything, possibly even a life that felt like prison. But in January 1977, Indira Gandhi declared that general elections would be held in March and the Emergency would end. Had she already sensed defeat or was it an act of arrogance? The political leaders were let out of prison, and campaigning for the coming election began in earnest. Several of the opposition parties formed a united front under Jayaprakash Narayan. JP had declared that he would not contest the election himself. He had no interest in holding office. Also, he was sick. His kidneys had failed, he needed dialysis, and he had been in a hospital in Chandigarh during his detention.

On the day the election results were to be announced, Jadu woke up early. Too early for any news on the radio. He went downstairs and wheeled his Vespa scooter out. He was going to drive to the newspaper offices and find out what was up. The roads were empty and, passing the shuttered shops in the early morning light, he saw the familiar posters and flags of various political parties. They were pieces of paper stuck on walls, no longer serving as calls to vote or to imagine a different future. The flags were like actors with makeup on their faces long after the play is over.

There was a crowd, about fifty people, gathered outside the office of the *Indian Nation*. Close to the main gate of the building where the newspaper was housed, a large black wooden board, almost twenty-five feet high, had been erected facing the street. The names of the major parties were painted in a vertical row on the left and a man standing on the boundary wall would every fifteen minutes paste a large sheet with a new number in a row on the right. It looked almost certain that Indira Gandhi's Congress was going to be defeated. All the political leaders who had been in jail had emerged victorious. The same had happened to those who had quit the ruling party and joined the opposition. In Sasaram, only a few hours away, Jagjivan Ram had already been declared a winner by a big margin. With every new sheet of paper that the man pasted on the board, a shout went up in the crowd. Jadu had been very young, in middle school, at the time India got its independence—the headmaster had given a sweet when the students gathered to sing *"Vande Mataram"*—and as he now looked at the changing numbers on the wooden board he knew that this was what independence must have felt like.

Then someone started shouting a slogan in support of Jay-aprakash Narayan, and everyone joined in. *Jayaprakash zindabad! Zindabad, zindabad!* The crowd had grown over the hour that Jadu stood outside the newspaper office and passing cars had to slow to a crawl. A group of young men, led by a long-haired fellow in a red shirt, raised slogans against Indira's son, Sanjay. The youth in the red shirt had got hold of a dhobi's donkey and hung a little board from its neck saying SANJAY GANDHI in Hindi. A ripple of laughter went through a part of the crowd. There was now barely any space to move on the road. Jadu decided to return home.

When he stepped into his living room he could hear the radio turned on high. Maya came out of the kitchen smiling. The new coalition of opposition leaders was on its way to a historic triumph and, according to the bulletin on the radio, the new leaders would take an oath at Mahatma Gandhi's memorial in Rajghat. Jadu found his daughter, Jugnu, doing her math homework, and he kissed her on the head.

In the weeks that followed, more changes were to come. Fresh elections were announced for the Bihar Assembly. Jadu's friend Ramdeo was nominated for the election from Barachetti. Jadu and Lallan Yadav decided to help Ramdeo with campaign work. They boarded a rickety state transport bus that took them to Gaya, and then they hired a pony cart to take them to Ramdeo's village.

It was hot. The monsoon rains hadn't arrived. A young man brought them bel sherbet in metal glasses. And then they were shown their sleeping quarters, a hut barely large enough to stand in, with two straw mats spread out on the floor on sacks of synthetic waterproof material used to store cement. A hand pump stood about thirty yards away. People took water from it to drink and to bathe. There were no bathrooms: Jadu and Lallan would need to go out into the fields.

Ramdeo laughed good-naturedly and said, "Get a taste of this life too. This is the real India."

Jadu smiled, silent, but Lallan said agreeably, "Gandhiji had said that India lives in its villages . . ."

That night, when an insect climbed inside Jadu's ear, he shook Lallan awake. Jadu could feel the creature burrowing in his ear canal. Perhaps it was frantically trying to find a way out and was trapped. Lallan lit the lantern they had been given. He could see nothing in the dark mouth of Jadu's ear. Stepping out of the hut in the dark, he plucked a blade of grass. If he inserted it into Jadu's ear, maybe that insect would find it easier to wriggle out. It didn't.

Jadu rolled on the ground, panicking, fearing that his brain would be damaged if the tiny invader had teeth or claws. Then, Lallan said, "Wait." He unscrewed the base of the lantern in the hut and emptied a spoonful of the kerosene oil on his palm. This he poured into Jadu's ear. The movement in the ear ceased immediately. When Jadu tilted his head, the oil dribbled out and so did a tiny centipede. It had drowned in the oil and was now dead.

Jadu was relieved. He wanted to laugh. He smelled of kerosene and felt that he would perhaps never get rid of its smell but he didn't mind. Lallan put the centipede on his index finger and examined it in the light of the lantern. He repeated what he had said only hours before. "Gandhiji had said that India lives in its villages. This poor insect, looking for shelter at night or something to eat, is an Indian too. *India Zindabad!* Long live India!"

———

Gaya was the closest town but it was more than an hour away. Jadu was asked to go there for an important task. Early in the morning he clambered aboard an overcrowded bus. His mission in town took five hours but at the end he paid a man for printing fifteen thousand election pamphlets. The paper used was thin, and the red color on the yellow ran in places, but it would work. The election symbol of Ramdeo's party, a farmer with a plow, was prominent in the upper-right-hand corner. The printer assured Jadu that glue would not damage the pamphlets. Each pile of ten thousand was packed tightly and tied with twine.

On the bus back to Barachetti, Jadu felt he was carrying essential supplies to the war front.

The next day, his work began. A cycle-rickshaw pulled by a man named Risal had been hired. Jadu sat on the rickshaw's passenger seat with a contraption at his feet, a loudspeaker attached to a car battery. In a cotton bag by his side were stacks of the yellow pamphlets. He spoke the same lines again and again into the microphone. *Friend of the poor, son of this soil, Ramdeo Manjhi. Give your valuable vote. Put your stamp on the symbol of the farmer. For a better future for everyone and not just for a few.* More than anyone else, it was the children, little village children who would not vote for fifteen years or so, who wanted his pamphlets. They followed his rickshaw from one end of the village to the other. Hours later, on the way back to Ramdeo's village, Jadu would find the pamphlets fluttering on the dirt roads. They were like fallen leaves, already faded, slightly soiled.

Whenever he saw a group of men seated together, under a tree or at a well, Jadu asked Risal to stop the rickshaw. Speaking calmly into the microphone, Jadu would repeat his words and then he would step off his seat and go to the villagers and give them the pamphlets. More than once the men would ask what the pamphlet said, and Jadu would point to the symbol and say this was where they should put their stamp on voting day. He was respectful toward the women. When they saw a stranger approach, they often averted their faces, drawing the edges of their saris so that only their eyes were visible. Whenever this happened, Jadu cautiously placed the pamphlets on any surface he could find near them and called them his sisters. He would urge them to exercise their right to vote and to vote for someone who knew their troubles and whose interests were close to his heart. *Ramdeo Manjhi, the farmer with the plow.*

At least once each day, and sometimes more, a jeep with the national flag flying from a bamboo pole lashed to its door would pass Jadu's rickshaw. A loudspeaker would be announcing the name of Ramdeo's rival or playing snatches of Hindi film songs. The moment he heard the jeep approach, Jadu would switch off his loudspeaker in order to conserve the battery. The jeep's driver, a young man who always turned grinning toward Jadu, had a *gamch-cha* tied around his head as if he was ready to wrestle. Jadu tried to look away when the jeep passed him.

On the fourth day, Jadu had to stop work because two news-papermen from Gaya, stringers for a regional Hindi daily, brought news of an accident. A child studying in the middle school had drowned in the river Falgu. He was an upper-caste boy and the parents claimed that his low-caste friends had pushed the boy into the water on the way back from school. They were responsible for the boy's death. The father of the dead boy, the journalists disclosed, worked for Ramdeo's opponent in the elections. The newspapermen wanted to know if Ramdeo would like to comment.

Ramdeo laughed at the question. He said, "Thanks to you, I have learned that upper-caste boys are now playing with lower-caste boys in our villages."

Jadu held up his hand. He said to the newspapermen, "Ramdeo Manjhi has no comment. Elections are coming. Please do not play with matches. No need to light fires."

Ramdeo said, "That is our comment. What Jadunathji said. He is my manager."

Ramdeo took Jadu to a hut near his own. He was looking for Aloki, one of the Dalit boys whose names were listed among those who had been in the river. The boy was tall for his ten years, thin as a stick, with large, nervous eyes. The two men questioned Aloki.

The dead boy's name, he said, was Neeraj. When Aloki and his friends were walking back from school, Neeraj had passed them on his bicycle and seemed headed to the river.

"Was he alone?"

"No," Aloki said. "There were two other upper-caste boys, also on bicycles."

"Did you exchange words?"

"No. Neeraj slowed down and acted as if he was going to spit on us. We stepped aside and let him pass." He said that there was no further interaction between the two groups.

A jeep was hired for 125 rupees. The first stop of the hired jeep was the dead boy's house. The upper-caste homes were built with brick. Still, it was clear that they would only have a few amenities.

The five or six men sitting on chairs outside the one-story house said nothing when they saw Ramdeo getting down from the jeep.

Jadu went up to the door and, speaking softly, asked if the father was home. The man's name was Jeetendar Singh; he was a tall, dark man, his head shaven that morning after the cremation.

Ramdeo extended his hand and said, "My condolences. Such a loss. It is difficult to say anything."

Jeetendar Singh gave his hand to Ramdeo and then looked at Jadu and Lallan. He had known Ramdeo ever since they had been boys in the village but he saw that Lallan and Jadu were city people. Warily, he pointed toward the chairs on which others were sitting, and said, "Please sit."

The men who had been seated so far stood up from their chairs. But the visitors couldn't stay. Ramdeo said, "The Block Development officer is coming to install a tube well in my village. I need to be there. I had just come to offer my condolences." Before getting into the jeep, Ramdeo turned back to face Jeetendar and all the other men, who were still standing. A few more had also appeared from the surrounding homes. Ramdeo said, "We have all grown up together here. Any one family's loss is our own loss. Please reach out if I can help with anything."

Instead of going back to his village, Ramdeo asked the driver to turn left on the road to Barachetti. It was clear that the boy's death and the lie about it was being used to solidify the upper-caste vote for the ruling party candidate. Ramdeo was going to take action against such a move.

The police station was next to a cycle repair shop. A large mango tree spread its shade over the blue metal gate that opened onto a short dirt driveway. Inside, the inspector appeared lost in the pages of the Hindi magazine he was reading. He was in his forties, with a pencil mustache that suggested he thought of himself as a man of taste. He addressed Ramdeo by name and asked if everything was in order.

Ramdeo said he wanted to file a report under section 153 of the Indian Penal Code.

The inspector's manner suggested that he thought Ramdeo

was acting in haste. He smiled a lazy smile. He said that Ramdeo should first tell him what had happened.

"As a candidate for the assembly elections, I have responsibilities . . ." was how Ramdeo began his speech.

He said that he had been contacted by members of the media. A rumor making the rounds was designed to cause social rift and lead to violence before the election. The accidental drowning of a boy nearby had been turned into a story about caste conflict. It was criminal to set one community or caste against another, et cetera.

The inspector opened a drawer and took out a book where he was going to record Ramdeo's complaint.

"Who do you want named?" The inspector asked this and then, still with his lazy smile, asked if Ramdeo wanted to name the ruling party candidate.

"Unnamed persons, please write that down," replied Ramdeo.

When the First Information Report had been recorded, Ramdeo asked Jadu to copy it down on another sheet of paper. This paper they took to the post office. From the public phone there, Ramdeo called the two main newspaper offices in Gaya and dictated his complaint to the subeditors present to take calls.

"Please print," Ramdeo said, summoning all his sincerity, "we must save democracy." At each newspaper, there were eager questions that Ramdeo was happy to answer.

It was clear even before he had got back in the hired jeep that Ramdeo had injected life into his campaign. He had taken what fate had thrown at him and hurled it back like lightning. The low-caste villagers all around Barachetti were going to vote for him anyway, but now he had made sure that not all upper-caste voters were opposed to him. In another ten days, stopping on his route on the Grand Trunk Road, Jayaprakash Narayan was going to address a rally at the local school grounds. Working hard on all the days that remained, Ramdeo would make his campaign stronger. And JP, who was popular among the upper-caste voters, would put his stamp of approval on it.

On their drive back to the village, the three friends began to laugh. This laughter came from a place of recognition. They were beginning to look at the election with the eyes of the others, including the police inspector they had met and the journalists from Gaya. They could now clearly see Ramdeo winning. This vision of the future was as real as a memory from their past. To Jadu it seemed that their story had come full circle: so many years after Professor Dey had taken them all to meet Tenzing Norgay, Ramdeo would return to the Raj Bhawan not as a shoeless student but as a democratically elected representative of the people. He would stand wearing a sherwani, or at least a silk kurta, and take the oath of office face-to-face with the Governor.

Jadu began telling them a story as the jeep traveled on the dirt road, lurching and leaping forward like a cow making its way across a ditch. It was a tale from the *Mahabharata*. During the great battle, the old warrior Drona was wreaking havoc against the Pandavas. Drona was a great teacher and he had taught the secrets of warfare to members of both the clans now locked in battle, the Pandavas and the Kauravas. Toward the end of the war, faced with Drona's tremendous skill and mastery, the Pandavas resorted to the propaganda preached by the charioteer in their army, the divine Lord Krishna. One of the Pandava brothers, Bhima, had killed the elephant that had the same name as Drona's son, Ashwatthama. When Bhima loudly proclaimed that he had slayed Ashwatthama, Drona asked Bhima's older brother, whose adherence to dharma was legendary and who always spoke the truth, whether what Bhima was saying was indeed true. And the older brother, speaking in the vague, stumbling way that truth-sayers often do, replied, "Ashwatthama is dead, the elephant and not your son." Lord Krishna had asked for the trumpets and conches to be blown so that the second part of the answer wasn't heard by Drona. Grief-stricken, he descended from his chariot and, setting aside his weapons, sat down in meditation. When Drona did this, the commander in chief of the Pandava army stepped forward and beheaded him.

Everyone in the jeep, including the driver, whose real job was as a government night guard at the irrigation canal station, knew the story that Jadu had just narrated. But they felt a great pleasure in hearing it narrated again. It was as if the story had given their actions a place in a larger story and they all belonged to an older saga about mankind. They felt this even though no one was sure whether Jadu was saying that Ramdeo and his friends had been wily that day like the Pandavas. Or that they had killed a Drona. Or an elephant, for that matter. There was silence after Jadu had finished telling his story. Not an awkward silence, just a silence filled with minds unraveling the thread of thoughts. After a while, Ramdeo said, "There is one story about Ashwatthama that has always been dear to me. I heard it during a performance in Gaya when I was a teenager and I have never forgotten it."

It was a story about Ashwatthama when he was still a little boy. He was playing with some friends who were drinking milk. Ashwatthama wanted milk too. But he was poor, the son of an ascetic. His friends were cruel. They mixed flour with water and gave that to him to drink. This act enraged his father, Drona, and he went to Drupada, his childhood friend who was now a king, to ask for cows so that his son could have milk to drink. Drupada refused the request for help, remarking that he could not be friends with a beggar. Drona resolved to seek revenge and the story that follows is an important part of the *Mahabharata*, but what had stuck in Ramdeo's memory was a poor boy's desire for milk—and his being mocked by being given flour mixed with water.

Again, there was silence at the end of the story, broken only by the jeep's driver sucking his teeth in sympathy.

———

The election for the Bihar Assembly wasn't the only new event to take place when the Emergency ended.

Censorship had been lifted. The newspapers could now report the truth. Writers were planning prison memoirs. One afternoon, Jigyasa showed up at Jadu's front door. He was there to tell Jadu and Maya about a public reading that the poet Renu was organizing on the following Wednesday at the Rabindra Bhawan. Famous poets were going to gather for the occasion. Raghuvir Sahay and Mahadevi Verma had already said yes; efforts were under way to get Kedarnath Singh and Baba Nagarjuna; there would be some local poets reading their new work too.

A lot of new energy had been unleashed with the return of democracy. Right from that March up to May, when it became too hot to do anything in the open, there were meetings of new groups that had been formed. These were not merely literary or cultural groups. A karate club for children began meeting on weekend mornings in the Gandhi Maidan; ditto, a walking club in the Botanical Garden; and in Lady Stephenson Hall, an organization put together a calendar built around an offering of art and cooking classes, and, only once each month, a discussion on astrology. Jadu felt that his life was being set to a new rhythm, a rhythm more akin to optimistic newsreels that were screened in cinema halls just before the main feature was shown. It was like a happy fantasy, unreal and unlikely to last too long. Also, Jadu worried that this fantasy wasn't too different from the one that he had been living in during the twenty-one months of the Emergency. During that period, the whole country had lived through an authoritarian leader's dream of clean streets, a population with a controlled growth rate, and trains running on time; and now the entire nation, or at least his own town, was suffering through a sedate middle-class drama staged by the hobby lobby with zero commitment to liberation and real change.

But then Jadu slipped into a fantasy of his own making.

Except that this was no fantasy, it was real. Jadu was sitting across from Ananya Ghosh. They were having lunch together. Jadu was telling her that when he saw her first after all these years, more than two decades, he didn't recognize her because she looked so much younger than he expected. And so beautiful too. He asked her a question, "What prompted you to write to us?"

What he was really asking her was why she had never spoken to him or his classmates when she was with them in Professor Dey's class. So many years had passed. So much had happened in the country.

But Ananya didn't answer. It was as if she was searching for an answer herself. Jadu was impatient. He broke the silence. "It seems a lifetime ago. It *was* a lifetime ago. What did you see when you looked at us?"

Ananya looked up at Jadu. She was laughing. "Why did we do anything at that age? Was there any explanation for what we did?"

This time it was Jadu's turn to be silent.

Ananya said, with seeming earnestness, "Did we know anything?"

Jadu said, "You and your sister appeared to know. I was the one who knew nothing."

Ananya surprised him now. She said, "I thought the same about you, that you seemed to know. You were so serious in class."

Jadu felt better now. He thought he could ask her more questions.

"What made you join the Ananda Marg? Was it like a cult?"

"I had a silly reason for joining the group," Ananya said. She said she didn't know whether or not it was a cult. She hadn't been in it very long.

"What was the silly reason?"

Professor Dey had given her a novel to read. *The Razor's Edge* by the British writer W. Somerset Maugham. A young American man comes to India to find meaning in life. He meets a saint during his travels and this leads to a spiritual discovery.

"You should read it," she said. "Then we can talk."

Two weeks earlier, Jadu had received a letter with an invitation to a gathering—except this time it was signed with a woman's first name. Ananya. No last name. He looked at the address on the letter. It was familiar to him. *Ananya Ghosh! Sukanya's sister, the unmarried one.* He had never forgotten the two sisters in *The Cherry Orchard*. Was it possible that her religious group had been banned by Mrs. Gandhi—and now the ban had been lifted?

Her leader had been accused of being party to some murder—and wasn't Ananya supposed to be abroad?

Was she still single?

He knew he had come to the right place when he saw Atul Tandon entering the gate of an old bungalow. Jadu hadn't seen Tandon for years. Inside, there was Lallan Yadav seated on the sofa. But no Ramdeo. He wouldn't have come even if Ananya had invited him. She hadn't, of course. Krishna Murari came, wearing a white cap, as if they were at a cricket match. Clearly, this was an invitation to a reunion, even if the other sister wasn't here with them. The bungalow was the one that old Dr. Ghosh had used as his home and clinic, but now there was a new modern structure looming behind it with its own separate entrance from the lane at the back. There was a sign indicating the entrance and hours for the eye clinic. The new house must have been built by Sukanya and her husband. It was a small gathering of friends who had known each other when they were young in Professor Dey's class, but the awkwardness of youth and its many uncertainties were now gone. There was a lot of laughter. A maid brought them tea. When they were to leave, Jadu said to Ananya that he had so many questions for her.

"Let's meet again," Ananya said. "Lunch in New Pintu this week?"

"Yes," Jadu said.

It had been simple. Ananya said that he should use the number in the phone directory under her father's name. Jadu let a day pass and then he called to confirm the lunch.

And here they were. Ananya was talking. A thought had entered Jadu's head. In asking him to read the Somerset Maugham book, Ananya was saying that she wanted him to come back and spend time with her. He wasn't going to be unfaithful to his wife, but it was pleasant, even thrilling, to be here with Ananya. This beautiful woman that they had all lusted after in their youth. Who had later gone away to—Seychelles, or had it been Switzerland?

"I will read the book. But I have one more question. Where were you all these years?"

"I was young and felt I was on a quest," Ananya said. "I'm talking about the time I had joined the Ananda Marg. In the beginning, I was here in Patna although I didn't live at home."

The ashram where she had lived was on the outskirts of Patna near the Kumhrar Park. Then, she had gone to Calcutta, to the Ananda Marg's headquarters on the banks of the Hooghly. After three years in Calcutta, she said she had risen in the ranks and become an administrator. "Then our guru was arrested, and a few of us fled to Pokhra in Nepal. We stayed there till the money ran out."

Another member of the group had arranged a visa for Ananya to visit Australia. She stayed in an ashram in Melbourne. Everyone else at the ashram had jobs in the real world, and so Ananya started teaching primary school.

"The Australian who had got me the visa said that he was in love with me," Ananya said. She laughed. "He had started in life as a bureaucrat, his job was to check tax returns, and now his ambition was to sing devotional songs in very bad Hindi." As he listened to Ananya, Jadu wondered what had happened to the Australian. Ananya was saying that she liked her work at the school. She loved the children and their questions.

"Wait," he said. "What happened to the Australian?"

"Oh. I didn't want to be a mail-order bride."

Still, she had remained in Melbourne. And then she got the news that her father had died.

A jailed comrade, someone from her circle in Patna, had read her father's obituary in the local paper. He sent her the clipping. The last line in the obituary said that Dr. Ghosh is survived by two daughters.

"I was devasted by this news, it cut me in half. This news had reminded me that I was still his daughter," Ananya said.

Jadu was nodding. Ananya said, "As shattering as the news was, it also freed me. I was so ashamed by then of what I had become that I had completely cut myself off from my family. After I got the news of my father's death, I began to plan my return."

But then the Emergency arrived. Ananya made a motion with her right hand, as if she were drawing a heavy curtain to shut out the light. Jadu understood that it would have been especially difficult for someone with her history to make an easy return to India at that time. Ananya said, "I didn't know what to do, or how things would change. And when things did change, I didn't wait. I was back here in five days. My sister was delighted. We are together now. I invited those who were in Professor Dey's class because I wanted to connect with the past."

A few days later, Jadu went to Ananya's home to pick up *The Razor's Edge*. Ananya came to the door, huge earrings dangling near her neck. She was wearing a cotton outfit striped black and white, a stylish variation on dungarees in an Indian style. After they had talked for a while, Ananya got up and withdrew Maugham's novel from her shelf.

Jadu opened the book. Professor Dey's name was signed on the title page. Under his name he had written, *Patna, 1951*. Ananya was saying something about how the book, when Professor Dey had lent it, was in pristine condition. But she had liked it so much, she had made marks with a pencil in different places. When she was rereading the book, the cover got scuffed and then torn. She had told herself that the book wasn't in any condition to be returned.

Jadu told Ananya that back when they were students there was talk among the boys that the Ghosh sisters had appeared in an ad for Bombay Dyeing. Ananya asked about Radha Charan's wedding. She said at one point that she had looked out of Professor Dey's classroom and seen the boats on the Ganga but never gone down to the river herself. They could go for a ride on a boat now, Jadu thought to himself, but remained silent. Ananya was looking at the mango tree outside the window and Jadu found himself talking about the trees in Khewali. In Australia, Ananya said, she had seen rows and rows of eucalyptus trees and also orange trees. At her ashram near Melbourne, she would be startled during her walks by the sudden explosion of wings and would look up to see a herd of parakeets taking flight. Can you say "a herd of parakeets," she wanted to know. "I don't see why not," Jadu replied unconvincingly. Ananya then spoke of having watched a film in Melbourne by the great Bengali filmmaker Ritwik Ghatak. The film was *Meghe Dhaka Tara* (The Cloud-Capped Star), shot in black and white. Ghatak was a refugee from East Pakistan during the Partition, and this had been true of Ananya's maternal grandfather too. The pain of the young woman at the heart of Ghatak's film *(Those who suffer for others suffer forever)* had touched her but what had really pierced her was the sound of her native language being spoken by the people on the screen. It made her want to come home. Jadu said that a group of students was planning a strike. Ananya said that she wanted to start a school for children: the focus would be on play and not on studying.

There had been no plot to the afternoon: the story was in their dialogue. Two decades late, this delayed conversation between two people from Patna. There was more to it than mere dialogue. It was a revelation, an outpouring, of personal histories. Ananya's voice in the late afternoon telling him about her life while all that was visible of the world outside was the gardener's brown back bent over an unseen patch. Caught in a tumult of emotion, Jadu held on to the sound of Ananya's calm voice. She had cut a large green watermelon and offered him a slice. And she had taken a bite from a slice she had cut for herself. Two shades of pink, the fruit and her mouth.

———

Maugham's protagonist was a young American in Chicago named Larry. The first sentence in the book that Ananya had underlined was on page 32. It was about Larry's smile: "It was not a brilliant, flashing smile, it was a smile that lit his face as with an inner light." Larry was an unostentatious young man on a singular quest, unattached to worldly pleasures, attractive to women and yet distant and untouched by them. Jadu was drawn to Larry's persona on the page despite being aware of the novelist's artifice. Midway through the book, Jadu came to the section that had many lines underlined by Ananya. In this section, Larry was recounting details of his visit to India and he revealed that he had spent time with a yogi. When asked what had attracted him to the holy man, Larry replied, "Saintliness." Spiritual accomplishment wasn't to be located only in tales from hundreds of years ago, tales of St. Francis or St. John of the Cross. There were saints in present-day India. That's what Maugham was saying. He also seemed to be saying that ordinary seekers could acquire some of the qualities of saintliness through meditation. The novel offered proof of this in the very next pages: Larry performed a little miracle, curing his friend's migraine. Jadu felt light-headed reading this.

After lunch, Maya was absorbed in a magazine while lying sprawled directly under the ceiling fan. Behind her head was the phone. Jadu picked up the receiver and dialed Ananya's number. This was the first time he was calling her from home. He was aware that this was unusual behavior, not at all typical of him. He was forty years old. Why was he behaving as if he were twenty?

The phone rang many times, giving Jadu time to practice his lines.

When Ananya picked up, Jadu said, "This is Larry calling."

"Larry?"

"Larry Darrell."

"Who?" She sounded genuinely mystified. Still sticking to English, she said, "What number do you want?"

Jadu introduced himself properly now in Hindi. He said quickly, "I'm enjoying *The Razor's Edge*."

They didn't talk for long. Jadu said he was only halfway through the book. Ananya said that they should talk when he had finished reading it.

"What was that?" Maya asked from where she lay on the sofa.

"I was just telling Ananya about the book she gave me."

"Why were you calling yourself Larry?"

Jadu didn't answer. The conversation with Ananya hadn't gone well. He had wanted to be humorous but, instead, he was awkward. Instinctively, he retreated. Drawing back into himself, he returned to Maugham's novel, and he was once again immersed in the flow of its narrative. Larry wasn't cynical or petty; he was never superficial. The disinterestedness he represented was perhaps a model that Jadu should adopt. Larry didn't pursue sex and yet he wasn't prudish about it either. There was a degree of freedom in his approach to everything, sex included. Jadu didn't mention it to anyone but, like Larry in the book, he started a daily routine of meditation. Around dusk each day he lit a candle and stared at the flame in silent contemplation. When thoughts came into his head, he allowed them to drift away. For some days, Jadu thought that meditation was shaping his body in such a way that he was becoming indifferent to heat or cold. He wanted to discuss this with Ananya. When he asked her about *The Razor's Edge*, however, and prodded her about what she had thought of Maugham's description of the yogi, she said that it was a very long time ago that she had read the book and she didn't remember much. She only remembered that it had affected her thinking and given strength to her resolve to be unconventional and to keep asking questions about the meaning of life. Jadu felt he had made a mistake in trying to find in the book a truth he was seeking about Ananya. After a few weeks, he gave up the practice of meditation. He didn't forget Maugham, though, and during the two or three more salons that Ananya organized at her home, Jadu would remember bits of the novel as he looked at his host standing in the light.

Fiction, or the idea of the imagination enlivening the narrative of life, was alien to Jadu the historian. However, it was from a novel that Jadu had borrowed feelings that he felt in his heart about Ananya. Perhaps his own life was becoming novelistic. Like the people in the novel Jadu was reading, Ananya represented worldliness: she had traveled to other places, she had crossed the ocean and lived in a foreign country, she had had relations with other men. Given the odd and unexpected bouts of emotion that buffeted him, Jadu now reached a realization: every object that caught his attention attracted an act of invention. Was this what romance really meant? *This is a leaf fallen on the earth.* Would Ananya have walked on it? *Here is a red flower.* How would it look in her dark hair?

A student was getting married and Jadu found the invitation in his office mailbox. On the card, embossed in gold, were two lines from a poem by Rabindranath Tagore: "I seem to have loved you in numberless forms, numberless times . . . / In life after life, in age after age, forever." Standing in the dusty office, rickety shelves crammed with yellowing files, the registrar's clerk working on his typewriter nearby, Jadu felt his heart knocking against his chest. This was because the phrase "in life after life" had made him young again. He was suddenly a new undergraduate drinking tea near the Ashok Rajpath gate of the college on a winter morning. The rickshaw carrying Ananya and Sukanya was coming close and now Ananya, instead of staring ahead of her, was looking straight at Jadu, just as she had done the previous week in the New Pintu restaurant.

He felt young, yes, but he also felt guilty. Maya had not yet met Ananya. When Jadu mentioned to Maya that he was going to meet Ananya again for tea, her face had remained expressionless. Jadu knew what this meant, and yet he felt powerless. He reasoned that he wasn't doing anything with Ananya, just sitting and talking over a cup of tea and a fish cutlet. There wasn't anything more to it, even if it felt nice to imagine that there was. Just the previous week he had said to his colleague Saeed Anwar, "Please tell me, Anwar saheb, do you ever think of love?" Anwar's beard was turning gray, Jadu noticed. Anwar embarked on a discourse about how "for health and happiness, it is necessary to strike a balance." Anwar meant that he cared for his aged parents, he was responsible for his three children, and he had to fulfill his obligations to his wife. "In order to lead a peaceful existence, all these needs and desires must be in harmony." This lecture bored Jadu. He wanted to talk about Ananya. Unable to share his secret with anyone, he began making short entries in a diary. It was just a notebook with a chocolate cover that had been lying unused in his cupboard.

The inspiration for it had come from a diary that Jadu had been reading for his research. Manu Gandhi, the young niece of Mohandas Gandhi, had been in detention at the Aga Khan Palace in 1943. She was fifteen years old. Both Mohandas and his ailing wife, Kasturba, were already prisoners at the palace. The British government had moved Manu to the Aga Khan Palace to care for Kasturba. Kasturba died the following year while still a prisoner. Manu had begun her diary on April 11, 1943. Jadu had come to her diaries in search of Gandhi's prayer speeches, which Manu had recorded, but he grew interested in the drama of a young girl's life. Gandhi, whom Manu called Bapu, urged all his followers to maintain a daily diary. He would on occasion inspect Manu's diary. Sometimes, however, she didn't submit to his demand. On May 21, 1943, she made an entry where she revealed she hadn't shown him her diary because she had written in it about how Gandhi hadn't allowed her to apply ghee to his feet. Manu produced twelve volumes of diaries. Either her later diaries hadn't been translated from Gujarati or that volume hadn't yet been purchased by the college library. Jadu made a note that he would wait to read the later volume too. Because, before the end of his life, Gandhi shared his bed with Manu and another niece. What had Manu written of Gandhi's experiments that tested his celibacy, his brahmacharya?

On July 25, 1943, Manu had written that she prayed to God that she not commit errors and give offense to others. While cooking the previous day, she noted in her diary, she had "slightly burnt" the vegetables. She had taken quinine for severe body pain. And then: "I have written these notes after a gap of many days—pages are expensive, aren't they?" This brief note by a teenage girl was the first entry copied down in Jadu's diary. He had liked it because he too didn't want to give offense and he liked the girl's sense of thrift. *Pages are expensive, aren't they?*

His entries included the following:

Nov 29, 1977. Jugnu high fever of 103.

Nov 30, 1977. Jugnu better. Bought jalebis 2 rupees and flowers 3 rupees.

Dec 3, 1977. India Coffee House. Speech by Upendranath Ashk. Ananya didn't like him, "masculine arrogance."

Dec 5, 1977. Patliputra Hotel. Tea with Ananya.

Dec 16, 1977. Restlessness. Have started reading *Shekhar: Ek Jeevani*.

Dec 19, 1977. "Man has places in his heart which do not yet exist, and into them enters suffering, in order that they may have existence." (Léon Bloy)

Dec 22, 1977. Extremely cold day. Prof. Prakash hosted reception for young poet Pash. Ananya brought me two books by Tolstoy.

Christmas Eve, 1977. At the farewell dinner for the Mountbattens on June 19, 1947, Pandit Nehru gave a speech in honor of Edwina:

"The gods or some good fairy gave you beauty and high intelligence, and grace and charm and vitality—great gifts—and she who possesses them is a great lady wherever she goes. But unto those who have, even more shall be given: and they gave you something that was even rarer than those gifts—the human touch, the love of humanity, the urge to serve those who suffer and who are in distress. And this amazing mixture of qualities results in a radiant personality and in the healer's touch.

"Wherever you have gone you have brought solace, and you have brought hope and encouragement. Is it surprising, therefore, that the people of India should love you and look up to you as one of themselves and should grieve that you are going? Hundreds of thousands have seen you personally in various camps and other places and in hospitals, and hundreds of thousands will be sorrowful at the news that you have gone."

A plan had been proposed for a New Year's Day picnic on the Ganga. Krishna Murari Sharma was arranging a boat. Maya said she was under the weather and Jadu dropped the idea. They took Jugnu to the Botanical Garden: a small toy train in the park took them past animals in caged enclosures. A bear, a giraffe, a tiger pacing back and forth on the dry earth. A few days later, there was another plan for a get-together. The film *The Day of the Jackal* was being screened at Alpana Cinema. English films would be screened in places like Delhi and Bombay; after a year or two, they arrived for a week's run in Patna. Jadu telephoned Ananya and wished her a happy new year. He told her that some friends were going to the matinee show on the coming Saturday. Jadu and Maya both went to watch the movie after leaving little Jugnu with her cousins. Lallan Yadav had bought the tickets by arriving an hour in advance and standing in line. Ananya came. She was meeting Maya for the first time; the two women seemed to be having a pleasant conversation. The assassin in the film was a mercenary hired by the military right in France, who believed that de Gaulle had given away Algeria and must be punished. His task was to kill de Gaulle. At one point in the film, the assassin, code-named Jackal, bought a big green watermelon and hung it from a tree in the mountainous wilderness. The Jackal was testing his rifle. When he blew away the watermelon, which exploded when the rifle's sights had been adjusted correctly, Jadu looked left, where Ananya was sitting. But she wasn't there. She had left the cinema hall at some point. He called her after they got home but there was no answer.

A week later, he sent a postcard. And then a longer letter, which also remained unanswered.

After that day, Jadu saw Ananya infrequently, and only at weddings. She would be standing among females but also appearing apart from them, and Jadu would be among the males. Their glances sometimes met and though they acknowledged each other they seldom got a chance to talk. When he saw Ananya standing apart like that, it occurred to him that in the society in which he lived stories never found their endings. But then he would doubt this judgment too, and begin to think of other things. It would be silly to walk up to Ananya and ask her, "Where did you go after the intermission during *The Day of the Jackal*? Was it Seychelles? Or Switzerland? How is the weather there today? Are you planning to come back ever?" Most of the time, though, when he thought back to that time he was looking for Ananya in all the rooms and on each street, and finding only her absence everywhere, he felt as if he had been suffering from a fever. He felt foolish but also terribly moved when he thought about that period. He kept up the practice of making entries in the diary that he had started during that time.

———

A few years later, Jadu had reason to think of Somerset Maugham's Larry Darrell again when a slim, bearded American man arrived in Patna. He was a historian from Michigan, his name was Reed Anthony, and he had come to Patna to study the student movement that had emerged under Jayaprakash Narayan some years earlier. He was new to Patna but he had done research in India before. In the early seventies, he had authored a study about textile weavers in Benares. Reed Anthony's interest was in history from below. He wasn't going to write a biography of JP; he was here to carry out research about the students who were his nameless supporters. Poor, unemployed youth, faced with a bleak and uncertain future, and yet with a belief in democracy.

The American was staying at a guesthouse near Gandhi Maidan and someone directed him to Jadu.

The boy at the tea shop next to the big peepul used to put cardamom in the tea. Jadu took Anthony there.

"Call me Reed, please," Anthony said. He wanted Jadu to dispense with his formal manner.

"Okay, Mister Reed."

"No, just Reed."

Then, Anthony began telling Jadu that his name on the train ticket to Patna had been spelled Red Anthony by the travel agent in Delhi. The mistake was repeated by the clerk at the local guesthouse. Jadu told him that he had an uncle whose first name was Lal, which, in Hindi, is the name for the color red. Lal Babu Kunwar.

They went to see Amitesh Sinha. He had been kept in jail for nearly two years, certainly for the whole period that Indira Gandhi's Emergency had lasted. His manner had changed by the time he got out of prison. It wasn't that he was tortured or had suffered greatly, it was just that he had matured as a politician. But is it maturity, Jadu wondered, if you grow more gifted at cutting ribbons at inaugural ceremonies or handing trophies to cricket champions? Amitesh had hoped that he would be given the Tourism portfolio. He wanted to travel and experience the rest of India and maybe the world. Instead, he was made the junior minister in the department of Information and Public Relations. Jadu congratulated him after he had been sworn into office and asked what his main job was going to be. Amitesh said, "The senior minister will control the press. My job will be to smile for the camera."

On the other side of a gleaming desk in the Old Secretariat sat Amitesh. He now sported a beard. He was wearing a white khadi kurta. He raised his folded hands and said to Anthony, "Welcome to Bihar, where the Buddha achieved Enlightenment."

Maybe he should have been given the Tourism portfolio after all, Jadu thought.

There was a small painted sign on the desk in front of Amitesh facing the visitor. It said in Hindi, PLEASE DO NOT, BY SITTING IDLE HERE, WASTE YOUR PRECIOUS TIME. Anthony surprised Amitesh with his knowledge of Hindi by reading the sign aloud, laughing at what he called *vyang*, or satire. Both men conversed only in Hindi after that.

The meeting was between Amitesh and Reed Anthony, but it changed Jadu's life. Amitesh helped Reed get access to JP's papers, which were being readied for transfer to the Nehru Memorial Museum and Library in Delhi. The professional relation that grew between Jadu and Anthony took on the character of a collaboration, and three years later Jadu got the chance to visit America as a Fulbright scholar. Their friendship had started with that afternoon's meeting with Amitesh; in the weeks that followed, Jadu and Anthony spent many days together, meeting student activists and young intellectuals. An unaffected closeness grew between them. Jadu took Anthony to the cinema to watch serious films like *Andhi Gali* and *Paar*—and the American would ask questions about urban poverty or about Naxalites—but what he really enjoyed, Jadu suspected, was Sridevi and her dancing in another film they watched and whose name Jadu immediately forgot.

Jadu also took Anthony to meet Saurabh Kumar Jigyasa. Jigyasa was heading out the door to a poetry reading and they went there as a group. The poetry stirred Anthony's soul and he offered to translate some of Jigyasa's poems. Jigyasa insisted that this would be impossible until Anthony had traveled with him to his village. The dust from its dirt roads must touch Anthony's shiny shoes. The village awaited his arrival. Anthony must taste the water from its earth and eat the food prepared by Jigyasa's seventy-year-old mother. He needed to hear a cowherd calling at dusk for a lost calf. Jigyasa had his own ten commandments for living an authentic life. Jadu went to Jigyasa's village with them. In Jigyasa's own home, Jadu found an air of tension. He was told that Jigyasa had urged his father to give away all his land to the workers who plowed the fields. When talking to the father, Jadu was surprised to discover that Jigyasa had been suffering from depression and had been given electroshock treatment over the course of the past year. How had Jadu or Maya not known about this? A year later, when Jigyasa committed suicide in Delhi while attending a language conference at Sahitya Kala Akademi, Reed Anthony published a touching obituary that put the poet's life in a broader context of peasant struggles and people's movements in modern India.

After his first visit to Patna, Reed Anthony returned every six months with his wife, Lucy. Jadu always tried to speak English with them, and they were as adamant about speaking in Hindi. Although the Americans acted as if Jadu was the host, and deserving of all their gratitude, they paid for all their expenses. The only thing Jadu didn't ask for was a salary and it probably didn't occur to Anthony that perhaps he should be paying Jadu. But then, during his second visit, Anthony offered to help Jadu with a Fulbright application to travel and teach in the United States. Jadu had heard of such scholarships, a colleague in linguistics had gone to Chicago for a year, but Anthony's suggestion opened a new world of dreaming. Jadu felt he was in a position to travel alone to America. Jugnu was now completing her undergraduate studies in Patna. She wanted to go to Delhi to study journalism for two years; she would stay in a women's boardinghouse and would have a measure of independence. This meant that her parents would also regain some of their own freedom. Jadu was stuck for a subject to research. When he admitted this, Anthony reminded Jadu that, in the nineteen twenties, Jayaprakash Narayan had traveled to America for graduate study, first at Berkeley and then at other universities. Did the youth movement in Bihar have any connection to the knowledge gained abroad? Jadu could work with scholars in Berkeley and elsewhere in the United States where historians were already producing research in what was coming to be called subaltern studies.

Jadu sent in his application, the pages typed by the stenographer, Badri Babu, who sat in the college's main office, all for a small payment of twenty rupees. Miraculously, an envelope came for him some months later from the U.S. embassy in Delhi, and inside, on a cream-colored paper embossed with a seal of an eagle holding arrows, an offer of a scholarship that would take Jadu to Berkeley. Another letter came from Reed Anthony in Ann Arbor.

He gave advice and assurances. He had also written that a package would be waiting for Jadu when he reached America; it would include a winter coat that Anthony had worn only a few times.

When JP had arrived in Berkeley from India in 1922, he found a job in nearby Marysville, earning forty cents an hour. It was farm work; he had to sun-dry grapes so that they turned into raisins. He slept in a shed with other workers. At Berkeley he washed dishes and waited tables in restaurants. Later he worked in a vineyard in the Sacramento Valley and, after that, in a fruit and jam canning factory in San Jose. But no such trials awaited Jadu. He had already paid rent for a small apartment and received printed sheets from the university office on Shattuck Avenue with information about nearby grocery stores and pharmacies. Over the next few days, he attended a total of nine orientation sessions meant to instruct him on everything from how to open a bank account to the process of getting an identity card and gaining entry to the library. After having passed the post office twice, he decided to buy an airmail form. In the letter to Maya that night he wrote that in the supermarket he had seen a bar of Pears soap on sale. That was the only item familiar to him. He had also found Colgate toothpaste, but the packaging was completely different. Although Jadu hadn't seen a tin of talcum powder, he had found a deodorant stick. He wrote that he felt he was living a new life because all the commodities he was using and even the food he was consuming were new. *The soap I ended up buying was the cheapest in the shop. The name of the brand is Irish Spring.*

In the library, he followed Reed Anthony's advice and began looking for records of the lives of thousands of peasants, mostly Sikhs, who had migrated to California even before JP and were often the subjects of racial attacks. On the street and on campus Jadu would sometimes come across white-skinned Sikhs who had a different look about them from those sardars he had grown up with. Hard to link them easily with the rough peasants who had come from Punjab at the end of the nineteenth century. That had been in 1899. A newspaper in San Francisco had reported the arrival of four Sikh men. Jadu found out that the first Sikh immigrants in the United States were farmers or laborers. In the lumberyards and sawmills in Oregon, Washington, and California, these men earned $1.50 to $2.00 a day. Most farmed the land in the Central and Imperial Valleys in California. Between 1900 and 1920, nearly seven thousand Indians arrived. But over the years, these growing numbers were perceived as a threat by whites who then passed exclusionary laws, in particular an act in 1917 that barred immigration from Asia. Most of the immigrants were workingmen, and those among them who were not single had been forced to leave their wives and children behind in India. The new laws made it more difficult, if not impossible, for the families to join the men. Jadu wasn't, of course, in the same position as those men, but he felt he could understand a bit of their loneliness. In a book he was reading, there was a mention that among these early immigrants from India, as late as 1930, there were only 100 women per 1,572 men. The process of immigration declined sharply after the racist new laws of 1917 and 1923 were enacted; many Indians returned home voluntarily. Others were deported or they died.

His papers were spread on a mahogany table in the library. An orange tree stood framed by the nearest window to his right. Jadu was reading from a stack of pages that presented yet another account of the first Indian immigrants. These papers were part of a typed collection of oral reports compiled by a retired postal worker in Stockton, a California town that was about an hour inland. The amateur historian's name was Darshan Singh and he was a Sikh. The oral reports he had collected were all brief memoir pieces: older Sikh inhabitants of the area, recalling life between the World Wars in California and what came later. Jadu was reading the reports but when he raised his head from his reading what he was most aware of was simply his comfort and delight at the chance to sit in the wonderful library. He was tempted to write to Maya and Jugnu, telling them about his good fortune. Would Jugnu ever get the chance to step into a place like this? During the winter in Patna, his feet would feel chilled when he sat in his own college library. And then came the unbearable heat of the summer. If he wasn't lucky enough to get a chair close to a fan, his sweat would drip down and dampen the pages of the book he was reading. Often, the electricity failed, and Jadu felt distracted or hungry.

The thought of food roused Jadu from his reverie in the cool interiors of Doe Library. He had been unadventurous in Berkeley. The only restaurant he frequented was the Indian place on Bancroft called Amber. And even those visits were rare. Mostly, he cooked khichdi in his tiny apartment. Or beans that he purchased in small tins. Rajma was here called kidney beans and then there were black beans, but that wasn't exactly kala dal. Nevertheless, how easy it was to open a can and heat the beans with a bit of salt and a spoonful of garam masala!

In his diary, Jadu would note down the $0.69 purchase of a can of beans. On another day, $2.20 for ten stamps. Or $1.05 for a dozen eggs and $1.09 for a half gallon of milk. For a quarter, Jadu could buy his own newspaper. During the first few weeks, his only nonessential purchase was a blue and yellow Cal T-shirt for Jugnu. That set him back six dollars. No one reading Jadu's diary would have known if on a particular day the sun had come out or whether it had been rainy, if he had worried about not having received a letter from home or whether he made a call on the telephone or, for that matter, if he had made a rich discovery in the archives. Jadu hadn't noted in his diary that he attended a tabla performance at the university by the legendary father and son duo Allah Rakha and Zakir Hussain—but he did remember to record that on that day he had bought bananas for $0.75 and yogurt for $1.29.

Jadu got up from his desk and smiled at the librarian to let him know that he would see him again soon. It was slightly windy outside, the wind stretching the clouds into long strips, but it was all pleasant. In ten minutes, he would be in his room. He had leftover rice and a pot of dal in the fridge. He passed Amber on his way home and the owner waved at him from the doorway. Pushing the maroon curtain aside, the man said, "Nice day." Jadu had a feeling that the restaurant owner was Muslim but they hadn't exchanged names so he couldn't be sure. The last time Jadu had eaten the buffet meal there, he had spread the page of classifieds in *The Daily Californian* on the table before him. He liked to compare what he was paying for his apartment with the new deals that were being offered in the area. That Sunday, however, what had caught his eye was a rectangle of prose that said: "Like to invite women 18–24 to try Indian food. Call Vijay, 849-3979."

Vijay must be young and unmarried, Jadu thought. Most of the students from India or Pakistan that he met on campus were younger than he was. When he saw the desi youth on the streets, in parks, even in his classes, he thought of his wife. Maya hadn't known this freedom when she was young. He wished she were walking down Telegraph Avenue with him to a café. Would they have looked like a couple in love? Jadu was conscious that he dressed more formally than the students around him. During orientation week, a woman from Bangladesh had asked him if he worked for the government. There was a program at Berkeley that was popular among government officers from the subcontinent. "No, I'm a Fulbright scholar," Jadu had answered stiffly. "I'm studying a chapter in history."

A chapter in history! The language of application forms. Clichés in the dull getup of office clerks. Jadu would have felt a greater sense of ease if he was expressing himself in Hindi. A conversational ease. But the language he used in the classroom even in Patna was English. When students in Patna stopped him outside class with questions, he would switch to Hindi because that was the language common to them, the one they were at home in. Such an anxiety not about English but about the places where it was spoken. When he had gone to Delhi to get his American visa, someone said that he should look at the cars and the trees outside the embassy. He would be questioned about them inside. Why? The man had said it was an "intelligence test" and it had struck him that power was always arbitrary. At the interview, they had asked about his knowledge of English and whether he taught in that language in Patna. "Yes, of course," he said, a bit too loudly. At Berkeley, he now spoke only English; it felt as if he was doing something new or strange, like wearing a hat. All his life he had gone hatless, his naked head and his full head of black hair, under the Indian sun. But here he was now, studying "a chapter in history."

As a part of his Fulbright obligations, he was teaching a class called Indian History, 1857–1947. Half the students in the class of twenty-six were white; there were three Black students and half a dozen who were from the subcontinent or born in the United States to desi immigrant parents. Jadu hadn't talked to them much but he was looking forward to telling them about the formation of the Gadar Party in nearby San Francisco in 1913. JP had met party members during his stay in Berkeley. Jadu would tell his students that Indian activists living here had smuggled arms to India to fight the British. If you thought about that for a minute, India didn't seem so distant or alien anymore. There was a history on these streets and in buildings that could still be identified.

A rebellious India. The India of the Gadar Party, he imagined himself saying, wasn't the India of incense sticks and yoga or vegetarian food that you encountered in Berkeley. It was scrappier and its goal was freedom for the masses. When classes started and Jadu shared this knowledge with his students, they seemed unsurprised. One of them was a girl from Calcutta writing an essay about her grandmother who had been a freedom fighter. She was from a prosperous Marwari family. The family had given money to the Congress Party and her grandmother, housebound until then, had stepped out on the streets in a white khadi sari. She sang the bhajans that Mahatma Gandhi had made popular. The grandmother was no doubt an admirable figure. In the classroom, however, when the girl spoke about her desire to write a novel about her grandmother, Jadu was not pleased. She had simplified the story of a whole country's struggles into a story about a woman one morning leaving the comfort of her home to join a procession. The story the student had shared was vague except for the colorful details: the garden where peacocks danced, the good food that the grandmother liked to cook, the color of her khadi sari. What irked Jadu was that the story ended with freedom not in India but in America, as if the freedom struggle had been fought only to produce this cheerful Californian.

Was this what the old woman's sacrifice had been for? He was being too judgmental, Jadu later thought to himself. But—wasn't he right? The fight in which millions had engaged had been replaced by a story about an individual—not even the grandmother but this girl herself, delighted by her visit to the distant homeland. He felt that here was another example of the old high school essay describing how the students had spent their summer: a time of adventure and visits to exotic places, a place called the past.

Instead of this girl from Calcutta, it should have been Jadu telling the story. This was what he told himself while eating his rajma and rice one night. He felt tempted to say to the young woman, earnest, bespectacled, so smug in her knowledge gained from a class in South Asian history, that he had been in jail during the Emergency. He knew he was exaggerating his own participation but he would like to ask her if she had any idea of what that time had meant. A police jeep at night dragging in its wake a sepulchral voice announcing the hours of curfew. Men from the Intelligence Bureau at your door at three in the morning, with their minatory knocks, bundling you into a blue van and taking you to jail. A curt call to a newspaper editor to tell them that this was the end. Not that this had been Jadu's own experience.

His own experiences would not fill a book: they had been so light and inconsequential, like a brief ripple on a lake's surface.

The Bengali girl in his class would not of course know the name Phanishwar Nath Renu, but what unforgettable stories he had written in Hindi and Maithili! Language as it was used in the villages of Purnea. He had fought alongside Nepali revolutionaries who had helped bring a measure of democracy in the kingdom. During the youth movement in Patna, only months before the Emergency arrived, Renu had shielded the frail Jayaprakash Narayan with his arm, preventing the police lathi from hitting the old man's head. Jadu would study Renu from a distance when they were together in the jail in Patna but didn't know what to say to him. He had read *Maila Aanchal.* He had watched *Teesri Kasam* when the film came out in 1966. Only once, after the prisoners had been given tea, and Renu was standing close to him in the line for the toilet, Jadu summoned strength. He bowed with folded hands and asked the writer how he was feeling. Renu was unguarded and quite unaffected. He said that the besan sabzi that had been served to the inmates the previous night hadn't agreed with him. For a moment, he appeared to be examining Jadu's face as if trying to recall if he had put him in one of his early stories. Renu passed his fingers through the curls that fell to his shoulders. He said that his long hair was dry and unkempt, and he wanted to know if Jadu happened to have any coconut oil or even mustard oil. But, oh, the misery of this sad and unlucky world, Jadu did not have any oil.

———

Early one morning Jadu opened his eyes and stared at the gray ceiling of his apartment in Berkeley. He had awoken from a dream in which he was on a boat with his father. Shivnath had tears running down his face. What had his father been so grief-stricken about? The dream did not offer up any details. Jadu could not even remember if there had been anyone else in the dream. He didn't get up from bed, turning over in his head the images he had seen so clearly as if from life. Jadu wondered if the dream really had been about his mother's death. Then, he remembered the page he had written in prison about the fire consuming her. Where was it now? He ought to have brought it with him from India. It had not escaped Jadu's notice that ever since he had come to Berkeley, he would wake up in the gray dawn and realize that he had been dreaming about Patna or Khewali. One night he dreamed of Professor Dey, and it seemed that Jadu and he were on a train passing through California, except that all the passengers who were sitting crammed on the floor of the car with them were Indians, poor Bihari peasants who were trying to escape a drought. So, in that case too, the dream was really about India. But what about exactly? The sad faces of the destitute, seeking a safe haven, why did they come to him here in his sleep?

On the radio the news was about a debate between George Bush and Michael Dukakis, the two men locked in a battle for the White House. Jadu was interested in the race but the candidates didn't hold his interest. All the intrigue, the drama of personalities, the conflicts of caste, that fueled the fights at home didn't translate here. From what he could tell, the real contest in American politics was between media images. Dukakis had appeared in a tank, a diminutive figure wearing a helmet, and all the conversation for a week or more had been about that image. Jadu made tea and sat down at the desk. The window overlooked the street, on which he could see students making their way to the university. He entered the feeling that had overwhelmed him during the dream from which he had awoken. The particulars of what he had written about his mother more than a decade ago escaped him now. He started writing about his father, whose tearful face had been so close to him in his dream just a few hours ago.

History doesn't repeat itself, but it forces you to remember. When my father was dying in the hospital, in September 1991, I thought of my mother's death and I also asked myself if my father found himself burdened by the same thought. My father, Shri Shivnath Kunwar, died at the age of seventy-eight from kidney failure in Patna Kurji Holy Family Hospital. By the time we brought him there, he was also suffering from hypertension, shortness of breath, and acute swelling of the legs. Every day there were new complications. Soon, as a result of sores in his mouth, he found it difficult to eat. Despite the care that the nurses took at the hospital, he also developed painful bedsores, which were wounds that would not heal until his death. During the last days, when nausea racked his body, and his limbs jerked uncontrollably, and he suffered from what seemed to be anxiety attacks, I wondered if my father ever felt that for him, too, the manner of my mother's death would have perhaps been preferable. My mother had died in terrible agony, but it was all over in minutes. I am confessing to a thought that troubled me during those days; my excuse is that I wanted my father's pain to abate or just end. By then he was complaining of an excruciating pressure on his chest and even greater difficulty in breathing. The doctor said that other illnesses ravaged the body after the kidneys stopped working: my father had contracted pneumonia and when he died the next day I felt he had at last found peace.

When I think of my parents now, it is not their life but their death that I think about. The fact of their death and their manner of death are most real to me: do I pay importance to those events because that is where their history ends? In my profession of history writing, this is called teleological thinking, where the end result governs the way in which we present everything that precedes it. But this kind of thinking, especially the importance I have given to my parents' death, would have been alien to their own experience. For them, death was a part of life, and life itself, the life of the soul, was eternal. I suspect they found support for this view in their faith but I also think they were encouraged by their own experience of death around them.

Death was so commonplace. The very young and the old were particularly vulnerable but even those who were hale and hearty could be snatched away. My mother had seen her own daughter perish from a mysterious illness but she regarded it as an ordinary occurrence. In my father's case, as a young man he had been struck by the fate of his elder cousin's family. When there was a terrible earthquake in 1934, the year before my birth, my father's cousin Raghunath was working for a legal office in Calcutta. He was informed by a telegram sent by his father-in-law that tragedy had befallen his young family and he must come to Muzaffarpur at once. Raghunath took a train to Patna and then crossed the Ganga. It was difficult for him to make further progress. At last he was able to hire an ekka and, sitting on this horse-driven cart for hours, he reached that part of Muzaffarpur where his father-in-law had his house. But nothing was recognizable anymore, all the usual landmarks either had vanished or were in ruins. More-over, he found his path flooded in places and he was forced to undertake the rest of the journey on foot. It had taken him two days to arrive at the house where he had last seen his wife and two little children alive. Raghunath's father-in-law was the only survivor in that house; five people, including his little girl and the boy who was still an infant, had died during the earthquake. I remember my father narrating to me his elder cousin's experience. In the years that followed, Raghunath remarried and had children. He established himself as a successful magistrate in Motihari and as the head of the joint family. But during those first few months of 1934, he was a man whose life had lost all purpose and meaning. He spent nearly a month at his father-in-law's home; the two men slept on two cots in the one room that had remained undamaged. Raghunath cooked the same simple meal each day for both of them. He would cook khichdi in a pot and then, without eating, leave for the Siddhi Ghat in Sikandarpur, where he sat for hours looking at the river. When he had first gone to the river, the day after his arrival in Muzaffarpur, it had looked as if the surface of Burhi Gandak was choked with corpses. As far as the eye could see, there were the bodies of the dead floating on water. So many dead.

Each day, Raghunath came back and kept coming back to the Siddhi Ghat until the river was a river again and his own mind permitted memories and new thoughts to flow once more. Whenever my father spoke about his elder cousin's experience, he always mentioned the river and the high vantage point at Siddhi Ghat, where Raghunath spent his days of mourning. What had taken his cousin to the river? It was the will to live, my father said. It is the essence of life itself, something elemental reaching toward light or joy. Raghunath had been able to turn away from the fallen walls where death had visited, and gone to the river to see what was lasting and eternal. What was lasting was change itself. So, that was my father, a teleologist of a different kind. My only hope is that this sense that he had about our existence gave him peace when he was himself dying, racked by pain, beside the window in Kurji Holy Family Hospital that overlooked the brown waters of the Ganga.

————

Part II

JUGNU

Never again will a single story be told
as though it were the only one.

—JOHN BERGER

I was a child when I first heard the name George Orwell. I was aware that when we were in the company of educated people in Patna, my father would tell them that he was born in the same hospital as Orwell in Motihari. I later found out that Orwell was indeed born in the same sleepy town as my father, close to our ancestral village, Khewali, but it is quite likely that Orwell's mother had given birth in the small bungalow that served as the Orwell residence. Richard Blair, Orwell's father, was a subdeputy opium agent for the British. The bungalow in which they had lived in Motihari, now a dilapidated cow shed overrun by pigs and stray dogs, was described recently in one Patna newspaper as an "animal farm."

My father taught history in Patna. He believed in the past and it would be only a slight exaggeration to say that he was suspicious of anything new. Unlike Orwell, my father was lucky to have lived to an old age. In his last days he was attended only by the teenager who had been his help for four years. I have been away, living and working for nearly twenty years in Atlanta. One morning during the pandemic, I was woken up by my phone ringing. I wondered whether it was my father and—this will be the greatest regret of my life—I let him go to voicemail.

I went to sleep again and called him back two hours later, after I had first made coffee. But my father didn't answer the phone. It was the boy, Pramod, who worked for him. He said that my father had just died.

Pramod's voice cracked and then he began to keen. Was he imagining my grief and then, moved by it, giving expression to that imagined sorrow? This thought came to me because I had been struck dumb. I mean that literally. I was not able to speak. And the boy, bless his soul, cried for me loudly in that house where my father's body lay. The sound of Pramod's sobbing filled my ears. I wasn't crying because a weight had entered my chest. A heavy fluid was filling up my lungs and I was finding it a struggle to breathe. After a long while, I told Pramod to stay calm and that I would find out and let him know who would pick up my father's body for the funeral. I called a newspaper editor I knew and asked him for the phone number of the Irrigation Minister, Ramdeo Manjhi.

Manjhi had been a classmate of my father's in college. He had been in the news several years ago when he said that he had grown up eating rats—he was from a family of Musahars at the bottom of the caste system—and he didn't see why rats couldn't be served in restaurants in a poor state like Bihar. In a state as food-starved as Bihar, field rats would be a source of protein. Then there was another scandal. His daughter—her name was Reena, or was it Rani?—had opened a telecom agency in Delhi and had been awarded huge contracts for government installations at suspiciously low prices. There were calls for Manjhi's resignation and a commission of inquiry had been instituted. Nothing came of it because the amount of money involved was so astronomical. People asked naïve questions about where Manjhi would have hidden so much illicit wealth. The truth was that his earnings were so monumental that he was able to put up obstacles and buy everyone's silence—judges, politicians, police, editors and other members of the press.

I got through to the minister's secretary, who called again to inform me that the minister had ordered a police escort for my father's body. There was a lot in the news about difficulties with the disposal of the dead if they had died from the virus. I work for CNN and our bureau in India had reported the case of a doctor in Chennai who had been treating Covid-19 patients and then died from the disease; the doctor was Christian and when his colleagues arrived at the local cemetery, there was already a crowd waiting there. They threw stones at the ambulance carrying the doctor's corpse. Another doctor, the dead man's assistant, was threatened with an iron bar. The group returned in the middle of the night to complete the burial.

I was asleep when Ramdeo Manjhi, the minister himself, called my number, unmindful of the difference in time zones. It was around two in the morning here in America. On the phone, Manjhi said repeatedly, "I had no news about this, I didn't even know that Jadu was unwell." To just say something, I said that I hadn't had any news either. It had come as a shock.

As I was now up, I called a cousin who ran a small business in Patna. For years, he had been planning to open a coaching institute, a training center where unemployed youth would learn to speak English and work in call centers, but for now his business provided tents to rent for weddings and funerals. I didn't need a tent. I was calling him because he was the only son of my aunt, my father's sister, who had died two decades earlier, blind in both eyes and crawling from one room to another. The cousin said that he had been informed about my father's death and asked when I was coming back. I told him that there were no flights due to the lockdown, I wouldn't be allowed into the country. Surely he knew this?

He said, "This is the problem with all of you who go so far away."

I tried to detect sadness in his voice but concluded that he was only complaining. After I had made the call, I realized I had nothing else to do. Like a magnifying glass, grief makes bigger the emptiness of life. With no more chores to do, I was left with my father's loss. I searched for the photographs I had put away in various places—albums, diaries, even my phone—where the past was stored forgotten. From time to time, I don't know why, I would glance at the dark windows. I knew it would be several hours before the sun came up.

The next day, my cousin texted me. He had sent photographs from the electric crematorium. My father's corpse in a white body bag. A police officer with a mask standing in the distance. Two men in blue protective robes with masks, and darker blue coverings on their heads, carrying my father's body toward the metal tray. At first, I didn't notice that one of the men in blue was the boy Pramod. He wasn't even kin, but how extraordinary his presence felt to me. He was like the son setting fire to the funeral pyre on the riverbank. This time I cried for him, sinking down to my knees in the kitchen, as if unable to hold up the weight in my hands. There was no one else in my apartment to hear me, and I didn't care anyway, and I howled like the women in the village back home who tore their hair and sat down in the middle of the road and screamed and asked *where are you taking him, please take me too, O Muneswar, O Parsuram, O Birua, my son, please, throw me into the fire too, I cannot live like this, please.*

All that crying must have helped because when I went to sleep I fell into a dream in which my father was alive again. It was early evening and we were sitting in chairs on the roof of the house in Patna, balancing on our laps plates of puffed rice, dry-roasted chickpeas, chopped onions, all mixed with a little bit of mustard oil and salt. This was my father's favorite snack, and I remembered liking the taste very much. My father was telling me a story about the time he had spent in Baghdad, where he had never actually been in real life, so that was how I knew I was dreaming. He was telling me a story about the grilled carp popular in the riverfront eateries in Baghdad. The fish would be splayed open, impaled on a skewer, and quickly grilled over an open charcoal fire. I think I knew what he was talking about because there had been a story broadcast on CNN about it: after the American invasion, the people living there had lost their appetite for the fish that, or such was the belief, fed on the corpses being dumped in the water.

An email arrived from the editor in Patna, the man I had called
to ask for Ramdeo Manjhi's phone number. The editor's name is
Nirmal Issar. He is a mild-mannered Punjabi who had always been
professional with me. In the past, we had corresponded on the
coverage of news and exchanged contacts. I never had a chance
to ask him what brought him to Patna. In his email, he inquired
about my father's funeral and asked if things had gone okay. He
wanted to know if I would write a short obituary for my father
that they could publish in the newspaper. This request posed a
problem. Despite what Pramod had said in that first phone call,
and despite even the photographs sent by my cousin, despite all the
sorrow I was feeling, his death still didn't seem quite real. It was as
if I could wake up from my troubled sleep and, of course, he would
be present as he had always been all my life. My writing about my
father's death would make everything terrifyingly true and per-
manent. In fact, I would be the agent of this change, I would be the
one responsible for killing him.

And yet the idea of his death was becoming tangible. I put on a
mask and went to the grocery store two blocks away to buy pack-
ets of tea. And because it was inadvisable to make more than one
trip a week while the infection was spreading, I began going up
and down the aisles. It took me a few minutes to realize that I was
buying what my father liked: green beans, potatoes, cantaloupe,
yogurt, almonds, honey. When was the last time I had bought
honey? I couldn't remember. The cashier was a tall Black youth
with high cheekbones and huge eyes. He was looking at me carefully. He perhaps sensed my pain, and my panic, because it felt to
me that I was exposed, and that I had plucked out my heart and put
it on the conveyor belt among the things I was buying.

Or maybe the young cashier was just showing professional
concern.

"Did you find everything okay?"

"My father has died, my father has died."

That is what I wanted to say to the boy in response. *Let him learn of my sorrow, let me show I value his humanity, that I trust he will know and understand.*

Instead, I nodded and felt tears roll down to the place where the mask bit into my cheek.

There was something else that was also happening to me. This new grief was opening other wounds. Many years ago, when my mother died, I had been in this country for only seventeen days. I had arrived to join a graduate program in journalism. More crucially, I had left behind a husband from whom I was trying to separate. The news of my mother's death shattered me. But I couldn't go back to India—I would be forced to find entry into a life I had done my best to escape. My mother was only fifty-two when she died. She had suffered from low blood pressure for a long time and though she didn't have any major ailments she had been confined to her bed for two months the previous year. That summer, a fortnight after I flew out of Delhi, my parents had gone to Saharsa to attend a cousin's wedding. It was hot, they were all crammed in tiny rooms in a relative's house, and I'm sure their meals were erratic. The marriage ceremony went on until one in the morning; my parents didn't go to sleep until three. The next day they took a train back to Patna. The following afternoon my mother climbed a few steps to the roof to spread on the clothesline an expensive silk sari she had hand-washed. My father found her on the roof. She had fallen down, already dead, the red silk sari clutched in her hand. The cause of death was "sudden cardiac arrest."

———

I remember the new black phone I had bought from Sears after my arrival in America: it had a button for redial and it retained in its memory up to thirty numbers. It could also save messages on voicemail. The phone had cost fourteen dollars. It had felt like a small miracle to me. You brought the light plastic machine from the mall and plugged it into the wall. A light wire went into the phone jack that the landlord had shown me. In India I would have had to wait for months for a phone connection; here all it took was a visit to the AT&T office across from campus and there was a dial tone on the phone by the time I reached home.

My first call was to my parents.

A fortnight later, the call from my father was the first time I had received a call from Patna.

I was happy to hear my father's voice but he kept clearing his throat.

After a pause, he said that he had some bad news.

When I stopped howling, my father became the historian who tells you that the present is always meaningfully born of the past. He said, "She kept herself alive to make sure that you had started a new life and were happy."

I was grasping at straws and my father offered me one. He said, "Just the other day, a piece of her gold earring fell out. I said to her that we could go to Alankar and get it fixed. She said no, I won't be needing this for long. I didn't understand her comment then, but now I do. I think she knew it in her heart."

My father, the Shakespeare of omens.

In the days that followed my mother's death, I sealed myself off from my grief. I began to feel less of everything. People will always tell you that they feel the presence of the dead when they are gone. Not me. I felt acutely that my mother had turned to ash and the wind was scattering her remains. But during these last few days, after my father's death, I have thought more about my mother. Alone in my apartment, I have remembered all the times I had rushed out of the house on my way to college, saying no in response to her saying that she had already made me a cup of tea. Just drink a cup of tea, she would say, and no, I can't, I would say and rush out. *How much time does it take to drink a cup of tea? Does it take longer than to drink a cup brimming with tears?*

I have bitterly asked myself if my poor suffering mother is going to forgive me wherever she is now as I sit pulling out my hair.

My father had borne witness to my mother's life and death—and now my father was gone too. Nirmal Issar was asking me to provide proof of my father's life. I got down to work because it had to be done. I wanted to pay tribute to my father. Issar had said he wanted eight hundred words, and if I found I had more to say, I could also go for twelve hundred words. My father had been a teacher and a guide to many in Patna and elsewhere, and this fact needed to be recorded, but I wanted to write about him also as a father. I had feared all my life that I was a disappointment to him. However, the truth was that he had praised me whenever I achieved any goals, however modest. To have him taken away meant that I was suddenly adrift and without an aim in life. I had all my life worked only for his praise, and he had been generous, and it was intolerable to me that the source of that flow had now forever been cut off. Like an actor robbed of an audience, I felt I was walking alone on a dark and empty stage.

Jadunath Kunwar (1935–2020)

A girl I had known in my childhood married a bureaucrat who was the first person I knew personally to have died from the coronavirus. I got this news from Facebook. In her Facebook post, the girl I had known in Patna when we were little, and have not seen for thirty years, described her husband as her teacher. That description puzzled me. I even found it annoying. Why would you want to describe your husband as your teacher? But my father, who died from Covid-19 the same week as my friend's husband, really was a teacher. He was a teacher to many, and certainly a teacher to me.

The story that my father repeated the most to me during his lifetime was one from the Mahabharata. *It was about Arjuna taking aim with his bow and arrow at a fish. The archery teacher Drona had tied a fish to a branch above a body of water. Drona's students were to look at the reflection of the fish in the water and release their arrows. He asked his students one by one what they saw when they took aim. Yudhishthira said he saw the sky, the birds, the fish. Others gave similar answers. But when it was Arjuna's turn, he said, "I see the eye of the fish."*

Drona commanded him to shoot and Arjuna's arrow pierced the fish's eye. Don't be distracted! *This was the message of my childhood. Stay steadfast in your journey to your goal. Don't lose your mental balance or your moral focus. My mother, sweet and wise and always supportive, had balked when I announced to them that I wanted to end my marriage, but my father, a man who was born in a hut to illiterate parents and had grown up in a rural milieu bound by tradition and religion, was unwavering in his faith in my thinking. He said, "You do not owe your husband or anyone else anything. Stay true to your life's intention."*

I am indebted to my father for saying that I was free. I wish every girl in Patna had a father like him. I wouldn't be where I am today had it not been for my father. I work now as a journalist for CNN in Atlanta. I was inspired to come here to the United States because during my youth my father had visited Berkeley on a scholarship. When I was growing up the story he told about Indians in the West was a complicated one. When India was still under British rule, and Indians were fighting for independence, a stay in a city like London or New York could well be a way to join a revolutionary movement. Not only that. More than once, my father told me that Gandhi wrote his book Hind Swaraj, *his call for home rule, while traveling from London to South Africa on a ship named SS* Kildonan Castle. *To move out of the house, to shed one's chains, to undertake travel, was to find new life. He didn't say all this, but I absorbed this lesson from the stories he told me.*

What is this grief that seems to be mine alone—attached to my feelings for a particular person, my father—and yet seems to cover like a giant cloud the whole universe right now? We are in the middle of a pandemic. My father used to so often repeat the story of the grieving woman who came to the Buddha. Her son had died and she wanted the Buddha to give her some medicine that would bring the child back to life. The Buddha asked the woman to bring him some mustard seeds from a house where there had been no death. The woman knocked on the door of one house after another—and after hearing in each house a sorrowful account of loss, she realized that grief had been a visitor to every home. I always thought that this parable wasn't so much about the presence of sorrow as it was about Buddha's style of teaching. How to invent an active-learning exercise. My father was a teacher and this story appealed to him. I don't think he would have known really what to do with me now, what to do with this extreme feeling of loss that has made me a cripple. To understand my grief, and to soothe me, he would have to convert his absence into presence. Not as a teacher, but once again as a loving parent.

In these days after his death, as I walk around my apartment by myself, my eyes swollen, my body hurting, feeling lost, there is another story from the Mahabharata *that sometimes comes to me. The blind king Dhritarashtra has retreated from his throne. He is living in the forest with his wife, Gandhari. Gandhari makes for a memorable character in that epic because, apart from bearing a hundred sons (and a daughter) for Dhritarashtra, she has also taken a vow of blindness. She has tied a blindfold over her eyes—to do what exactly? To assure her husband that he is not alone, or to forge a bond with him, or to present a perverted model of matrimony, it doesn't matter. Dhritarashtra and Gandhari are in the forest with Kunti, the mother of the heroic Pandavas. The Pandavas are the cousins of the Kauravas, and the* Mahabharata *is an epic description of the battle between the two clans. (The Pandavas win, with some Kissinger-level duplicity on the part of their charioteer and adviser, Lord Krishna.) And in the forest with Dhritarashtra & co. is also the old and eminent Vidura, the embodiment of wisdom and truth, who happens to be uncle to both the Kauravas and the Pandavas. In the story, as I remember it, Yudhishthira, the eldest Pandava, comes to visit the elders who have exiled themselves in the forest. Upon not seeing Vidura, Yudhishthira inquires after him. Dhritarashtra replies that Vidura has been practicing a terrible penance, neither eating nor drinking, simply wandering in the forest.*

Then, Yudhishthira is told that Vidura has been seen naked, covered with dust, nothing but skin and bones. Yudhishthira begins his search and, finally, catches sight of Vidura. He runs after him. Vidura, stop, I'm your dear Yudhishthira. *They both keep running deep*

into the forest until Vidura stops and leans his back against a tree.
I am Yudhishthira. *Vidura fixes his unblinking eye on Yudhishthira
and using his yogic power he enters Yudhishthira's body limb by limb.
Vidura gives Yudhishthira everything—his life, his organs, his wide
erudition, his brilliance. It is this behavior that makes many readers
of the* Mahabharata *suspect that Vidura was, in fact, Yudhishthira's
father. Or perhaps they are led to this conclusion because there is a
description in the* Upanishads *of what a man nearing death is to do:
he should lie on the bare ground, and make his son lie on top of him,
saying,* Son, I give you my organs. *The son should reply,* I accept.

*This terrible pandemic prevented me from being with my father
when he was dying. I would have liked to cover him with my body and
when he said,* Daughter, I give you my organs, *I would have liked
very much to reply,* I accept. *There is the pain I feel in my entire body
about not having been given the chance to conduct this ritual of transfer, to be able to assure my father that though I myself was no longer
young he would continue to live on through me. At the same time, I am
aware that all the story of Vidura's death in the* Mahabharata *does is
dramatize a process that very often has gone on over a lifetime. A lifetime of toil and sacrifices for my sake. All his life, my father imparted
to me his learning, his love, and the fruits of his labor.* I accept, I
accept, I accept.

———

On my office listserv, there was mention of a local cop who was
reading Dr. Seuss stories to elementary school kids from his squad
car. Before the lockdown this cop had been assigned to a school in
Marietta and now his readings were being watched by the students
on their home computers. On Facebook a doctor at the Grady
Hospital recorded a video saying she wanted everyone to stay at
home instead of going out to get their hair cut or their nails done.
Health workers were putting their lives on the line while there was
a widespread shortage of protective gear: the doctor revealed that
she herself had worn the same N-95 mask at the hospital for fifteen
days. In an op-ed written by an astronaut, there was a suggestion

for those who were finding isolation oppressive. The astronaut in space had craved nature, the color green, the smell of fresh dirt, and the warmth of the sun. In his op-ed, he advised people to go outside.

The weather in Atlanta was getting warm but often we had rain in the afternoon. A small dogwood under my balcony glowed with red flowers. There was a terrible thunderstorm late one evening. Clouds raced across the low horizon, which had turned dark. I heard a crash outside. And stepping onto the balcony, I saw that about fifty yards away there was a sweet gum tree that had lost a branch. In the dusk all that was visible was the soft phosphorescence of the leaves. When I came out again the next morning, I saw a bird with a red crest busy on the sweet gum. There was the long white gash in the wood. The bird was tapping the bark with its beak as if testing the quality of the timber. I took a picture and an app on my phone identified it as a pileated woodpecker. A common bird in Georgia but I wasn't sure I had ever seen this energetic visitor before. A question appeared on the screen. Did I want to save the picture?

I thought of the pictures from my father's cremation. There were so few pictures of us together. Most pictures I have even of myself are from my middle age and later. There are a few from when I was little, small black-and-white rectangles with yellowing borders, bearing the thumbprint of passing time. These photographs show me standing with my parents, the family resemblance expressed mainly through a shared awkwardness. Do I have any pictures from college in Delhi? I remember one from a class visit to Surajkund; I am standing next to a red vintage car from the nineteen forties. I had asked a friend with a camera to take a picture because the car's owner had told the people ringed around his car that Jawaharlal Nehru had once ridden in it. The photograph is from 1989, I think.

Humans take a total of 4.7 billion photographs every day. You can see people on the streets removing their masks and holding up their phones to take a picture. I read some months back that a tourist fell into Mount Vesuvius while attempting to retrieve his phone, which he had dropped after taking a selfie. In the Surajkund photo I'm wearing the red sweater my mother gave me; it never fit me properly and made me feel ashamed. I hadn't fallen in love yet except with pictures in magazines. But I remember that time well, the sense that anything I was doing was wrong. The way I cut my hair, my choice of sandals, the glasses I wore. You were always being told that there was something about you that wasn't right. As if from the way you walked or dressed or spoke, Shah Rukh Khan was going to stop you on the street and ask if he had met you before.

I have a photograph from that period where I'm standing next to a boy with a light beard. He is wearing glasses. We are both standing next to a poster for a sarod recital by Ustad Amjad Ali Khan. The boy's name was Jatin and he was a fellow student in Delhi. What made him special was that though we didn't know each other well—we certainly weren't lovers—he used to write me letters. Jatin's father was a government doctor in Chittaranjan Park. Jatin wanted to work as a journalist, but he believed his true calling was to be a poet. His poems were full of vague abstractions; all the words in those short chopped-up lines had the look of people waiting quietly at a bus stop in the half-light. The poems said nothing much, they didn't speak to me at all, and yet I understood that Jatin was trying to tell me that he was a young man who felt things deeply. His letters were more intelligible in comparison. Maybe this was because his letters seldom contained his own words. We were both shy and it was easier to discuss films or books. Jatin wrote letters quoting from the books he was reading. I would find a yellow postcard waiting for me when I came back from my classes. Example: *"I'll study people!" he pledged. "People, just as they are." And that was the beginning of his education.* In the week after: *It is death to mock a poet; / Death to love a poet; / Death to be a poet.* Or, two days later: *What was youth at best? A green, an unripe time, a time of shallow moods and sickly thoughts.* Annoyingly, there was no mention of the book or the author. Even though I saw that Jatin meant for the borrowed lines to serve as introductions to his own imagined self, I complained. I wanted to advance my education.

And as a result, Jatin started adding names to the quotes he sent. Saul Bellow had written in *Humboldt's Gift*: *Once you had read the* Psychopathology of Everyday Life, *you knew that everyday life was psychopathology*. I didn't want to cede too much power to Jatin and yet I was intrigued and asked him to tell me about Freud. Instead of his having to explain anything, Jatin felt it would be better if he gave me the book of Freud's selected writings. He had bought it from the secondhand bookstore on Janpath. I opened the book when I was back in my room and a letter fell out. At first I thought Jatin had written me a letter and had put it in the book as a surprise. But the envelope had his address on it. I hesitated and then plain curiosity got the better of me. There was a handwritten note pinned to a poem:

> *Dear Jatin, You do show potential for good poetry, but only if you realize that you suffer from one major flaw that seems to have gripped modern poetry everywhere—a lot of words and little meaning. These poems do make interesting reading, because words have their own peculiar beauty—but because of a deliberate obscurity or a confusion of ideas and images, these poems have no lasting value, nor do they have any depth of feeling or thought . . .*

I stopped reading. I was experiencing a sense of wrongdoing, of course, but I also felt sympathy for Jatin because these words were precise and accurate. When I carefully refolded the note, I saw that the address on the back of the envelope said Editor, *Lyric* Magazine, Chetan Enclave, New Delhi. The thought crossed my mind that I could just throw the letter away; then, perhaps, Jatin would not be embarrassed. Rather, I would not be embarrassed. But what if he was aware that the envelope had been inside the pages of the book? He would find it missing, and immediately grow suspicious. And, maybe, just maybe, the letter's presence wasn't entirely accidental. Perhaps Jatin had wanted me to see it. He had wanted me to share his pain. Or, instead of sharing his pain, at least relieve it—maybe by just saying that everything the editor had written was false and inaccurate. In the end, I did nothing, and said nothing. In fact, I felt that the book contained a secret that was taboo; I replaced the envelope inside the book and never opened its pages again.

When passing a cup of coffee, or when exchanging books or even letters, my fingers brushed against Jatin's hand. But there was no other intimacy. We had never kissed. During each of our interactions, I reminded myself that in meeting Jatin so often, even in my regularly receiving letters from him, I had gone far beyond the experience of my parents. I was quite sure my mother had known no man other than my father. The thought that often came to me during those weeks and months was that I wouldn't know what to say to my parents if they found out about Jatin. *He is a friend. He is reading Homer these days. I learned this from his letter in which he has recorded some phrases he liked ("rosy-fingered dawn," etc.).*

For my part, I wanted to appear interesting to Jatin and when I read anything unusual, I asked myself if I could use it in a letter that I sent him. In the college library, I came across a magazine article about a new book. A few years earlier, a photographer at the Los Angeles Olympics had taken pictures only of the losers at the games. Using a 1920 vintage camera, this man exposed the film for a longer time, up to five seconds, believing that this better captured the sense of loss. He had recorded not the looks of triumph but faces rearranging themselves for life following a defeat. I photocopied this news item and mailed it to Jatin.

The next week, another postcard from him. This one informed me that Franz Kafka had written in a letter to his fiancée, Felice Bauer: *And then, if all goes well, I shall be back in Prague tomorrow afternoon, and race from the station to our porter. Letters, letters from you!* Upon reading this, I realized that Jatin had enjoyed receiving my letter and I was also aware that a letter was expected from me. What to write in return? I liked getting Jatin's letters, even when they were unsatisfying, but I couldn't summon any poetic thoughts of love or longing. In my letter, I mentioned the smell of the rain, the three-legged cow standing unmoving near the fence, and the fact that the woman who prepared our food in the hostel seemed to believe that anything left only half-burnt was possibly only half-cooked.

In response, another postcard. *Yesterday, Felice, I received your letter unexpectedly; when I got home at seven o'clock in the evening, the porter's wife handed it to me downstairs. The postman had been too lazy to climb to the fourth floor. How serene and sweet your letter is!*

So far Jatin had complained that I didn't write him often enough, and then the situation reversed. He wrote infrequently and letters didn't come even when he told me in class that he had already posted me a letter. I suspected he was lying and didn't know why he was doing it. Perhaps he felt I was more interested in journalism than I was in reading Borges or Hemingway. I wasn't sophisticated or artistically inclined. It was a humid evening in early July. Jatin said he wanted us to get ice cream. Inside the air-conditioned store, the glass walls dripping with moisture, Jatin said he was leaving for America. He was headed to graduate school in a place called Urbana-Champaign. Why had he not told me about it earlier? He said it had been a tense time for him, he had first been told he had received admission and then only later that he had also been granted financial aid. When had he finally found out that he was leaving? Jatin hesitated. He said that it was some days ago. I left the half-eaten cup of ice cream and walked out.

I didn't respond when another postcard came. I felt cheated. Jatin had written that he would stay in touch when he was abroad. Acting out of anger, or only despair, I decided I would never talk to him again. The truth was that even though it was I who had turned away, his departure left me feeling empty and depressed. One or two more letters came from him. I remained faithful to my promise and though I read his letters I didn't write back. However, I kept the photograph from that one time several of us had gone to Pragati Maidan to listen to Ustad Amjad Ali Khan. It's not that I still had strong feelings for Jatin or wanted to be with him; it was more that whatever had happened between us had meaning while it lasted, it had colored my days, and I wanted evidence of it. It was as if I were being a good reporter, taking notes. For the same reason, I didn't throw away his letters either. I found the book of Freud's selected writings that I had never returned, the one with the editor's letter of rejection inside it, and I put all of Jatin's post-cards like bookmarks between its unread pages.

————

There is another photograph that I had overlooked earlier. I am eleven. I am holding up for the camera a polythene bag filled with water. Although the photograph doesn't reveal it, I know that there are fish swimming in that bag. I have just come home from the pet shop.

Water as a preservative in which swims a memory of the child that I was and the woman I then became.

I was a quiet girl in school, shy, holding close a sense of privacy that is less important to me now. I grew up without a sibling. If a girl has no brothers, brothers who are loved more and provided special treatment, served their meals first or sent to a better school or expected to work at important jobs, how is that girl to learn her true place in society? I was lucky to not receive that kind of education. I was loved by my parents and I believe I had a happy childhood. As a girl, all I lacked was an aquarium where I could watch fish swimming. I wanted a small aquarium with tiny fish and a little machine blowing bubbles. That was my greatest wish.

When I was ten or thereabouts, floodwaters entered Patna, turning whole mohallas into lakes. Water climbed up the steps to the home of our downstairs neighbors, a Catholic couple called Mathew and Alphine. They brought their baby girl to our floor and took shelter with us. For a week, we lived together. I liked their baby very much. After a week, the water receded, leaving the walls and the floors of their apartment stained brown with mud. In their plastic bucket, Mathew and Alphine found a fish swimming in the floodwater. But it wasn't an ordinary river fish. It was white and streaked with a brilliant red. We had never seen anything like it. My father took it in a jar to the local pet shop, where the owner said that this was certainly a fish that had escaped from someone's aquarium. That fish brought me luck. My father bought for me a small aquarium. We brought colorful fish home in a polythene bag. Every day I fed tiny flakes of food from a plastic bottle to the dozen red and blue guppy fish we now had in our house.

I was happy and there was nothing to make me question my place in the world I inhabited. This changed with the onset of puberty. I was expected to stay indoors, and I think I accepted this change without complaint. When my father had been jailed for a fortnight following student protests, I was still a young girl, but to have a real sense of what a prison means I had to grow into adulthood and experience it firsthand on Patna's streets.

In the late seventies and early eighties, Patna was still a very conservative place. My father went alone to the Shiva temple in Kankarbagh on Mondays. Alone because my aunt Lata, my father's sister, once told him that unmarried girls should not be worshipping Shiva. I had seen married women lustily rubbing the phallic *shivaling*, and I understood it had to do with a plea for their husbands' potency. Or for becoming pregnant. On Saturdays, we went to the Hanuman temple. Occasionally, my mother and I would watch a movie, but only the matinee show. These were considered safer. I never mentioned to my mother the groping hands that searched for me in the dark—that sudden, painful intrusion, I resented it deeply, especially because as soon as the film started, I would slip into that imaginary world unveiled on the screen. I never complained to my mother; I feared she would put an end to our outings. Or, who knows, maybe she was aware of them and, like me, resigned to a certain helplessness.

For the most part, we stuck to the television at home. We acquired our first TV set when I was in my late teens. Another few years passed and the city became thoroughly criminal, with a spate of kidnappings and random killings. Shops pulled down their shutters as soon as darkness fell. When passing through slow traffic, we drove with the windows up and the doors locked. The rapid, urgent instruction from one or more persons in the car, "Keep driving. Don't slow down. Drive, drive."

I was enrolled in Patna Women's College for my B.A. in English Honors. As I wanted to get out of the house, journalism felt like a practical choice. I was taking courses in English literature; the first editor I went to meet assumed I knew how to use the language. He asked me what I wanted to write. A small item had appeared in the inside pages of one of the local papers, *The Searchlight*. One Mr. Tribhuvan Das, 57, had been reinstated by the Bihar Education Department in his position as a clerk twenty-one years after he had been dismissed for misappropriation of five hundred rupees. The report explained that Mr. Das had taken the money for his daughter's medical treatment and had returned the money voluntarily two days after having taken it out of the office funds. I told the editor that I wanted to seek out Mr. Das.

I found him in a small flat in Patna's Kidwaipuri. He wasn't expecting me. He asked his wife for a shirt and hastily put it over his vest, which had holes in it. Only then did he ask me to sit down. I said I wanted to know a few more details about his story. What was his daughter's sickness all those many years ago? Tuberculosis. Did she recover? Yes. Where was she now? In Dhanbad. Her husband was a foreman in the coal mines and she had a twelve-year-old son. What were some of the struggles he faced when his job was taken away? Mr. Das turned to look at his wife, who was even tinier than he was, a little bird with its head sunk into its wings. She sat on a stool placed a bit behind her husband's chair. From her stricken face, it was clear that she was unable to answer my question.

Mr. Das opened his mouth to speak and a cry gurgled from his throat. He tried to stifle the sound with words. Words like "Only God knows what those first years were like" and "I spent three years knocking on one door after another."

How did you survive?

"We didn't."

That was my first piece of journalism, a report about a father and a daughter.

I was filing brief reports in Patna while still trying to attend my college classes. The nuns had us reading Daniel Defoe, Henry Fielding, Samuel Richardson, Jane Austen and the Brontë sisters, Charles Dickens, Thomas Hardy. The classes weren't inspiring; everyone took notes to use during the end-of-the-year exams. I found the life I was discovering on the streets more real than the ones I was asked to read about in my classes. My teachers didn't like me. I told Sister Rosalyn that I was interested in living authors and showed her a letter I had received from Günter Grass. She didn't know who Grass was.

In a magazine published in Calcutta, there had been a story about Grass spending several months in that city. He had been to Calcutta before too and his description of it in a book had upset some people. "This crumbling, scruffy, teeming city that eats its own excrement is determined to be cheerful. It wants its misery to be terribly beautiful." I was curious and decided to get in touch with Grass. Where to send a letter? I sent it in an envelope addressed to the reporter from *Ananda Bazaar Patrika* who had written the Grass story. Grass's wife was acting in the Bengali version of his play *The Plebeians Rehearse the Uprising*. It didn't occur to me to read the play or to wonder how Ute Grass was in a Bengali play. Instead, I thought, here is a famous writer from Germany who is visiting the slums in Calcutta. What does he notice in the narrow alleyways? What could I learn from his way of seeing? It wouldn't do to hide my motives. I decided to be direct and invited Grass to Patna, taking care to mention that it was the capital of India's poorest state. I wanted to learn from him how to write about the poor in our city. The early age at which the poorest youth got married in Patna, resulting in the premature start of the next generation in the form of underweight, malnourished children. Migrant poor from the villages surviving with any available ad hoc work, a vast underclass beset by deprivation and disease. Long lines of men urinating on boundary walls all over the city, piss flowing between their legs, while dogs or cows wandered nearby. How would Grass put this into words or find a larger meaning? I hadn't expected Grass to respond to me but there was a letter from him two weeks later. He had addressed me with the generosity of an older writer. He had written that he wanted me to make the discoveries for myself. On a separate sheet he had made an ink drawing and sent it as a gift. Three tiny children, looking like bedraggled monkeys, taking shelter from the rain under a banana leaf that they clutched above their heads. My father felt that Grass was a foreigner only interested in Indian squalor but I was convinced he was drawing what he was seeing.

After my graduation, my father brought me to Delhi because I had been admitted to Jamia Millia to study journalism for my master's degree. One of my father's former students was now a lecturer at Shyam Lal College and my father treated him as our local expert. *You are now a Delhi native. Who will know better than you?* This man, bald and with his belt tight over his paunch, was as lost as we were but he tried to look competent. (At one point, my father looked at the signboard outside one of the places we visited and asked if "P.G. Hostel" referred to "postgraduate" or to "paying guest." The man clearly had no idea but, unable to decide what was right, he wobbled his head shyly and said, "Both.") He took us to one private hostel after another and then, exhausted, we settled on the home of a retired couple who provided board and lodging to six female students. My father had been saving for years for just this—to pay the college fees in Delhi and to be able to say to my mother and his friends that he had found "suitable accommodation" for me in Delhi. He was clearly very proud that, like him, I had studied in Patna, and then, unlike him, I had gone further and was now going to get a degree in Delhi. But how was my difference to be understood? Through the achievement of what in his mind constituted a superior style of living. At each hostel we visited, he had asked the same questions: 1. Is your bathroom clean and without leaks? 2. The room doesn't get too hot, does it, and do you have round-the-clock electric supply? 3. In the meals you provide, do you also give fruit? (And, as if the person hadn't understood the English word *fruit*, he would specify: "banana, apple, oranges, papaya, or mango.") Most of the landlords actually let him recite the whole list. In the days and months that followed, I was often tired and hungry, and soon afterward, my father left for Berkeley, but what would come to me, at odd times, was his list. *Banana, apple, oranges, papaya, or mango.*

I spent two years in Delhi and once I had earned my master's degree I returned to work in Patna. There were so many people in Delhi from places like Patna, and I could have stayed, but my mother was unwell. I had to return home. Or at least that is what I told anyone who asked. The truth is that I was unsure about what I wanted from life. My classes had been demanding, and I felt I had learned a lot, but I had done very little journalism. There was no time for it. For my thesis, I had done research on lunch provided in government schools. This work was hobbled by academic demands and I was certain that it would not get published. I applied for a job at *The Illustrated Weekly of India* and received a rejection two weeks later. I didn't think I had it in me to apply for another job. My best chance was to come back to Patna and stay with my parents; freed of the demands of paying for food and an apartment, I could calmly go about finding work. Patna had changed a lot, it had witnessed an explosion of luxury stores and coaching centers, its inhabitants introduced to a fast-paced urban life. Hordes of young men and even a few women out on the streets, at least near the commercial sites. Despite all my uncertainty I felt hopeful.

Back when I was climbing into an awareness of what it meant to be a woman living alone in Delhi, I saw myself as if on the set of a play. It was all so unreal or seemingly staged in a time different from the one I was meant to be living in. Place yourself in the audience, take a seat in the dark, say, in seat C9. You are looking at my life at that time. Light filters onto the stage from a dirty window on the side and falls on the old, sagging furniture in the living room. Sitting on the small sofa in the middle is a young woman in a plain dress. More than the room, she seems to occupy the silence in it. If I were seated next to you, say, in C10, I would find it difficult, from my imagined place in the audience, to say what the woman onstage, who was really me, happened to be thinking. All I would know was that nothing very bad had happened to her, but nothing good had happened in her life either.

But then, Ranjit came into my life.

———

Ranjit was short and fair-skinned with large eyes and a pleasant laugh. When I started working at a newspaper on Buddha Marg, he was one of the people with whom I spent time. He had studied in an English-medium school, and I liked this about him; he quoted lines from T. S. Eliot's "Waste Land." How many people were there in Patna newspaper offices quoting Eliot or Yeats? I later realized that these names were already dated in the late nineteen eighties but I didn't know any better. I also liked that while others shouted when they talked on the office phones, Ranjit talked softly. His father worked for the state industries and handicrafts department; the family lived in government quarters near the Botanical Garden. Although Ranjit owned a Bajaj scooter, he sometimes borrowed his father's old Fiat car when he wanted me to go somewhere with him. There weren't many places for us to visit. I had told him how my father used to walk beside the Ganga when he first arrived from the village, and so that was where Ranjit and I often went. Just going to the river and sitting on the steps near Patna College. On special occasions, we hired a boat for an hour. And by doing this, for such were our assumptions, it became clear to us that we were going to get married.

When Ranjit was courting me, he saw me as a desirable, magical creature, as if I were a deer with golden spots. In those days what I felt most keenly was his desire for togetherness. Without me, he was incomplete and this incompleteness caused him pain. The evidence for this was so palpable that I told my mother that there was a young man at work who was interested in me. She asked me about his caste and I told her that he was definitely upper-caste. I didn't tell her that Ranjit mocked the Dalit subeditor who manned the night desk. He had said that the man's ancestors had washed clothes on flat slabs of rock for centuries—but that didn't give the man the right to try to clean Ranjit's copy.

Instead, I told my mother that Ranjit had given me to understand that he was related on his mother's side to the Chief Minister, Jagannath Mishra.

"He is a Brahmin," my mother said, and then asked me if Ranjit had siblings. I said no, and she asked me nothing else about him for several days.

Ranjit always had schemes. One day he asked me what time my parents and I would be at the Hanuman temple on Saturday. I didn't know why he was asking me. Next Saturday morning, when my father and then my mother had raised their arms to ring the massive bell and then bowed their heads in front of the idol, accepting the *prasad* from the priest, they saw a stranger come to them and bend down to touch their feet. He had a serious expression on his face when he was doing this but he then turned to look at me and smiled.

I was smiling, too. I was impressed by his boldness.

"This is Ranjit," I said to my parents with subdued excitement.

My father nodded his head, which meant my mother had revealed to him already what I had told her. Ranjit now stood with folded hands as if he were still facing Hanuman's idol. After a moment, my mother asked him if he came to the temple often.

"Yes," Ranjit said, and then softened the lie by adding, "as often as I can."

When we were coming out of the temple, my father stopped to buy a kilo of laddoos. Holding up the box of sweets, he invited Ranjit to come to our home for a cup of tea.

"Come now if you are free," my mother said.

How easily had Ranjit plotted all this. I felt light-headed. In the kitchen, while preparing tea, my mother said that although he was short, Ranjit was fairer than I was. She then got busy making lunch because how could she let him leave without having eaten.

In the living room, sitting across from my father, Ranjit was listing all his family's political connections.

When I saw him at the newspaper office on Monday, Ranjit said that he had held my father spellbound with his performance. He had started with his freedom-fighter grandfather and then mentioned the names of several other notables, including a man from his district, though not related to him, who was the current Minister for Agriculture and Land Reforms in the state cabinet, before rounding off the list by mentioning his mother's maternal uncle, however distant, who was the Chief Minister of Bihar.

For my part, I hoped that because it was going to be a love marriage instead of an arranged one, the dowry that Ranjit's family demanded would be reasonable. Or maybe they wouldn't ask for anything at all. I was disappointed. The list that arrived asked for a lot of things, including small items like a table fan. Didn't they feel shame in demanding even an alarm clock? A decision had been taken and my father was prepared to defend it. With characteristic stubborn optimism, he said that it was a relief not to be asked to gift an apartment in a city or a plot of land. In fact, my father was impressed that they had only suggested, rather than required, that he buy a car for Ranjit two years down the line. But then my father ran into bad luck. He was carrying the cash that Ranjit's father had wanted for the dowry in a cloth bag on the bus and it was stolen. I could imagine exactly what had happened. My father, detached from the cash that he had withdrawn and was supposed to give away, had already forgotten that it even existed at all. It would have been terribly easy for any alert thief to slice through a bag of thin cotton resting on the metal floor.

Ranjit never humiliated me about the way in which my father haggled during the weeks after he had lost the money. At the same time, it was clear that not once had Ranjit counseled his father to forgo many of his demands. Maybe he felt he was powerless. To me he said that we shouldn't try to step onto a path where elephants walk, and this argument, I don't know why, had appeared rational to me at that time.

Already everything that was happening seemed larger and stronger than I was. One evening I went with Ranjit to Shilpee Emporium on Ashok Rajpath to pick up three new saris that my mother had left there to be embroidered for the wedding. We sat on wooden stools while the kaarigar finished work on a green sari for us, and, turning to look at the man next to me, I didn't recognize him. Why was he going to be my husband, this near stranger, and why not someone else? Ranjit never admitted to any doubts about what we were doing but I often had the feeling that I was living my life at a distance. It was as if the wedding that was about to take place were in reality a story about others that I was reading in the newspaper, and, like everything else that one found in the news, this wasn't anything good.

If my father felt that I had abandoned him when I got married— left him alone in the field of battle to fend off the vultures—he didn't say anything to me. Except when I was about to get into Ranjit's old Fiat after the wedding, my father suddenly had tears in his eyes and he said he wished he had been able to gift me a car. I experienced such helplessness in that moment. A confusing flood of emotions overwhelmed me. My marriage with Ranjit had reduced my father to this position, a beggar; maybe my father was reminding me, or more likely himself, that he had done nothing but provide for me all his life. The thought came back to me more forcefully that Ranjit should have said no to the list of demands that his family had drawn up. A new gold chain had been put around my neck and I felt like cattle. I felt angry with Ranjit. My father's abrupt declaration surprised me so much, and filled me with such unexpected shame, that I couldn't even assure him that he had given me everything I needed. I said to him that if he cried, it would be difficult for my mother to remain calm. I didn't want to cry but tears came unbidden as soon as the car joined the traffic on the road.

————

Ranjit liked talking to the legislators. His reports in the newspaper carried the byline "By Our Political Correspondent." But he also filed the column that was for some reason called "Tailpiece." He asked people to share jokes they had heard and he put them in the paper.

> *Before passing the sentence, the judge asked the prisoner: Have you anything to offer in your defense?*
>
> *The prisoner replied, No, sir. I had five hundred rupees and as my lawyer has already taken it I have nothing to offer you.*

When I read these bits, I always saw in my mind Ranjit's long teeth and gums so pink they looked new.

One day the Chief Minister made a call—this was about two months after our wedding—and Ranjit was transferred to the newspaper's Delhi bureau. We were able to get out of the house in which we had been living with my in-laws in Patna. As no call had been made on my behalf, it was expected that I would find a job by myself in any of the other newspaper offices in Delhi. Or, as my mother-in-law suggested, maybe instead of looking for a job I could take this opportunity to have a baby.

Ranjit told his mother that he needed to settle down in Delhi first. And it would help matters if during this time I took up a job too. Ranjit's mother had a maid in her house, a young Christian teen who had come to her a couple of years earlier from Khijri in Jharkhand. It was decided that this girl, Sudha, would come with us to Delhi. She would keep house and we would work. I was happy because in Patna I felt I had been married to Ranjit's family; in Delhi, I was a newly married woman looking for curtains for her apartment. I began loving Ranjit in a new way.

We were looking for furniture and a colleague of Ranjit's took us to Kirti Nagar market, and then in a few days, we also got a phone line even though we could make only local calls. I wasn't going to get a job at the English dailies right away; instead, I became a reporter at the Hindi newspaper *Amar Ujala*. My salary was much less than what Ranjit was getting. He laughed and said that every bit counted, and what I was getting would pay for the maidservant. This was cruel, and inaccurate too, but I had stopped protesting at these remarks. He was being paid more than he got in Patna, and it was a big help. Ranjit was kept busy by his boss. He was sent to cover the riots in Aligarh, the renovation of the Taj Mahal, and student protests over the government's reservation policy to help those belonging to lower castes. When Ranjit attended press conferences given by personages like President Giani Zail Singh, they left him feeling excited and gave him the chance to repeat stories about the fine-quality tea served on Raisina Hill. He came back from Madhya Pradesh and filed a report that all the Adivasis had fallen prey to propaganda and become communists. As a joke, because Sudha was also an Adivasi, a Santhal tribal, he took to calling her by a new name: Comrade. Ranjit believed that half of the Adivasis had said yes to the missionaries and converted to Christianity; the other half had chosen Marx and become bloody-minded communists. I don't believe Sudha had any idea that Ranjit was mocking her or what the word *comrade* meant. She would smile shyly and go back into the kitchen.

As the days passed, my own work grew more absorbing. At my newspaper, we worked in a large room on the second floor with the big, dirty windows opening to a noisy street. In the summer, we had air-conditioning. For our reports, we were given few column inches. I wrote stories on the rise in polyester prices, the protest about firecrackers for Diwali, the death of the writer Ismat Chughtai. Plus a long piece that was a review of a play that also called for investigative reporting. The play was called *Kamla*, and it was based on an event from over a decade ago, when a journalist had bought a woman named Kamla for a bit over three hundred dollars at a flesh market in Dholpur. He had then returned to Delhi with her and called a press conference to talk about human trafficking. In the play, the high point was the conversation between the journalist's wife and Kamla that first night at the journalist's home. The journalist and his wife have had a fight and Kamla asks how much she, the wife, had been bought for—and then Kamla makes a suggestion that the two women could share the man between them. For my story I had gone to the orphanage where the government authorities had sent the real-life Kamla. The previous day I had watched the play which was supposed to represent her, and now I found an angry, withdrawn woman. After half an hour of sullen interaction, Kamla began to speak about the insult to her freedom. Why was she kept caged here, she wanted to know. I tried to be provocative. I asked if she would like to go and live in the journalist's house. She said no. This was the story that got the most letters and phone calls at my office, but I didn't know if, at the end, I too had simply used Kamla and got recognition for myself without changing anything for her.

During those days in Delhi, Ranjit and I would come back home in the evening from work and Sudha would have a meal waiting for us. In the morning, it was her job to make tea and then have our breakfast ready. She would also prepare a light lunch that she had packed for us by the time we left for work. On weekends, there were no relatives to entertain like there had been at Patna at the home of my in-laws. Ranjit was a cricket fan and twice I went with him to sit in the stands at Feroze Shah Kotla. On some evenings, we walked to a nearby park and then came home. With Sudha sitting on a chair behind us, and Ranjit beside me on the sofa, we watched movies that were being shown on the TV channels. Brothers lost at birth were reunited, a brother avenged a terrible wrong done to his father or a sister, a young man who was dying gave the gift of life to everyone with his joy.

One film that we watched on TV showed Naseeruddin Shah taking his son to the lake at Purana Qila. So, we also went there on a Sunday and took Sudha with us because I thought it would be a break for her. The pedal boats for hire were simple, leaky devices outfitted with painted metal frames in the shape of swans. Sudha was a comely, dark-skinned girl, and she wouldn't stop smiling when we went round and round in circles on the water. Ranjit had bought her an ice cream bar from the vendor at the gate. He asked her if she could possibly have experienced this pleasure in Khijri. She didn't reply, staying silent, smiling. As I looked at her, from nowhere came the thought that I wanted the best for Sudha, and perhaps I should help with her education, but if I was going to have a baby after a year or so, I would need her to be at my side to keep the household running. It had been chilly in the morning but now the exercise had made me warm. I took off my red sweater and gave it to Sudha to hold. We were all quite happy, the pedals treading under our feet, the boats with their mute swan-like faces turning in a large circle in the dirty green water.

We returned home and I helped Sudha make dinner. We were about to finish eating when Ranjit got a call from his editor, Surinder Minhas. A separatist militant group had killed seven Bihari migrant workers in a quarry in Kashmir. Ranjit was being asked to leave for Srinagar the next morning. The murder of the workers would be the hook, but Ranjit was to file a report on Pakistani support for fundamentalist groups. There were a couple of people he needed to speak to. He could be back in a day, two at most.

Ranjit was a fairly balanced person; I wouldn't have married him otherwise. But I had noticed that there was one point on which he became someone else. Yet, why do I even say that he became someone else—this too was a part of who he really was. The belief that was ingrained in him, and of course there were many like him in the country, was that Kashmir was a part of India and anyone who even spoke of protecting human rights there was a traitor. I had stopped arguing with him on this subject. It is quite likely that he was outspoken on this issue at work and that was why the editor had given him this story.

Ranjit left for the airport at nine in the morning and at noon my father called me from a phone booth outside Kurji Holy Family Hospital. My mother's blood pressure had fallen steeply, and the doctors were going to check her heart. He said that he didn't want to disturb my schedule, but he was helpless, he wanted me to come to Patna. He complained that my mother wasn't accepting help from him. She was refusing water because she didn't want to urinate in a pan that he was holding for her. I began to cry when my father said this. I told him that I would catch a train that evening if I could get a seat and be there by late morning. I knew I needed to go when I heard him say, "You will get a seat, you will get a seat. Tell them your mother is in the hospital and will die otherwise."

It was almost one in the afternoon the next day when I stepped off the train and found my cousin, my aunt's teenage son, waiting for me on Platform No. 1. He took my tiny suitcase from me and asked if he could take me straight to the hospital on his motorcycle. Although my mother appeared frail as she lay on the hospital bed, all the test results on her heart had come back normal. She smiled when she saw me. I took one look at my father and realized that perhaps he had needed my help more than she did.

Ranjit called me before his return flight took off from Srinagar and I told him that I was probably going to stay away longer. My own editor had said that I could take a week's leave. Ranjit asked how much longer would I be away and I said I didn't know. He was tender and full of sympathy. I felt a pang of guilt in my heart but I had the comfort of his understanding. Soon, I said in response, soon. We will be together soon.

———

A man had come to our door in Patna early in the morning. I didn't recognize him. It was Parvez. We had all been colleagues at the local newspaper office before our move to Delhi. He had put on a lot of weight since the last time I saw him. He must have just woken up because he looked disheveled. He asked me if I had heard from Ranjit and I said no. He looked down at his feet. I asked him why he was asking. I thought Parvez wanted me to take something to a relative in Delhi. Maybe he had contacted Ranjit and was curious if I had been informed. But why had he come so early, and why was he embarrassed to talk to me now?

He said, "Last night a thief tried to get into the house. Ranjit was there and has got injured."

"What do you mean—whose house?"

"Your flat in Delhi," Parvez said. And then added, "Nothing was taken by the thief and he ran away but he has hurt Ranjit on his hands."

Ranjit hadn't called us.

I hadn't heard the phone ringing even once in the living room.

I shouted for my father, and he came out of his room. He was getting ready to leave for the hospital to sit with my mother. I was to follow in an hour with food and tea.

Parvez touched my father's feet. He said, "Chachaji, please excuse me. I have brought bad news when you are already in a difficult situation."

My father was looking at me. I asked him whether he had heard the phone ring. He shook his head and I went over and picked up the receiver. There was a dial tone. The phone was working.

I didn't ask Parvez if Ranjit's hands were hurt badly. Instead, I said to him, "When did he call you?"

Parvez said, "He called me at one in the morning. I haven't slept since."

———

Ranjit was not at home. What was equally disturbing was that, despite our calling so many times, Sudha never picked up the phone. We had asked her not to answer calls but, surely, she would have known what to do in an emergency. When I called Ranjit's office, Surinder Minhas said Ranjit hadn't come to work. I asked if he could send someone to our flat to check on him. I was going to try to return to Delhi as soon as I could.

My father didn't go to the hospital that morning. Instead, he thought it best if I left for Delhi. He tried to get me to fly back to Delhi but the ticket for that day would cost more than fifteen thousand rupees. I was able to call my cousin and ask him to drop everything he was doing to find a travel agent who would get me a reserved seat on a train to Delhi that night. Two hours later, he had a ticket for me on Vikramshila Express. And then Minhas called to say that the apartment was sealed: a heavy lock was on the door with a yellow paper from the Delhi police pasted over it. A policeman was standing guard outside the house. Then the editor said that he felt I needed to return as soon as possible. From his tone, and particularly from his reticence, I sensed that things had taken a more serious turn. I was afraid to ask anything else. I feared that perhaps Ranjit was battling for his life in the hospital, and Sudha, the caring and responsible girl, was at the hospital too, bringing him food and taking away his bedpan.

But why hadn't Ranjit dictated my father's phone number to Sudha and asked her to call me from a public call booth?

In the evening, at the train station, where I had been taken by my cousin, my father suddenly appeared through the crowd. In his hand he held two packs of Frooti mango juice. His face was haggard and creased with worry. Wordlessly, he put the juice beside me on the train seat. He was quiet for a while and then he said that he had known Parvez's father in college. The older Iqbal had been my father's junior by a couple of years. Parvez's father had practiced law from his Rajendra Nagar residence for close to thirty years. I was getting impatient with this historical narration but then my father said that Parvez's brother-in-law was a police officer in Delhi. Here was the point he had been building toward. I saw that he was trying to comfort me. He said that the reason Ranjit would have called Parvez instead of us was because he wanted the police to help catch the thief who had attacked him.

It was so late at night when it had all happened, my father continued, that it was very likely Ranjit hadn't wanted to alarm us. Except, the longer my father spoke, the less assured I felt about his reasoning.

The train pulled away from Patna and soon gathered speed. In a short while, the conductor appeared with his small entourage of passengers holding currency notes between their fingers. They all wanted a reserved seat and had calculated what would be a fair bribe. After two hours, I drank mango juice from one of the packs my father had brought for me. I missed him and felt bad for having brought more sorrow into his life. There was in my handbag a copy of *India Today* that my cousin had given me. I started reading a report on police killings of Sikh extremists and then stopped. I stared out the window. Sparks flew past in the night air. A few seats down from me four youths were playing cards. They sat with their knees touching, a surface like a table made for their cards by spreading a towel on their laps. The sour smell of alcohol floated in the air. Later, after eating the dinner served in a dirty tray, I unfolded my blanket but sleep didn't come. And yet I must have fallen asleep because near two in the morning I woke up with a jolt. The train had stopped at Kanpur station. Right across from me on the platform was a public phone and my impulse was to jump down and try to call our home in Delhi. But where would I find change for the call? Although there were several porters and passengers milling around, it was the middle of the night and I couldn't risk it. I turned away from the window and tried to go back to sleep.

At the train station in Delhi, I found an auto-rickshaw. The morning was chilly. The driver had a shawl wrapped over his sweater and a woolen muffler tied like a turban over his ears. When I went up to our apartment, I was immediately aware of a problem that I had ignored so far. There was a lock on the door but it wasn't the one we used. As Ranjit's editor had informed us, a piece of yellow paper with writing on it and red wax had been used to seal the lock. I had imagined I would speak to the police constable and explain that I had returned home but there was no sign of him anywhere. It was not the most logical thing to do but I knocked on the door. What was I thinking? That Sudha would open it from inside, smiling in welcome? As if in response to my knocks, down the corridor, the door of N23 opened. It was Mr. Shingari's teenage daughter. Earlier that year she had been admitted to Sri Venkateswara College to study commerce. She looked at me with curiosity, and then without saying anything or acknowledging me, she passed me by quickly. I was taken aback—we always smiled or said hello—and I wasn't able to ask her if she knew anything about Ranjit.

It was still fairly early and Ahuja Stationers wasn't open. I used to make all my long-distance calls from there. And so I walked further on to Melody Sweets. They had a public phone. I also asked for tea. I dialed the number I had for Ranjit's editor and heard the phone ringing in his house. Surinder Minhas answered in a voice filled with irritation, but his voice softened when I said my name. I had arrived in Delhi, I told him, and the apartment was locked and there was no policeman around. Where was Ranjit? Instead of answering that question, Minhas said, "Come to my house and we will go and visit him in the hospital together."

Ranjit was in Ram Manohar Lohia Hospital. He looked away when I came into the room. Minhas touched Ranjit's shoulder and said, "You are looking better today." Then he said that he would come back in ten minutes and left us alone. While I was with Ranjit, a policeman put his head in and then withdrew.

"Show me your hands," I said.

But they were heavily bandaged and there was nothing to see. I asked him if he was hurt anywhere.

The policeman came back into the room. He said, "Not allowed, madam."

"What is not allowed?"

"Visit not allowed, madam."

"This is my husband," I said. I began to shout. The policeman said something about following orders. I must have been shouting loudly because two nurses came rushing in, and then behind them, Surinder Minhas. He put his hand on my arm and said, "Come out for a minute. I'm making arrangements. Don't worry."

All this while, Ranjit had not spoken a single word. It was as if the thief had also cut out his tongue.

When we got outside, Minhas said, "The situation is complicated. I will explain it to you."

I was trembling. I realized this when I sat down in Minhas's white Maruti. I said, "What is going on? What are you not telling me?"

Minhas said, "Have faith in God. I will explain everything. I have called a man to meet you at my residence. He has all the correct information."

I hadn't ever heard anything more stupid. I just wanted the plain facts. Even if the police were investigating a case, what was wrong with the family member of an injured victim visiting him? We were passing the Asian Games Village by now. His fat jowls shaking, Minhas said stupidly, "Please wait. Have faith in God."

At his house, as soon as we entered, Minhas asked his wife for tea. A tall man with a thin mustache was sitting in his living room on the orange sofa. He was wearing a button-down blue shirt and had a notebook in his hand. I thought he was a journalist but he said he was the inspector in charge of the police station in our area. His name was Rohit Garg. He opened his notebook and said, "Do you know a man named Deepak Mintz?"

I said I did not.

"Why are you asking me?"

Garg ignored my question. He said, "Does the name Dulu mean anything to you?"

I said, "Yes, that is the name of Sudha's brother. Sudha is our maidservant. What has happened?"

The last I had heard Dulu was working at a printing press in

Ghaziabad. He was a clever young man, with an air of intensity about him. I had only met him a few times, and always briefly, when he came to pick up his sister on occasional Sundays. From everything Sudha had said about her brother I knew that he had educated himself despite the family's poverty and had received a scholarship from the Christian priests in Jharkhand. The owner of the printing press in Ghaziabad had given Dulu a place to stay at the press. Despite his young age, he was regarded as a foreman. Sudha often spoke of the trust and love that the owner of the press had for Dulu.

"The man you know as Dulu," Garg said, "his legal name is Deepak Mintz. Sudha Mintz has filed a police case. She has accused your husband, Ranjit Pathak, of raping her. She left your home on the night of the incident and went to Ghaziabad to get help. The attack on your husband was by Deepak Mintz."

I looked at Minhas. He was staring at the carpet. His wife hadn't come out of the kitchen with the tea. I guessed she didn't want to see me either. I wanted Minhas to look at me and I wanted him to tell the policeman the truth. Had he even spoken to Ranjit? If they spoke to Ranjit, he would tell them what had actually happened. Why only Ranjit, I would also like them to ask Sudha. That would clarify matters.

I said, "Where is Sudha?"

"She is in our care," Garg said. "We have arrested Mintz till the investigation is completed. Your husband is also in our custody. You will need legal permission before you can visit him. There is no provision for making a hospital visit. Please do not do it."

I felt that my feet had turned to stone and that I couldn't move.

Garg got up and stood towering over me. I believed there was something else I needed to ask him but couldn't remember what it was. He tore a corner of a page from his notebook and wrote down the phone number of the police station.

When he was gone, Minhas said softly that Garg had told him the lock on our apartment door would be removed by the evening.

I hadn't moved from my place.

"You should rest," Minhas said. His wife stepped out of the kitchen and very gently, very quietly, as if trying not to wake me up from a deep sleep, put a cup of tea next to me.

———

The lock wasn't removed from the flat that evening. I walked over to Ahuja Stationers and tried calling the number that the policeman Garg had given me. There was no response, and I felt I was being punished. For a moment I thought I should catch a train back to Patna. In other circumstances I could have asked one of the women I worked with. I didn't know what was true, and the fact that I didn't know how to prove my husband's innocence confused me, and this confusion was a matter of great shame to me. Of course, I trusted Ranjit and wanted to defend his name. However, because of the terrible way Garg had spoken to me, and all the earlier shouting in the hospital, the humiliation of it all, I didn't think I could tell anyone what had happened or ask for help. I don't think I had ever felt so alone.

When I told Minhas on the phone that I was getting no response at the number that Garg had given me, he insisted that I come back to his house. He said this was important because he had something to talk over with me. I said I would but he needed to tell me right then on the phone what he had found out. My whole being resisted any mystery now. I didn't want any surprises. There was sudden hope in my heart, maybe he was going to give me some good news. Instead, Minhas said that a rival newspaper in Patna was going to print a story about Ranjit the next day. If I had family members that I wanted to warn, I should perhaps call someone there.

Then, he added kindly that I could make the calls from his home. His wife was going to expect me for dinner.

When I reached Minhas's house, I called my father to tell him everything. I tried to be direct. My father said nothing at first and then asked if I still wanted to go back to work. I said I did. He asked, mildly, if I wanted to return to the old job in Patna. I said no. In that office, Ranjit and I had worked together. It would be impossible to go back there.

To prepare my father for the worst, I had presented him with the damning details of what I was certain that the newspaper would say. He had accepted it whole. I had hoped he would tell me how the police had been mistaken, but it was clear he had decided that Ranjit was in the wrong.

I couldn't now tell my father that I had to stay in Delhi to help Ranjit. Ranjit needed me. He hadn't been given a chance to clarify anything.

I didn't yet have access to the flat, I told my father, my things were there. For several reasons, I would need to keep the flat. If only for a while.

And then, as if to make a concession to his truth, I told him that he should avoid Ranjit's parents. He should not answer their calls or admit them into the house. I wanted nothing to do with them.

The police removed the lock after another day. When I was alone in the flat, my thoughts also turned to Sudha. Did she know that I had come back to Delhi? Sudha was a very good girl. I wished I could speak to her. The policeman Garg had said that her brother was in their custody. Where had they put Sudha? All these questions reminded me of something else. I had exploded when the constable at the hospital asked me to step out of the room. But just before that happened, I had asked Ranjit several questions. He had refused to answer them; he did not even meet my eyes. For so many days now I had been flailing, trying to save myself from drowning in doubts, and when I recalled those moments in the hospital room, I suddenly felt as if I were being pulled down into the depths, the dark waters closing over me. I found myself waking up from sleep, screaming.

A few days later a journalist from Patna called me at my office. She said that Satish Pathak, Ranjit's father, had made a statement that his son had been framed. According to my father-in-law, his son had woken up and confronted the burglar. Sudha was awake. In fact, she had let her brother into the flat. Dulu Mintz had a knife in his hand and he attacked Ranjit. And then the brother-sister duo had gone to the police and told an elaborate lie. The journalist said that Satish Pathak had petitioned the court to get Sudha Mintz arrested. Could I offer a comment?

I hung up.

A week later, when I came home from work, I saw Ranjit's father in front of my locked door. A suitcase stood beside him. He saw me and I turned around and walked down the stairs. I went to my colleague Nidhi's flat and didn't come back home for four days. My grandfather's kidneys failed and I went to Patna; I didn't even wait for him to die, leaving for Delhi after only two days, because I didn't want to see anyone, or be seen by anyone I had known in my previous life.

A month later, when I started applying to journalism programs in America, I hadn't yet initiated divorce proceedings. At the end of each day, I had little energy to do anything that was not absolutely necessary. I continued to go to work. One afternoon, when I was on my way to Yamuna Vihar in an auto-rickshaw, I saw Sudha walking with a white plastic bag in her right hand. I had recognized her walk. There was traffic but I didn't care. Avoiding cars and a DTC bus, I crossed the road, shouting Sudha's name. Then I saw that this girl was someone else. What did she think when she saw me burst into tears? There was nothing to do but get back in the auto-rickshaw and go on to the mall opening where Narasimha Rao was to cut the ribbon. The auto-rickshaw driver, an old man with a white stubble on his cheeks, looked at me in the rearview mirror and asked in Hindi, "*Aap ne samjha woh aapki saheli thi?* Did you think she was your friend?"

When I got the acceptance letter from Emory, I ran down to Ahuja Stationers to call my parents and give them the news. My father answered the phone. I asked him whether it would make my mother sad if I gave her the news myself. She mostly stayed in bed

these days. My father congratulated me and after we had talked
a bit he said calmly, "Before you go to America, we will file your
divorce petition right here in Patna."

When I was paying for the call, the old man in a white kurta
who always sat at the counter in Ahuja Stationers, and whom the
workers there called Papaji, turned his watery eyes to me and said,
"Please bring sweets for us next time you come to make a call."

How many conversations had he overheard in the past? The old
man would turn his head away and look inside the store but he was
always listening. There was a red LED strip on the wall in front
of him; it showed the phone number that had been dialed. Because
my calls were long distance, the glowing red digits showing the
phone number were replaced by changing digits that indicated the
cost of the call. Both Papaji and I would watch the red strip during
my calls. He must have formed a story in his head about me.

A young woman comes to Delhi from Patna. A man is often with her.
The man's occupation is not clear but the woman soon finds work in the
offices of the newspaper Amar Ujala. *One day, during a call to Patna,*
she reports that they have bought a dining table from Kirti Nagar. Also,
new curtains. She says to her father that he had already given her every-
thing else that she needed. But then something terrible happens. There
is sickness in the family in Patna but something bad, even unnameable,
has taken place here in Delhi too. When she comes to make a call, the
woman looks as if she is recovering from a long illness—and that this
is her first day out after falling sick. The man does not come to the shop
anymore. The young woman had an Adivasi maid who also had made a
few calls. She spoke in a strange language. What happened to her? She
is gone too.

For at least two months, the police have been involved in the young
woman's life. She mentions on the phone that she was interviewed by the
police. More than once. She tells her father that she will not hire a lawyer.
She says that she has done nothing wrong, and she had not been charged
in the case. She wasn't even here. She says she feels bad about the girl;
she wants to help but the girl's whereabouts are unknown. The woman

makes an international call very early one morning and during that call she speaks only in English. She uses the words "financial aid" often and says "thank you" more than once. For once, she looks happy after a very long time. Then she calls her usual number in Patna again. She talks to her father always, never her mother. She gives her father the news that she is going to study at a university in America. Her father must have asked if the university is in New York. The young woman says no, not in New York, it is in Atlanta, Georgia. That is where CNN has its headquarters.

———

From Calcutta I sent a telegram to my father in Patna. VISA GRANTED. Two days earlier, my application had been denied. The statement of financial aid from Emory wasn't enough for the officer at the American consulate. Her name was Livingston. She said a bank document was needed to show that I could afford other expenses. The next afternoon a fax from my father arrived at the hotel and I went back to the consulate. The fax showed that my father had named me as the owner of the flat in which my parents lived. When the officer stamped my passport, I felt only overwhelming relief. At that moment, I radiated goodwill for the entire universe, and, overcome by an upsurge of fellow feeling, I asked the officer about her name.

"Are you related to Dr. Livingston?"

She didn't look surprised at the ridiculous question. She said, "Actually, I am Polish-Russian but everyone in India asks me the same question."

When I stepped out of the consulate, I felt that if I clapped my hands, water would splash in a million shiny drops and turn the streets into a magical garden. Couldn't people tell from the look on my face that I had the visa? Such elation. At the post office I wrote my two-word message on the telegram form and slid it beneath the glass window to the clerk. He was an older man, wearing a brown kurta. His face remained serious behind his glasses. A cigarette packet lay on his side of the counter. I wanted him to share my joy. But why would he? He probably had family members who loved him and whom he needed to take care of. This thought stabbed my heart. I was going to abandon my parents. That was the truth of it. I hadn't looked for a public phone booth from which I could have called Patna because I didn't want my parents to hear the joy in my voice.

In the morning it had rained and during the afternoon the sun came out. I walked beside the Hooghly and in the evening I took a ride on a tram from the Esplanade that showed me the lighted Howrah Bridge over the river. My hotel was near the Rabindra Sadan stop on the metro: when I saw Tagore's sketches and poems on the walls of the station—such an elegant display of culture— it was easy to imagine that I was already in a foreign country. The earliest train on which I could find a seat for Patna was the Delhi Express. For the entire trip, I slept with my head away from the aisle; my passport was under my head, secreted inside the pillow-case. At every station, there was a crush of pilgrims in orange garb, with their adorned bows made of bamboo; they were all headed to Sultanganj, where they would pick up water from the Ganga to take to the temple in Deoghar. I was separate from the pilgrims and their frenzied longing. Not only because I wasn't wearing orange but because my wish had been fulfilled. I woke up some-time in the night. The train had stopped. Then with a lurch the carriage was moving again. Outside in the dark I heard the sound of running feet. That person was not going to make it. The train pulling away from the station, the train always pulling away, and the rush of feet in the night. The panting desperation of so many needy others. Did the feeling of guilt return to me, the guilt of leaving? Yes, it did.

At home, I learned that my mother had consulted an astrologer to find an auspicious day for my departure the following month for Atlanta. Everything that had happened in my marriage with Ranjit had made my parents cautious. The astrologer had declared that I was going to be a widely traveled person. Any warnings, I asked. My mother said that the astrologer had said that when I travel I should make sure that the moon isn't to my left. She hesitated. Then added that the astrologer had also said that I should be careful and not quarrel with anyone in America.

As I was going away soon, I wanted to spend the rest of my days with my parents. And so, I did what had seemed unthinkable only months earlier. I came back to Patna. My mother was happy that I was leaving the country—my marriage with Ranjit and what had happened during it had devastated her. She never spoke about it. On my second or my third day home, she gave me money to buy new clothes. I didn't take the money; I didn't need new clothes. I told my parents I had this sudden feeling that I didn't know enough about my hometown, that I needed to explore it and find its secrets, fix it in my sights, talk to everyone I had failed to notice so far. I needed to do it—I felt this in my bones—before I left.

Did I already know in my heart that I would not come back for so many years? It didn't occur to me then but I think my father knew this before I did. One evening, I forced him to come out with me on a boat for a brief trip on the Ganga. My mother refused, saying she preferred to sit in the cane chair near a fan and read a magazine, but I said to my father, "It is hot here in the house and by the time we are on the water it will really be pleasant. Let's go."

A boy, barely fourteen, started a loud motor and asked us to climb in, and after he had untied the boat, he jumped in too. He wore a blue cotton shirt unbuttoned, revealing his skinny black chest, and I was struck by his air of indifference that bordered on a kind of daring. It was as if he knew how insignificant we were, or our worldly affairs were, and how meaningless it all was in the end. He sat on a bamboo platform nailed into the boat's bow and hummed a tune while looking around. Now and again, he patted his hair like a star about to step out onto the set of a film.

Soon, we had moved away from the stench of shit near the riverbank and were floating in the middle. My father grew talkative. First, he pointed out the hospital where my grandfather had died. Then came the college where my father had taught. And then, the hostel where he had stayed when he first came to the city. Pointing to a tall building painted pink and gray, he said that right behind it was the apartment where my mother and he had first lived. I hadn't seen much display of affection between my parents, and such gestures were hardly the norm among families in Patna, but now, as I looked at my father, I saw his eyes were glistening. I turned my eyes away and gazed at the distant rooftops that were catching the light from the setting sun.

That night when the three of us were eating chicken biryani and papad with lemon pickles that were dear to my father, he cleared his throat. I thought he was going to say something but a minute passed and he didn't speak. And then he cleared his throat again so loudly, pushing the phlegm stuck in his throat, that I thought something was happening to him. I looked up, alarmed, and saw my father's cheeks bulging. He was trying to stop himself from crying.

He said, his cheeks shining, "I failed to protect you. This marriage should not have taken place. When the money was stolen, I ought to have turned back and come home. It was a sign."

I was shaken when I saw my father's tears, but his irrational remark, full of the nervousness and superstition that were becoming more and more a part of him as he aged, rescued me from my fears about breaking down and crying.

Laughing, but only halfheartedly, I said, "No, no, there was no way any one of us could have foreseen what happened. You should not torture yourself."

My mother was silently crying by now.

I was desperate to rescue them from their sorrow. I spoke bluntly. "Ranjit never harmed me physically. He has no doubt harmed Sudha, but she reported him to the police and I hope that means she is fighting back. She is a survivor."

I paused and they didn't say anything. So I added, "And I, too, am a survivor, in my own way. But I have made a change in my life. I'm looking forward to resuming my education."

The impromptu speech helped my parents, even if I felt emotionally spent myself. We returned to our meal.

My father would later make the same sound with his throat when he called to tell me about my mother's death. And, quite unself-consciously, I was sure, he repeated what he had said before I left India. This time, after my mother's sudden death, he said, "I didn't do enough. I should have kept her alive until you came back."

"You are not a doctor and you are not God," I thought to say later on. On the phone, however, I bawled. I must have been shrieking and it worried him because he again tried to impress on me a sense of destiny. He said that my mother had willed herself to stay alive until I left for America. By doing what I was doing, I was fulfilling her ambition for me.

I turned over all these memories from long ago while sitting at my small dining table eating yogurt and honey after my father's death. Whether it was summer or winter, my father had yogurt and honey in the morning. There was a reason why I was thinking of his saying to me, so pitifully, that he ought to have protected me. During recent years, he had surprised me by making comments in favor of the leader in power in Delhi. I never protested. These conversations with him were so precious to me, and our connection so necessary, that I didn't want to waste any effort on asking my father what had changed in him over the last few years to make him so accepting of a demagogue. I had a crude theory in my head; I hadn't shared it with anyone because I was afraid I would appear patronizing. My father was an educated man and a scholar in his own right but he had grown up in a hut in a village. At heart, he was a peasant. In his old age, and utterly alone after a lifetime of teaching, he was entirely at the mercy of television. The media in India had become increasingly hypernationalist and hostile to dissent. Had my father found in the certainties of the television anchors berating the nation a measure of stability that he had perhaps lacked in his own life? I hadn't said anything to him and yet I had imagined the scene so many times. I wanted to say to my father, just as he had said after my mother died, "I didn't do enough to protect you. I left you alone. Now you listen to these men who shout about the enemies they see everywhere. It is my fault. I should never have left you. You were all I had after my mother died and you have become someone else."

But it would have broken his heart, and mine, if I had said anything like that and so I kept quiet.

––––––––––

One item I did not buy during my first visit to the grocery store after getting news of my father's death was peanut butter. I should have. A jar of peanut butter was the only edible thing that my father brought back with him from America. At that time, I was finishing my coursework in journalism in Delhi. It was 1989 when my father returned to India from Berkeley and I was twenty-four years old. He had been away for a year. I find it appalling to think of it now but I had written to ask my father to bring back several packs of Wrigley's chewing gum. In my small room near Jamia Millia, where I was a student, I had fantasized about the Double-mint chewing gum flooding my mouth with its fresh sweet taste and fragrance. However, when I looked in my father's suitcase, I didn't find it. I was disappointed but couldn't ask my father why. I understood intuitively that it wouldn't have made sense to him to buy it; I'm sure he hadn't ever chewed gum in his life.

After landing in Delhi on a Cathay Pacific flight just before dawn, my father spent a few hours in my boarding room and then took a three-wheeler to Paharganj to catch a train for Patna. Before leaving, he had extracted the jar of peanut butter and presented it to me. He was smiling. I had seen it in his suitcase during my earlier search but didn't exactly know what it was. My father said, "I got into the habit of eating this while I was in America.

Spread it on bread and eat it. A good food to have before you go to the college." I tried it the next day and found that the butter stuck to my palate. After a couple of days, however, I grew to like its taste. It wasn't until I had made the journey to Atlanta many years later that I got the chance to have peanut butter again. During my graduate student days at Emory, because money was scarce, I always had peanut butter in my kitchen and, sometimes, even in my backpack. Which is all to say, a story that had started with my father's journey to America had now become mine and I was completing it.

When he was at Berkeley, my father used to mail me an occasional letter. I liked the quality of the paper and my father's regular handwriting, which always appeared decisive to me. However, his letters didn't tell me much about his life in America. I had no idea if he missed us, although I'm sure he did, or whether he had made any friends there. I could see that he always tried to give me a sense of what it would have been like for me to be a student at the university in Berkeley. He told me about the class he was teaching and his research schedule. So, that was another story that started with him—and some years later I was able to write about my classes too. Except that I was aware how little I was telling him in my letters. And there again, I was following his example.

A few months after my father's return from Berkeley, I came back to Patna from Delhi with my journalism degree. Soon, I was to start working in a newspaper office. One evening I went with my father to the Bankipore Club. A local group of intellectuals who ran a group called Explore had invited him to speak about his Fulbright experience abroad. What my father said surprised me. Like many others who teach, he was comfortable in front of a crowd. But the surprise lay in what he was telling us, things that had never entered any of the letters he had sent home. He recited a poem by the Marathi Dalit writer Daya Pawar; the poem was addressed to a high-caste friend who had traveled to America to do graduate work in chemistry. This friend had written a letter to

Pawar to tell him that Indians in the United States were treated like dogs—this was in the fifties, I imagine, before Ravi Shankar had played with the Beatles and Hollywood had sold Gandhi with popcorn to millions. In his poem, Pawar had described himself standing beside a dusty bush in Nasik reading the long letter that had come to him from America. His joy made him cry. In his reply, he wanted to be honest. I felt so damn good, he wrote in his poem. Now you've had a taste of what we have suffered in this country for far too long.

There were people in the Bankipore Club audience exchanging looks and puzzled smiles. A man, a famous cardiologist wearing a blue suit, had brought his teenage son with him; no doubt, this man was looking forward to sending his son to America. Most of the men and women sitting in the hall, though maybe not all, of course, belonged to the upper castes. They probably expected to hear tales about Americans asking the visiting Indian about the magic and mystery of temples and tigers. Instead, here was my father lecturing about caste.

The talk took a darker turn.

Thirteen months before my father's arrival in America, an Indian man named Navroze Mody went to a bar in Hoboken. Mody lived in Jersey City. When he came out of the bar, he was accosted by about a dozen youths and beaten. Mody died in the hospital four days later. He was thirty years old. My father said that there was a group in Jersey that called itself Dotbusters—the name a reference to the bindi worn by Hindu women on their foreheads. A handwritten note sent by this group had been published by a local paper. "We will go to any extreme to get Indians to move out of Jersey City. If I'm walking down the street and I see a Hindu and the setting is right, I will hit him or her."

A silence had fallen among the members of the Bankipore Club audience, although I also heard gasps and sighs.

Why was my father doing this? He hadn't told them about peanut butter. Nothing about the pleasure of watching a retrospective of Shyam Benegal's films at Berkeley, the depiction of village life in those films reminding him of his childhood in Khewali. No word also about his friend Reed Anthony visiting him and driving him in a hired car to see the old-growth forests in the Humboldt Redwoods State Park. They had traveled up the hills of Northern California to vineyards where they sampled wine. The research he had done at the university and the comforts of its library. When he was about to return to India, my father had invited to dinner the librarian of the South Asia wing, and this man, Cecil, had brought him a gift, a book of Tamil poems translated by the great Indologist David Shulman. None of these memories, which he had narrated to my mother and me during the weeks after his return, were shared with his audience. When we got back in the car to make our way home, I smelled the sour odor of my father's sweat. The air was warm and I didn't know exactly why my father was silent.

Earlier, when he had finished his speech, a man raised his hand and said, "You have shared your thoughts on our societies. But can you say something about your journey itself?"

In response, my father laughed derisively. He said to the man, "Kedar babu, our journeys are not journeys to the moon. There is no escape from society."

The man who had asked the question didn't oppose my father's statement. I was relieved. I hadn't wanted an argument.

My father had more to say. "I will tell you what I mean. Our government is worried about loss of foreign exchange. We are allowed to take only thirteen dollars. I had to change planes in Amsterdam. You cannot leave the airport, of course. There were four hours to kill. There were other Indians at that airport waiting for their flights. It was only we Indians who stood hypnotized in front of the glass shelves of the shops at the airport. Watches, perfume, jewelry, fashionable clothes. These were all beyond our meager means. We wanted to save our dollars. I didn't eat or drink anything, waiting to be back on the plane because I knew I would be offered food."

211

Did the others see my father as clearly as I saw him? I couldn't
be sure. He wasn't a tourist or even a traveler at the airport; he
was like a patient in the waiting room outside a doctor's clinic.
This is what I wanted to tell the man who had asked the question
about the journey. What is wrong with you all? If you are seated
in the waiting room at the doctor's, you are nursing a sickness and
you know that others are sick too. You just want to get better, to
be healthy again, so that you can get up and go to work. That is
why you are here. You breathe in the sad air of scarcity. The goal
isn't to get up and sing and dance. They couldn't have expected a
jaunty travelogue from my father. The poverty of his childhood
defined him utterly. It was a part of him and he was never going to
embrace luxury.

This also meant that a certain quality of thriftiness, if not also
deprivation, marked my own upbringing. My father had always
repeated, somewhat mechanically, a line that he attributed to Gandhi. "How many things can you do without?" I have never checked
to see if Gandhi did indeed ever say this. And wouldn't he have
said, instead, "How many things you cannot do without"? It is a
truth that defined my father and I don't want to discover in my
middle age that this was a lie.

A younger man, maybe a student, had then raised his hand. He
wanted to know if my father had been surprised by anything in
America.

"I could tell you about big cars and broad avenues but, to tell
you the truth, they weren't really a surprise," my father said. "In
fact, aren't those things precisely what we expect to find there in
California even without having visited it? I'll tell you what never
ceased to surprise me. The toilets I had used all my life in India
were small and often damp if not also dirty. But what surprised
me was that even middle-class Americans had bathrooms in their
homes that were dry and often stocked with books and magazines.
Several bathrooms even had photographs or art. And also air-
conditioning. I was born in a hut and my village still doesn't have
electricity. Those of us who have air-conditioning have machines

in our walls. In America, it was quite common for homes to have central air-conditioning. I'm sorry if what I'm saying itself is a surprise because I'm talking about ordinary things, but yes, I was surprised how cheap chicken was, how much Coke and beer people drank, the easy availability of fruit. The waste visible everywhere, especially in the use of cars. You might have wanted me to talk to you about American cars, but I couldn't believe that so much of the beautiful landscape across the country had been turned into highways and paved with concrete. I saw a society that was hostage to the automobile."

A young woman, who was clearly a student, smiled ingratiatingly and said to my father, "Sir, I had heard that Jayaprakash Narayan had been a student at Berkeley and that is why you had gone there too—"

My father said, "JP sailed to California to study chemical engineering and other subjects at Berkeley. But the place was too expensive for him and so, after only one semester, he moved to Iowa State University. Then, he moved again, this time to the University of Wisconsin, Madison. In Madison and in nearby Chicago, JP spent a lot of time with Indian students and often got into situations in which he got a taste of class inequality and racial prejudice. That was also where he read Marx and became a communist. He could have gone on to study at the Oriental University in Moscow but he couldn't raise the money required for his passage. Four hundred dollars. You must understand why this was so: America was headed toward the Great Depression and it was difficult, if not impossible, for JP to get a job. We know from reading his memoir and his papers that he went from one factory to another looking for work. He found their gates shut. For a time, he worked as an usher in a cinema hall. When his mentor in graduate school, a professor named Avrom Landy, joined the Ohio State University faculty, JP followed him. After earning his master's in sociology there, JP returned to India in 1929. He was later to say that in America he had worked in mines, in factories and slaughterhouses. He had worked as a shoeshine boy and even cleaned commodes in hotels. All his experiences there made him a Marxist but he was also a nationalist and a Gandhian. Did you know that he was close to Gandhi? In fact, while he was away in America, his wife, Prabhavati Devi, lived mostly in Gandhi's ashram."

An old man with short gray hair and a green khadi kurta was seated in the front row. He cleared his throat and, out of respect, the people around him fell silent and looked at him. My father bowed to the man. He said, "Professor Trivedi . . ."

The old man didn't keep sitting. He stood up and, turning first to the front and then halfway back, he made it clear that he was only appearing to address my father. His audience really was everyone else in the room. As he spoke, he patted his green kurta, first near his heart and then his stomach.

"You have laid out many interesting facts about America, showing us in a way what is often overlooked. I'm thinking now, however, of our own country. While you were at Berkeley, there was a massacre of Dalit peasants only an hour away from here. Eighteen men and women were shot by the private army of a landlord. The whole Dalit *basti* was torched. You were talking a minute ago of Indians looking at watches and jewelry in the glass cases at foreign airports. You were talking about air-conditioning and cars. These realities are far away from the lives of the Dalit peasant in Bihar. Many of us don't pay heed to those realities. I want to ask you how we are going to change the thinking of our people not about America but about India. That is my question."

Someone laughed at the back. My father remained silent, and so the first man's snicker was echoed by others. The question was treated as a final challenge, a stunning rebuttal, that had completely foxed the speaker. A show had now started in earnest. Who was going to be the winner?

My father waited a moment longer, maybe surprised by the laughter, and then he said, "Professor Trivedi, you have been teaching for much longer than I have. What can I tell you that you don't already know?" He folded his hands together and bowed to the audience and stepped off the wooden platform on which the lectern had been placed. It was an abrupt, maybe even rude, departure and, after a pause, there was a bit of applause from different parts of the room.

When we got in the car, my father said nothing. Was he angry about the way the audience had behaved? I stayed silent as we passed Gandhi Maidan and then Rajasthan Hotel, where two nights earlier my parents and I had tomato soup and excellent tandoori chicken with naan for dinner. My father drove in silence. And as we drove the silence grew and became complete. Where was my father taking us? This wasn't the way home. He drew up in front of the Khadi Gram Udyog store in New Market. Turning off the engine, he said, "Come."

He said to the bearded salesman that he wanted to look at khadi kurtas for himself. The one he liked was a pale blue kurta with thin pink vertical lines. "What about you? Let me buy you one." I said no at first, and then I said yes. The salesman extracted a pile of neatly folded kurtas from a shelf that said in dirty letters LADIES. The kurta I chose had delicate red flowers block-printed on the marigold-colored background.

In the car, my father laughed and turned the car around. We were now going home. When we edged out into the opposite lane of traffic, a rickshaw passed too close to us and I was afraid the car would get scratched. But we passed unscathed. My father said, "When Professor Trivedi was talking, I decided I wanted to buy a new kurta. I liked the green kurta he was wearing."

He laughed with greater freedom now.

We were passing the wide-open expanse of Gandhi Maidan. There were a few kites in the sky. My father said, "You saw today that people love to talk. They will say anything—just because they have been given the opportunity."

I stayed silent. I didn't want to say something just because I had been given the opportunity. But he was my father. I could say anything to him. I said, "I saw your friend Ramdeo Manjhi on TV the other night. He was good. If you are at that level, it is perhaps unavoidable. You are always talking to an invisible audience."

My father said, "Let me tell you a story."

In the library at Berkeley, he had watched a documentary about Indians in South Africa. In an interview, a man named Laloo Chiba spoke of his work as a militant in the antiapartheid struggle. He was an expert at planting bombs at state installations. On the night before Nelson Mandela's first court appearance in 1952, Chiba bombed an electrical substation. Mandela was sentenced to life and deported to Robben Island prison. Chiba was later arrested too and spent eighteen years on the island alongside Mandela. Chiba was from Gujarat, as was his wife. Families of political prisoners were allowed rare prison visits, sometimes once a year, but they were to speak in either Afrikaans or English. Chiba's wife only spoke Gujarati, so the two of them would sit silent, looking at each other with tears running down their cheeks. It went on like this during each solitary visit year after year.

My father said, "That is the story I wanted to tell the people when I heard them asking their questions at the meeting today. There they were, holding their cups of tea, biting into their samosas, and wanting me to give glib answers. It occurred to me that I should just tell them that I watched a documentary when I was in Berkeley. I wanted to tell them Chiba's story and ask them to think for a minute about what it means to not be allowed to say anything."

Words are slippery and we cannot trust our memories but I seem to remember that when my father told me this story it occurred to me that there were so many things he had shared neither with his audience at Bankipore Club nor with members of our own family. And did I also think that with his death—it is possible that I was thinking even then of his death because I had this sense that I was going away from India—all that was stored in his memory would be lost forever? When I reflect on language and silence,

I'm reminded that my father and I never said "I love you" to each other, nor did we ever hug or demonstrate any intimacy. It wasn't part of our custom, or at least the customs of his generation; if I had children, they would have had a different relation to him. My father had cried in front of me but we hadn't used words like *crying*. Both of us noticed each other's tears but there was no shared language to name our tears or sometimes even the emotions from which they sprang. Soon after my father's death, I heard a white woman, an American, being interviewed on our channel. She was elegant and elderly, with thin lips, and she was saying that there weren't enough books about friendship. My father's death was still like a bruise, a shade of blue darker than black on my skin, and when I heard the woman's words on TV, I wondered whether she would grant that my father and I had been friends even if we hadn't hugged or shared a beer together or liked each other's photos on Facebook. Isn't that what you are supposed to do in America if you are friends? I switched off the TV because I didn't want to experience that feeling of loss widening further and further in my heart until it was wider than any ocean.

There was the time when I had first put an ocean between my parents and myself. My father traveled to Delhi to see me off on the flight to Atlanta. A small prayer book clutched in his hands while we sat in the taxi to the airport. Three hours after my flight he would be on a train taking him back to Patna. I had never flown in a plane before. The flight from Delhi had landed in Doha. I was to change planes there. The plane to Doha was filled with Indian workers who had work permits granted to migrants. The passenger in the seat next to me said his name was Mohammed Musa. He was from Siwan district in Bihar. I could sense that he was reluctant to talk to a female, particularly a stranger, but I couldn't help observing that he watched everything I did out of the corner of his eye. He watched me lower the tray and also switch on the reading lights. I translated for him when the flight attendant asked him in English what he would like to drink. Perhaps this was his first time on a plane too. I couldn't ask him that question—I wasn't preparing a journalistic report. Nevertheless, I learned a few things about him. Musa said he was going to be away for six months. He was going to work as a welder at a construction site. He said he had family at home but didn't explain whether he had a wife and small children waiting for him in a village near Siwan. Musa wasn't used to handling a knife and fork. He would have resented the drama if I had suddenly said to him, "It is okay, it is okay. We didn't grow up using these things. There are a hundred ways in which the outside world will try to humiliate you but never, never let them rob you of your dignity."

After the plane landed, he followed me into the airport but I showed him the sign for transfers and explained that I was continuing my journey and that was why I had turned in to the corridor on the right. He needed to go left. His ticket in his right hand, his face a mask of seriousness, Mohammed Musa went in the direction of his new life. I wished him a safe stay and he thanked me politely and called me his sister.

There were many other things I didn't report to my parents because I was busy experiencing my new life.

An Indian student at Emory, a PhD candidate in biochemistry, was my host for my first five days in America. Each summer, the International Students Office contacted older graduate students and made arrangements to welcome the new incoming ones who didn't have housing for the fall. My host's name was Renuka Agarwal and she was from Meerut. Renu also helped me find a sublet in an apartment where the leaseholder was a female Russian student who was her lab partner. It all worked out very well. I was swept into a life of classes, homework, and, when I had time, cooking and cleaning. In India I had worked as a journalist for years, but in America I found the ways of preparing copy refreshing and new; the rules as well as the language were different here. The situation was challenging and much to my liking because the assignments I got in class gave me a reason to discover my new surroundings.

Bill Clinton, the Governor of Arkansas, was leading in the polls for election as president. In late October he was addressing a rally at Woodruff Park and all the fifteen students in Professor Sund's newswriting class were required to go and file a thousand-word report. I saw Clinton from a distance, his youth reminded me of Rajiv Gandhi, who had been killed the previous year. Except that Clinton had more charm. I wondered if this was inevitable in a country where more people had television, or where there was more mixing among the sexes, and women had greater freedom. I didn't ask this question in my report. Clinton had appealed to the younger members in his audience by speaking of a better federal loan plan for getting an education. In my report I contrasted Clinton's proposal for better education with that of the Chief Minister of my home state of Bihar, Lalu Yadav. Yadav had mocked our interest in information technology during his election campaign by famously asking voters if a computer could give people milk. Instead of computers, he wanted more cows. He had also made fun of villagers who had appealed for roads to be built to connect their villages with the world. If you have roads, Lalu said, the police will be able to catch you faster. You won't be able to escape.

There was another Indian student in my class. His name was Piyush Tyagi and he was very different from me. Piyush had come to this country when he was nine. His family had sold the little property they owned in Haryana and filed a case for political asylum because Piyush's uncle, his father's elder brother, had been killed by terrorists in Gurdaspur. The family had ended up in this part of America because their landlord in Punjab had a cousin who ran a trucking business out of Richmond, Georgia. Now the elder Mr. Tyagi worked as a meter reader in Augusta and on weekends he put in more hours as a parking lot attendant. Piyush was younger than I was and I liked him because he was blunt and cynical. He didn't harbor hypocrisies. There was a roughness in his manner and also a great deal of sensitivity. I was talking to Piyush once and praised his father. I said that I admired a man who had been a head salesman at a bicycle selling shop in Punjab and in this new country had been unafraid to wear a uniform and tramp up and down the streets noting down numbers from electric meters. Piyush gave a bitter laugh. He said his father was a flop. Before leaving India, he had boasted that once he reached America, he would probably become a bank manager or run a luxury hotel. There had been no practical basis for such plans. Piyush said that it was his mother who had pushed his father out of the house and forced him to take the job. Piyush had a younger sister, who was disabled, and still in high school. Piyush's mother had felt that this daughter would have a more meaningful life in a rich place like America. This was why they had left home.

It always appeared to me that Piyush carried a bottled rage inside him and I wondered whether he was from a low caste. I wanted to say to him, *I'm on your side*. It turned out that it was just my prejudice to imagine that his anger was that of the low-born. Piyush was a Khatri, from a merchant caste; although he had grown up poor, he had some rich relatives. I found out these details about him and the family not from Piyush but from a piece he wrote for *The Emory Wheel*. I read the essay and was shocked by its candor. I remember thinking that this was the way one could be honest. And yet, when I told Piyush that I had loved his piece and wanted to talk to him about it, I felt I couldn't breach the walls of politeness I had built around myself. So, I ended up talking to him about his style of writing instead. Near the beginning, Piyush had written this line about their rooftop apartment in Gurdaspur, which had a sink attached to the outside wall: "Each night my father would stand before the sink, the sky full of stars, and brush his teeth till his gums bled." How had he arrived at this startling line? Piyush said that one of the courses he was taking that semester was all about writers reporting about war or work. In writing his essay, Piyush said he had followed the example of the Russian writer Isaac Babel, who wrote short stories about his experiences in the Red Cavalry. Piyush pulled out a book from his navy backpack.

"Babel's sentences embrace opposites," he said. Then he chose two lines to read out to me in a declamatory voice, one finger of his left hand pointed upward like Socrates moments before taking the cup of poisonous hemlock: "Savitsky, Commander of the VI Division, rose when he saw me, and I wondered at the beauty of his giant's body . . . His long legs were like girls sheathed to the neck in shining riding boots."

A few days later when Halloween rolled around, Professor Sund had a new assignment for us. We were to file another report, this time about what we observed at Halloween. I accompanied my housemate, Lena, to her lab. Her whole team of lab assistants, most of them doctoral students from other countries, was unable to get away from the tests being run in the lab, but they had all dressed up in costumes and brought bottles of wine. I asked Lena's colleagues as many questions as I could, about their home countries, their favorite festivals, and how much they had spent on their costumes. Before I came to this country, I hadn't even heard of *Sesame Street*, but when I saw a giant yellow creature in Lena's lab, I learned about Big Bird. My report focused on Lena's colleague Marcos, who was from Cuba, and I thought I had done a good job of showing why Marcos had chosen to dress up as a character from a television show for kids. But the following Monday, Professor Sund told me that a few nights earlier a Japanese exchange student named Yoshihiro Hattori had been shot to death in Baton Rouge, Louisiana. Hattori was on his way to a Halloween Party when he got the address mixed up. He rang the bell at a house where he wasn't expected. The owner came out and shot him in the chest. Hattori had dressed up as John Travolta's character in *Saturday Night Fever*.

I worried that Professor Sund was telling me that I had been shallow. On the very first day of class she had told us about Gene Roberts, a former editor at *The New York Times*, whose first job was writing farm columns for a small newspaper in North Carolina. Roberts's editor was Henry Belk, who was blind. Roberts remembered later that when he showed up for work in the morning, Belk would call him over and tell the young reporter that his writing was insufficiently descriptive. "Make me see," he would order. "Make me see."

Now, upon learning about the shooting of the Japanese kid in Baton Rouge, I wondered whether Professor Sund was asking me to make her see. Or, maybe she was asking me to open my eyes and see the reality of the world around me. I was a newcomer in America, I didn't feel I could speak authoritatively about this country. Also, the truth was that I was very happy to have come here. But I took Professor Sund's lesson to heart. For that whole semester I became a victim detective. At dinners cooked by Renu, to which other international students came, I would ask if they had experienced racism. Had a professor made a derogatory comment? Did a stranger in the shopping mall say something insulting? Was a white friend guilty of an insensitive observation?

One of the students I met at that time was a Pakistani girl called Azeen Bamji. She was quiet and pleasant, focused on becoming a doctor. Her grandfather had migrated from Bombay to Pakistan at the time of the Partition; twenty years later, Azeen's parents moved from Karachi to Stony Brook, New York, to get their advanced medical degrees. In a few months she would be applying to medical schools herself. It is possible I had asked her questions like those I have listed above and she had probably smiled and answered that everyone had been nice to her. Almost ten more years were to pass before she was forced to change her mind. This happened a few months after the terrorist attacks of September 11. Azeen was stepping into her car with a bag of Mexican takeout when a middle-aged white man wearing a camouflage hunting jacket fired two shots at her before leaving the scene in his truck. Witnesses said the shooter had said, "Go back to the desert, you fucking terrorists." This time I was able to do a story on her. Azeen was a pediatric dentist in a Jacksonville suburb, and, unfortunately, the bones in her right hand had been shattered by the bullet from the Mauser M2. When I asked her to describe her attacker, Azeen said, "I didn't get a good look. I didn't even see his gun." Then, she added, "I don't think he saw me either. He only saw my headscarf and began to scream."

———

One class assignment was modeled on a magazine profile we had discussed in class: instead of sitting down for a dull, prepackaged interview with a Hollywood star, the reporter had asked the actor if he could go with him while he shopped for vegetables. The idea was to observe the interviewee making real choices. One of my fellow students, John Crowley, went to the train station six days in a row: he would get into a taxi and ask the driver to name a place in town which told a personal story. A place that the driver, rather than the passenger, wanted to visit. John said he would pay for the trip, of course. Some drivers were puzzled but John explained that it was for a class. *Take me to the hospital where your child was born or your high school where you played football or where you go on dates or whatever. Tell me a story about this place and what it means to you.*

I wasn't as creative. I chose the dour owner of Krishna Groceries. She was a middle-aged Indian woman and sat behind the counter surrounded by the narrow shelves of merchandise that threatened to tilt and bury her. The shelves were piled high with everything from cumin seeds and asafetida to cheap bamboo flutes and sour-smelling cotton outfits. Next to her sat a portrait of a plump man with a shy smile. He wore a red embroidered cap on his head. Often, an incense stick would be burning under the portrait. I said to the owner, "Behenji, I come here as a customer all the time. And today I want to buy a bottle of Patak's curry paste. But I also have another request. Can I ask about you and the story of this shop? I have to write a paper for my journalism class."

The woman made a face. She was suspicious but I couldn't guess what she was suspicious about. I felt I hadn't been a good journalist. A better journalist would have taken a different tack perhaps.

Turning toward the smiling man in the photograph, I said, "I see this picture each time I come into the shop. Can you tell me who this is?"

The woman's face grew even sadder. "That is my father," she said. "He gave me the money to start this shop. He was going to come here. We are from Raipur in Madhya Pradesh. He was on his way to Delhi to come here when he started feeling unwell. He didn't get a chance to come to America."

I was nonplussed. Her unwillingness to talk had been replaced by a show of sorrow that didn't brook polite journalistic queries for a student paper. I was engaged in my own little drama about what a journalist is supposed to do in such a situation.

"Are you alone?"

There was a pause. Then she glanced at me before looking away. She said, "I came here with my husband. He developed bad habits."

Another pause. "I have a son. He is twenty years old and works in Tampa."

"That's good," I said. "What does he do?"

"He works in a Radio Shack store."

"That's very good," I said. I was trying very hard.

She looked at me for a long while this time. "What is good—he has a white girlfriend and doesn't talk to me anymore." It was odd. For a moment, and just for a moment, I think both she and I had the same absurd thought—even I, older though I was, would have been a better match than that boy's white girlfriend.

I realized I should leave. I asked the woman her name.

"Savita Shukla," she said.

And then as if that wasn't what I had asked her really, she went on. "We are Kanyakubja Brahmins with roots in Benares. My uncle was the head priest at a temple in Dwarka and my maternal uncle worked in the Allahabad high court."

The conversation felt uncomfortably like a badly written film script. Another ten or fifteen years would pass and I would be watching a movie in which Aishwarya Rai played the role of a grocery store owner in San Francisco. When the woman in the film gave her customers spices like "sandalwood to dispel painful memories, black cumin seed to protect against evil eye," I would remember Savita Shukla in Krishna Groceries and think that the movie in which she was living wasn't so bad after all. I mean that her real life wasn't hokey and didn't turn her story into bloodless bathos. I'm sure that Savita kept the Aishwarya Rai film on her shelf of shiny videos, but I hoped to God that she hadn't subjected herself to its cut-rate magical realism aimed at lifting the unsuffering masses into the zone of the spicy sublime.

But all this was many years later. On that day I came out of Krishna Groceries wanting to tell Piyush of my encounter with Savita Shukla. I don't think any of my American friends, or even my roommate, Lena, would understand the forces at work in that conversation. As expected, Piyush found the exchange hilarious but he thought I had been a poor journalist. He laughed when I told him that Shukla had said that her husband had developed bad habits. *What were they? And where was he now? Had there been a legal separation? A death?* I shared with Piyush some of what I had written but he wasn't impressed. "There was so much to talk to her about, man. What about that uncle who was a priest? How many women did he impregnate on the temple premises?"

Piyush was being cruel but I recognized the truth in what he was saying, of course. I had often asked difficult questions in my work in India and wondered now whether I had become more diffident or uncertain after my arrival in this country. How could this be possible when I knew I had cut my old ties and felt lighter? There had been other changes in my life, less dramatic but also important. For half a credit, I had enrolled in a swimming class. The following summer, or certainly the year after that, I would learn to drive. But during that conversation with Piyush, I didn't have a ready answer for his questions. In nearby Virginia, a woman named Lorena Bobbitt was in the news for having used an eight-inch carving knife to cut off her husband's penis. She then drove away with the severed appendage before tossing it in a field from the window of her moving car. Bobbitt complained that her husband had abused her for years, hitting her and raping her. I hadn't had that experience, but I thought of Sudha. Dulu had perhaps also wanted to castrate Ranjit, and that was why Ranjit's hands had been cut badly as he tried to defend himself. These thoughts passed through my head as I spoke to Piyush. Here was the main difference between us: unlike him, I hadn't written out of my anger or my shame. In fact, I was afraid I had been downright sentimental. Ranjit had once appeared in my dream. He apologized to me and then looked down at the floor shyly. And so tawdry, and even reactionary, was my subconscious that from behind Ranjit, Sudha appeared. She was holding a child in her arms, and she was smiling. The three of them stood together, as if posing for a family photograph in a studio.

I was certain that Piyush never had such dreams. I asked him what he had done for the assignment. He shrugged and said that he had interviewed his father about his workplace. Each weekend, in a parking lot on Prescott Way, Madan Mohan, his father, sat in a little kiosk for part of the day and then late into the night, handing out tickets. The parking lot abutted a strip club called Bottom Line. Piyush had asked his father about the strip club, as he was interested in the men and women who frequented it. Were there regulars, for instance. At the end of the interview, he had asked his father if he had visited Bottom Line himself and how had he liked it.

Madan Mohan had answers for his son's questions but he also had a story to tell. The story was offered at the end of the piece that Piyush had titled "My Father and the Bottom Line." One of the strippers was a young woman named Annie. She came out to smoke during her breaks; she didn't like standing alone at the back of the club under the lights. Annie often strolled over to Madan Mohan's kiosk and talked to him. Annie had the gift of curiosity; she asked questions. Piyush's father wanted him to know that customers who left him a tip or those who misbehaved—one of them had waggled his head and called him "Fucking Gandhi" when he couldn't understand Madan Mohan's accent—didn't matter much. Madan Mohan had stepped inside Bottom Line a couple of times but only for a few minutes. The last time was when a car's alarm went off and he went looking for the driver. Annie was dancing, naked except for her tall boots, around a shiny metal pole. But Annie was interesting in other ways. Piyush was conscious that his father was always boasting but there was modesty in his description of what Annie spoke to him about. "A desirable woman who was dancing naked just a few minutes earlier but here she is asking me about the difference between cheese and paneer."

Madan Mohan had repeated, "She asks questions, and I answer them. I find it very pleasant."

Piyush laughed when I handed his paper back to him. His laughter had a hard edge. He said, "My mother also asks questions, but my father doesn't find that very pleasant."

That night, as I was about to fall asleep, I thought of what Piyush had said and then I guess I closed my eyes and dozed off but was awake again. A memory had come back to me. My aunt Lata, my father's sister, was talking to my grandmother in the village. In later years my aunt was to become blind with cataracts and crawl sideways on her bad knees. But back then, she was still young and I would have been in my early teens. When I woke up from my nap, I saw my aunt combing my grandmother's hair on the other cot in the room. They were talking about my father and a woman who had once been in an ashram. I knew the woman they were talking about. Her name was Ananya and she had a quality that marked her as different from the other women in Patna. My aunt was telling my grandmother that my parents had fought over my father's friendship with Ananya. There were weekly meetings at the woman's house. Apparently, my father took a journal with him during his visits. There were discussions, readings, and, on occasion, they wrote together. My aunt was laughing. There was cruelty in the laughter, cruelty toward my mother. Maybe that is why the conversation had been forgotten—and yet preserved in the hidden recesses of my memory. My grandmother had stayed quiet during that conversation. My aunt was telling her that my father had said that he liked talking to Ananya; there were some people that you liked talking to more. That was all. And my aunt laughed again but my grandmother didn't.

She asks questions, and I answer them. I find it very pleasant.

————

Professor Sund told the class, You have to learn to be a good listener. Wait for the money quote. Texas Guinan was an actor who had said, "A politician is a fellow who will lay down your life for his country." A politician named Earl K. Long, an aging member of a political dynasty in nearby Louisiana, had told his interviewer, "When I die—if I die—I want to be buried in Louisiana so I can stay active in politics." More recently, the Republican Pat Buchanan had mocked the Democratic candidate for president by saying, "Bill Clinton's foreign policy experience stems mainly from having breakfast at the International House of Pancakes."

The professor was saying that everyone had a story—in that sense, everyone you spoke to was a writer. Maybe that was true, but I wasn't always sure I was a writer myself. When I started as a journalist, I knew that turning a government release into a few column inches of newsprint didn't make me a writer. Going out into the city, to a cooking show to talk to an enterprising housewife, didn't challenge me with writerly demands either. My questions were usually those that I knew my editor wanted me to ask, and the answers that I received were similarly uninspired, either too short or too long, in any case, merely small advertisements for the self. It wasn't until I started doing longer stories, reports in which I would arrange material in an interesting way, creating an arc with a beginning, middle, and end, that I felt I was doing real writing.

In teaching us about approaches to journalism, Professor Sund recounted the following story from a textbook: A new reporter at *The New York Times* turned in a piece about an alcoholic nun who counseled other nuns with a similar problem. The story didn't move past an editor, who told the reporter, "As it stands you have a moderately interesting interview with Sister Doody. You sat in a chair, and she sat in a chair and you had a chat. That's not very good, considering the story material." Among the questions the editor asked the reporter and which Professor Sund wanted us to remember were the following: "Did you talk to any nuns in treatment?"; "Where is the anguish, the embarrassment, the guilt?"; "It doesn't sound as if you had done any real reporting, digging, pushing. Where are the people, the quotes, the color?" I understood in an abstract way what my professor wanted from me but the anguish and the guilt that I was most conscious of were my own: I had left my parents behind, my mother had died soon after I left, and my father was living alone.

Sitting in Professor Sund's class, I so badly wanted to know how to find truth in words. I was dimly aware that while dealing with questions of craft in that class, I was fulfilling the dreams of my parents. My father had said more than once that his dream was to write a book like Orwell's *Homage to Catalonia*. Orwell, he had claimed, had been born in the same hospital as he was in Motihari. And my dear mother had also harbored an ambition to write. She went to poetry readings and discussions with my father's friend Saurabh Kumar "Jigyasa." I would come upon her during silent afternoons or some mornings, an aura of stillness around her, bent over her diary. She wrote only in Hindi, her lines arranged diagonally on the page, her sentences dense with symbols and signs. I didn't find easy entry into my mother's writing. I believe she was writing her sentences under an intense pressure of thinking and feeling. When I turn the pages of her notebooks now, although it is an act that requires a lot of courage on my part, it seems to me that the words want to break free, and breathe free, and, finding it difficult to do so, they are caught in a terrible, suffocating tussle with meaning and space. Jigyasa was a well-known published poet. Did my mother share her writing with him? Or with my father? I don't know. I should have asked my father when he was still alive.

I have with me in Atlanta three of my mother's notebooks. During one of my visits home some years ago, I just took them from the closet where they had sat for years. One is a small diary, smaller than a paperback novel, with a pale green plastic cover. In it are small poems that my mother wrote after she made the pilgrimage to Deoghar with my father. I was a small girl then and didn't go to Deoghar with them. I remembered their trip because till then I had not known that children could be separated from their parents. At that age, I was obsessed with stories I had heard about the cruelty of stepmothers. In the *Ramayana*, the stepmother had sent Lord Rama away into exile in the forest for fourteen years. Stepmothers were cruel even to the gods. But clearly I had been paying attention to the wrong thing. My parents had left me in the village and, if I remember right, I had decided that my grandmother was in reality my mother. So, that was my association with Deoghar and then, in my thirties, I first saw these poems that had been composed by my mother. They were written in a style unusual for her. Her sentences, even in the letters she wrote to me, were always lyrical, but in these poems the language had been stripped of any ornamentation or opacity. It was as if on her pilgrimage my mother had found a calm space for giving voice to a simple faith; what is equally clear is that her faith is rooted in her desire for love.

I'm amazed that the air of reverence with which God was treated in our society is replaced in my mother's poems by a more personal entity who was divine and yet drawn on a human scale; the relationship between the poet and God is often sensual in these lines which appear addressed to a lover. Too late now to ask my poor, dead mother if she had intended these poems for publication. I just want to acknowledge, and honor, the yearning for love visible in her words. And not just love, skill too. My mother was a frail creature, troubled by disease and by the traumas of loss, first the loss of her father and then her young brother, and who knows, if she were stronger and had survived, she would have public accomplishments to her credit. I can imagine her wan smile if I were to say this to my mother. Her death took her away from me, and it is true that it brought me closer to my father. I'm no poet, nor a translator, but here are a few of her short poems from that Deoghar series, which I have rendered in English:

1.

On the road to Deoghar
All the hills are shaped like temples.
The black tarmac
A snake uncoiling from your neck, O Lord.
The sudden rain showers
That catch us midjourney,
The Ganga flowing from your hair,
Soaking me to my skin.

2.

I wake up in the dark
Before dawn.
The white flowers
Fallen during the night
Light a path
To a small temple
Where you wait,
A black stone.

3.

At night in our roadside tents and inns
I can feel the weight
Of the burdens carried by our fellow beings.
But my heart is free, O Lord. I want
Nothing. I am walking
To Deoghar, a long journey.
You are not there, I know.
You are here with me, all the way.

4.

The sky is blue like your skin, Lord Shiva.
All I desire is to be like this red earth
Lit up, radiant, under your gaze.

5.
A sickly dog
Runs alongside
The pilgrims
Who believe
They cannot
Be touched
By anything unclean
Like love.

6.
On our way home we find
The train station is crowded
Like your temples.
One train arrives, another departs.
An eternal story.

———

A month before Ranjit was arrested in Delhi, I had started following the news of a Soviet cosmonaut in space. His story was being reported in our newspaper. Sergei Krikalev had been told to stay in space until further notice. He was unable to return home because the Soviet Union had fallen apart while he was in space. After I learned what my husband had done to Sudha, and he had been taken away to prison, I was living alone. At night, trying to push myself to sleep, I would often think of the cosmonaut surrounded by uncertainty and the unfathomable unknown. I felt a kinship with him. When Krikalev was finally allowed to return to earth, he had been in orbit for ten months. The country he had left was now split into more than a dozen nations and even the name of his hometown had changed. His delayed return led to other problems. He had been expected to serve in the military reserves and the authorities were going to issue a warrant for desertion until they realized that their reserve soldier was not even on the planet.

I know our situation was very different but whenever I thought of the day I had come back to Delhi and learned about Ranjit's crime, I felt that I was now alone in this new life, orbiting in empty space, and that in time, when I was allowed to return, it would be to a different country from the one that I had left.

And then, during my second year at Emory, I became close to a classmate. His name was Motley Mitchell. Motley was from Baltimore, where his mother lived with his two younger sisters. Motley's father had been a star football player in high school and then worked as a porter at the Baltimore airport. He had managed to send Motley to a good school and then, before his death from heart disease, seen him leave for college on a Pell grant. Motley was a strange first name and I asked him how he had acquired it. He said that the name had belonged to a famous Black player named Marion Motley, who had helped desegregate American football. In fact, Motley's full name was Marion Motley Mitchell. But he went by his middle name now, having dropped his first name during his twenties when, in nearby D.C., Marion Barry, the mayor, was caught smoking crack cocaine in a hotel room.

Over a succession of many days, I had noticed that Motley sat next to me in the Journalism and Ethics class. Professor Stenger liked to set us up in pairs to debate opposite sides of an issue. I enjoyed going head-to-head with Motley. "Is it ethical for a journalist to pay an interviewee?" I said no. Motley's viewpoint was that it depended on how much the interviewee was asking. Did they need to buy food? A burger, for instance. Then, sure.

The professor disagreed and it was understood that I was supposed to side with him. But in my heart, I was with Motley. When class was over, I tried to tease him. "Motley, let's go and get that burger."

He laughed. "Only if you let me interview you."

While we ate burgers at a popular nearby joint called the Blind Pig, Motley asked me questions to which the answers were: I am twenty-eight years old, I am from a town in eastern India, I am separated from my husband and, in fact, am in the process of getting divorced. He wasn't able to wheedle out of me the reason for this divorce. As a part of his interview technique, Motley shared that he was two years older than me, his mother and sisters lived in Baltimore, and, before his recent, prolonged breakup, he had lived with his last girlfriend for five years. His ex was an Ethiopian nurse named Seble, who had moved to Roanoke to work at a hospital there.

When I read what Motley wrote for Professor Sund, I saw that he had absorbed her lessons better than I had. He wrote a piece about having attended a screening of *Schindler's List* at a local, predominantly Black high school. This was after a national controversy had erupted the previous month in California on MLK Day; a teacher took his Oakland high schoolers to a screening of Spielberg's film but the manager of the movie theater was forced to stop the projector and ask the students to leave. This was because other patrons had protested that the students had laughed when a Nazi soldier casually shot a Jewish woman in the concentration camp. The students were accused of racial insensitivity.

Motley had done the digging in his conversation with students after the screening at the school in Fairburn. There was anguish and guilt, of course, but also a push for understanding instead of pat condemnation. A teenager had said that the swift execution had made him think not of a distant place but of his own neighborhood. Another said that he didn't know enough about what the Nazis had done and he would like to know more. Motley asked him if he knew about the lynching of Black folk in the area and the boy said that he knew very little. So, Motley was also addressing a question to his readers. How is a boy who knows so little about his own history supposed to know a lot about what happened elsewhere? A third student had said that he wouldn't have laughed at the scene. He saw such violence outside his home every day. What touched me was a female student's explanation for what happened in the theater. This student had told Motley that she really did believe the boys had laughed. When Motley asked her why, she replied that if the boys hadn't laughed, if they had shown in any way that they had been touched, they would have been laughed at in turn. It was a mechanism that was probably the result of a need to survive. Motley asked her to say more and he wrote that she went silent and then said simply that it was so tough out there that you weren't allowed to be sad.

In time, I would learn to do the digging too. I mean, in my interviews. But with Motley everything became easier after we had slept together. Where did I find the courage, and, more than that, the sense of freedom to become this new person with him? I don't believe it had anything to do with America; it had more to do with a sense I had of myself as a person finding a new footing. I was away from the habits of my youth and my upbringing. I had wandered out. And now it was as if I was free to choose an identity that was more suited to me. I chose a bolder self. When Motley asked me when I would be able to go for lunch with him again, I smiled and pondered the right response. I wanted to go, of course. Professor Stenger's class met twice weekly. We could go after one of his classes.

Motley asked, "Tuesday or Thursday?"

"Both."

He smiled a deep, mysterious smile, then chuckled softly, and said, "Okay."

Those first weeks with Motley. Whether I was attending lectures with him, or going for walks in Piedmont Park, or even doing something silly like visiting a museum dedicated to Coca-Cola, I felt full of energy. It was as if I were running on a dirt road toward an open field, soft sunlight warming my back, the taste of fresh-cut sugarcane on my tongue. Or the taste of jaggery, which I had often seen being prepared in wide shallow pans over roadside fires in Khewali. Yes, that was it. In my imagination, I had taken Motley and placed him in the remembered landscape of my childhood. But that is how natural it felt for me to be with him: it was as though he had been there forever in my past and it was always just the two of us. All my friends, including Lena and Renu, but also others like Piyush, accepted Motley in our circle.

As we were so often seen together, they invited him to all the parties. In turn, he had them over for meals he cooked on Thursday nights. Stirring a giant pot with one hand while with the other he tipped a bottle in his mouth. A warmth in the press of bodies in the room, Erykah Badu and Tracy Chapman playing on the stereo, and then, right there in the middle of the packed room, if two or three people decided to start dancing the music would switch to Prince and Michael Jackson. And, always, before the night ended, Barry White's "Can't Get Enough of Your Love, Babe."

I had made the discovery that to be with a lover erases the *presence* of what had been in the heart before: only rarely during that entire time was I reminded of my earlier life with Ranjit. When Motley stepped into my life, the effect was startling. Even the possibility of what had been there with Ranjit—the existential fact of my married days—somehow grew remote and receded in time. It grew small like a tree or a bush on the far horizon from which I was traveling away in a fast-moving car. Yes, I would now and then archly invoke the past—"the ex liked this fruit, and that is why I avoid it now"—but only to set it more firmly in the distance. Except that now suddenly there was traffic between the past and the present. Had it not been for Motley, I would not have remembered what I once valued with Ranjit and then fought so hard to forget. I'm thinking of the moments when being with Motley produced an ache in my limbs and in my heart, such that I feared my core was melting, and, once or twice, other memories returned. There was a power outage on our street in Patna one night. Ranjit and I had stepped out of our apartment to get some air. At the corner in a pool of blue light stood an ice cream cart, and we stopped to buy a chocolate bar. We kept walking a few more minutes till we reached the edge of the market. A flower stall was lit up as if for a wedding. How did these people have electricity, Ranjit wanted to know. These shopkeepers were all aware that he was a journalist and there was a lot of banter. In the end, the flower seller either forced Ranjit to buy a jasmine garland for me or maybe Ranjit paid for it after haggling about the price. I braided the jasmine in my hair. When we were back home, groping in the dark staircase for the banister, Ranjit buried his nose in my hair and his invisible hand found my breast. The half-forgotten smell of crushed jasmine on my bed that night flooded my nostrils when Motley turned me on my stomach and I had my face buried in the pillow.

———————

In November, during the weekend of my birthday, we drove in Motley's car to Savannah. I had never stayed in a bed-and-breakfast before. The room was quaint and elegant, and when we were woken early by a thumping against our wall because the couple in the next room was having sex, my first thought was that Motley shouldn't have wasted so much money. I was annoyed but then I started giggling. There was so much noise, and so close to our heads, that I whispered to Motley that I wanted him inside me. He laughed and then began to kiss and touch me. The racket near our heads continued unabated and we laughed at the absurdity of our situation. But we were also being turned on by it, at least in my case. At first we tried to be quiet and then we didn't care. Later, we put on some clothes and drove out to the nearly deserted beach, where we strolled for an hour. I told Motley that my father might have called to wish me happy birthday. Lena, my roommate, would probably be in her lab. And my father would have tried again. I said that my father would be concerned upon not finding me; when I returned to the apartment, there would be his voice on the answering machine. Motley suggested I call my father from a pay phone there in Savannah. But I explained that I had no idea how many quarters such a call would require. A single call to India could end up costing up to five dollars if it went beyond a couple minutes. What I didn't tell Motley was that I had not mentioned him to my father and I didn't want to lie to him, or at least not yet, about where I was that day and who I was with.

For the rest of my time at Emory, Motley was in my life every day and night and then, when we received our degrees, he was offered a job as a managing editor at a newspaper in faraway Rochester, Minnesota. He wanted me to come with him and this idea, which did tempt me more than a little, plunged me into a crisis. I wasn't going to repeat what had happened before in my life; I wasn't going to move for anyone. We were having breakfast when he said gently that I could fly out with him to help choose an apartment. I think he was surprised by the sudden and decisive firmness of my reply. Motley had an impressive face, the flat plane of his cheekbones pierced by the sharp cuts that were his eyes, and he let a tear roll down his face. I didn't want to be reminded of my past. I said to Motley that we would always remain in each other's lives as friends but I wouldn't move from Atlanta. I had already worked as an intern at CNN for a semester and my bosses had told me I could find employment there. My father was all alone in India, I told Motley, but I had left him behind so that I could follow my dream of becoming a journalist.

I think Motley understood what I was saying. He was moving away to cold Minnesota because he had to support his mother and sisters. He started clowning. *Man, we is tropical. I'm frightened of snow.* And yet, a hollowness entered my heart the week before he left and neither he nor I would stop crying before we went to sleep in each other's arms. One night, he brought home a video of a film called *Mississippi Masala.* In the movie, a Black man played by Denzel Washington is in love with a girl called Mina, who is of Indian origin. Her family is part of the mass of Indians kicked out by Idi Amin from Uganda. Now they are in a town in Mississippi running a motel. The Indians are hostile to the idea of Mina being in a relationship with a Black man. Motley put the video on pause. Although he was smiling, I knew that he was serious when he asked me, "Is that why you don't want to come with me to Minnesota, honey?"

But he knew that I had my own reasons.

I drove Motley to the airport on the day he was leaving. I was sad, of course, and so was Motley, but he was trying too hard to crack jokes. We had breakfast in one of the airport restaurants—framed photographs on the walls of football players and airmen—although

I hardly ate anything other than the hash browns on my plate. Motley kept up a steady stream of wry observations about the people around us while I slipped deeper into silence. What was he even saying that morning? I don't remember. I only remember the futile smiles and his glances. We went to the departure gate. I asked myself if I could say to him, "Will you just shut up for a minute? This is breaking my heart." I was angry with him but maybe I was angry with myself: I was suddenly unsure whether I was doing the right thing. This relationship was ending. I was angry that this was the price I had to pay. At the gate, just before boarding, Motley said, "Say something, Jugs." And I barked a laugh and said something miserable and ugly like "You have been talking enough for both of us." Motley, bighearted Motley, enveloped me in a hug and simply said, "I am sorry. I will miss this tongue of yours." He kissed me on the forehead. As he was pulling away I reached up to pull him back and kissed him on the lips. Tears sprang to his eyes but he was already leaving and I turned away too, my eyes on the frayed carpet so that no one saw me crying.

Every day we talked. Some days, we fought because we were unhappy. After six months of doing this, we began to find a balance in our distance. We said to each other, over and over, that we were each other's best friends. Motley talked about all his new friends, including the women he was meeting, so that I wasn't kept in the dark or, and this might have been his thinking, that I wasn't surrounding myself with delusions. I always made it a point to be generous and encouraging.

All this time, it was true that I had still said nothing to my father about Motley. One day he called me from Rochester to ask if my father or anyone else could confirm a story about Martin Luther King during his visit to India. When introducing MLK to his class—this was at a school for Dalit students—the Marathi teacher had said that the civil rights leader was a fellow untouchable. It was said that MLK was shocked at first, but then saw the aptness of the comparison. Motley asked if I could check with my father if this was a factual account. I didn't dare. I didn't want the thought to enter my father's head, if and when he met Motley, that he was from an untouchable caste. I flinched from this recognition. I didn't believe in caste but here I was trying to protect my father from what I imagined was his bigotry. These thoughts created a disturbance in my mind. I was conscious that it might have pleased my father to know that I was loved and cared for by someone I also loved but I was frightened too. I was afraid that my father, despite his love for me, would say the wrong thing about Motley or his race and then my love for my father would diminish and this I would find intolerable. It was a weakness on my part, and I was aware of it, but I also felt helpless.

Unknown to my father, however, Motley had a role to play in his life. On my birthday, the first one after he had moved to Rochester, Motley sent me a care package. He must have made a list to demonstrate to me that he remembered what I liked. A handwritten letter affirming our friendship, a maroon cashmere cardigan, a tin of Darjeeling tea from Harney & Sons, a pack of peanut M&M's, a bar of 90 percent goat-milk soap, and, as a joke, three edible condoms. Included in the package was a book that Motley had bought from a secondhand bookstore in Duluth. The book was written by a British woman in the nineteen seventies. She had been married to a Bengali engineer and both were arrested on the charge of conspiring against the Indian state. The writer's name was Mary Tyler and she had been imprisoned for five years in Hazaribagh Jail in Bihar. My mother's side of the family had a small, crumbling house in Hazaribagh; my maternal grandfather once worked as a revenue official in that town. With my parents, I had visited Hazaribagh long ago for the wedding of a cousin who now lived in that house. I read the book with great interest because I'm always impressed when a writer brings alive on the page the reality I have seen with my own eyes. I don't mean anything like state power or oppression, though that might be true too, but things like the traffic on the streets, the heat and the dust, and the speech of the shopkeeper selling Disprin for your headache. Tyler had evoked for me the sights and smells of home, even though what she was describing was a prison and her characters were mostly wardens and prisoners. The book was about the seventies, and my father had spent a few days in prison during that time, and so, as soon as I had finished reading it, I wrapped it and mailed the package to Patna.

How long did it take for the book to reach my father? As on previous occasions when I sent him anything, I would worry for a few days, and then the worry would fade, and still later, after enough days had passed, I would start despairing. This time my father called to say that not only had he received Tyler's book but he had also already finished reading it. I asked him if he had liked the book. He said yes and then quickly added that it had given him an idea. If a foreigner could come to India and write a book about what it meant to have been alive at that time, why shouldn't he, my father, attempt to do the same? He would return to the book he had always wanted to write. A history of the youth movement in Bihar under Jayaprakash Narayan. A lot of time had passed since the seventies, he said, and of course a lot had changed. I asked him to give me an example of the changes that he had in mind, and he said that those who were in prison then were in power now. They were now sending others to prison.

A long time ago, he said, he had read a book by Somerset Maugham. In that novel, an American man had come to India and found a spiritual experience. My father said he should have begun work on his own book back in the seventies, when he had read that novel.

Had he had a deep spiritual experience?

My question gave him pause. He said mysteriously that there had been awakenings. Did I know that Gandhi had come to Motihari, the town near our village, to launch his satyagraha and had been detained by the British for a night. This happened long before his birth. But, he said, Gandhi had been a spiritual presence in his life. My father then began talking of his childhood, the terrible earthquake in the year before his birth. His journey to Patna to get an education. So much had changed in his lifetime. His friends in college, Krishna Murari and Ramdeo, had been in and out of political office during the decades that followed. Amitesh, my father's student, was a very powerful man in politics now. I asked my father if he had taught the man who was then the Chief Minister of Bihar. He said that Lalu Yadav didn't attend classes when he was a student, and so he couldn't recall if Lalu had ever sat in a class of his.

My father had read countless books in his life, why did this one touch him so deeply? Had there been other occasions when his life took a turn because of a book? A different, quite superficial and sentimental, thought had come into my head: Tyler's book had brought together the two men who mattered most to me. Motley had found the book and now it had reached my father. Was I becoming superstitious like my father by thinking that the universe was bringing these two men together, without their knowledge, at that present moment?

As if he had read my mind, my father said, "A thousand books, or over a lifetime, many thousands more. They can pass through your hands. But at the right time, one book finds you and changes you forever." He could have been also talking about people. I was thinking of Motley. A part of me acknowledged that I had come into contact, professionally but also personally, with so many men, and a few of them had shown some interest in knowing more about me, but I had turned away and then, maybe because it was indeed the right time to do so, I had let Motley enter my life.

My father was still speaking at the other end. He said, "I was reading this book you sent me and then a memory came to me. I remember like it was yesterday. The youth movement had started in March of that year. I'm talking of 1974. In early June, the students organized a march to the Raj Bhawan. That is where the Governor lived. I had gone there, as a guest, decades ago when I had first joined Patna College. This time I was a part of the march. The students had collected signatures from all over Bihar calling for the removal of the government in power. The demand was for fresh elections. The signatures were on sheets of paper that had been collected in huge bundles. Too many bundles for a rickshaw.

A truck was hired to carry the bundles of paper. The procession made its way from Gandhi Maidan to the Raj Bhawan. There were many leaders here in Patna that day. Jayaprakash Narayan submitted a memorandum to the Governor along with the bundles of paper that were hauled up the steps by a small group of students. Among those countless sheets of paper, one signature was also mine. That is the scene with which I will begin my book."

————

My father was a historian. He was committed to a narrative of what had occurred in the past. I liked to read him, even though his language was often stiff and academic, because he was concerned with the mystery of the past and connected it to our present. He had surprised me by telling me the story of his one signature among the truckload of papers presented to the Governor in Patna. It was almost as if he were writing like a journalist. I wasn't ready to see him as a fellow member of the tribe to which I belonged. This was because he remained professionally inclined to tell the story of progress, and to locate in its trajectory a narrative of greatness. Yes, small people also found a place in the story he was telling, but they were extras. I was one of them.

One day on the phone from India he read to me two paragraphs from his book. A group of protesters in the summer of 1974 clamber onto a ferry crossing the Ganga. In the middle of this throng, quiet and dignified, is the elderly leader Jayaprakash Narayan. When the ferryboat begins to move, the breeze is strong and JP wants to find a more sheltered place on the deck. When he comes around to the back, where the tea stall is located, he is offered a chair where a man and his daughter are sitting. JP asks the girl how old she is and what it is that she is reading. She says she is nine and she is reading an Amar Chitra Katha comic about the life of Rabindranath Tagore.

When my father read out this part to me, I interrupted him. I pointed out that I used to have that book—and then I asked if that girl was me. He said yes and then went on reading to me.

The girl shyly shows JP the cover of her comic book. The leader compliments the girl on her choice of reading material. He asks her if she knows that Tagore's poems were chosen by two countries for their national anthems. She says no, she doesn't. JP smiles and tells the girl, although the young students crowded around him are his true audience, that it is an irony of history that the poet who thought nationalism was an evil epidemic, a force that had divided humanity and caused so much suffering through wars, should be the person whose compositions were adopted as the national anthems of both India and Bangladesh.

For many years that followed, the writing of his book absorbed my father's energies. He didn't write every day, he told me, but his diary was always beside his bed. It became routine for him to read a paragraph or two when I called him every month. The men he had known during the Emergency, and those youth leaders who had been in jail during that period, were now in power. The story of these men—there were no women among them—that was the history lesson my father was offering to his imagined reader. He was describing a conflict: there was a true sense of empowerment among the lower castes but the men from those castes who had found political power were often thuggish and even feudal. My father was harsh with Lalu Yadav, who was now the Chief Minister and amassing a huge personal fortune, but he was kinder to his old friend Ramdeo Manjhi. I didn't argue with him, accepting whatever judgments he had formed. My heart was thirsty for any scrap my father shared unguardedly about himself. I caught a few glimpses of my mother and, here and there, mention of my own professional life, but it was all written from a kind of scholarly distance. When I heard his words, I discovered that what they recalled wasn't my life but, instead, the past when we were together: from halfway across the planet, my father was calling me back, even if momentarily, to a life we had shared. His need, and my guilt at having abandoned him, these were the twin axes of the story I was telling in my head. The rest was peripheral.

To put it another way, the content of what my father was reading to me didn't matter. Our lived experiences—no, my mother and I—were spectral beings haunting the margins. There was more in his memoir about the manufacture of jute in his village and the role it played in British India than there was about my jaundice when I was seven. And yet I know, of course, that he loved me more than any miserable length of jute. Even in those mentions of professional achievements which earned my father's attention, I could hardly recognize myself. For instance, in the paragraphs in which he had described my visit to the Martin Luther King memorial in Atlanta. The report had been broadcast on CNN on MLK Day. As a new CNN bureau had just been opened in India, my story got a lot of play. It began with a shot of Mahatma Gandhi's statue in the King Center and showed footage of MLK's visit to the Gandhi memorial in Delhi thirty-five years earlier. ("To other nations I may go as a tourist. To India I go as a pilgrim.") The only detail that had snagged my father's interest in my report was a photograph he had seen in my footage of Dr. King removing his shoes at Rajghat. It had impressed him that a foreigner had followed an Indian tradition that showed respect to sacred spaces.

There was no mention in the book of my marriage to a rapist.

My father's memoir was never published. The rejections left him without any anxiety or bitterness and this did not cease to amaze me. Then, just before the Olympics were to take place in Atlanta, he said on the phone that he would like to come for a visit. "I will see the city where you live and I would also like to show my book to a few American publishers." A pause. "I could stress the connection between Mahatma Gandhi and Martin Luther King. What do you think?"

My heart sank. The possibility of his finding a publisher here in America was even more remote than it had been in India. I didn't know what to say. He had tried to tell the story of our nation at a point in time; but the story he was really telling was about the deaths of his parents. He didn't know this, however, and I couldn't say it to him. Out of the simplicity of his heart my father said, "I remember the report you did on Martin Luther King's visit to India. Why don't you do a report on Jayaprakash Narayan in America? He can be just an example. You can have me as someone who speaks about the youth movement in Bihar." Again, a moment's silent pause. I had been unable to say anything. He went on, "There were so many Indian leaders who studied in the United States. Babasaheb Ambedkar, for instance. He was at Columbia University. Ambedkar's fiftieth death anniversary is coming up in December." I told my father, laughing, that he was talking like a television producer. He laughed, too. Then, I said, "The city will be crowded during the Olympics. Roads will be blocked. It will be chaotic. When the Games are over, you come here and we can take a tour of all that has been built new."

During the Games, a bomb exploded in Centennial Olympic Park. I was at the CNN Center and I heard my colleague in the next cubicle shout, "Oh my God." I got up to look at the monitor. A woman was dead, impaled in the head by a nail, and then they said that a Turkish cameraman had suffered a heart attack and died. When it was morning in India, I called my father to give him the news. He said, "We took the right decision." He spoke as if he and I were aware that the bombing was going to happen and had subsequently made the right choice. He arrived in Atlanta two months later. All his life in India, my father had traveled by train. It was unsettling for him, and in the beginning maybe even shocking, that when I had come to see him in India, I had taken a flight from Delhi to Patna. After I landed in India, he would have preferred that I board a train for the twelve- to fifteen-hour ride home. He might have added that it would be good for me to see the country again, but what he really meant to say was that it was important to save money.

I was glad he had flown to Atlanta. It still felt like summer and my father enjoyed eating the sweet and heavy Georgia peaches with vanilla ice cream from the nearby dairy. His observations were full of wonder. "There must be minerals in the soil or they use a superior fertilizer to produce fruit so good. What do you think?" He didn't ever again mention wanting to be interviewed on any show or getting my help finding him a publisher for his book. I felt relieved, and also guilty. And, more than anything else, his silence made me think that he wasn't as simpleminded as I had assumed. He was sensitive and had seen my awkwardness as a kind of refusal. And he had stepped away, graciously and kindly, so that I wasn't awkward anymore. He had felt the need to visit me, having insisted on paying for the airfare himself, and now sat at a wooden table at the Holy Cow Organic Dairy on my street praising the miracle of mulch.

One Thursday afternoon during his visit, I was going to drive out to Riverdale to interview doctors and nurses about a patient who was suffering from dementia. I mentioned this to my father when we were having lunch. The patient who interested me was a retired schoolteacher. He was aware of his memory fading and also of a decline in visual perception. In response to his deteriorating condition, he had begun drawing maps. The maps he drew were highly intricate attempts to preserve the past: his memory of the design of his home, the school where he had taught for thirty-two years, the streets around the home where he had lived with his wife in Athens, Georgia. After finishing lunch, I went to my room to change. When I came out, my father looked up from the sofa and told me cheerfully that he had drawn a map of our village, Khewali.

I looked at it. It was a pencil drawing on the back of a sheet where I had noted the phone number of a local museum. I was unable to smile in return because I was wondering if my father thought he was losing his memory.

Or, worse, if he really *was* losing his memory.

I said, encouragingly, without even having had time to orient myself within the space of the map, "Well, looks like you seem to remember everything."

He was smiling. He said, "The X is our home."

I looked closely and found the X. The long rectangle of the shed in front where the animals were kept. And it helped when I saw the pond and then the temple. These were familiar landmarks. My eye returned to the pond and I saw that he had drawn the champa tree whose flowers used to fall in the water. I used to wonder as a child if the fish thought someone had dropped food when the flowers fell.

I could make out trees in the lower right-hand corner. The rosewood trees lining both sides of the path—on the route my father had taken as a boy to the middle school—led to the tarred road where one could get a bus. I told him that I had recognized those trees. This pleased him. Pointing with his pencil, he showed me the flour mill on the left, the tightly packed huts of the daily-wage laborers who mostly belonged to the *chamar* caste. On the right, close to the top, the rectangle that represented the landlord Ram Kinkar's home. My father had drawn lines across all the patches of land that were cultivated for crops.

Going back to the X, I saw that he had drawn a series of spikes next to the house.

"Oh," he said, in response to my question, "that is the bamboo grove next to the shed where the cattle are kept."

But I didn't remember the grove or on the opposite side of the road a clump of trees. I also saw that he had left the fields on the left without the lines. Had he forgotten about them? I was now looking at the map a bit more critically. Where was the tailor shop? Or the post office that had been there ever since I was in my teens? No sign also of the small store that sold provisions, including spices and grains, and, in recent years, other things like flashlights and batteries and now the prepaid recharge cards for mobile phones. I didn't ask my father about these missing pieces because I saw at once that he had gone back to his childhood. He had drawn from memory a remembered village. It was a perfect representation but an outdated one.

———

The living room in my apartment was divided from the dining area by a four-feet-high wooden construction that had drawers for cutlery and utensils on the side facing the kitchen and bookshelves on the other side, where I kept my books and alongside them a few photographs and stones and seashells. There was a photograph of my parents there, an early photograph showing them sitting on the lawns of Bankipore Club, colored lights around them, at a reception for a wedding. I had found the five-by-seven print in my mother's album during one of my visits and brought it back with me to Atlanta. Next to that photograph was another framed photograph. This one was of Motley and me beside Lake Lanier. The picture had been taken by his newspaper's staff cameraman, Chip Striker. Motley had his arm around me and I was laughing, and, in the distance, there was a boat that was about to enter my left ear if I didn't move. Motley and Chip were going there for a story and Motley had asked me to tag along. I felt bad; I had to take sick leave from my work. The story that Motley was filing was an unhappy one. A four-year-old boy had drowned in the lake and his father had dived in to find him but somehow failed to come back. While Motley and Chip went to talk to the police and medical authorities, I sat at a bar near the water's edge, shielded from the summer sun by a huge orange and blue umbrella. Chip took the photo when they came back to pick me up. The wide edge of the umbrella is visible in the photograph. Motley is wearing a white cotton shirt with pale green dots, and a soft collar that cannot hide his strong neck. I have sunglasses covering my eyes, but my mouth is open and my teeth are showing because Motley has said something funny. My father must have seen the photograph but he didn't ask me about it and so we passed twenty days of the thirty-one days of his trip without having once spoken about Motley.

I was in my teens when I once heard my father telling our dinner guests, maybe it was Mani Uncle and someone else, my mother was there at the table too, of course, that Nehru had loved Edwina Mountbatten. At the final reception for the Mountbattens before they left India, Nehru had given an after-dinner speech. My father had quoted Nehru's words ("The gods or some good fairy gave you beauty and high intelligence, and grace and charm and vitality . . .") so that he too was delivering an after-dinner speech for his own guests. And I had received through his words the lesson that love exists between people but is only rarely acknowledged: it is given expression, if at all, perhaps only as regret. I couldn't have shaped this lesson in so many words but that is the principal emotion I appear to have absorbed from that evening.

I couldn't talk to my father about what he had meant. Even during this visit, there was a practiced, even unconscious, reticence on so many subjects. There were times, however, when I felt that my father was offering me pages from his memoir. On one occasion, driving back from CVS, where we had gone to buy him an elastic bandage for his swollen ankle, my father started on a story about his friend Ramdeo. He had written about Ramdeo in his book, he said. There was something special that Ramdeo had done after he got his first ministerial post. Unlike the upper-caste politicians, he hadn't gone to a temple to make a show of thanking God. Instead, he had gone to a village near Barachetti to put a garland around the neck of a man whose name was Dashrath Manjhi. Dashrath had been born in 1929. An ordinary villager who had accomplished an extraordinary feat: over the course of twenty-two years, Manjhi had carved a road through a stone mountain, a distance of over a hundred meters, using only a hammer and a chisel.

"Do you know why Dashrath Manjhi undertook this task?"

I said I didn't. I hadn't even heard his name.

"His wife fell down on the mountainside and there was no way to take her to town," my father said with great emotion. I glanced at him to see if he was crying. "No one would help. So he decided to cut the mountain in half."

My father went on like this. He spoke as if he were reading out a Wikipedia entry. But he was my father and I was moved by what he was saying. He was sitting in my car and telling me a story about the triumph of the oppressed. But the pain I felt deep in my heart came from the sense that my father was telling me that he had loved my mother. When he was in the thick of his description, I wanted to stop him and tell him how much I had loved Motley and still did.

Then there was the time when I was taking my father to an Indian restaurant called Mitali for dinner. The restaurant was located off the Buford Highway, which was the route I took to get from work to my condo in Doraville. I pointed out the immigrant businesses (Chinese, Mexican, Indian) and said something about people working hard to find prosperity. My father affected an austere tone and said that wealth is a mirage. He asked if I was aware that his former student Amitesh Sinha was now a junior minister in the central government in Delhi. I said I was. I had seen a news report when he visited Washington. *India's state minister for finance Amitesh Sinha meeting the U.S. Secretary of Labor, Robert Reich, and the discussion of a new India–U.S. deal affecting pharmaceuticals, agricultural machinery, intellectual property, diamonds, spices, mineral fuels, H-1B visas.* A tall Indian man in a black sherwani next to a short, bearded man in a suit and tie. What had I thought when I had seen the photograph? I had thought, not without pathos, of my father as a marginal man. The men he had taught, and had once wielded influence over, had now claimed power. They affected the lives of millions of people, even the destiny of an entire nation.

I asked, gently, "Do you ever see or talk to Amitesh Sinha?"

Too quickly, and with a poisoned bitterness, my father said, "He is a crook."

We parked and began walking to the place where we were going to eat. The fresh air energized my father. There were people on the sidewalks, shoppers and diners. It was a lovely evening, balmy and scented with a feeling of leisure. My father returned to the theme of politicians. As if to tell me that knowledge will always triumph over power, and that language is not a slave to any sovereign, he became satirical, sounding more amused than bitter. He was speaking in Hindi, which he knew no one around us would understand, and his voice grew louder as if he were onstage. It was as if he had become a satirical poet whose performance he had watched during his early days in Patna, reciting lines at a *kavi sammelan* in front of an enthralled and laughing audience.

"I have come to Bihar after hearing the call of the people. How politicians hear the call of the people, this is a trade secret and cannot be shared. The call of the people is sometimes like the bleating of a lamb. The lamb is calling for its mother but it is the wolf who arrives instead. Even if the lamb stays silent, the wolf comes and asks, *Did you call me?* The lamb says, *No, I didn't even open my mouth.* The wolf says, *In that case I must have heard your heart's call.*"

The food was excellent. We ordered only vegetarian dishes because my father had given up meat some years ago. I had also found that vegetarian items were always better prepared in Indian restaurants. I could manage meat dishes well at home. Here we ate mattar-paneer, fried okra in mustard sauce, a cauliflower dish that my father especially liked, and, over his protests that we were squandering money, I also told the Nepali waiter to get us malai-kofta and dal makhani. It was the dal that my father blamed later, the item that had tipped us into wasteful excess, after we had returned home and my father, unspeaking and expressionless, rushed to the bathroom. He came to me after fifteen minutes with his trousers and underwear bunched up in his hands.

He said, "Can you put soap in your washing machine? I had some trouble."

There had been an accident, and my nostrils caught the smell of shit. I tried to take the clothes from him but he wouldn't let go and so I turned the knob to hot and poured the detergent into the machine and waited for him to lean over and lower his clothes away from view as if he were dropping them into a deep well.

———

On the twenty-first day of my father's stay, a Thursday, Motley called. He said, "Jugs, I have a plan. Hear me out first."

He was in Baltimore, visiting his mother. But the following day he was going to fly to Atlanta. He had booked two rooms in a motel in Savannah, a room with two beds for my father and me and another room with a single bed for himself. I was to pick him up from the airport and we would, the three of us, drive to Savannah. Motley chuckled in the silence. "I'm calling to ask what kind of food your pops would most enjoy. I'm about to make dinner reservations."

"When did you buy your ticket to Atlanta?"

"Maybe a month ago, I think?"

"So, before my father even got here?"

"That's right. Are you mad?"

"No, of course not. Thank you. But I'm paying for the hotel."

"You don't have to."

"I want to."

"Okay."

"Maybe Southern?"

"What's that?"

"Oh, the food we should offer my father. A peach cobbler, for sure."

I told my father that my friend Motley was coming and that we were going to Savannah. I pointed at the photo on the bookshelf. Yes, yes, my father said agreeably. Did he sense my joy? I was smiling but careful not to show my excitement. At Hartsfield airport, however, I grew nervous. For so long I had tried to be loyal to my father, wanting to shield him from the actuality of Motley. After Ranjit was gone, my father must have thought of me as a widow. Maybe this thought was merely in my head. I was like a nun, a nun devoted just to the church, and that church was my father. But perhaps I was the only one who was worried. Motley gave me a hug and then shook hands with my father, who smiled in return. As we drove out of the city, Motley took on the role of tour guide, pointing out places to my father and delivering brief commentary. I had printed the directions from MapQuest, but I got distracted and took the wrong exit. I thought we were completely lost in inner-city Atlanta but Motley recognized the place. He said to my father, "I once wrote a news report about that building and then that one across the street."

He was pointing to a five-story-high building, dilapidated and dark, with a dull brick façade. On the other side stood a yellow structure, which was in better condition but it was clear that it was a warren of tiny apartments. Motley said to my father, "Something terrible happened here, sixteen, seventeen years ago. Someone was killing Black children here in Atlanta. About two dozen of them disappeared one by one. Sir, have you read the writer James Baldwin?"

I had read Baldwin, but my father hadn't. He hadn't even heard the name. He shook his head and Motley said, "Baldwin was a famous Black writer. Back when the children were dying, he came down to Atlanta to write about them in *Playboy* magazine." This time he looked at me to check if it was okay that he had mentioned *Playboy*, but the name probably meant nothing to my father. Or if it did, he didn't show it.

Baldwin died in 1987. At that time Motley was interning at a newspaper while still in school. The paper's editor sent him to do a story on those families that had faced the terrible loss of their children. Motley had spent days visiting the buildings near where we had parked.

When we got back on the highway, my father asked Motley whether the police had found the killer.

"Yes and no," Motley replied, and it occurred to me that my father probably hadn't heard that expression before either.

A man had been arrested, Motley said, but his connection to the murders was never clear. The accused man certainly couldn't be linked to all the deaths and disappearances. Making his voice go all professorial and sounding more like a public speaker, Motley said that Baldwin's own report tried to draw attention not to the deaths but to the lives of Black folk, and the violence and neglect that often afflicted them. My father was absorbing all this knowledge and said nothing.

When we had gone farther, Motley broke the silence again. He was making an effort, I could see that. A warm feeling of love washed over me. Motley was riding shotgun, my father associating the act of sitting at the back with privilege and comfort. I would have felt awkward even patting Motley's arm in appreciation while my father could see us. Two unmarried people exchanging gestures that would have struck him as intimate. Such was my naïveté. I kept my eyes on the road.

"You have taught people all your life," Motley said to my father. "I think you will like this story about Baldwin."

The tale that he embarked upon began with an introduction to the history of the Rosenbergs—Julius and Ethel Rosenberg, who were communists, and convicted of helping pass American nuclear secrets to the Soviet Union. The Rosenbergs were executed for their alleged crimes. The electric chair. They left behind two sons, small boys, one aged ten and other maybe seven or eight. This happened during the height of Cold War paranoia and extreme distrust of anyone with leftist sympathies. The injustice done to Ethel Rosenberg was especially wrong. She was most probably entirely guiltless. But there she was, dead, the papers reporting that she was given five electric shocks and smoke had risen from her charred flesh. The reason why he was telling the story, Motley explained, was that the Rosenberg boys were then adopted by a family friend whose name was Abel Meeropol. And Abel Meeropol, Motley said, after my father had asked him to repeat the name, was also the man who was James Baldwin's teacher when Baldwin was in school. Before his death, Meeropol wrote a letter to his former pupil, who was now a famous writer. Meeropol had never forgotten the small boy with big eyes. In particular, he remembered one incident. Meeropol had asked each boy in his class to step up to the blackboard and describe a scene from nature. Young James had chosen a winter scene in the country and the phrase he had used and which the teacher hadn't forgotten even after all these years was "the houses in their little white overcoats."

"Isn't that remarkable?" Motley asked my father, half-turning in his seat, even though it was difficult for him to do so.

"Yes," my father replied. And then added, "We talk of teachers influencing their students but, of course, students influence their teachers too."

"Isn't *that* right? That's the truth!" Motley said, nodding gravely, as if my father had said something profound. I looked at my father in the rearview mirror: he had been listening to Motley's account with great interest. I felt at that moment that I could tell him at some point about Motley and me, and that it would be all right.

After a while, a comfortable silence grew in the car. And then it was my father's turn to tell a story.

"My friend Mani Shanker was driving in his car near Jamshedpur. His wife and two young daughters were with him. They stopped near a bridge and walked down to the river. The younger daughter was standing on a rock when her foot slipped. She said, Papa. And Mani reached out for her in the rushing water. Neither of them knew how to swim. And, unfortunately, Mani's wife didn't know how to drive their car. She walked with the surviving daughter for miles until she reached a phone. I was sitting down to eat when her call came. By the time I got there it was evening and the police had recovered the bodies. I was the one who gave fire to my friend's funeral pyre. Jugnu's mother said to Mani's wife that they should come and live with us for a while but she refused. Jugnu was three years old at that time. For the next four or five years, I always sent money for the surviving girl's education. She is doing very well now. But what I have admired the most is that Mani's wife went through teacher's training and then became a teacher so that she could support herself as well as her daughter. Education saved her and her family. And she learned to drive too."

I had known about the death of my father's friend. This was because a black-and-white photograph taken in a studio with the two young men dressed in graduation robes hung in my father's study. I wasn't aware of these other details. I had met the daughter, her name was Shobha and she worked as a lawyer in Ranchi, but I had never known that my father had supported her studies.

Motley was new to all of this, of course, and my father was taken aback a bit by his question. "Were you and your friend Mani political allies?"

"No," my father said, shaking his head. And because that was inadequate as a reply he said, "We had come as students from the village to the city. We had helped each other out, and shared things too."

There was a silent gap now in the conversation.

Then my father added, "Poverty was our politics, if you can call it that. We were poor. It bound us together."

Again, Motley was nodding his head.

My father sighed and said, "Mani Shanker was a good singer."

Motley and I stayed silent. A memory came to me from afar of an afternoon in Patna. I was alone in the bedroom in Patna where my parents slept. I must have been five. Was this during the summer holidays? I looked at the photograph of my father, his chin raised, and standing next to him Mani Uncle, who had been dead for some time now. I tried to imagine the worst thing that could happen to me. I told myself that both men in the photograph had died. My mother too. They had been pulled into a whirlpool in a river. My parents were dead and I was an orphan. That is why I was alone in my room. I had moved myself to tears and then I was full of sobs. But soon enough, suspicious of what I was asking my imagination to do, I had stopped and considered the excitement and the fear I had forced myself to feel. No doubt I was too young to understand this pantomime of sorrow but when exactly did I cease engaging in these rehearsals? We were now driving through the Georgia countryside, passing billboards for Bible worship and churches, and smaller signs outside little farm stands announcing sales of strawberries and peaches. I was suddenly back in the moment when my father had called to tell me about my mother's death. The shock had been real and unexpected. The news had left me feeling abandoned and alone on the shore of a desolate white and gray salt plain of grief, yes, but it had also given me this deep and irrational desire to know in advance when my other, living parent would die and the exact manner of his death.

I glanced up in the rearview mirror at my father. He was looking at the back of Motley's head. He said, "The poorest of the poor
in India are the untouchables, the Dalits. Gandhiji called them
Harijans. Compared to them, Mani and I, upper-caste men, were
like millionaires. The difference is that striking. Do you follow
what I am saying? I had a friend in college who was from a caste
that is so poor that its members are called rat eaters. My friend's
name is Ramdeo. He is a well-known political leader these days. I
want to tell you a story.

"Twenty years ago, I went to his rural constituency to campaign
for him in the elections. His opponent was an upper-caste man
named Brijmohan Singh. Brijmohan was a landlord. One of his
sharecroppers was a low-caste man, a *chamar* whose family had
traditionally skinned dead animals and made leather goods. This
sharecropper asked Brijmohan for some payment or a larger share
of his produce, I don't quite recall the exact details. But listen to
the part that I remember well." (Motley now half-turned in his seat
again to look at my father.) "First, Brijmohan asked his men to beat
up the poor sharecropper. He was a young man, strong and resil-
ient. He had a bit of an idea of the world outside the village. During the harvest season he had once journeyed as a migrant worker
to Punjab. Brijmohan had wanted the matter ended quickly and so
he got the man beaten. This young man's name was Bhikhna. The
beating resulted in a broken left arm for Bhikhna. He was told that
the next time both his arms would be broken.

"When his arm had healed, Bhikhna stole a pair of bullocks
from Brijmohan's farm and drove them through the night to a
trader who put them on a truck and sent them to a market town
called Siwan. With the money in his pocket, Bhikhna returned in
the morning to the village and told his wife to tie up one change of
clothes in a bundle and come with him. They walked out of their
village, which is also my friend Ramdeo's village, and they waited
for a bus on the highway. The highway is called National Highway 83, and they were waiting there when a white Ambassador
stopped near them. Bhikhna asked his wife to run away and hide in

the sugarcane fields. He said he would come and find her. And then he waited for the man who had come out of the white Ambassador. It was Dubey, the manager of Brijmohan's farm. Dubey put out his hand and asked for the money that had been given in exchange for the stolen cattle. When Bhikhna reached in his pocket for the cash, Dubey shot him in the chest twice. They found the wife and killed her too. Before shooting Bhikhna's wife, they handed her a country-made pistol and, grasping her hand, they made her shoot the pistol in the air. The police were given this pistol as evidence. Bhikhna had stolen from Brijmohan, they claimed in their version of the story, and his wife tried to kill Brijmohan when he asked for his money. That was the end of the story. This was the man that, just two years after the incident, Ramdeo defeated in the election."

After a pause, Motley said to me, "Jugs, man, you are from the badlands. I'm never going to mess with you."

We had been driving for two hours. I saw a sign for a rest stop and asked aloud if we should pause in our journey. Motley said he wanted coffee. When I crossed into the right lane and began to slow down, a truck drew out from behind me, its horns blasting. My indicator was flashing, and I had every right to start lowering my speed. I gave the truck driver the finger but I was rattled. In the tense silence, my father, who had said nothing to me in the previous weeks about the photograph in my living room of Motley and me, now spoke up awkwardly. "It is not really badlands. You and Jugnu must come to Bihar. I will be your guide there."

After parking the car, I told my father and Motley to go in while I looked in my bag for a couple of things I needed. When I found my pocketbook and stepped inside the rest stop, I had the unexpected pleasure of seeing the two men I loved going together into the men's room to relieve themselves, one man bulky and protective, holding the door open for the other who was old and limping slightly.

———

My father didn't come back to America after that visit. When I urged him to make the trip, he would always have an excuse. The weather wasn't right; the exchange rate was likely to improve next season; he didn't like the way his ankles swelled up during the flight; it would be easier, he would say, if I came to Patna instead. Luckily for me, I could go to India for work. For the previous few years, the bureau in New Delhi had been producing reports that were broadcast worldwide. I only worked on features about the southern states in the U.S., but after a few years had passed, my boss, whose claim to fame was that she regularly jogged with Jane Fonda, said to me that I should look into connecting more actively with the Indian bureau. I was now an American citizen and I could cover stories on the subcontinent. As I was distracted and didn't plan early, I missed the opportunity to do a story when India and Pakistan celebrated their fifty years of independence in 1997. But two years later, when there was a discussion on international coverage at the year's end, a global roundup, someone brought up a cyclone that had hit Odisha on India's eastern coast.

"A warning about climate change," my producer, Terrence Laffey, said. "In a few years, the rising waters will drown Bangladesh." Laffey's office had Dylan posters and a guitar in it; he always used the word *riff* when he meant *write*. Everyone around the table was listening to him with concerned expressions on their faces. Laffey looked at me with his gray eyes, and I saw an opening. It was a good idea, I conceded, but we could do better. The Kargil War had just been fought between India and Pakistan that summer, and I said that the enmity between the two nuclear-armed neighbors posed an even more immediate threat to the world. Could I go and interview the women widowed in the Kargil War between the two countries?

It was a selfish argument that I had presented: it allowed me to travel to India. A team from Delhi flew with me to Patna. After putting down my bags at my father's house and sharing a meal with him, I picked up my team from a hotel near Gandhi Maidan and we went in a hired SUV to a small town that was an hour away. We were going to meet Rajkumari Devi, the young widow of Raghubar Prasad, a soldier from the 1 Bihar Regiment killed on Jubar Hill. Rajkumari was a slight woman, shivering in the cold, with steel in her voice. Speaking to the camera she said that the government had erected a memorial to her martyred husband at the town's only crossroad but, she added, they had spelled his name wrong. Raghubar had been turned into Raghubir. She went on. Perhaps they had got her name wrong too. All the promises that had been made to her, that she would be given a new ration card that would allow her to get food grains at subsidized rates, had not materialized. It is possible, she said, they had sent it to the wrong woman. She had received an initial amount of money that she had used to cremate her husband's mutilated body and then to pay the rent on the room she and her one-year-old child were living in. A man had given his life for the country, and just because he was dead, did people in power think they could lie to his family members?

I liked Rajkumari's anger. It freed her from the helplessness that could be projected onto her, and I suspected it freed me from my own helplessness too, from my inability to be able to do anything concrete to get her immediate assistance. Over the next ten days, we interviewed twenty more such women. Driving up and down the Grand Trunk Road, visiting villages and small towns where poor peasant families had lost sons, husbands, fathers. Women would press into my hands the letters their husbands had written before their deaths, and I found the hope and despair in their lines powerful and moving. Dead men were speaking to me from the other side. They asked about harvests, the recurring cough afflicting the eldest daughter, the father-in-law's gallbladder, the money sent the previous week, their plans for the younger sister's wedding, the complaints received of fights with the elder brother's wife, the child who had been born three months back, the photograph received of the baby. And when my team and I crossed over

261

to Pakistan on the Delhi-Lahore bus we met widows, fewer in number because of problems of access, who shared similar stories of how a war fought to the north had blasted apart their lives and their hopes for the future.

Our first visit was to a village outside Lahore where Nasreen, a local journalist in her early twenties, brought us to a buffalo shed. The ground was muddy and there was smoke from a dung fire. I recognized the smell of burning dried dung from my own visits to my father's village. Two men, one old and bearded and the other young and bearded, appeared and spoke with the journalist in Punjabi. They looked toward the hut behind them and appeared concerned. We might well have been a medical team visiting a patient who was too weak to come out. Then the journalist explained the problem. The widow we had come to meet couldn't step outdoors on account of purdah, and the cameraman, because he was male, wasn't allowed to step into the hut. Kirk, my cameraman, worked out a plan with Nasreen. He put the camera on a tripod and fiddled with the settings. All that Nasreen had to do was point it at the interviewee and press a red button. I held the mic in my hand and had headphones wrapped over my head.

The girl we were interviewing—she couldn't have been more than eighteen or nineteen—sat on the floor. Her name was Rabiya Sheikh. Rabiya wouldn't get up from where she sat. I asked her to move closer to the door so that we would have light falling on her face. It was awkward, and sad, to ask her any questions. She told us that she had learned of her husband's death (she called it *shahadat*, or martyrdom) when an army jeep came with a letter for her brother-in-law. Rabiya's husband, Sikander, had written the letter a few hours before his death. He had written that Captain Altamash would give the family 2300 rupees; Sikander's mobile phone as well as his clothes were to be given to his elder brother; if the army or government gave any money, it was to be used to buy more buffalo so that Rabiya would not know any want; at the coming Eid festival, the family was to donate a certain amount to the local mosque in his memory. At the end, I had Nasreen tell

Rabiya in Punjabi that we had come from across the border. We had met widows of the war there. Did Rabiya have any words for those women?

Rabiya looked at the light falling on the ground through the open door and refused to say anything for the longest time. Nasreen repeated my question but Rabiya was unyielding. For the first time, she looked up at the camera and said, "Why should I say anything to those who took away my husband?" She had lost enough, a lot had been taken from her, and I just didn't feel it was my job or my place to also take away her hatred of those she saw as her enemy.

Then, on to a town called Kasur, to the south of Lahore, to meet the widow of a pilot, Mushtaq Jani, who had been killed when his plane was hit by a missile fired by the Indians. Were the women on one side of the border different from those on the other side? No. I felt this very strongly when I heard Aliya, a solemn and beautiful woman, who was seated on a sofa across from us, say that she wanted to be alone with her four-year-old son and not have much to do with anyone in her family other than her old mother. I asked her why. Aliya said that she had gone to a cousin's wedding recently and her aunt had pulled away the bridal clothes. She didn't want Aliya's touch to pass any bad luck to the cousin who was about to get married. When she entered a room, voices fell silent and people looked at her with suspicion. I wanted to know if Aliya could share any of her husband's letters. She looked down at her hands, which were clasped together, thin, elegant fingers, a small emerald ring on the ring finger on her left hand. She said no. And then said that she could share the last letter she had written to Mushtaq, which was returned to her from his squadron with a few of his belongings. The early evening light was slanting through the window. Kirk kept the camera running. Aliya returned to the place on the sofa where she had been seated earlier and handed me the letter in a pale yellow envelope.

She looked away from me, unable perhaps to bear a stranger's eye on what was intimate and now so laden with grief. I felt I was trespassing when I unfolded the page, but I read out for the camera the following lines near the end—before I returned it to her, my voice shaking with tears: "Let's sit on that ugly, cramped balcony again and drink tea and watch the squadron's planes taking off. I want to hear you sing your favorite song. Come back in one piece. Life is so difficult. It was bearable with you around."

From Lahore, we flew to Karachi for more interviews, and from Karachi we caught a flight to London, and after a three-hour layover, another plane to Atlanta. Onboard the London flight, I watched the new Austin Powers movie, but when I was drifting off to a fitful sleep in the plane's darkened cabin, my thoughts went back to a woman's question in Karachi. Her name was Qaiser and she was the thirty-one-year-old widow of subedar Muhammad Zaman, killed when an Indian grenade exploded near him during close fighting on a hill in Batalik. Qaiser was a middle school teacher. We met her in the school where she taught. In the empty classroom, despite the camera and lights trained on her, she appeared calm and unfazed. We were talking and Qaiser asked me in an even voice if I was married and if my husband was alive. I was caught by surprise. I told her I didn't have a husband anymore.

Qaiser misunderstood me. She said, "I'm sorry. Did your husband die in the war too?"

"No," I said. "I'm divorced."

"Does your former husband live in America?"

Yes, the thought did cross my head: I'm the interviewer; I'm the one supposed to be asking questions. Your job is to answer them. But I liked her air of calm, which was more like a feeling of confidence, and I was curious where she would go with this exchange. Suddenly, I felt we were equals and I wanted to be open with her.

"No, he is in India. He is in jail."

Qaiser now looked at the camera and then back at me.

Since she wasn't saying anything, I said, "He committed a crime. But we need not waste time on him. Let's return to what we were discussing. Do you have anything to say to Indian women who have lost their husbands in the war?"

"Yes," Qaiser said in a level voice. "I feel I know you because your suffering must be like mine. In the time since my husband attained martyrdom, I have been thankful to Allah that I have my job. I love my students and I haven't made the mistake of trusting anything that the politicians have said to me. They have done nothing. I have the support of my two sisters but, in the end, I have learned to be strong by myself. I never want to think I have shed my tears in vain."

When she was done, I tried to hide my own tears from her. And then we hugged. Later, on the plane, I thought that I hadn't been entirely accurate in my answer to her question. Ranjit had come out of prison recently. He had served a little over nine years in jail. My father had sent me this news. I heard it with mixed feelings. More than anything else, the news made me wish I knew where Sudha was, and I hoped to God that she was well. I was aware that when I had answered Qaiser in the way I did, I was acknowledging something that I hadn't done in front of others ever before. I was telling myself that I needn't hide the fact that the crime belonged not in any way to me but to the man who had committed it. I had nothing to hide.

Husbands. Fathers. How they had populated the world of the stories I covered! I approached such men as enigmas. Each woman I met during my reportage defined herself in relation to these figures in her life, even though sometimes she succeeded in eking out her own independence. In fact, I felt that even when such women appeared most attached to the men around them, and their situations had turned dire because of the condition of the world, I understood that it was the woman who was strong and keeping the world together. She was able to do this because she clutched with one hand the flag of her freedom. During one of my subsequent visits to India, this would have been in 2005 or 2006, I was driving with my team on a highway in Kashmir. It was narrow and we were behind an army convoy. The highway branched away to the right, and our hired car turned left onto a gravel road. No longer were we forced to look at tense soldiers standing upright in those trucks, black bandannas tied on their heads, gun barrels poking out from under the green tarp flapping in the wind around them. Instead, there were doves bathing in the dirt and beyond them apple and almond trees.

Earlier that same day we had interviewed a woman who had founded an organization for the young men who had been disappeared by the government. We had collected footage of the unmarked graves. There were a lot of dead in Kashmir but now, in the village where we were headed, close to the Pakistan border, we would be looking for someone who was still living. A woman named Saira who, when we arrived at her door, was hanging her children's laundry. She guessed right away that I was a journalist and that I was there to ask her about her husband, Tariq. Saira said her husband was at the police station and would be back soon.

Tariq's parents were from the same village. However, they had migrated to Pakistan around 1953 and Tariq had taken on Pakistani citizenship. He was Saira's cousin, the son of her mother's first cousin, and they saw each other frequently, or at least when the two countries weren't fighting a war. In 1987, Saira and Tariq got married. According to the police, because Tariq was Pakistani, he was a terrorist and he was to be taken to the border to be deported the next morning.

While we waited, a family of ducks emerged from the apple orchard. And behind the drying laundry, we could see sunflowers. Saira brought salted tea for me and for my camerawoman, a young Bangladeshi American named Amina Aktar. And then Saira said that her son was learning English. The boy was only five. He was asked to show us his notebook, where he had copied down a poem by Longfellow. By the time Tariq returned from the police station, Saira had prepared mutton yakhni for us, fragrant with cardamom and ginger in a spicy yogurt sauce. The rice she served had saffron in it. We were all sitting on carpets and while we ate Amina shot some footage of us from the window. I watched Tariq eating his meal hungrily, and wondered whether he was thinking that he was eating one of his last meals in his home. This terrible thought made me appreciate the taste of what I was eating even more. After lunch, I asked Amina to choose a place in the apple orchard where I could interview Saira and Tariq sitting together. I asked them about their married life so far, their young son, and what the future held for them now. Tariq kept saying that he had put his faith in God. He would grant wisdom to our fellow creatures and then the couple would find relief. But Saira would have none of this. She wanted to know why in a poor country where there were few or no resources for education and health care, the government was spending so much on an army that behaved in all matters like an army of occupation. They were taking her husband away the next day, she said, and she would be alone now, bringing up her son by herself. How was the security of the nation strengthened by throwing out of the country a man who grew apples?

While Saira was speaking, and we were recording her words, I wondered whether she was helping her cause by being so critical. But later, in the car, I began to think that Tariq hardly mattered. The strength I had seen in Saira, the boldness of her statements, came from the fact that she had chosen a separation from that fake husband that was the State. She had declared her independence from the pretense of protection that the government offered her. Saira knew that the armed State was a bullying husband, and all its laws were nothing but a system of excuses to support its abusive behavior. She was not going to be a silent and submissive victim.

After the show aired, I called Saira from Atlanta. I still had her number in my notebook. She laughed when I said my name. The whole village, she said, had watched the report on Kashmir. She appreciated what I had said about Tariq's cruel deportation and, laughing again, the fact that I had said she was a good cook. I asked Saira if Tariq was going to be allowed to come back. No, she said. Then she said that she was planning to sell the orchard and the house. She would move to Pakistan with her son. Providing information that she hadn't shared before, Saira said that on her father's side she had a cousin who, like me, was a television journalist. He lived in Srinagar with his family. This cousin was a man of influence and a real crook and, Saira suspected, he had prompted the police to deport Tariq. This journalist-cousin had his eye on Saira's property. But she had seen through his designs and was waiting to discover whether she could find a better buyer. Then she said that she was glad I had called.

"You had liked this place when you visited, you looked really happy among my trees," Saira said, laughing. "You buy the apple orchard. I will give you the house very cheap. You can pay me in American dollars."

————

How much loss can a heart take, and what are the ways in which love outlasts loss? I had done stories on factories and fields, on hospitals and schools, but what I liked the most were stories about people, what brought them together and what pulled them apart.

Near the close of 2016, after that disastrous election, I flew from New York City to India. A colleague's daughter was getting married in Mumbai. Both bathrooms at the back on the Air India flight were out of order. The doors had *not working* stickers pasted over their metal handles. Identical stickers from different days stuck on top of earlier ones. In the op-ed that I had already begun to compose in my head, I was going to write that the bathroom doors were *festooned* with yellow stickers. The plane hadn't taken off yet from JFK; the bathrooms weren't working, and I felt I was already home. Even the blue carpets in the aisles exuded a fecal odor. The flight attendants, betraying a suspicious expertise in the situation, walked down the aisle with the nozzles of air fresheners aimed only inches from the floor. My neighbor in the next seat, a businessman from Surat, was amused by my agitation. He soothed me with the news that the previous month an Air India flight that had taken off from Mumbai for London was forced to return because a rat was racing up and down the length of the plane.

I wanted to breathe. From my handbag I extracted my notebook and wrote down what I was seeing and feeling, as if the tiny page that fitted into my palm were a window I could open. When I began to write I was struck by the absurdity of my situation. Here I was, an Indian living in the West, returning to India for a few days. How crude, how banal, to have become that person who complains loudly about the smell of shit. Trump had just the previous month been elected president and if I made demeaning comments about India, weren't newspaper readers in Mumbai and Delhi going to judge me harshly? I was sure that on Twitter a troll would provide a link to my op-ed and paste a picture of the White House underneath with the question: *Are you sure the smell isn't coming from there?*

The hotel in Mumbai, where the wedding was being held, faced the sea. The lounge had impossibly high ceilings that gave the plush interior a false sense of quiet. Young women in peacock-blue and orange saris stood behind the reception counter. The large glass windows framed a view of the swallowing darkness, but close by, where the land ended, there stretched an undulating, glittering necklace of white lights. The wedding guests, some of whom had traveled huge distances and were counting the time zones they had crossed, sat on sofas holding drinks in their hands. Two Arab men in their spotless white robes turned away from the check-in desk and regarded our group. Had they not seen all of this before? No doubt some of the gold on display on the bodies of my fellow guests had been purchased in Dubai and Abu Dhabi.

In this last month of the year, hordes of desis settled abroad returned to India and you could hear the twang of stretched-out Westernized syllables in upscale restaurants, chic boutiques, and colonial-era clubs. The talk was always the same. A mix of arrogance and condescension accompanied by an ability for unceasing wonder at how bad things were in some places. As it was, those who spoke in English in India generally spoke louder to their children, to waiters, and even to strangers, but the assault on the ears was especially painful when the face was brown and the accent was American. Despite my long years abroad, I hadn't acquired the accent yet. Still, it struck me that I had become one of those that

I had so far been railing against. Who was going to save me from such a crushing solitude?

A waiter came by with a tray filled with dainty little sandwiches and then a couple of minutes later another one stopped by to offer a colorful, thoroughly exotic description of something small and elegant looking at the end of a toothpick. The woman seated next to me was older than I was by at least two decades; from her air of reserve, I guessed that she was a teacher or a bureaucrat. At her request, a waiter brought her a pot of green tea and she sipped solemnly from a delicate china cup. I was drinking jalapeño margaritas and felt sociable enough to address my elderly neighbor. It turned out she was a doctor. She said her name was Ranjana Ghosal.

Did she live in Mumbai now?

"No," she said. "I live in a small town very far from here."

I asked her the town's name. She said, "You won't know the name. Khunti, it is close to Ranchi."

I heard the name and felt a loud drumbeat in my chest. Khunti was very close to the village where Sudha was from.

Ranjana Ghosal had been a doctor in that small town for fifty years. I asked her, sounding like a journalist, what had been the major changes during all the years she had lived in Khunti.

"You will hear many people who are sitting around us complaining that when they stepped out on the hotel's terrace they could not find a Wi-Fi connection. The trauma of bad connectivity in the jewelry market. That there is no HBO. Well, when I went to Khunti we were decades before the internet. Actually, there was no TV, and not even telephones for everyone. There was a telephone in the Civil Lines office. The particular distraction of watching sitcoms on TV wasn't to come until two decades later, although you could go to Ranchi to watch a movie in a theater. But where was the time to travel for an hour or more each way on the bus? We were in the middle of hills and iron ore mines. Thick sal forests surrounded us. I didn't own a car for a long time.

"To make matters worse, there was famine in nearby parts, in

Palamu, which gave an excuse for the government not to pay us on time. Salaries were delayed and the officials held up funds. I would have to use my own money, or borrow it, to buy what was needed in the clinic. Anything from a bar of Lifebuoy soap to penicillin for common infections. Or streptomycin for my tuberculosis patients. A life of scarcity. But there was one bit of pleasure in our lives, a nice thing to look forward to, and this was that we played badminton each evening. The subdivisional magistrate was a man in his late twenties named Kumar Raghuvansh. He was married and didn't have any children when we first met. This man and his wife were very kind to me. The badminton court was in the open, on a part of their three- or four-acre official compound. We played under lights with the magistrate's staff bringing us iced lemon or orange squash in the summer and milky tea with ginger and cardamom in the winter.

"A young Adivasi lecturer would come on weekends and after our badminton games we ate together. Chicken was cheaper there than in places like Patna. Fresh vegetables. We ate well. I liked this man, the Adivasi scholar, who was good at many languages and also played the flute. His name was Ram Naresh Nag. We fell in love and he and I got married. That was in 1971. Raghuvansh, the magistrate who had become our friend, was from a small royal family but he was committed to the people. At the time, Adivasis were displayed each year on Republic Day in Delhi as simple tribal folk with bows and arrows, the bare-chested aboriginal people who loved to sing and dance. Adivasis had their educated leaders even then; we didn't know about them, we were just privileged outsiders, *dikus*. But Raghuvansh was interested in the history of rebellion among the Adivasis and he was writing a biography of Birsa Munda, who had been hanged by the British. I liked to see the two of them working together. The magistrate's father had been the ruler of what was once a small principality under the British and his grandfather had attended Queen Victoria's coronation as her guest. He had gifted an elephant for the ceremony. You can see the giant, placid creature in the archival photographs of the royal event even if it is difficult to make out Raghuvansh's ancestor in the crowd. Birsa Munda was unknown to Indians at that time; now you find his portrait hanging in the halls of the Parliament in Delhi. That process of his discovery began in those years in Khunti when Raghuvansh would go into villages and examine the dusty government gazettes from decades ago to find out more about Birsa Munda and his fierce fight against the British."

The doctor described the collaboration between Ram Naresh and Raghuvansh on translations from Mundari and Santhali to Hindi or English. And on Sundays the drives in Raghuvansh's Ambassador for picnics to nearby falls—Dasham, Perwaghagh, Panchghagh—passing peacocks and surrounded by the noise of water falling on giant rocks.

"Your question was about what I remember of the past. And I don't know whether I'm answering your question. Do you want me to go on?"

"Yes," I replied. "Please, please go on." It wasn't the alcohol, I was convinced that it was her story, her voice, warm and steady like a candle flame on a still night, that kept my attention focused on what she was telling me.

"I said earlier that it took too much effort to drive all the way to Ranchi to watch a Hindi film. While that is true, we still made the trip on several occasions. When that happened, Ram would wait for us in Ranchi. Those were the years when Rajesh Khanna was the most popular actor in Bollywood. The driver and the magistrate sat in the front seat of the Ambassador; the magistrate's wife and I sat at the back. Ram would meet us at the cinema hall. We always ate aloo-chaat and drank Coca-Cola before the film started. Afterward, we went to a restaurant for dinner before driving back.

"Ram stayed in my flat after we got married. We had a civil ceremony. My mother wasn't opposed to my marrying an Adivasi but the rest of my family was. My two maternal uncles were angry with me. They saw the dark-skinned Adivasis and thought of them as savages. My father had died when I was young and these uncles had assumed charge. But my mother was financially independent; she taught in a school in Patna.

"Do you know what a softie is? There is a shop in Ranchi called Firayalal. It had a new machine for making softie ice cream. Ram, his friend Subhas, who was a teacher in Saraikela, and I went on two rickshaws to Firayalal to have softies after we got out of the magistrate's office. You wanted to know about the past. Well, there you have a little glimpse of what weddings were like in those days. We didn't have the money to meet like this in five-star hotels.

"The war with Pakistan happened, the war that led to the liberation of Bangladesh. I was asked to report to the army camp nearby where Pakistani prisoners of war were kept. It was winter. The prisoners were courteous and I had to do a quick medical examination to determine whether or not they needed treatment. Most of them only wanted to be able to make the announcement on radio that they were alive and well. The radio announcement was broadcast also from a loudspeaker on top of a pole in the field where the prisoners sat in the sun. The prisoners heard their own voices from the loudspeaker—name, father's name, name of village or town, regimental identification, and a short message about health and well-being—but I couldn't understand how the announcement was also reaching the families in Pakistan. Raghuvansh, the magistrate, assured me that it was."

———

The doctor had stopped speaking. A waiter in a maroon jacket had come to us to say that the party was moving outside to the pool. The two of us got up from our sofa. Despite her age, the doctor held herself erect as she walked ahead of me. Her hair was gathered in a small bun. I wondered what she was thinking. I had only just met her but I was taken with her. I was unaware just how this transition had happened but mentally I had put her among the old women from Bhopal who, during an earlier visit, I had seen protesting outside the Supreme Court in Delhi. They wanted justice from Union Carbide. There had been no cleanup even though three decades had passed since the gas leak; new generations of children were still being born with deformed limbs. These old women seemed to have their own minds, their own strength, they were not owned by any party or political group; they had taken what life had thrown at them, over many decades, and they had hoarded their tribulations, and used this startling inventory of defeats and small triumphs to remind themselves and others that they were survivors. Nothing would move them, and they wanted answers. At the backs of their minds, maybe there was also the thought that of course it could not be long before they would be dead and soon forgotten. And so, they were afraid of nothing.

When we stepped out, I saw that a raised platform, decorated with flowers, was in place at the near end of the pool. Drinks were being served by a bartender standing under a festive umbrella bedecked with ornate flowers made entirely of sequins. We walked over to the chairs at the other end of the pool. White lights glowed underwater while the breeze ruffled the pool's surface as if it were fur on an animal's back.

"What have you been drinking? I think I'll have one too."

The doctor took a sip of her jalapeño margarita. She smiled and nodded, and then looked around.

"Tell me," she said, "because you have lived both here and abroad. Do you think that because weddings in India take so long to complete—do you think that is the reason why marriages last here so long too? In the West people probably get married in an hour and then divorced in a week. Or that is what many of us believe here."

I laughed with her. And then she calmly, unaffectedly, went on with her story.

"Soon after I got married to Ram, a government order informed me that I had been transferred to Dhanbad. I didn't want to go. I had established myself in Khunti. The town was changing, growing fast, and I thought I was needed there anyway. I resigned from my government job and started my own practice in a rented room next to a machine parts and hardware store. Instead of calling the clinic Nursing Medical Home, Ram wanted me to call it Narsing Medical Home. Narsing is a Munda name popular among the Adivasis—it was also the name that had belonged to Ram's father. Ram was playful that way. He said that just because of the name my clinic would be liked among his people. I accepted his suggestion.

"My assistant at the government clinic agreed to work for me part-time. His job was to come in the evenings and serve as dispenser of medicine and blood tests. He was from Deoghar and his name was Adishankar. His wife had died recently and he had a little daughter. She came to the clinic with him and kept us amused, dancing the little filmi numbers, her hips moving this way and that. Adishankar was an efficient man, good at administering injections or swabs but also handy with tools. The table fan is making a ticking noise? Let Adishankar take a look! There is a water leak? Wait for Adishankar. If I rented a car, for myself or a patient, Adishankar was there as a driver. He had of course never owned a car, and he had never been employed as a driver before. Where had he learned to drive? I asked him but he just smiled.

"And I had a female nurse, who was Adivasi like Ram, and also like him a Christian convert. She has remained with me all these years, a small, hardworking woman, ten or twelve years younger than me. Her name is Maryam. Over the years, I began to think of her as my shadow. So many times, when I was delivering a baby, or performing a minor surgery, I felt that she knew exactly what I was going to do next.

"The story I want to tell you is about change, and the first inkling I got of it came from Maryam. She told me one morning that she had eaten a heavy meal the previous day. This was most probably in August or September in 1990. I remember that Rajiv Gandhi was the prime minister. He hadn't been killed in that bomb blast yet. I asked Maryam to tell me about the occasion for the feast. She said that her brother had become a Hindu at a ceremony organized by his employer. Everyone had been fed. There was a feast with rice, dal, two different vegetables. For dessert, sweet jalebis.

A priest had done a puja. Her brother had been given a new name. His name, which had been Peter, was now Ramsewak. Maryam began to laugh. She said that Peter's employer, Anil Sharma, had washed Peter's feet before the puja. The washing of the feet signified that after a long journey Peter had returned home: he wasn't a Christian anymore and was back to being a Hindu. It could be argued that the Adivasis had never really been Hindus, but politicians like Sharma had their theories.

"Peter now had three names. The name that the padre called him and which was on his ration card; the new name that the *diku* Sharma gave him; and his oldest name, his tribal name, Donka, that he had from his childhood. Maryam thought it was funny that all the four men who were converted were Anil Sharma's employees. Peter drove one of the two buses that Sharma owned; another, an Oraon man, was the cleaner on the other bus; and two others worked in Sharma's grocery store, Mata Top Quality Kirana.

"Long before Peter started working for him, Anil Sharma had come to my clinic. By the town's standards he was a prosperous man, but he had a rough look. His family owned a gas station in Jamshedpur, and his older brother was active in politics there. Sharma's two buses plied the route daily between Ranchi, Khunti, and Jamshedpur. When Sharma came to see me at the clinic the first time, he had in his hand what looked like a wad of raffle tickets. But no, he was collecting donations for our local Hanuman temple and for organizing devotional meetings during which the faithful would sing bhajans. He wrote out the amount you donated and gave it to you with a flourish that suggested you had bought a ticket to heaven.

"Sharma was chewing paan and wearing a yellow polyester shirt unbuttoned at the top. He implied, or did he say it more explicitly, that I had enough money to support the community because I had carried out abortions.

"But abortions had been legal for more than a decade! I don't think I pointed this out to Sharma in response. I guess I was numb with surprise or fright. A schoolteacher had recently come to me wanting an abortion because she said she had been raped by a colleague who taught physics at her school. She didn't want anyone to know. Had word got around? Did Sharma have something to do with what had happened to her? There was another case. A local railway official's wife, newly married, had also wanted an abortion. She said she would like to be able to tell her husband that she had suffered a miscarriage. I went ahead and did what she wanted.

"Now, Sharma was sitting in my clinic making what seemed like a veiled threat. I felt I was being blackmailed just because I wanted to protect my patients. I stayed quiet for a few seconds, but Sharma was already trying a different method of attack. He said he was sure that my husband, Ram, supported his church, that the local Christian church had a lovely, shining dome, and wouldn't it be nice if I also supported the house of worship of my own faith. The Christian church got money from Germany, from far-off United States, he said, how was Hinduism to survive without support either from outside or inside the country?

"I found Anil Sharma bullying and insulting. I don't think I had ever met anyone who inspired so much anger in me even when he hadn't said a word yet. I think it had to do with his brazenness. He was a rude and unsavory character. When he produced his badly printed pink ticket, I didn't want trouble and so I thought it better to pay a large amount and get rid of him. Our friend, the magistrate, was long gone. He had been promoted and had been given a desk job in Patna in the rural development department. I would have been ashamed to tell him what was happening in our town. Each Dussehra, I made the payment that Anil Sharma wanted and if there was some relief for me, it was that for several years, till Peter's death, Sharma didn't come to the clinic himself but sent Peter with that scrap of paper that looked like a raffle ticket and which I quickly threw away.

"Maryam and I had both thought it funny that Peter had to change his name. Maryam is nothing if not a practical person and she accepted what Peter had done. What she hadn't expected, and what surprised her, was how Peter himself would change. He was ambitious, he was making money from his driving, and he wanted to please Sharma. I was told that on the six- to eight-hour round trips on the bus each day, he would play for his passengers these cassettes of so-called holy men and women delivering fiery lectures on how Hindus had been crushed by Muslim invaders and their temples destroyed. Peter learned from these cassettes that after arriving on these shores the foreign missionaries had destroyed the culture of the Adivasi tribals by converting them to the Christian faith. His passengers heard these lectures too, and, whether they believed it or not, Peter told Anil Sharma repeatedly that he understood that his return to Hinduism was indeed a homecoming.

"During that time, there were riots in different parts of the country. There was trouble in Jamshedpur, and curfew was imposed in Ranchi, but we were left untouched.

"But the following year, during Holi, there was a clash in town. A group of youths in a car threw colored powder on strangers in a lane and shouted slogans that led to a fight. It was a scuffle between Hindus and Muslims and, as the fighting heated up through the day, Anil Sharma and his men got involved. Peter too. I should tell you that Peter wasn't religious at all. The devotional meetings and bhajans were not for him. He liked that he had influence, and he certainly wanted power. I'm sure he entered the fray that night in order to play a role in the violence and emerge victorious. Unfortunately, the scuffle took a bad turn. A Hindu man lost an eye. By that night, everyone was in a frenzy.

"I was told that Sharma was roaming the town in an open jeep haranguing small groups of Hindu youths to kill Muslims. An eye for an eye was the slogan now. Swords, spears, iron rods were put on display. The new magistrate, a young Sikh fellow, saw the conflict spilling out of control when Sharma's procession reached the Muslim area and the mob torched a police vehicle. The magistrate ordered the policemen to fire over the heads of the rioting mob. But a bullet found Peter. Overnight, he became a martyr.

"For Maryam, there was the pain and grief of losing her brother.

But what was a different kind of pain was that Peter was taken away from her and turned into a symbol. Despite the curfew, two men from Sharma's kirana store came to ask Maryam for a photograph of her brother. She gave it to them. In no time, the photograph had been enlarged, framed, and garlanded. In the Hanuman temple near the town's central chowk, the photograph sat on a wooden stool. Incense sticks lent the air a sickly-sweet odor. A Hindu shrine had sprung up around Peter's framed portrait and the police didn't dare remove it. Anil Sharma had a new loudspeaker installed over the temple and people sang bhajans. The state elections were still eight months away but people began talking about how Sharma would be the most popular candidate from the area. Just around then I began hearing from my husband's students that he would make a good rival candidate, but Ram dismissed the proposal. I hated the idea, sure that it would spell trouble."

––––––––

The groom's party was now entering the hotel. The doctor said that she would talk to me after we had witnessed the preliminary ceremony. We both moved with the crowd to greet the guests. A wide, curving ramp led from the pool to the path below, where the groom's party had gathered. The groom's name was Paritosh. He was seated on a horse, which stood at the bottom of the crowded ramp. A small stool with three steps had been placed by the animal's side but there was to be a wait as a few rituals needed to be performed. Paritosh worked for Google in San Francisco, where he presumably used a car instead of a horse. I assumed that his life was distant from the past in which anyone dressed in a knee-length sherwani and wore a bejeweled sword at the waist. But he now sat astride the horse with those trappings and a tall magenta turban on his head. Over his face fell a curtain of small white jasmine blossoms: the groom, like a woman lifting a veil in a Rajasthani miniature, parted the strings of jasmine every two minutes to acknowledge a friend or a family member. His teeth were perfectly white and the impression of his smile lingered under the jasmine.

Did the doctor guess what I was thinking? "Handsome boy," she said.

She was still looking at the groom. She added, "Ram used to say that the difference between Christians and Hindus is that while Christians put a Christmas tree in their homes, the Hindus plant one on a horse and bring it home to marry their daughter."

I said to Dr. Ghosal, "I would have enjoyed meeting Ram."

I spoke those words with great sincerity because I meant them. The doctor looked up at me, not out of surprise, but simply out of a sense of shared feeling, a feeling perhaps also of deep loss.

She said, "It is very crowded here. Let's go back and sit down."

Inside, in the lounge, the doctor began to speak again.

"Ram was a complicated man," she said. "I complained that the Adivasis were being fed lies by people like Anil Sharma who distributed cassettes that distorted history. Ram must have been concerned but he was quite calm about it. He said that his hero Birsa Munda had told his followers that the guns of the British police would turn to wood and their bullets become water. Were they not lies? There is no field of politics where truth is a given and everyone agrees on it. For their part, Birsa's followers believed that the authorities couldn't arrest Birsa. He would turn into a log. Even after his arrest, there were all sorts of rumors. That there was only a body of clay in the cell, Birsa had escaped and taken refuge in heaven.

"I guess Ram was saying one couldn't be fanatical about truth," the doctor said.

She went on, "I tried to argue with him. What about the conversions or counterconversions—were they not attempts to spread hate? Here again he appeared unperturbed. If a tribal man or woman saw reason to convert to Christianity, or, for that matter, to Hinduism, if that was what it was that Anil Sharma wanted him to do, Ram thought it was okay. Birsa too had converted to Christianity and then gone back to his traditional faith, worshipping his Bonga Buru, and even then, his method of preaching was what he had learned in the Christian missions. Birsa was also influenced by the Vaishnav preachers and wore a dhoti dyed in turmeric and the sacred thread worn by many Hindus. And, let's not forget he also attacked the priesthood of the tribal bongas.

"Ram's strategy was to always argue against a too rigid or what he called authoritarian definition of culture or history. In the public gatherings organized by newspapers or the district administration, he became a trickster figure embarrassing his opponents by pointing out how reality or our lived existence was so much richer than what their ideology dictated.

"Ram had enemies on all sides. Once, Maryam reported that during a meeting in town Anil Sharma's brother from Jamshedpur had pointed to Ram's picture in the newspaper and asked why the caption didn't say that this was the poisonous snake of the forest, the Nag or the King Cobra. I didn't tell Ram this. He lived in his own world. He was trying to teach his students, poor and from a background without books, with limited resources in a provincial college, the writings of philosophers like Edward Said and Michel Foucault. One summer he adapted, in both Hindi and Mundari, Hannah Arendt's *Eichmann in Jerusalem*. He was a great admirer of the novels of Albert Camus. I'm painting him as someone very serious. Ram would joke that he was exactly the kind of Adivasi that the government in Delhi wants to display on Republic Day. He would say, I'm a living, walking, talking, dancing stereotype. Ram loved the taste of *mahua* and would accept it at any hour of the day. And when he was really drunk, especially during festivals, he danced through the night.

"People have become more aware of their rights; but I wonder whether we know more of our own history. Once, at a gathering organized by a municipal councilor, Ram said that what had happened in the country during our first war of independence, in 1857, had been inverted in recent times in the drive to build a temple at Ayodhya. After Ram had presented this analysis, and was leaving the meeting, someone threw a brick at him. It hit his shoulder and I was just thankful it missed his head. I didn't look at the brick again but I was later told that these were special bricks with जय श्री राम written on them in Hindi. These bricks were headed to Ayodhya, where they would be used to build a Ram temple.

"I have told you so much," the doctor said. "I should stop now."

The mention of the brick thrown at her husband's head had an ominous ring to it. I said, "Doctor, if you don't mind me asking, how did Ram die?"

She looked at me. "We have been trained to talk about death, we are used to it," she said. "But I'm tired. Let's talk tomorrow." The wedding guests had free access to a yoga clinic in the morning and the doctor was planning to go to it. She said she would talk to me in the afternoon.

When I woke up in the morning, I was conscious that I had been dreaming. But I couldn't recall more than a detail or two. I was on a bus. There had been an accident on the road. I knew I was in India. While I was safe, maybe the bus or another vehicle had killed an animal. The passengers disembarked and there was a roadside dhaba nearby selling tea and sweets. Flies buzzed around the plates of sweets. I wanted to sip my tea but the milk had curdled and I threw it away.

With free time before me, I sat at my computer and searched for Ram Naresh Nag. I found a picture of him playing the flute. Then I saw a story with the headline ADIVASI SCHOLAR AND ACTIVIST MURDERED. I didn't feel like reading the story. The temptation was strong but I decided I would return to it after I had spoken to the doctor. A few seconds passed. I asked myself if I should search online for the doctor's name. I hesitated because while the doctor knew that I was a journalist I hadn't told her that I was already shaping a story about her in my head. She didn't know and most likely didn't even suspect that I was sitting in the hotel room contemplating searching online for the details of her life, which I would then make public.

Promptly at three, as we had decided, I saw the doctor coming toward me in the hotel's restaurant. She looked altered, as if she had aged more during the night. Maybe it was only tiredness owing to travel and the setting. I got up from my chair and asked her if she was well.

"No," she said plainly. "But here we are."

She asked for tea.

While she poured tea, a silence grew between us.

"Thank you for talking to me last night," I said to her after a while. "You were telling me about your husband when we parted."

"I remember," she said. "I was thinking all night about what I wanted to tell you. I'm not a writer. It is not always easy to line up the past so that it leads to the present."

I waited when she fell silent and then she spoke again after gathering her thoughts.

"When Ram died in March 1997, I kept doing my work at the clinic, even though I felt hollowed out, not just alone but also very old. For the first time in my life, I felt exhausted. Maryam was my big support, never shirking her duties, and yet finding the resources to attend to me too. There were other blows. Three years after my husband's death, Adishankar, my assistant, discovered that he had cancer. All those years of smoking. We had worked together for close to thirty years. I was stricken. His wife had long been dead and the daughter who had been his life had been married for a few years. I looked at the X-rays and the report he brought from the oncologist in Ranchi. It looked bad. One month, three months? I told him that he should rest at home. We would take care of things in the clinic and we would also take care of him. He fell at my feet, crying. I thought he was afraid of a painful death—who wouldn't be? But no, he was asking for forgiveness.

"I kept asking him what he wanted to apologize for, but for a long time I couldn't hear him above his crying.

"He said that some men had come to his house one night during Dussehra, back when Ram was still alive. They had taken him to the home of an inspector in the Home Guards. Anil Sharma was there too. They were waiting for him. The policeman asked Adishankar if he recognized Anil Sharma. Sharma was friendly at first. You do good work at the clinic, he said to Adishankar. You are going to get your daughter married off soon. If you need help, if you want to hire our guesthouse, let me know. We will give it to you cheaply.

"Adishankar said he stood with his hands folded. No, *maalik*, I don't need anything, sir.

"At which, Anil Sharma laughed. He said to Adishankar, But I need something from you.

"By now Adishankar had stopped crying. He could not meet my eyes. He still sat on the ground, and addressed my feet.

"Anil Sharma had said to him that he needed to discuss the matter of Ram Naresh Nag. Sharma told Adishankar that he needed to talk to Ram for ten minutes in private. He had tried, he said, but not succeeded. This talk was necessary. It was urgent.

"Sharma said, But you drive him sometimes from one place to another, don't you?

"Adishankar began wailing now, but I don't know whether I could even hear him above the thumping of my own heart. After all these months and years, I was finally learning how Ram died."

The doctor said she tried to come back to the present. "Why didn't you tell me, Adishankar? Why didn't you tell the police?

"He attempted to touch my feet again.

"Why? I must have been shouting by now. He looked at me for the first time. He said, *Bola ki hamari beti ko uttha lega. Hum ko phir khali uska nanga body dekhne ko milega.* They said they would take my daughter away. That the next time I saw her it would be her naked corpse I would be looking at.

"I didn't want to hear any more. I told Adishankar to go away."

———

"The very next day, the deputy superintendent of police and a magistrate went to Adishankar's home. He gave a sworn statement describing how he had gone late one evening to Anil Sharma's shop and told him, while buying a prepaid calling card, that the next morning at eight he was to drive my new car to Tamar. There was no further conversation.

"In the morning, Adishankar drove out with Ram. A few minutes after eight, just where the road splits left for Dasham Falls, two men stepped out on the road, waving down at the ground. Adishankar hadn't even come to a stop before they opened the doors and quickly got inside. One sat in the front and the other at the back. From what he heard the man in the backseat say, Adishankar could guess that the stranger was pointing a gun at Ram. The man in the front, maybe thirty-five years old, a *diku* with a light beard, slapped Adishankar.

"Drive, *haraami* bastard.

"They drove for five minutes before they asked Adishankar to stop and wait on the other side of the road for a bus that would bring him back to Khunti. Adishankar told the magistrate that he had taken the bus as directed and he had come to report the matter to me at the clinic.

"I should tell you what happened when Adishankar had made his sudden appearance that morning, looking wild-eyed, telling me how two strangers had taken Ram away. I called the superintendent of police, a young and decent man named Menon. He said he would alert the police at the checkpoints on all highways. He also sent me his official jeep to bring me to the police station. By the time I reached there, Menon and his team were getting ready to leave.

"Please wait here, Menon said to me. We have received some information. Would you like tea?

"I said I didn't want tea. I told Menon, You will have to take me with you. Please.

"Did we drive outside town for fifteen minutes? Twenty? The driver had switched on the siren in the jeep and I found the noise deafening. There was no conversation among the men. Then, a man seated in the back said, Yes, drive to the left. I can see it.

"I could see nothing. My car, which I had bought six months

earlier, was a red Maruti. The police jeep drew close to a car that was a mix of pale brown and gray. About twenty villagers stood nearby. Speaking either to me or to his constables, the superintendent of police said, *Dekhiye, metal bahut garam hoga.* The metal will be very hot.

"I'm a doctor. It seems I see death every day. But this was new to me. The glass on the windows of the car had exploded or melted, I don't know, and I was to believe that instead of a tall man with beautiful, nearly shoulder-length hair, the charred, unrecognizable skeleton inside was my husband. *No.* The police officer's hand was on my arm, but I only wanted to say *no.* Can you be sure? It was only a minute ago, well, just that morning that I had seen Ram wearing a light blue, half-sleeve shirt, and a navy blue vest. This sounds terrible but I thought they had set fire to a short Adivasi man—Mundas aren't tall, though Ram was. He also had lighter skin. How could Ram have shrunk like this? Instead of my red car there was this ash-brown thing—except that you could see flecks of still red paint in the front, especially in the middle of the hood.

"Everyone was standing back. In my mind, or maybe even out loud, I kept saying, No, no. Instead of this no, all the silent people around me were waiting for me to say yes and to make it all real for them. But does horror become real because you are told that they had locked the doors of the Maruti before throwing a burning rag in the fuel tank? No. It never became real to me. And it never became real enough for others either. So three years after the crime had been committed, on the basis of a dying man's confession, the government authorities arrested Anil Sharma. His lawyer argued that the case was baseless and, besides, his client was suffering from diabetes and should be released. Sharma was in prison for two months and then the government accepted defeat. No other witness would come forward; the police never found the men who had abducted Ram in the car and then murdered him; the defense produced witnesses who exonerated Sharma. Adishankar also died. During his last days, I took care of him—I was helped by his daughter, who had meant the world to him when he was alive."

The doctor was catching a flight to Delhi and then after spending two days there she was going to board a flight to Ranchi. I knew I would never see her ever again. She had been generous, extremely so, in talking to me, a stranger. Was I being vain in imagining that she had narrated her story to a journalist so that it could be shared with others? I waited another day. Then, sitting down at my computer, I searched online for her name. There was nothing except a link on the *Dainik Jagran* website, in the regional Jharkhand issue of the Hindi paper, a report from some years back. A small, not very consequential report, and yet, I felt it important to extend our conversation just a bit. Perhaps distance or time would provide a different conclusion to our story. To emphasize this point, I sent the doctor an email inquiring, in the manner of the conventional journalistic interviewer, whether she had any regrets about her past. I also asked her to comment on the newspaper report. I told her I would write a report called "Narsing Medical" about how a remote town fell under the sway of a violent and extremist way of thinking. I wasn't sure how good a correspondent she would be but after four days I saw her reply in my inbox.

Under the subject line Re: Narsing Medical, she had written, "I am happy to have had the chance to talk to you. In the normal course of my life, given the pace of work, and the wretched conditions in which people around me survived, it is impossible and even unnecessary to examine one's motives. I have not been a character in my story, but you made me see myself as one in what I was telling you.

"The news item you have mentioned refers to the death of a thirty-year-old woman in my clinic. It is accurate in telling us that she had lost a child in an accident at the Panchghagh Falls. What is its point? That a woman who had suffered a calamity was then not saved at my clinic? I cannot speculate on the motives. The reporter was searching for a cause.

"What he has missed is the extraordinary events that happened prior to the woman's tragic death. The woman's child was three years old. He fell into the water when his mother's foot slipped on a rock at the Panchghagh. The water moves very fast there. It was Christmas and so there was a big crowd at the waterfalls. But others got involved too. All along the narrow river, at regular intervals, ten or twelve men formed a slow-moving line, everyone joined by a rope they held in their hands, using their feet as net to catch the boy. They found the child's body, so that the parents' agony could find a resting place. Even in that short time, the river fish had already eaten his eyes and the father said that the boy's eyes had been received by the river goddess. I was just impressed that, long before the police could act, the people had got together and helped find the boy.

"The mother was brought to the clinic because she was in pain. She was clutching her stomach. Her brother felt that she had hurt herself during her fall. But the woman told me that this pain, nearly unbearable, had been with her for several days. The smallest pressure on her abdomen where the appendix is located made her cry out in pain. There was no time to lose. I asked Maryam to prepare her for surgery. But it was too late. Her appendix had already ruptured, the abdominal cavity was severely inflamed, and the infection had spread. We gave her antibiotics but to no avail. She was also anemic. A history of abdominal disorders as well as her recent attack of pneumonia suggested a weak immune system. I couldn't save her.

"I am a doctor. My job is to heal. What has perplexed me so much all my life as a healer is that I have seen the most violent, the most brutal people, I'm talking now of those who have the actual power, act as if they are the ones carrying the biggest wounds in their histories and in their hearts. Can you please explain this to me?

"When I look at these people, and some of our leaders are among them, I feel that theirs are wounds I can never heal because there is no medicine for bad faith. These are people who are lying to others, and they are also lying to themselves. No mirror in the world can show them their true face. And at the end of the day, this knowledge is the only medicine I now have.

"You have asked me if I have any regrets. In my professional life? No. In my personal life? Yes. I wish I could have saved Ram.

"Less than three years after Ram was killed, there were riots in Gujarat. Everyone knows of the two thousand Muslims murdered by mobs of zealots but there was a Hindu woman killed in the riots who has a near-sacred place in my heart. I read about her in the papers. Her name was Geetaben. She was lynched in Ahmedabad, her clothes torn off, her head bashed in with a brick. They did this to her because she was trying to defend her Muslim lover. They gave a Bharat Ratna award to the man who was Prime Minister at that time, and there were no awards for the dead woman, and, one could add, no help for her either. So, please, put that at the top of my list of regrets. I regret not being there, as a woman, as a citizen, as a Hindu, although I don't know what that means these days, to help Geetaben. I regret not having been Geetaben for Ram."

———————

Every time I went to India, I would buy a small gift for Motley. He appreciated anything I brought back for him, a cotton kurta, books, bowls carved from walnut wood. A sociologist I was interviewing once offered me tea whose delicate taste and light golden color appealed to me, and when I asked him about it he smiled and said it was Darjeeling tea from the Makaibari estate. I asked where I could buy this tea, and he gave me a phone number, and that evening I picked up two bags from a home in New Friends Colony, one for Motley and one for me. That might have been the same visit during which I met the doctor at the wedding in Mumbai. She had revealed so much to me about herself, and our society, but I hadn't had the courage to ask her if she had ever come across a woman named Sudha Mintz. I had always wanted to find Sudha, to learn what shape her life had taken; I had been trained as a journalist, I could look harder, but I was aware that she had taken steps to shield herself from Ranjit and me. I didn't want to intrude on her privacy. I never saw Sudha again and perhaps that is the reason why I never published the doctor's story.

One of the last stories I did cover in India before the start of the pandemic was in 2018. A left-wing journalist named Gauri Lankesh had been killed outside her house in Bengaluru in September 2017. This murder was one in a chain of killings of progressive intellectuals. The case hadn't yet come to trial, though several arrests had been made. All the arrests pointed to the involvement of fundamentalist Hindu groups. On the anniversary of Lankesh's killing, my report was broadcast on CNN. On this visit, I bought a sweater for Motley—and for Sandra, a girlfriend that he had acquired, I bought a stylish blouse made of Mysore silk. Sandra was a middle school teacher in Minneapolis. Motley had been dating her for a few months now, and everything he had said suggested that she was a warm and loving person. But this time, Motley called to say that maybe he could send the blouse back. Would I be offended?

I knew it wasn't the blouse. I waited. His voice came on again.

"It wasn't working out," he said. "But it wasn't me who ended it."

"Was it your snoring?" I laughed.

"I don't know. She said she was finding it hard to stay committed in the relationship."

Two months later, I drove up to Baltimore to celebrate Thanksgiving with Motley and his sisters. I had made a reservation at a Days Inn, which I then had to cancel because the whole family protested that there was enough room at home. I saw immediately that Motley was unwell. He said he was stressed at work and one night during the summer had woken up with the feeling that his eyes were leaking blood. He had still been with Sandra then. On that night, she was asleep next to him, and he shook her awake. She said his eyeballs were swollen and bloodshot, and she dressed and took him to the emergency room. While these symptoms were new to Motley, at the hospital the Nigerian doctor proposed that the underlying condition was perhaps common among the males in Motley's family. Motley responded that there were no other males in his family. The doctor shrugged and asked if other people in his family had diabetes. Motley admitted that he had heard talk of that disease when he was growing up. And now during Thanksgiving, Motley's old mother, seated on a sofa with a blanket spread over her lap and her legs, said that her husband's heart disease had been a result of diabetes. Loose lips wet with spit, but sounding like a police detective in a potboiler, Motley's mother said, "Diabetes was the killer, it was the killer in this house."

Earlier that year, in April, a story I had done on medical malpractice in Georgia and Alabama was nominated for a Peabody Award. The story was called "Unhealthy Hospitals." The fact that I had spoken to so many doctors, and discussed conditions affecting neglected Black populations, gave Motley an excuse to treat me as an expert. He would call and say things like "Earlier I had put on weight. But now, I'm losing a lot. Are they also giving me medicines for weight loss? Can you shine some light on this?"

I indulged him. We were no longer talking about pleasure, all our talk now was about reducing pain. Motley said he was seeing a good doctor, he swore he was telling me the truth, but if that was true why was he asking me these questions. I took his calls seriously because I saw that he was sick. And probably lonely, which I was too. But a definite change had come over him quickly; there had been a swift decline, and I wanted to be there for him. In recent years, I had occasionally gone back to thinking, with a faint hope, that maybe we would get together again. I had managed to articulate this thought to myself even when he was with Sandra. With his illness, however, that thought had left me. There had been a shift. I had become more conscious of our mortality, and this realization had freed me. I was no longer going to be a partner; I could only be a caregiver. And so it happened that when I got a call the following spring, at 7:00 a.m. on May 9, 2019, from Motley's sister, telling me that Motley had suffered a stroke, I said I would fly to Minnesota to be with him.

Motley was in the hospital but his sister arranged for the key to be left for me at the front desk in his apartment building on South Chicago Avenue in Minneapolis. That same morning, his sister had flown back to Baltimore. The entire left side of Motley's body was immobilized and his smile drooped on that side. In a week's time, he would receive physical therapy but right now he had a catheter attached to his body. I called my father from the hospital, to tell him that I was in Minnesota taking care of Motley. I didn't need to tell him that I was looking after him as an old friend, a loyal and caring friend, and not as a lover. This thought made way for another in my head. Did my father feel that I should come to India and look after him instead? If he did, he didn't say anything. He asked one or two questions about Motley and then fell silent. After a while, trying to change the topic, he said that all the talk in India, and I think he meant all the talk on his television set, was about the elections. Modi was going to win. I ended the conversation quickly, telling my father again that I was calling from a hospital. I didn't think I needed to ponder the question that now, late in his life, my father was feeling victorious because a propagandist turned prime minister was returning to power.

Motley's apartment was on the sixth floor, overlooking the busy street. When I woke up each morning, I drove his car over to the nearby lake for a walk. My breakfast was simple: cream of wheat with raisins and a banana. For at least half an hour, I read alone. I was reading an environmental history of China, from the ancient period to the present. When I left for the hospital, I took with me a novel about two teenage girls who are friends until their friendship falls apart. I was alert to the fragility of relationships and our deep yearning for companionship. Motley would often listen to podcasts, he told me, but when I was there, I read aloud from the *Star Tribune* to him. He said he liked to listen to me reading. I was using most of my vacation days during this visit, ten days at a stretch.

It was true that I had, years ago, made love to that body, skin slick with sweat and semen, but now it was as if that body, and mine, had changed completely. I would place my palm on Motley's forehead, as if I was checking to see if he had a fever, and I murmured sweet nothings to him. I caressed his cheeks and, bending, kissed his head. He had acquired a new, medicinal scent but his skin, warm against my lips, brought me comfort. I would put my hand in his hand, and he would wrap his swollen fingers around mine; if he dozed, I felt his fingers jerk and pull on mine and my heart would race in a panic because I was afraid that he was maybe drowning in a dream. When I held a cup of water with a straw near his cracked lips, or wiped down his face and neck with a warm wet towel, I also thought of my father's body, a body close to death. Is this odd, I asked myself, and answered no. I felt close to Motley, caring for him, and I felt close to my father while providing care to my friend. Not once did I say anything about this to either man, but I believed that at some level my actions, which I thought of rather nobly as my service, would be translated into feeling and communicated to one, if not both, of them.

There were repeated assurances by the doctors that Motley would recover from the stroke. There were complications, it wasn't only the heart, the kidneys got affected too. I flew to Minneapolis and took turns with his sisters sitting next to his bed. I chose the night hours to sit vigil. He faded in and out of consciousness. I'd begin to say something hopeful—*Don't give up, you will get better*—but inevitably my voice cracked and I would start sobbing. Then, all I could say was *I love you, I love you so much*. His lips would move then, he would try to say shush, a sibilant whistle emerged from his tired mouth, and he would say with great effort, *Love, love*. Just that one word, nothing else, as if it would take too much scarce energy to say those other smaller words, *I, you*. Motley died before the end of the year. His sisters brought him to Baltimore for the burial and his mom saw her son getting put in the ground next to his father. I felt odd because I was the only one there who wasn't a family member or a childhood friend. None of his girlfriends had shown up, perhaps they were not even informed or invited. This meant that some of the older relatives—men as well as women—stared at me. I stared back.

Months later, a friend posted a poem by Yevgeny Yevtushenko on Facebook, writing that in this year of losses this was the poem she had put on her refrigerator. "When people die, they do not die alone. / They die along with their first kiss, first combat. / They take away their first day in the snow . . . / All gone, all gone—there's just no way to stop it." These were the lines that opened the flood-gates. It was a short poem, maybe twenty lines, and I read those lines again and again. I thought of Motley and our first kiss at the Blind Pig. The feel of his fingers entwined in mine, his deep and extraordinary kindness toward all who came in contact with him. Which made me think also, of course, of all the others who were dying around us, alone. All those irreplaceable, incomparable lives, and my father among them. My father remembered Nehru standing on an open jeep, throwing back to the crowd the garlands made of roses and marigolds he had been given upon arrival at the Patna airport. My maternal uncle's body returned to the family in a casket packed with ice after bullets had raked his body in the fight with Chinese forces. Three years later, my birth. What memories did my father have of that little occasion? I didn't know and now I couldn't ask. That was what the poet meant, that no person died alone, all his memories died with him.

A year before his death, my father surprised me by saying that one day when he was in the Kali temple near his college, the Ganga just a stone's throw away, he had felt a presence beside him. It was his sister, not the one who had lived, surviving until old age, but Laali, dead at two after being licked by a fox. She was just a spirit and yet, remarkably, she had aged and was now an old woman. Her face was in the dark. However, her identity was unmistakable. He spoke confidently to her, "Laali, is that you? I know it is you. We are meeting in God's temple. Be at peace." He asked her without speaking what it was that she wanted from him and whether she was okay. She said in a clear voice that he heard inside him, close to his thudding heart, that she was fine but she missed him, her elder brother. Later, he saw her in his dreams, a gentle, benign presence. Laali was a tall woman, tall like Madhubala in the movies.

Motley came to me in my dreams. Once, in deep December or early January, he appeared dressed for summer. He had gone out on a boat and caught a large spotted bass. When he showed the fish to me, he smiled and asked if I had any regret that I hadn't caught any fish. He didn't ask the question unkindly but I knew in my dream that he was asking about something else. Of all the dreams that I remember or have forgotten, I have often returned to this one.

Four more months would pass and I would have an answer for Motley's question. *I have thought about it, Motley, and I don't think I need to ponder it anymore. I don't have any regrets about that relationship because I don't know what would have happened if we had been together. This is something I'm certain about—you had needed the job, and I had needed mine, and I was never going to move to a new place without any friend or support. But, because of what happened recently, I know what I really regret. My father has died and on the day that he died he called me on my phone. He was not in the habit of ever calling me. That was my job—calling him and asking him how he was. I heard the phone ringing and was tired and I didn't get up. I said to myself that it could well be a sales call. If it was my father, I said to myself, he would leave me a message and I would call him back when I woke up. And I did call him back but it was too late. I got the boy, who gave me the news that my father was dead. But here's the thing, Motley. My father has never, not once, come in my dreams to ask if I regretted not answering the phone when he called. Nevertheless, Motley, my dearest friend, I regret that you are dead. In May this year the police murdered a man near the street in Minneapolis on which you had lived. A white police officer pinned down a Black man on the street, he put his knee on the man's neck for nine minutes and twenty-nine seconds. The man lost consciousness and was soon dead. I'm telling you this because when I think of all the people, especially Black people, killed by the police in this country, my own little regrets fade in importance. Once I start thinking in those terms, I go back to my father's death. No, wait. You remember the video I once sent you of the Indian man, a fifty-seven-year-old grandfather named Sureshbhai Patel, who was slammed on the ground by two cops in Alabama? The man had arrived in America just the week before. He was going to spend time with his grandson, a toddler. The cops came looking for him— he was taking a walk near his son's house, looking curiously at the houses as any newcomer might—because someone had called to say that they had seen a suspicious man in the area. "A skinny Black man wearing a tobog- gan."* Hey buddy. Where do you live? Where you going? *The video from the police car's dashboard camera looked like a home video from the early seventies: fuzzy houses in the background, a sky that is a satu- rated green, camphorweed lining the sidewalk, a thin man with his arms twisted behind him and then within seconds thrown face-first onto the hard ground.* You wanna stand up? No? You okay? Can you stand up? You understand English? No? *Sureshbhai Patel was paralyzed after that assault by the cops, who, incidentally, were acquitted in court. One judge said that the victim had committed a misdemeanor by leaving home without identification. And the federal case was declared a mistrial: all the non-Black jury voted to acquit; only the two Black female jurors voted to convict. I didn't want my father to visit me after I had watched that video. He didn't come again and now I'm seized by the moment when I imagine him dying in his bed alone. And then I think of all those who are dying every day all around us in this pandemic because the people in power, including the narcissistic kleptocrat in the White House, didn't value public health over profits and their manifold mendacity. All those reports of nurses holding a phone to a dying man's or a dying woman's ear so that their loved ones could say goodbye to them. And the anony- mous burials or cremations of all these bodies because it was considered too dangerous to hand the bodies over to the families. No, my grief is neither special nor unique. So, my answer to you, dear Motley, is that I wish you were around, of course. I'm okay, I'm doing fine. I love you and I miss you. I wish we had more time but this is only loving desire and not a bit- ter longing for what could have been. Mostly, I want you to know that I am without regret. All I feel, often, or at least right now, is rage.*

———

A journalist in Lucknow tweeted his falling oxygen level. He had repeatedly appealed for help but none came. His last tweet was sent when his oxygen level was down to 31. Then, nothing. I told Roberta that I wanted to go to India to cover this surge. We had a team there on the ground, but this was a big story. Roberta said that Christiane Amanpour was in London and it was quite likely that she would take a quick flight to Delhi. I doubted it. Roberta was my producer now in Atlanta but had been a young assistant to Amanpour two decades ago in New York. More than once, she had told me about her boss in Bosnia during the war. Despite the fact that her helicopter had come under fire, Amanpour was determined to get the story. The pilot asked people to disembark and lighten the load but she clung onto the straps and then spun it into a mantra for younger journos. *When you've got a helicopter taking you to a news story, you don't get off.* As a result of her determination, Amanpour was able to file a report on the hidden concentration camps run by the Serbs. While Roberta was talking, I could suddenly see Amanpour standing on a boat on the Ganga, the burning pyres of Varanasi behind her, the posh accent delivering news about the fresh two hundred thousand cases of coronavirus in the country.

Two days passed and it became clear that no one wanted to risk it. There was a strong chance that flights would be canceled out of India very soon. Roberta sent me a text. If Amanpour went to India she would need to be in quarantine for ten days upon her return to London. She wasn't going to even try it. Over the past few weeks, over fifty local journalists had died in various parts of India. After the text, there were three urgent email messages from

Roberta, beginning with: "Jugnu, do you still want to go? You have family there, don't you?"

The flight from Atlanta took me to Zurich and then to Doha. Another change of planes there for the last leg of the journey. Flights were already being canceled and I was advised this was the best way to get into Delhi. I was carrying my Covid vaccination card but was required to take the antigen test on arrival; it helped that I had an Overseas Citizenship of India card. Standing ahead of me in the line for the Covid test were two Indian men whom I had seen on the Zurich-Doha flight and then on the one to Delhi. The men, who could have been brothers, looked dazed with grief, appearing wild-eyed and rudderless in their movements. I saw that their passports were maroon; no doubt they were citizens of one of the countries of the European Union. The older one wore an expensive linen jacket and from the gray beard beneath his mask I guessed that he was Muslim. While waiting for the results of our tests, I turned toward them and asked what had made it necessary for them to return home during such a difficult time. We were all wearing masks and I also had a plastic shield in front of my face. The younger of the two looked at me blankly for a moment, as if trying to understand whether he had failed to recognize this middle-aged woman speaking to him, and then said simply, "Mother."

The other man dropped his eyes to the blue carpet.

I didn't want to leave them stranded in their grief. I said, "It is terrible, it is terrible. My father . . ."

The younger brother took out his phone from his jacket pocket. He said, "Look at this."

I didn't want to touch the phone but I bent toward his extended arm. He was showing me a video that he had come across on Twitter that day. A young woman was speaking into the microphone held by a journalist in Lucknow. Behind her was the well-lit entrance to a hospital. She was saying that her father was in the hospital, struggling for air. She had been paying forty thousand rupees daily to the hospital but they had already run out of oxygen twice that day. The young woman's voice from under her mask came out all choked, as if she too was gasping for breath. Her hand went up to her throat. She said that the Chief Minister of the state had announced that anyone complaining of oxygen shortage would be arrested.

Her voice rose higher. She removed her mask and said in Hindi, "I just want to say, I'm standing right here in front of the hospital. My father is on the fourth floor and he is in desperate need of oxygen. But come on, you fucker, I'm here. Try to come and arrest me."

I looked up at the faces of the brothers and I couldn't bear to imagine what they were thinking. "I'm sorry," I said, "I'm so sorry."

It turned out they were Marwaris, not Muslim, and owned a diamond business in Brussels. The older brother had migrated there as young man twenty-five years ago, and the younger one had followed sixteen years later. I told them I was a journalist for CNN. And then felt empowered to ask if their mother had died from the virus. They nodded.

I too had a video on my phone. But I didn't think it was right to share it with them. The video had been uploaded on Instagram by a bright young journalist I knew. My friend's video was from when she had gone to a mortuary in Patna where an old man had died from the coronavirus. The corpse was inside a blue body bag on a stretcher; the bag had been opened at the top so that the head was visible. In the video, you could see three middle-aged men using their phones to take pictures of the dead man. The men's faces bore a family resemblance but what also united them was that all three had freshly shaved heads—this was because their mother had died of Covid the previous week. And now their father had met his fate. Turning her camera to the oldest son, my young friend asked a question to which the answer was that the brothers had uncovered the body to make sure the medical staff had not stolen their father's kidneys or his eyes.

It was late evening when I came out of the airport in Delhi. The warm air engulfed me. Under the soles of my feet the asphalt still seemed to be releasing the day's heat and I thought of the crematoriums in the city in which the metal had begun to melt. The taxi that I took to the Oberoi Hotel passed a crematorium on the right, and I made a quick mental note of it. Two minutes later, after a temperature check at the door, I was in the cool hotel lobby, which smelled of roses. When I got to the room and switched on the TV, there was a cricket game in progress. I was surprised that it was a live match, being played under lights and without spectators, in the same city where I knew even wood for the pyres was already scarce. I switched the TV off and gulped down a whole bottle of water that was waiting on the counter. With nothing but my notebook and my press card, I left the hotel and started walking toward the glow in the distance.

Back in Atlanta, when Roberta had asked if I wanted to go to India, and didn't I have family there, I hadn't gone into complicating details. The previous year, during the first wave of the pandemic, my father had died. I could not enter India during the lockdown. A first cousin in Patna, who had kept my father's ashes, had posted a bad photograph of my father last May. He had also posted a photograph of an earthen pot with a red cloth tied around its mouth. His status update on Facebook read "I hv Jadu Uncle's mortal remains. May God bless his soul. Rgds."

Roberta was right. Spread across small towns in Bihar, I did indeed have a tattered extended family with whom I was fitfully in touch through Facebook updates about weddings and birthdays and car purchases. They believed in posting loud GIFs in lurid colors saying LOVE or WOW and instead of coming up with words they used animated bouquets of flowers. So, I had this Facebook family in India and also the man who was once my husband but with whom I had not been in touch for nearly thirty years. For so long it was only my father who had mattered and as the hours passed on my flight to Delhi, I often caught myself talking to him in my head, telling him that I was coming home. Before I returned to Atlanta, I was going to take his ashes from my cousin's house and scatter them in the waters near Allahabad.

A uniformed doorman asked, "Taxi, madam?" and I shook my head to say no. The sloping circular driveway of the hotel delivered me to the road that would take me to the crematorium. I walked past a bank of boutique sari shops on my right that resembled medical clinics with their masked attendants looking out silently at me from behind glass. The road with its lanes going in the opposite direction was on my left, the traffic thin, only a few cars hissing past me. The news reports from our bureau had said that the fires burned all day. The glow from the crematorium was now closer and I could make out the tall marble pillars at the entrance. It seemed to me that the fires had never stopped burning all this time that I had been away. I wanted to go and stand near the flames and see the shrouded bodies and the faces of the bereaved and remember my father.

It wasn't a great distance, fifteen minutes of walking at most, but perhaps because of the jet lag, I quickly felt exhausted. The water I had drunk in the hotel room had done nothing. My mouth was dry now. However, I wasn't going to turn and go back to the air-conditioned room and the bottles of Himalayan spring water on the dark counter. In fact, I was walking faster. It was as if my father's body were still burning. I had to reach the crematorium in time so that I could learn to read from his glowing bones everything about who I was.

———

A few months ago, the cop who killed George Floyd was convicted. By the time that happened I had filed reports on the second wave of Covid from five cities in India. There was always a chance that I would not be able to leave immediately, and I had to spend time in quarantine in a naval hospital in Miami when I returned. The window in the green wall of the room where I was required to stay looked upon a navy yard where two white boats sat serenely in the water like two retirees in white bathing suits resting with their backs on beach chairs. The news that I was paying attention to on social media was from all over India. My body kept its circadian rhythm aligned with the time in India so that I was up all through the night doom-scrolling on my phone. It felt to me that Indian society's own circadian rhythm remained bound to its ancient inequalities. The thousands of bodies found buried on the shores of the Ganga were mostly of the lower caste. The men from the bottom rung of the caste hierarchy were the ones left working around the clock at crematoriums, and now they were asking when we get the virus and die who is going to cremate us? I saw a tweet from a young Dalit engineer in Pune who was trying to reach his parents in Muzaffarnagar. The couple had contracted Covid. Then the young man, desperate to reach home and unable to do so because of travel restrictions, tweeted that his mother had died but his father needed help. He then uploaded a response he had received. A stranger, an upper-caste man, had tweeted back that the engineer should relax as his parents were probably already in heaven cleaning latrines.

Over the course of the last few days, my mind has gone back to the trip we took to Savannah—my father, Motley, and I. During the conversation in the car, Motley had told my father about Abel Meeropol and his young pupil Baldwin. The story had fascinated the teacher in my father. The two men then returned to that story during dinner. We were seated outdoors at this lovely restaurant, old oaks around us dripping with Spanish moss. Motley looked happy that his story had found a home in my father's heart. He said, "There is something else I haven't told you about Abel Meeropol."

Motley told us that Abel Meeropol was also a lyricist and a songwriter. His most famous, most mournful song was "Strange Fruit." It was sung by the great Billie Holiday. Meeropol had been inspired to write that song after seeing the photograph of a 1930 lynching of two Black men. Motley recited two lines of the song, about blood on the leaves, and bodies swinging from the trees, and the feeling it inspired was so real, so visceral, that my father looked around us.

It was only later, Motley said, when James Baldwin was in late middle age, that he came by the knowledge that it was his own high school teacher who had written that powerful anthem of protest. That is what Motley told us, or that is how I remember it. And it is too late now to ask Motley. But what I keep thinking is that, of course, it is logical that the man who wrote "Strange Fruit" was also James Baldwin's teacher. The earth's shadow falls on the moon and then during the nights that follow the moon shines: Meeropol, in his experience with the Rosenbergs, had experienced a darkness and his student Baldwin, somehow, had later glowed. But what are we to make of more ordinary lives? That is what I cannot get away from when there have been so many deaths over the past year and a half. How to remember them for the experiences they accumulated over a lifetime of living and hurts? I'm trying to understand how to mark the life of my father who died alone.

I have a memory from when I was seven. My mother had cut away the skin of a mango and was now slicing the fruit. I was filled with a sense of happy anticipation. My father looked at me and asked me if I was hungry. When I said yes, he turned to my mother and said something that I haven't ever forgotten. I remember it because it had struck me as a statement that put my seven-year-old body at the heart of our family life, which, at that time, could well have represented the whole universe to me. What my father had said was that during the length of his early life, he had witnessed how his parents' lives were governed by the needs of the livestock they owned. The times at which his parents had woken, or washed, or prayed, or eaten had all been determined by the clock that ruled when the buffalo and cows had to be given fodder and water. Unlike his parents', his own life, my father said, was governed by when his daughter was to be fed. *This* was the change from the village to the city. It is possible my father was exaggerating, or even just joking, but the child that was me accepted this as a profound truth about the change that had overtaken the lives of my parents.

I never forgot these words and remembered them again when I was a student at Jamia in Delhi and outside the window of my rented room I saw across a bare patch of scrubland a group of migrant women and their babies. The women were daily-wage laborers at the construction site where a private hospital was being built. There were three or four infants who slept in improvised hammocks that the women had fashioned by tying sheets between the slender trunks of acacia trees growing nearby. Once during a squall, two of the women took refuge from the rain under the same bus shelter where I was standing. Each woman had a baby at her waist; the rain had released something in the two women and they were laughing. I asked them questions. They were from a village near Jodhpur and they had fled from their homes because for the third year in a row there had been a drought in the region. Every year the desert kept coming closer and these women, no longer able to till the land or tend cattle, had come to Delhi; they were good only for doing cheap manual labor at urban construction sites. I saw that this was a different move from the village to the city. What had been disrupted was not just the hours of the day but the cycle of seasons itself. Droughts and floods had intruded into the lives of the people like never before. For the women who continued working deep into the winter, with their children sleeping in blankets by the wayside or crawling around when awake, all of their time from now on and forever would be only one season, a long, leafless season of want. A person like my father leaving his village for the city could have believed that he was escaping, leaving his past behind, but not these women—they were visitors from the future toward which we were all being thrown, an overheated planet and a promise of deprivation for all.

———————

Back in 2015, I had reported a story on a small artist collective from Delhi that had made a video called *Strikes at Time*. My report was about a show at Georgia Tech; the three members of the collective, two men and a woman, had come from India to present the work in different media. In that video, the audience heard and read the words written by a factory worker named Heeraprasad, the words he recorded in Hindi every night in his journal in the early part of the twentieth century. Each entry details some of the day's expenses, often accompanied by a thought startling in its lyricism, and ending always with the same words. *Everything else is ordinary.*

TUESDAY
Left for duty in the morning.
Medicine for myself, for 32.50
rupees.
4 rupees on bus fare, oranges
for 8 rupees.
20 rupees on photographs.
The next episode of a story can
be written only when you stake
your life, your own self. I am
proud of my abundant poetry.
Everything else is ordinary.

WEDNESDAY
Stayed at home today. Ate and
drank all day; it was intoxicating.
Got my slippers mended.
When you are searching you have
to get up and move. The very
idea of endeavor lies outside all
boundaries.
Everything else is ordinary.

After I came back from reporting on the Covid second wave in India, I began to put together what I had assembled there, a document offering testimony about people's daily expenses and their struggles during the pandemic. I wanted to do this story because it was essential to preserve the record. As it was, the government in Delhi denied that there had been any deaths during the second wave because of oxygen shortage: the junior health minister said in the Parliament that "no deaths due to lack of oxygen have been specifically reported." Earlier, the Chief Minister of Haryana had said that the dead were dead and gone, what use was it to talk of them, let's move on.

In my report, ordinary people recount their struggles to get help for their dying loved ones. They talk about their long wait at a hospital, and then at another hospital, or two more, or, as in one case, five hospitals, and then again at the crematorium. A young woman who had watched her brother-in-law die on the floor of the emergency ward of Deen Dayal Hospital spoke to me.

Did an ambulance come when you called? How long did it take to arrive? How long did it have to wait outside a hospital?

Was there a doctor available at the government hospital?

What did the private hospital charge you? How much did they ask for at first?

How long did it take to get a death certificate, and how much did it cost?

Does the certificate mention that the death was due to Covid?

Was it possible for the family to receive the financial help promised by the government if one of the earning members had died of the virus?

Were you able to cremate your relative? Did you have to bury him or her outside the village?

How much did the wood cost?

I sought answers to these questions and others. Although I didn't say this in my report, I believe strongly that we are in touch with a great astonishing mystery when we put honest words down on paper to register a life and to offer witness. Everything else is ordinary.

When I was in Patna during this last visit, I tried to bring order to my father's apartment, donating his clothes and throwing out the piles of yellow, crumpling newspapers. I took his books to a community library in Mukherjee Nagar. I saw that in the journal sitting on my father's side table, he had recorded in neat rows the money spent on items bought by the boy Pramod as well as details of other expenses, everything from lightbulbs to medicines for arthritis. How we spend our money is, of course, one way of measuring how we spend our lives. This accounting is present even in the letters my father wrote to my mother. I wasn't able to bring myself to read them but I did open one because it looked old, the faded blue paper already brown at the folds. The letter had been written almost exactly a year before I was born. My father had traveled in a group of faculty and students from his college to Delhi and other cities. The postmark on the envelope said Ahmedabad, which is where the group must have gone late during the trip. My father reported that at Chandni Chowk in Delhi, after a visit to the Red Fort, he had bought a pair of Kolhapuri chappals for my mother. Earlier in the evening, the students, all young men, had wanted to see Miss Olga, the famous trapeze artist, in the Russian circus. The large red tent was in the field outside the Red Fort. My father sat with the boys in the closest seats, which cost three rupees each. Miss Olga swung into the empty vault of the huge tent—supported by nothing more than the loud music, a violin recording being blasted from the speakers—and she never missed her target. The boys sweated with tension, but Miss Olga did not. She shone like a distant star in the heavens. The chappals had cost fifteen rupees. My father wrote that the leather chappals had mirrorwork on them, and they were just the right size for my mother's small feet. He had held the chappals and felt the light weight of her feet in his hands. The train ticket to Agra had cost thirty-two rupees. They had arrived in the evening and then gone straightaway to see the Taj Mahal. My father noted for my mother's edification, and possible amusement, that the marble monument had been built exactly 333 years ago. And then he observed that the Taj Mahal had looked beautiful, silent and naked, in the moonlight. He hoped that it would stand there forever.

———

Part III

JADU

In life, no story is told exactly the same way twice.

—JANET MALCOLM

Jadunath has had a dry cough for several days now. A cause for worry during this time. During Holi, when news of the sickness started coming in, he touched his forehead now and then to reassure himself. At unguarded moments, dread, like a spasm, swept over his body. After a week or two, that fear went away. But then, not long afterward, the cough started.

He turned eighty-five this past January. On first opening his eyes these last few days, he has felt okay, rested. The feeling of tiredness overtakes him when he tries to leave his bed. For a week, the fever has come and gone, and he has found himself sinking into exhaustion, a feeling of fatigue like no other. Before long, maybe an hour, sometimes less, his breathing becomes wheezy, his lungs imitating the sound of two pieces of paper being crinkled together. Jadu uses the inhaler his doctor has given him, and his head falls back on the pillow. His breathing is shallow and labored and futile, as if he were blowing into a balloon with a tear in it. As he lies unmoving on his bed, the thought of death once again comes to him from afar, like the sound of a car alarm in an otherwise silent city.

———

Jadu remembers. He was nearly eighty when one night he watched a TV documentary about the conquest of Everest. There on the screen was Tenzing fresh after his successful climb with Hillary.

Jadu had lost several teeth by then but, in the documentary, Tenzing was still young, with glossy black hair and brilliant white teeth exposed in a smile.

When Jadu had switched to that channel looking for something to watch, he saw the summit shining in the dawn's pink light and a voice was saying that Edmund Hillary was a beekeeper in New Zealand; he learned that Hillary had later also gone on expeditions to both the South Pole and the North Pole. After describing how Hillary and Tenzing Norgay had stood on top of the world, the voiceover informed Jadu that on the peak there were winds of up to a hundred miles per hour. The two climbers had needed oxygen because the air is so thin at that altitude that the lungs and brain cannot function properly. Hillary and Norgay had climbed to the same unimaginable height at which jets flew in the air.

The documentary explained how the world had learned of the successful ascent in 1953. James Morris, a journalist from the London *Times*, was among the members of the team waiting at the base camp at 17,900 feet. The team decided to hurry back to civilization so that the news could be sent to London in time for Elizabeth's coronation. It took a day and a half to climb down to the nearest village. From there, a runner took Morris's message to the home of the British High Commissioner to Nepal. The streets of Kathmandu were packed with foreign journalists but Morris had followed an elaborate code so that no one else would get the scoop. His message to the High Commissioner read: "Snow Conditions Bad Stop Advance Base Abandoned Yesterday Stop Awaiting Improvement." The British High Commissioner was a man named David Summerhayes. He looked through the codebook. Once deciphered, the message said: "Summit of Everest reached on 29 May by Hillary and Tenzing."

It took a few minutes to radio the message to London. The crowds waiting for the coronation outside Buckingham Palace heard the news from loudspeakers. The London newspapers the next morning said THE CROWNING GLORY: EVEREST CONQUERED.

Morris, the journalist, later underwent gender-reassignment surgery in Morocco and wrote several books about travel. Her name since 1972 was Jan Morris. A tall, distinguished-looking woman with long snowy hair swirling around her head was walking across Jadu's television screen to accept an award for literary achievement. As James, he had been married to Elizabeth Tuckniss with whom he had five children; after becoming Jan, once the laws of the land allowed, Jan and Elizabeth became same-sex partners living together. And suddenly there she was, Jan, speaking to the camera. "I am now ninety," she said. "The Everest expedition altered my life so much. Now I'm the only surviving member of the expedition, and I miss them all."

On that distant afternoon when they had visited the Governor House and met Tenzing Norgay, the students returned to the college and sat down on the green lawns with Professor Dey. Jadu wasn't sure he had learned what *high tea* meant—but now he was pierced by a desire to reach across the years and address Professor Dey. *Oh, if Professor Dey were still alive!* Professor Dey, sir, this is what I have learned in my life. That there is no end to living. Things keep changing, people change, in ways that you had never expected or even imagined.

I'm the only surviving member of the expedition, and I miss them all. Look at me, Professor Dey, sir. That is what Jadu wanted to shout across the years. He felt the same as Jan Morris. He was almost eighty. Over the years he had lost nearly everyone who was with them in the room when they met Tenzing Norgay. Jan Morris had led a rich and varied life. It was extraordinary, by any measure, but even Jadu, with his very ordinary life, had witnessed so many changes. He was born in a hut with a thatched roof in a village in Champaran. He hadn't seen an electric lightbulb until he was in high school. The village in which he was born still did not have electricity or water supply. The children of his cousins in the village were old men now, with grandchildren, and while they still relied on kerosene lanterns and hand pumps, they also used cellphones and owned motorcycles. Jadu had succeeded in leaving the village. And others, less fortunate than he, had done the same.

The granddaughter of a man who had labored in his father's fields was now a librarian at Delhi University. Many years after Professor Dey's death, Jadu wanted to tell his old teacher that he had received a Fulbright scholarship and had traveled abroad to study and teach for a year at University of California at Berkeley. That was in 1988. How could he have said to the eager young faces in the classroom in Berkeley, and to what purpose, that for a long part of his early life, when he had to shit, he walked out with a lota of water in hand into the fields of sugarcane or corn?

All those years ago in that classroom in California, one of his students named Joey Tirglia had shown him a picture from the Kumbh Mela of a naked sadhu pulling a car with a chain attached to his penis. Joey was a cheerful student, better prepared to crack a joke in class than to offer an incisive observation; his father, he had told Jadu during one of their conferences, had moved to Arizona from New Jersey two decades ago to set up a chain of pizzerias.

"I don't mean to offend you, but is this real?" Joe asked Jadu, a bit of mischief mixed with curiosity.

Jadu said yes but what he had wanted to say was, "Wait, think of the things that have happened to you today. All sorts of things that could make a man in my village Khewali wonder if everything you had experienced was real. You got a phone line without having to fill out twenty forms or bribing anyone; your elected representative didn't get his rival murdered; clean water and electricity are available to you at any time of the day or night. Compared to these things, the man pulling a car with his penis is quite ordinary." By which Jadu didn't mean to accept that everywhere you looked on the streets of Indian cities, cars were being pulled by ropes tied to genitalia. In cities and towns and villages on different continents, the everyday acts or encounters of all kinds of people inspired wonder about this world. Jadu wasn't thinking of a man walking 1,350 feet above the ground on a wire stretched between two towers, nor of an anonymous woman in a video from Madhya Pradesh scaling the walls of a nearly dry well to fetch water for her family. Instead, Jadu just wanted to ask if it wasn't quite amazing that he and that kid in Berkeley were even in the same room and having that particular conversation about a car being pulled by a priest's penis.

Jadu could have told Joey Tirglia about Mr. Shukla. Soon after arriving in Berkeley, Jadu had run into him at a lecture by the visiting Indian historian Romila Thapar. Mr. Shukla was around Jadu's age, short and bespectacled, with a perpetual smile on his face. He had lost some of his hair on the top and so wore his remaining hair long, the curls kissing his shoulders. When they first met, he came and shook Jadu's hand with a smile, making him wonder whether they had known each other before. Jadu was surprised and pleased but also a bit confused. Mr. Shukla said that he was from Allahabad. He was employed as a lecturer teaching Hindi but he wanted Jadu to know that his real identity was as a writer and an activist. During subsequent meetings, over cups of tea that Mr. Shukla made in his small kitchen, using loose leaf Lipton tea that he bought from an Indian store, Jadu learned that he had faced arrest in Delhi during the Emergency and was forced to escape to the United States. As a young man, Mr. Shukla had revolted against the conservative culture of his Brahmin family. He had been born in a clan of distinguished priests, but he had become a radical, a Naxalite. His op-eds had been published in prominent left-leaning newspapers and magazines in India. After he had come to know Mr. Shukla, Jadu read several of these pieces; they offered pointed arguments and were unwavering in their commitment and demand for democracy.

After the Emergency ended, Mr. Shukla could have gone back to his professor's job in Delhi but he didn't. He liked it here in America which, he said, was the only imperial power left today and needed to be fought from within. At Berkeley, not too long after his arrival in the country, Mr. Shukla had met a Japanese student named Himiko. She was thirteen years younger than he; she was learning Hindi because she wanted to visit those places in India that were sacred to the Buddha. The apartment that Himiko was renting was larger than Mr. Shukla's and he had moved in with her. He couldn't marry her because he already had a wife and an eight-year-old son in India. In time, he also had a child with Himiko, a girl whom they named Mayumi. Mr. Shukla told Jadu all this quite plainly, looking him in the eye, not inviting or even expecting any judgment. Jadu became aware that his heart was beating fast from the surprise, or the shock, of what was being revealed to him. He asked where Himiko was now, and learned that after five years of living with Mr. Shukla, Himiko had gone back to Kyoto. She had taken Mayumi with her. And then, after a year had passed, Himiko wrote to say that she had met a Japanese man, a fellow Buddhist, and was going to marry him. Except that the child was an obstacle; Himiko's new man had an ascetic temperament and wanted to wander the world without children disturbing his equilibrium. Himiko had asked if Mr. Shukla would be able to take custody of Mayumi.

Of course, the answer was no. But this was Jadu's answer, and in his head only. Because Mr. Shukla went on to tell him that for the past fifteen months Mayumi had been living with his wife and son in Allahabad. She was learning Hindi. She was already able to communicate in it, Mr. Shukla said, not wanting to hide or muffle the note of pride in his voice. In fact, he added, if Jadu came to his apartment on a weekend morning, he would be happy to make a phone call to India and Jadu could test Mayumi's Hindi.

Jadu never did speak to Mayumi; he didn't want to. He couldn't imagine what she had gone through, the long journey between the impossible choices that life had offered her. A girl from Kyoto eating roti and dal in a hot room in Allahabad, not too far away from the site of the Kumbh Mela. That is where the picture was taken of the sadhu pulling a Maruti with a chain attached to his penis. *So, what do you want to know about what is real, Joey Tirglia? And what do any of us really know?* If you want to find out what is real and at the same time unbelievable, go and ask Mayumi that question and let's hear what she has to say. And please address her in Hindi, if you possibly can.

He stays there in his bed until the boy comes in to ask if he should bring tea. Jadu is often harsh with the boy, and can see fear in his eyes. He tries to be gentle. When he replies to the boy's queries without impatience, he can see the boy relax. A hint of a smile appears on the boy's small, dark face. It takes just a little—two or three exchanges—for the boy to start to giggle and want to play the fool.

"Should I buy cauliflower?"

"Yes, if it is fresh. No dark spots."

"The milk might go bad."

"Okay, get it. Small pack."

After a brief giggle, "You have never asked me to buy ice cream. Shall I get some today?"

Jadu's anger flashes, and then is gone. "I cannot have it, you idiot. But you can buy one for yourself."

The boy is eighteen. He doesn't look it though, perhaps because of a malnourished childhood. He came from a village near Saharsa four years ago. Jadu's daughter had an old friend who was very resourceful (*resourceful* is one of Jadu's favorite words in English) and she had found the boy. The boy's uncle was her gardener. Acting out of simplicity and her own lack of education, the boy's mother had sent a request to Jadu. Would her child, when he wasn't doing any household chores, be able to receive lessons in reading and writing from him? But Jadu had a better plan. A local charity ran a neighborhood school for both children and adults employed as domestic help: the school was open from one to four in the afternoon. The boy proved to be a quick learner. If Jadu wanted him to buy a whole list of things, he spelled out the names and the boy wrote it all down on a scrap of paper. Jadu's daughter was in another country but telephoned the boy regularly and talked to him first before asking him to hand the phone over to her father.

Today the boy has come into his room to ask if he needs anything, maybe a cup of tea. There is a smell in the room but the old man hasn't noticed it. To the boy's eye, the man on the bed, a sheet crumpled over his sunken body, has slipped into a delirium of irreparable decay. But he thinks he detects a slight movement of the head that says no to his question about tea. And then the boy sees the old man's body convulse before collapsing back into the sheets.

––––––––

Some hours earlier, Jadu had decided he would ask the boy to call his daughter if anything went wrong. In fact, when he woke up, Jadu wanted to talk to her. He had risen from a dream. A taxi in which he was riding had brought him to the train station. A large train station, bigger than the one in Patna. He didn't recognize the city, or the surroundings, but he could see the travelers and the smoke from the trains. From the way the people were dressed it was the nineteen sixties or maybe the early seventies. He looked at the taxi driver and asked him a question.

"Is the taxi meter okay?"

"Is the country okay?" the taxi driver had asked in response.

This reply had left Jadu nonplussed. Where had this exchange occurred? He wanted to call his daughter and ask her. Unable to understand anything, he felt he must be dying and that was why memories were coming back to him. But for the past several years, he had rarely called his daughter himself; her calls came regularly and, unwilling to intrude, he now decides it is better to wait.

He has told the boy to not to speak to his daughter about his illness. He knows he could dial 104 for any nonemergency complaint arising from the illness. In the public announcements, they have mentioned that if senior citizens need medicines the police in town will help. Call 104.

He doesn't know the number to call, however, if there is an emergency. Was one given out?

Jadu is troubled by the feeling of breathlessness that has now come back and he thinks of a particular dog he used to pass in the park when the parks were still open. He would see a servant in an orange sweatshirt taking that dog out on walks, an old German shepherd with its back bent, its back legs stiff. Neither the animal nor the caretaker ever covered much distance. When Jadu passed him, the dog never showed any curiosity, remaining focused perhaps on its own loud breathing.

A new thought has introduced panic into Jadu's mind. What was the thought? It has come and gone. He doesn't know how much time has passed. Is it past dinnertime already? He has been sleeping a lot. The boy must have come and asked about food, and when Jadu didn't respond, he would have retreated instead of daring to disturb him. After some time, Jadu remembers the thought that had caused the panic. The newspapers have reported that once your condition worsens, you are put in isolation—relatives are not allowed in because of the high risk of infection. This new disease is relentless. If you don't recover, the oxygen level in your lungs keeps going down and you slip into a coma. No chance of saying goodbye.

Acting contrary to what he has felt and believed during the last several days, he reaches under the far pillow for his phone.

He clears his throat several times. Then, looking intently at the screen on his phone, he presses his thumb on the green circle beside his daughter's name. So far away, where it is probably not yet morning, her phone is ringing. While the phone continues to ring, he has a conversation with her in his head. *Yes, I'm calling you because you need not worry about me.* But she will be worried. In fact, she will know from his voice that he is unwell. *No, this is just a cough. I felt strong enough to listen to the boy read the newspaper this afternoon. He is doing well. You will be impressed.* She will say that she is going to talk to the boy too. She had been busy with work. *There are reports that it has affected many people in America too. Are you staying safe?* She will probably say that she doesn't need to be so worried about herself. You know that it is the old who are vulnerable. She will no doubt speak of the cases she herself has seen during her reporting.

A mechanical voice comes on the phone to tell him that the person he is calling is not answering the phone. Even before the message has begun repeating itself—or is that only in his head—he feels himself slowly sinking into sleep. There is a sound outside his door. Is his daughter here from America? Except the sound is not at his door but near his dark window, a sleeping bird flapping its wings and settling into the nest above the ledge. The disturbance has woken him up and he has become lucid again. *Of course, it cannot be his daughter.*

Every day people are dying but not only of this disease. Last week, in the newspaper that the boy was reading to him, there was news of the death of a famous actor in Mumbai. This talented man looking out from his photograph with his large, soulful eyes (another actor called them *morpankhi-aankhen*, "peacock-feather-shaped eyes"). That actor was more than three decades younger than Jadu. Such a tragedy, the death of those who had spent so much less time on this earth than he. The obituary described a few of the roles that the actor was famous for. An underworld gangster in an adaptation of *Macbeth*, a police inspector, a taxi driver, a Bengali immigrant in America. Did the actor ever tell himself, perhaps trying to seek consolation on his deathbed, that he had played so many people on the stage and on the screen, he had inhabited so many lives, indeed, he had lived so many more lives than his fans?

Perhaps he didn't. The actor probably thought only of his loved ones and the lives that would go on, painfully, without him. In bed, staring at the ceiling in the same way that he imagines the actor might have done on his hospital bed, Jadu thinks of the roles he has played in life. Son, husband, father, teacher. For a minute or two, he sees himself in a grainy black-and-white film. He is in college, where he has arrived from the village. He is in a crowd, rushing to catch a boat, his head bobbing among other heads. He is lighting the pyre on which his wife's body lies. Is this what one does before death? Just the other day, he was reading about a judge who had died under mysterious circumstances in Nagpur.

The judge, presiding over a case in which a powerful leader of the ruling party was accused, died suddenly when attending the wedding of a colleague's daughter. The judge's family raised concerns about the medical report that had been filed. But then nothing happened. What were the judge's thoughts in his final moments?

What a cliché—final moments.

———

When he awakens—he has the sense that perhaps only a little time has passed—he tells himself that he is not afraid. He has no further ambition, and no further responsibilities. He had read somewhere that for years before suicides kill themselves, they start giving away things. But he is doing the opposite. He wants to collect all that has gone into his making, all that history, which is what matters to him now. The exhaustion he feels doesn't allow him to shape a story; all he is able to summon is a set of memories that appear unconnected. He is thinking of journeys. Standing on the deck of the ferry taking him across the river to his village, the day after his graduation; or sitting near the window of the train at night on his way to Sugauli, small sparks flying past, the wind in his hair; with his wife in the bullock cart, the day after his wedding, being driven to the village from the train station in town and a boy on the dirt road holding up a silver fish for the bride to admire.

The endless travel through the years, the back and forth. What does it matter that he has to go on yet another journey? Although Jadu is not panicked at the thought of his death, he isn't ready yet. As he thinks again of the newspaper photo of the actor who died recently, he remembers that the first real-life hero he met was the mountaineer Tenzing Norgay. In contrast, he has himself led an ordinary life. One is taught to think of such a life as one without heroism. But that cannot be correct—no valor maybe, but such a life has courage too. The strength of will required to get out of bed and put on your shoes.

Courage—and cowardice. There was that one incident. The

young man's face comes swimming before his eyes. More than thirty years have passed but Jadu remembers clearly the moment when he realized that the money was gone. The taste of metal in his mouth. He had looked around like a startled bird, its feet trapped in the net. Then, he was shouting for help. There at the crowded bus station, in the afternoon light, he had sunk to the ground, holding his head in both hands. *Help! My money! My daughter's wedding . . . !* A man touched his shoulder to ask a question. Two women stopped close to him. He was unable to say anything. The crowd grew and then a man, stocky and wearing a blue cap, appeared in front of him holding a young man by the neck. Jadu noticed that the man had interlaced the fingers of his right hand with the fingers of the youth's left hand.

The man in the blue cap was saying, "How much was stolen?"

"My daughter's wedding . . ." That was all that Jadu could say.

How had the man decided that this thin youth was the pickpocket? From the circle that had formed around him, a dark-skinned man with a stubble on his face stepped forward and slapped the youth. It was an unexpected blow and the young man staggered back. He kept standing because of the other man's grip. A small, thin figure standing behind the youth now hit him on the head with a slipper. Jadu didn't say anything because he believed, or half-believed, that these people who were hitting the boy must know something that he didn't. He hoped the money would be found soon.

The youth was screaming that he didn't know anything about the money. A man no older than Jadu himself brought Jadu a glass of water. And said gravely, "Even if he took the money, they pass it on to the accomplices. There is always a gang." Jadu didn't understand what he was being told. The man in the blue cap said, "Please get up. Go to the police, so that your complaint is registered." When he left, the youth was on the ground. He was being beaten and there was blood on his face. He had first pleaded his innocence, repeatedly saying that he wasn't a thief, but by now he was just shouting for his mother.

Jadu wants to shut off the flow of memories when he remembers that afternoon. As if he were closing a book and turning off the light. He then makes an effort and asks himself to consider joy. No denying that there was joy in his long life. At the thought of joy, he thinks of the years of his youth, when life seemed to be endless, a long straight road lined with sunlit trees. He thinks dutifully of his wife, who died long ago. And his daughter. He thinks of all the things that made her happy when she was a child. His daughter's life has had its ups and downs like all other lives. This thought gives him pause. It is a distraction, like a tiny splinter under his skin.

The greater truth is that at this moment he feels distant from both sadness and joy.

This sense of detachment is his reality now. This is what he thinks for a while before he is undone by an overwhelming chill and nausea. He fears he is going to lose consciousness. His eyes are shut and he knows that there is something more he wants to say to himself, but recognizes that it is just out of reach, like a string of dazzle on a river's dark surface.

Then, Jadu is a boy leaning over a small pond that his father has constructed outside their unfinished house in the village. After the bricks are baked in the fire in a field nearby, three hired help bring the bricks to be soaked in the water. The cracks in the house are being repaired and a cement ceiling added for the two rooms to be built on top. This is the reason for the bricks. Jadu wants to seize the string of light he sees in the water. But he tips over and falls in the dirty pond. Shivnath is angry.

But Jadu hasn't fallen in the water yet. He hears his sister Lata calling him but on turning toward her he sees it is his friend from college, Ananya. She is smiling and saying something that Jadu cannot hear and he turns his eyes back to the water. He sees a school of tiny fish cutting the dark depths with light—their colors are brilliant, their movement electric and full of energy, and they appear almost within reach. With his right hand, Jadu touches the water's surface, which is cold. Attracted by the ripples, a snake emerges from the water and before his mother can move to protect him, the snake is there in front of his face, its head dancing in the dank air. The numbness he is feeling means that the snake has bitten him. His body, still that of a boy, is now at long last tipping into the water.

———

Part IV

MAATI

I sat on a gray stone bench
ringed with the ingenue faces
of pink and white impatiens
and placed my grief
in the mouth of language,
the only thing that would grieve with me.

—LISEL MUELLER, "WHEN I AM ASKED"

Ghaziabad. I am sitting away from the rain on the veranda of the printing press. It is late afternoon. The leaves of the lemon trees are wet. I was born in this building in 1992, in a room that is in the middle of the set of three rooms on the left. My mother called me Maati but that was just her name for me. Some years later, when she took me to a nearby primary school, she put down my name as Karuna, which means compassion. We are Adivasi people, the indigenous people of India, although a popular name for us, popular among others, is tribals.

My mother's name was Sudha Mintz. I do not know my father's name because the walls of our home have never heard that name spoken.

My uncle Dulu was the manager of a printing press. He had started work there as a daily wager. This is the story that has been told to me over and over since my birth; this is also one of the few stories that I actually also believe. When I was seven, my uncle took out a bank loan and bought the press from the owner, who was dying from heart disease. We all lived together in this row of rooms jutting out of the press. From my window, I had a clear view of the Hindon River.

The school I attended as a girl had broken furniture and lights that didn't work. There was another school just ten minutes away where, through the metal gates, you could see flowers and a fountain sending up sparkling water. I could sense inequality, but didn't understand it. When I was a little older I also became aware of the great churning in our society. The castes at the bottom of the social hierarchy were rising, and they didn't hesitate to fight the people above them—or assault those below them, people like us, Adivasis and Dalits. This didn't prevent other people from reminding me that we were given a place each year in the Republic Day parade to sing and dance. A teacher told the class that the portrait of the Adivasi leader Birsa Munda, who had fought against the British, had been in the Parliament building in Delhi for a decade. She looked at me and said, "You should be happy. You have nothing to complain about now."

My mother never got married. She didn't want to. My uncle joked that in solidarity he hadn't married either. The two siblings divided between themselves the task of supervising workers and dealing with clients. When there was time, my mother tended to the flower garden, roses, dahlias, bougainvillea, rajnigandha, and, just outside the front door, a row of flowering jasmine.

The printing press was the only real world I knew. Once, when I was quite little, a young man, who I was told was my cousin, arrived from the village where my mother had been born. Actually, he didn't come—he was brought. An old man, whom I was asked to call grandfather, and an old woman, whose name I have forgotten, brought him to the compound of the printing press. The next day the two returned to the distant village, leaving the youth with us. His name was Junul. I would later realize that he was just a boy, though to my eyes at that time he appeared to be a grown-up. What had happened to him? Junul was having trouble walking. His right arm was fractured and there were bruises on his left side, a broken rib or two. In any case, as a result of his injuries, he wasn't able to use a crutch. I learned from listening to my uncle talking to my mother that the boy had gone into an army camp and asked for his goat to be returned. What I also learned from listening to the talk of the grown-ups was that if you are unable to walk, if the parts of your body that you must keep covered are bludgeoned, you will be unable to have a child or even get married. I concluded then that there were people in the world who would do things to you that sent you to a world without children. A place where I had no place. I built a wall around this knowledge and never visited it except in nightmares that faded after a few years. Eventually I forgot about all of this and remembered it only when I was in college and reading a short story about a Santhal rebellion.

When I was growing up, it was important to me that I did well in my studies. And the years of my life arranged themselves neatly like words on a printed page. I became the most educated member of our family when I cleared high school, and I didn't stop there. After I had received my bachelor's degree in social welfare, I considered becoming a teacher but decided to work at the press instead.

In the courtyard of this building, I planted lemon trees in large pots. Straw curtains provided shade in the veranda where all the workers could sit on cane chairs and read newspapers and books. This is what I believed I could do: provide chai and sweet buns at a nominal price. And more than that, the idea of free time. That was where I started; the fight against what in the social welfare textbooks they call alienated labor.

On Saturdays, the press would close at noon. With my uncle and my mother, I went down to the river and ate fried fish from paper plates that we discarded on the banks where once the Mughals used to picnic.

In my early teens, a strike was called at KPT Steel Ltd., the biggest factory in the area. Our work tripled because the union asked us to print all their posters and pamphlets. As long as the strike lasted, while the workers stayed idle, we worked the hardest. Then, the owners brought in thugs from Haryana who attacked the strikers with iron rods and sticks. All I know about printing I learned on the job, but what I learned most was how you to have to fight for the world you want.

Once, for a wedding, we went to Khijri. It was the time before

Christmas. From Khijri, a taxi took us to the village in the Saranda forest where my mother and uncle had passed their childhood. The forest was dense with towering sal trees. Five tiny blue and yellow birds flew ahead of the taxi for more than a mile as if they had waited all morning to perform this task of showing us the way home. The village was just a group of huts surrounded by green fields and red hills. It was beautiful but it was clear that my mother and uncle had left this life behind them. I had never thought that the city was ours and the village that had till now, in a vague way, represented the idea of home—that idea now faded from my heart.

My mother had a childhood friend whose daughter was getting married. That is why we had come. After I had been among my people in the village, and seen for myself what gets to be called their simple life, I was able to understand why arrogant fools in the city never failed to condescend to me. Long ago, when I was in the final year of high school, a boy had stolen my notebook and drawn a dirty picture in it. Do your people not go bare-breasted in the forest, he asked me with a smirk.

When I was old enough to vote, I did. But the candidate who won the election in Ghaziabad was from the right-wing party. In the next election, he won again. I took on more responsibilities at work. Every Tuesday, the workers' newspaper was printed at our press. Everything that the outside world considered necessary or even inevitable, the newspaper showed was only the workings of chance. Or worse, manipulation on the part of those with power. Everything that had previously been deemed impossible, the newspaper argued was attainable. I had done only printing work so far but then I started writing in the newspaper too.

In 2014, I got married and gave birth to two daughters, one who is now five and the other three. I moved into the flat my husband rented in Raj Nagar Extension. Every morning I brought my daughters with me when I came to work so that they could play with my mother. The girls took turns watering the plants.

The everyday struggle and, of course, the work continues like before but with the girls there are new needs, new demands. Also, a new alertness. Every day you read in the newspaper or see when you turn on the television what can happen to a girl.

In the middle of a workday in 2017, sitting in his office chair, my uncle Dulu died from a heart attack. In another life, he would have died years earlier, toiling in the field or in a dark hut.

Not long after that, my husband was involved in an accident and after a brief period of bedrest he was able to return to work. It was only when he was healthy again and back at his factory that I realized I was no longer young.

I grew old with my mother. We talked and were together all the time. You do not see that kind of relationship on television. In the shows on TV when women are together, their talk has the shine of new coins. Lot of tinkle. It wasn't like that between my mother and me. We needed to talk about births and deaths, people and disease, works and days. I would make tea for us and she sat in her garden pulling weeds or she rubbed oil in my older daughter's hair. The words that passed between us were familiar, well worn, and black with use. We would discuss the quality of the tea that we were drinking, the heat that had burdened us all week, or the price of sugar, but we knew, of course, that we were talking about births and deaths, people and disease, works and days.

Covid came. The press was shut down. As a result of the countrywide lockdown, many of our workers couldn't return home. Nearly twenty of us cooked food together. There were no vaccines but things improved for a while.

And then came the second wave. I knew a young businessman who owned a travel agency that operated tourist buses from Delhi and Dehra Dun and Haridwar. He used to get his brochures printed at our press. Both his parents fell sick from the virus. He had money and was able to get them beds in two different hospitals. Both were in intensive care. Then there was a power failure at the hospital where his father was being treated, and one by one the oxygen machines came to a stop. Eleven people died. The businessman's old father was the only survivor. But the father told his son that he had lost the will to live. Within a week, both the businessman's parents were gone.

I was very scared for my mother, and then she too fell sick. Although we were able to get her to the hospital, there were no beds and no oxygen cylinders available. I spread a sheet on the floor in the waiting area and my husband helped her lie down. In the final half hour before all my fears came true, we watched three other patients die waiting for help. Then, it was my mother's turn. No one deserves to die like this. Panting, rubbing their heels against the hospital floor.

My older daughter was with us. I had left the little one with a worker but brought the older girl, thinking that she would be able to comfort my mother. A mistake. It was terrible for the child to witness her grandmother's agony. But she tried. She massaged my mother's feet while I tried feebly to pump her chest. I did not cry. There were so many others around us who were trying to make it through the night.

Now and then my mother comes back to me in my dreams. She is alive again but these are not happy dreams. It is almost the same dream every time and, inside this dream, it is a shock for me to discover that my mother is not dead. The truth that lies in wait for me is that we have sent her away somewhere. We have made her mad, she is speaking unintelligible words, her gray hair hangs loose around her face. At times, it seems she is back in an empty field near Khijri. There are trees nearby and small hills. It is clear to me that I haven't been visiting her, and, indeed, that I had forgotten her. Where does this dream of abandonment come from? I wake up shaken, feeling guilty and sad, but the dream makes me angry. I feel I have cheated myself in my sleep. It is not we who ever left my mother's side; we were trying to save her. She died fighting for breath. Where were those leaders who had been telling us that there were vaccines for all? That the crisis was over and that there were oxygen cylinders for those who needed them? I don't ever see their faces in my dreams. I don't understand why my unconscious has been deceived. I have seen those politicians talking on my television screen but they are absent from this drama that unravels in my head each night. Instead, I'm alone in what looks like a forest clearing while my mother howls and I realize that I had forgotten that she was still alive.

Meanwhile, the world is returning to what it believes is normal. By the time the next elections come, we will be told that the government had the best strategy to defeat the virus. Everyone who needed it got aid; there was enough oxygen. And that as a nation we won the fight.

My older daughter came back from school last week and said that her teacher had taken them to the Hindon to plant saplings to prevent erosion. I smiled to show the child that I was pleased. My mother once told me that when she was growing up in the village near Khijri, the huts they lived in would almost completely be made from leaves. Everyone was skilled at making huts out of leaves. If a roof leaked, the man who had made the hut was excommunicated for a month. He needed to show that he could build a perfect roof of leaves before he was allowed back in society again. That world is now gone although I must add that the papers sometimes report stories of people fighting—with bows and arrows, but also with guns—in the Saranda forest. They don't want their land taken away by mining companies. No ugly brown gashes dug into the sides of the hills that are then blown up with dynamite, miles-long strips of forest disappeared on the backs of trucks headed for timber mills.

I think of my mother's village every time I see the giant rolls of paper brought to our printing press. In the course of my life here in Ghaziabad, I have seen trees in nearby forests replaced by the chimneys of newly built factories. I look at the new factories and karkhanas spewing smoke and worry about the world in which my children will live. I learned from my mother that this is what the citizens of a defeated nation must feel like as they watch their soldiers bound in chains and marched outside the city gates. The people know that their country has changed forever. Huddled in their homes, alone or in quiet groups, they wait for a signal, a shout, a call, or a cry, even a wailing or a howl, so that they can believe that not all is dead.

And then, from somewhere far or close, a word arrives.

———

Acknowledgments

For their support in writing this book, I'm grateful to the Corporation of Yaddo as well as the Cullman Center for Scholars and Writers at the New York Public Library. I want to thank David Davidar, Levi Irie Hafez, Diana Miller, Emmanuel Iduma, Hemali Sodhi, Jay Mandel, Jenny Offill, Jordan Pavlin, Josh Begley, Kiran Desai, Nicole Winstanley, Pujitha Krishnan, Ravi Mirchandani, and Teju Cole. And I also want to record the unpayable debt I owe my family, especially Mona, Ila, and Rahul.

Sources

The author gratefully acknowledges his indebtedness to the following texts in the writing of this book:

Christopher Rand, "The Story of the First Sherpa to Climb to the Top of Mt. Everest," *The New Yorker*, May 29, 1954.

Pramod Mishra, *Dark Lotus*, unpublished memoir.

David Boyk, "Collaborative Wit: Provincial Publics in Colonial North India," *Comparative Studies of South Asia, Africa and the Middle East*, Volume 38, Number 1, May 2018.

Sumit Sarkar, *Modern India 1885–1947*. Delhi, McMillan India, 1983.

The Diary of Manu Gandhi 1943–44, edited and translated by Tridip Suhrud. Oxford: Oxford University Press, 2019.

Bimal Prasad and Sujata Prasad, *The Dream of Revolution: A Biography of Jayaprakash Narayan*. New Delhi: Penguin Random House India, 2021; and Gyan Prakash, *Emergency Chronicles*. Princeton, New Jersey, Princeton University Press, 2019.

Irawati Karve, *Yuganta*. First published in 1991. Hyderabad, Orient BlackSwan, 2016.

Jatin quotes from James Michener, *The Fires of Spring*; Robert Graves, *Oxford Addresses on Poetry*; and Oscar Wilde, *The Picture of Dorian Gray*.

Melvin Mencher's *News Reporting and Writing*. New York, McGraw-Hill Education, 2010.

Akhil Sharma, *Family Life*. New York, W. W. Norton, 2014.

Mary Tyler, *My Years in an Indian Prison*. First published in 1977. New York, Penguin Books, 1978.

Harishankar Parsai, *Inspector Matadeen on the Moon*, translated by C. M. Naim. New Delhi, Katha, 2003.

Robert Reid Pharr, "Little White Overcoats," *The Berlin Journal*, Volume 34, 2020–2021, pp. 10–13.

The poem by Yevgeny Yevtushenko from which Jugnu quotes is titled "There are no boring people in this world" and translated from the Russian by Boris Dralyuk. Thanks to Eileen Chengyin Chow for this poem.

The detail of camphorweed came from a poem by Divya Victor about the assault on Sureshbhai Patel. See *Curb*, New York, Nightboat Books, 2021.

Strikes at Time (2011) is a work of art by the RAQS Media Collective.

Sarah Lyall, "The Many Lives of Jan Morris," *The New York Times*, April 25, 2019.

Gauri Deshpande's poem "Female of the Species."

Amitava Kumar is a writer and journalist. He was born in Ara, India, and grew up in the nearby town of Patna, famous for its corruption, crushing poverty, and delicious mangoes. Kumar is the author of the novel *Immigrant, Montana*, as well as several other books of nonfiction and fiction. He lives in Poughkeepsie, New York, where he is the Helen D. Lockwood Professor of English at Vassar College.

A NOTE ON THE TYPE

This book was set in Janson, a typeface named for the Dutchman Anton Janson, but is actually the work of Nicholas Kis (1650–1702). The type is an excellent example of the influential and sturdy Dutch types that prevailed in England up to the time William Caslon (1692–1766) developed his own incomparable designs from them.

Typeset by Scribe, Philadelphia, Pennsylvania

Printed and bound by Berryville Graphics, Berryville, Virginia

Designed by Anna B. Knighton